I0677096

THE
HUMAN
EQUATION

KENNETH TAM

SETTER CAINE
FIRST LORD OF THE ADMIRALTY

THE
HUMAN
EQUATION
THE FIRST EQUATIONS NOVEL

KENNETH TAM

ICEBERG

Published in Canada by Iceberg Publishing, Waterloo

Library and Archives Canada Cataloguing in Publication
Tam, Kenneth, 1984-
    The human equation : the first equations novel / Kenneth Tam. -- Special
ed.
Includes the novella entitled The quest.
ISBN 978-0-9865017-1-5
    I. Title.
PS8589.A7676H85 2010   C813'.6   C2010-900083-8

Copyright © 2003 Kenneth Tam

This is a work of fiction. All characters and situations are either the product of the author's
imagination or are used ficticiously. Any resemblance to actual persons, living or dead, events,
locales or businesses is coincidental. No part of this book may be reproduced or transmitted
in any form or by any means, electronic or mechanical, including photocopying and recording,
or by any information storage or retrieval system without written permission from the author,
except for brief passages quoted in a review.

Iceberg Publishing
55 Northfield Drive East, Suite 171
Waterloo ON N2K 3T6
contact@icebergpublishing.com
www.icebergpublishing.com

First trade paperback printing: August 2003
First pocket paperback printing: May 2005
Special international edition: January 2010

Cover Artwork: Wesley Prewer
Cover Design: Kenneth Tam

For
Richard Joseph Barron,
my grandfather.

Rest well.

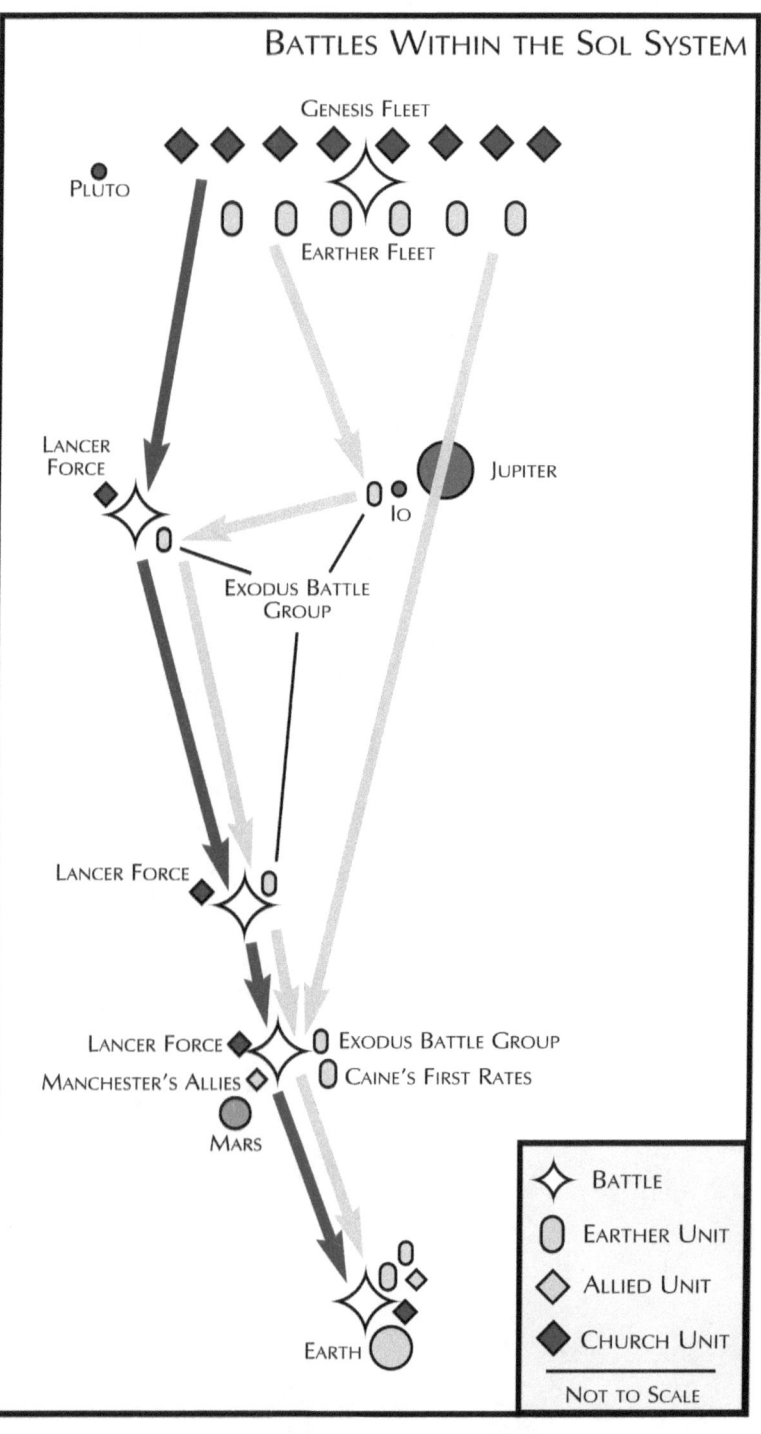

BATTLES WITHIN THE SOL SYSTEM

GENESIS FLEET

PLUTO

EARTHER FLEET

LANCER
FORCE

JUPITER

IO

EXODUS BATTLE
GROUP

LANCER FORCE

LANCER FORCE

EXODUS BATTLE GROUP

MANCHESTER'S ALLIES

CAINE'S FIRST RATES

MARS

EARTH

BATTLE

EARTHER UNIT

ALLIED UNIT

CHURCH UNIT

NOT TO SCALE

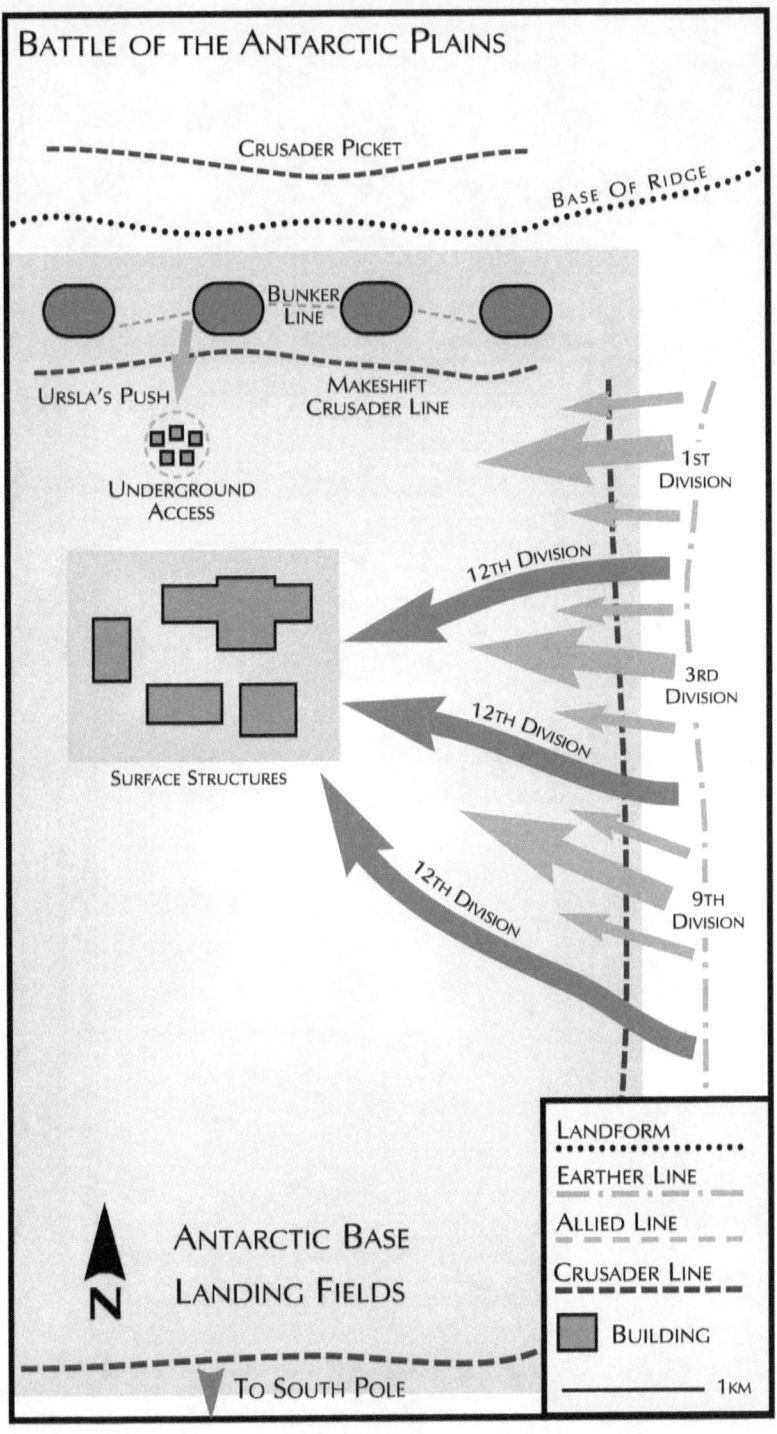

FOREWORD

I've been living with the Earthers for just over ten years now. In 1999, I was moving from one part of Canada to another — from Alberta to Ontario. As my family and I drove for five days across country, the combination of my recent absorption of C. S. Forrester novels and my desire to try writing something different than what I'd been working on up to that point (see Defense Command), led me to write a prologue about a character named Setter Caine, sitting in a pinnace and looking out the window as he cruised to a ship for a mission that was going to change his life. I was sixteen at the time.

Reflecting on that time, I see some interesting correlations between what I was doing and what I was writing. I began this book while I was looking out the window of our family station wagon. Canada was flying by as we headed towards a new life that would take everything I'd learned in Alberta and Newfoundland and use it for things I couldn't have imagined. Setter Caine began by looking out the window of his pinnace, heading towards a new mission that would harness all his training and see him launch into adventures unlike anything he could have conceived of — for better or for worse.

I was set to grow, and so was he.

The *Equations* are about Setter, and about his Earthers — a race of beings who can quite rightly be called 'too good to be true'. They are better than humans in every way imaginable, and worst of all, they are understanding of human flaws, and want to help us get better. They have the same idealistic outlook on the world that I had when I was sitting in that car, at the age of sixteen. They believe that good will prevail; they believe all the hopeful things that we humans grow out of as we age.

The story of the *Equations* novels is about how those seemingly naive beliefs can possibly survive when the Earthers face war and conflict on a massive scale. Setter Caine and his people are about to storm into the middle of a very messy fight with some of the most dangerous aliens in the cosmos — humans — and they're going to do it with the innocence of youth. How long before the luster starts wearing off their world view?

I invite you to come along for the ride, and see for yourself. I've learned a lot from the Earthers. I've grown alongside them, and I think where they've ended up is a pretty strong reflection of where I've ended up as well. So if you're planning to join us for part of the journey, or all of it, I hope you enjoy!

•••

A quick word about this new edition of *The Human Equation*. Aside from an updated look and format, this edition features a couple of pieces of new content. The first is this Foreword, which, if we're honest, isn't much of an added bonus. The second, however, is something I'm quite excited about: *The Quest*.

If I had one regret about *The Human Equation* in its first and second editions, it was that the book didn't spend enough time with the humans — it didn't go into as much depth about their hugely dysfunctional society as I would have were I to write it today. There was a reason for this — the book is more about Earthers than it is about humans — but as we go on in the series, and see how humanity is continuing to fall apart, I've had moments where I wished I'd set things up more explicitly at the beginning.

I considered doing a rewrite. I contemplated adding chapters to *The Human Equation* and doing a new, expanded edition... but when I talked to readers, I got some rather forceful feedback. Some liked the idea, but the vast majority were in the 'Solo fired first' camp — no messing with the original. A compromise had to be reached, so I took the ideas I was kicking around for those rewrites and put them together in a novella. Hence, *The Quest*, which occupies the last fifty-odd pages of this edition.

This story will take you into the midst of the human fleet during the events of *The Human Equation*, and show you how everything seemed to Audrey DeBrooke, a skipper who we come to know even better in books to come. You also get to meet Zed Dune, a character created by my good friend Wes Prewer, who figures largely in spinoff *Equation* stories, and in the later books of the core series.

I won't editorialize what you should expect from *The Quest*... I'll just say that it fits in quite neatly with the developments of the next book in the series, and it previews many of the social problems that humanity will be dealing with throughout.

The Genesis Fleet really wasn't a pleasant place to be during the Quest...

Before I wrap up this Foreword, I have to extend my gratitude to many people who had a part in this series.

First thanks go to my old comrade Cody Herauf. Cody originated the Kroggs and the Larosians, and he very kindly provided them to me for this series. Though we won't hear much more than whispers about those two alien races in this book, they factor hugely in those to come, and they provide the context that makes the events of *The Human Equation* possible. As ever, my thanks to Cody for his involvement.

I don't know if I can say enough to thank my good friend Wes Prewer for his involvement in the *Equations* series. He's been with us since the books were first released, and in 2005 he started producing ship artwork to use with the

Canadian pocket paperback editions. Since that time, he's stuck with us, and his classically austere renderings appear on the covers of every book in this special edition series.

Wes is also a talented writer, and his spinoff novel *Retaliation* added new characters and plots to the *Equations* universe, making a very positive impact. Wes' continued involvement and enthusiasm has made the growth of this series possible in ways we couldn't otherwise imagine. Many thanks indeed.

And then there's my elite friend Peter Caron, whose keen tactical mind helped me figure out the action of this book, and whose contributions to the series as a whole have been absolutely fundamental. I'll point out some of his specific suggestions in the forewords to the books in which they play out; for now, suffice to say that without his constant willingness to be a sounding board, this series probably would have hit a roadblock long before it ever saw print. I'm eternally indebted.

From friends to family: my Iceberg Publishing partners are my parents, Jacqui and Peter Tam. Without these two, there wouldn't be a series, and there wouldn't be a company. More than that, without them I doubt I'd be any sort of writer at all. Constantly supportive, challenging in a nonaggressive manner, and wise beyond most people's understanding of the word... I could not ask for better family. Period.

Lastly, I have to thank Atlas. Atlas was a dog, and when *The Human Equation* first came out, he was alive and well. In the years since, his era has come to an end, but his legacy is lasting. I learned a lot about the Earthers' innocent-yet-wise philosophy by simply observing him. He was my friend through the sorts of dark times when only a dog can stand to be your friend, and he taught me a great deal. If you come to know the Earthers, you'll come to know Atlas... and, I think, you'll come to know a lot of those 'inferior' species we take for granted, but who never seem to give up on us.

For now, though, I hope you enjoy this first step into the *Equations* universe, and that I see you again next time!

PROLOGUE

The Earther Fleet hung like a cloud of silver before a mat of stars, grav anchors down to keep it from shifting against the push of speeding interstellar particles. Six hundred years in the making, it was a magnificent sight for First Space Lord Setter Caine to behold from the view port of his pinnace. Ships of the line, frigates, and sloops all stood together in squadrons, awaiting the order to begin. He would give that order in about seven hours. Six hundred years of anticipation, and *he* would be the one to greet history.

Caine turned his attention back to the inside of the pinnace. He was alone in the luxurious cabin, which was just as well since he needed the time to clear his mind... to ponder. He glanced down at his hands. The excitement was coursing through his body but the gray, furry hands were steady as rocks, the fingers well in check.

He adjusted his collar, checking his reflection in the mirrored glass of the view port. A seasoned wolf face peered back at him — long, young looking, with dark amber eyes, a distinguished gray color, attentive ears, and shimmering teeth.

The fact that he was a product of genetic mutation no longer worried Caine. He'd come to terms with the reality that a virus had created his race to replace its lost human hosts, though he liked it no more than he ever had. In any case, the issue was now irrelevant — he was alive, he was here, and he was ready.

Standing slowly, he paced the pinnace compartment as he began to reflect on the past. His thoughts continued to return to the nature of his mission, and that took him right back to the end of the humans and the beginning of the Earthers. By the human calendar — or at least the one the Earthers had adapted — it had been the late twenty-first century CE.

Humanity's last round of terrorism and religious warfare had resulted in that species' destruction at the hands of a self-aware plague. The 'Omega Virus' had been created in the labs of human fanatics, and after wiping out primates, its intelligence had allowed it to fall upon the larger mammals of order Carnivora — the canine, feline, and ursine families — in an attempt to make them into a fresh 'food' supply. Ultimately, it had caused them to mutate into more humanoid beings.

Curiously enough, the plague appeared to vanish before it could destroy its new hosts. So the newly created race prospered, its members learning from the records and technology left by humanity, their new intelligence allowing them to avoid the mistakes the human race had made and to prepare for 'the return'.

And dealing with that return was Caine's mission. The humans had been able, despite the plague, to send a colony ship to a distant planet. The ship was full of individuals who had been conditioned to believe that Earth was a religious Holy Land and that it was the will of the Gods for them to return and retake it.

The Earthers hadn't liked the sound of this mission. As they matured and came to terms with their identities, they'd learned about the humans' destroyed civilization. They'd also decided the humans simply could *not* be allowed to almost destroy Earth again.

So the Earthers had made a decision. The calculations left by the humans indicated that, based on estimations of technology and distance to their adopted world, they would likely return some 700 years after departure. It would take them that much time to reach their destination, establish a home, and create the means to return. Which meant the Earthers had a comparable amount of time to prepare.

They adopted a common human language — English — for their new communication method, as their mutated bodies were quite capable of the speech patterns, then began to learn and innovate.

Now, seven centuries later, the fleet waited. It was a forceful deterrent to the irrationality humans had displayed in the history books, and would allow the Earthers to protect their planet, regardless of what the humans attempted. And if the humans proved more peaceful than expected, the Earthers would be glad to welcome them home — but to coexist with the ecosystem, not to dominate it.

The judgment would fall exclusively on Caine's shoulders. As the First Lord of the Admiralty, the 1,834-ship Navy was his responsibility. He was the one who would first meet the humans when they came and he, more than any other, would be responsible for what transpired.

The pinnace made its final approach to *ENS Orion*, the fleet's flagship. Classified loosely as a First Rate ship of the line, it actually could have been *two* such vessels. With 175 guns instead of the standard 100, the ship was well above the requirements for a First Rate, not to mention being fast and powerful. Caine would no doubt meet the humans from *Orion's* bridge, and he couldn't imagine a better ship for the job.

Bosun's pipes twittered as Caine entered *Orion's* main landing bay, and an honor guard of 300 marines snapped to attention. Thunder crashed as their boots came together in unison, their well-trained movements a credit not only to the ship, but to the Earthers as a whole. There was no punishment in the

Navy — none at all. Every member enlisted voluntarily and there had never been a single disturbance in 600 years of growth. Not *one*.

There were more important things to do than fight each other. Despite their predator ancestry, squabbling simply wasn't part of the Earthers' nature. Somehow, the mutations had accounted for that cooperative sentiment. Earthers were simply *above* trivial conflict.

Orion's Captain — and Caine's Flag Captain — snapped a crisp salute. Labrador Forepaw was brilliant, skilled at organization, motivation, and command. He was superior to every other Captain in the fleet, and like any Earther, he kept his wits about him. Forepaw had worked with Caine before, and the First Space Lord was glad he had been able to give him command of *Orion*.

Caine returned the sharp salute with well-honed muscles and the advantage of 116 years of experience.

Have I been in the Navy that long? Seems like only yesterday when I was a midshipman on the old Suffolk!

With a keen eye, he looked over the assembled officers in the landing bay. All were crisp and proper, dress uniforms well presented, the powerful royal blue and brass buttons of the Earther Navy well displayed. The double-breasted tunics were a tradition of the Navy, as was the official ceremony meant to welcome a flag officer to his ship.

"Permission to come aboard?" Caine said in his measured, somewhat soft tone.

Forepaw nodded, "Permission granted. Welcome aboard, sir."

The salutes all came down in a most orderly fashion and flanked by Forepaw, the First Lord advanced from the pinnace through the channel between ranks of marines.

This is a good ship. I'm glad I'll meet the humans aboard it.

Caine stepped into the lift at the far side of the landing bay, waited for Forepaw to join him, then smiled ever so slightly.

"A fine crew, Lab," he said quietly.

Forepaw grinned at his old commander — his old friend.

"The *best*, and I don't mind saying so."

Caine nodded with satisfaction as the lift rose through *Orion's* massive hull. The size of the First Rate ensured at least three minutes to the First Lord's quarters.

"There's no ship better for meeting the humans," Forepaw added, pride in his voice.

Caine glanced at the schematic of the massive ship on the wall of the lift, smiled again — a little more obviously — and nodded.

"I couldn't have said it any better, Lab."

CHAPTER 1

A cloud of starships drifted around a large gray station, orbiting a lush green globe which, in turn, rotated around a cool but determined sun in a lonely system. The cloud consisted of a wide variety of ships, ranging in size from Destroyers to Superdreadnoughts to the most powerful Colonizers.

This force had been built for a specific purpose, to return to and recolonize the foreign planet Earth which had borne the ancestors of its creators. By no means an easy task, but the fleet's leader was confident in his ability to see it through.

Lord High Chancellor Harvey Bingham was the religious and political patriarch of the colony set on the rugged jungle world Genesis. At rest in his cabin aboard the Crusading fleet's flagship — also blessed with the Holy name *Genesis* — he was contemplating the importance of his Quest, this most Holy Crusade to Earth. It had been prophecy for more than 600 years, and many obstacles had been overcome before it could be made a reality.

Bingham found himself involuntarily cringing at the thought of his people's defeats at the hands of the alien Larosians, and the alliance Genesis had formed with the sinister but accommodating Kroggs. They'd seen very little of the Kroggs and the Larosians of late — those species had become too overwhelmed by their own war to bother with Genesis and its 'small' fleet.

Alliances to Hell, now that our fleet is not so small we can stand up to the Larosians without Krogg help. That is beside the point in any case. We are returning to Earth, fulfilling a most Holy Quest. And we will protect both our Crusade and our home with our new fleet!

It was confident rhetoric which Bingham firmly told himself he believed, but somehow a piece of him refused it. Not that he would admit this doubt — he was the representative of the Gods, of the Holy Unity National, the leader of the Church. He simply could *not* be weak in his faith.

He slowly steadied himself and began to look through his fleet's statistical reports. He was, admittedly, not a military man. The figures of supply, tonnage, armament... most went over his head. He liked to show himself off as quite knowledgeable in all subjects, but his experience here was sadly lacking and he had no spare time in which to enhance it.

Bingham generally left the strategy to his fleet commander, ArcGeneral Hastings. She was a genius in her field, though, like all of the Naval class, was somewhat weak in faith and therefore inferior. Hastings had proven herself time and again in past actions against the Larosian squadrons — each subsequent encounter a *less* one-sided slaughter — and had shown that she was capable of using resources wisely.

Why couldn't there be at least one victorious ArcGeneral with more definite faith in the Holy Quest? Ahh, but those Naval heathen have no faith. They are inferior, and so they are treated. Our mission may rely in part on them, but it will be the Church that proves most important to the Quest!

Alas, there was work to be done. Bingham settled into his chair and let three hours pass before the Genesis Fleet boosted out of the system.

Caine was hard pressed to contain his eagerness.

"You can run out the guns, Captain Forepaw," he said mechanically, and 175 mark XIX energy cannon slipped out of the sides of *Orion*, the ship's gunports sliding apart to give them clear firing arcs.

Those words had brought excitement to ships' crews since the beginning of the Earther Navy — they meant action, or at least *simulated* action. Under normal navigation, a ship's maneuverability could be severely limited by the drag of tiny particles in space, even using deflector fields to minimize it. Having 175 massive energy cannon barrels sticking out the ship's side would make that problem significantly worse. As such, ships had been built on the base philosophy of the eighteenth and nineteenth century human sailing navies — particularly the Royal Navy of Great Britain, arguably the most successful of all time.

Ship classes, traditions, and many Naval ranks were borrowed from that service, and at present the Earther Navy could almost be considered a futuristic copy — and not a cheap copy either. The Earthers had made great progress in energy technologies, allowing them to build energy cannon with incredible firepower and great range. They also developed a space travel system based completely on energy fields, allowing them to travel light years in hours, even minutes.

A ship the size of *Orion* carried a dozen energy conversion reactors — half for its gun armaments, three for its normal space drives, and three for its operating systems. Each generator only needed to work at two-thirds efficiency to give *Orion* power to fight and fly.

"Target drones locked sir — three ships marked with Second Rate signatures," the Sensor Officer reported calmly.

Caine nodded. He was going against protocol by commanding *Orion* himself — it was tradition that the Captain of a ship had the final say in operations, but he knew Forepaw respected his love of ship command, and his need to, on occasion, take the bridge himself.

Now Caine's mind began to take full measure of the situation as it would be if those drones were real warships — Second Rate ships of the line. *Orion* was a First Rate — the biggest class of ship ever built — and could outgun any one of those lighter but still potent ships in a broadside fight. Indeed, in a straight battle it could doubtless knock down a pair of Second Rates while only suffering moderate damage. But the third ship could cause problems.

Caine's mind leapt to a decision, "Focus fire on the lead two — fire as guns bear. Helm, ninety degrees starboard, up angle twenty. Prepare reverse by 180 to port."

There was a shriek as the gunner's fire klaxon ran down through each gun deck, accompanied by quick orders. The port broadside fired unevenly as each gun crew trained its individual cannon on the targets and 'painted' them with laser tracers.

Even staggered and drawn out, the fire from *Orion's* 75-gun broadside was enormous, filling space with raw and deadly energy. Seventy-five guns were almost as many as a Second Rate carried in total, not just mounted on one side.

The helm turned hard over as the broadside entered recycle mode, recharging its guns for the next shot — they'd be out of action for a little under fifteen seconds. The guns mounted on *Orion's* bow slashed into the enemy formation, and then the ship, turning hard over to present its starboard broadside, accelerated across the drones' flight path. The starboard 75 guns loosed their energy salvos in near unison as the targets crossed their line of fire.

Scanners were momentarily blurred by the mass of energy, and Caine waited anxiously with *Orion's* crew. Finally, after an all too lengthy pause, the scanners cleared and the remnants of the enemy squadron were visible.

The lead Second Rate had been completely destroyed — no mean accomplishment, even accounting for a massive gun armament like *Orion's*. The second ship was clearly missing a third of its forward hull; it was in poor condition to fight a sloop, let alone the menacing First Rate it was challenging. The last ship in line was showing minor damage, but it had been shielded from the main fury of the broadsides by its two fellows.

Both survivors then turned to bring their broadsides to bear. From the nearer's opening ports, forty-two mark XVI cannon emerged — smaller models than the ones *Orion* mounted, but still quite powerful. Its crippled compatriot turned as well, presenting what broadside it had left — nineteen mark XVII cannon, slightly larger weapons, but of little importance in its beleaguered state.

"Power spike!" the Sensor Officer barked. "Incoming!"

Caine's mind was ahead of the report, "Hard to port, down angle fifty degrees. As much speed as we'll carry, Master."

Orion, despite its massive size, was quick at the helm. It turned and dove as the salvo raced down on it at near light speed.

"Starboard broadside charged," the First Lieutenant reported in a clipped tone. "Gun Captains report ready."

The drone's simulated energy barely missed *Orion*. What little of it hit glanced harmlessly off the shields.

"Cruising Master, take us back over to starboard. Lieutenant, fire as you bear to starboard. Primary target the undamaged Second Rate," Caine spoke with the steadiness of experience.

Orion once again demonstrated its quickness at the helm as it reversed direction and then adjusted course to bring its starboard batteries to bear. A staggered broadside of real energy crashed outward as each gun came around — unlike the drone's simulated blasts, *Orion* fired a fully charged broadside. Again the shot crashed into the Second Rates, and again the frenzy of energy blanked out the screens and resulted in a tense waiting period.

Careening through space at 78 percent of (adjusted) light speed, riding an energy field from its engines, *Orion* finally caught the sensor data. The crippled Second Rate was totally gone, and the previously undamaged one had been raked so terribly its reactors had all shut down — an almost impossible occurrence as they, like *Orion's*, were redundant and well shielded.

A silent but potent atmosphere of triumph filled the ship as it once again proved its invincibility. Caine simply sat in his command chair next to Forepaw and absorbed his pride with a smile.

After a few minutes the air cleared, *Orion* turned towards the waiting fleet and accelerated away from the drone's wreckage. Another First Rate — the 150-gun *Agamemnon* — passed them on the way out. It was that ship's turn to attempt the same feat *Orion* had just managed.

Not an easy act to follow, Caine thought quietly.

Orion always stole the show.

CHAPTER 2

The Genesis Fleet could achieve speeds that made interstellar travel practical through the use of massive fusion drives which pushed its ships into a state of 'flux'. The energy released by the fusion plants on a human ship altered the matter of a starship so that its total *mass* was less than matter dictated. In fact the ship no longer *had* mass relative to the rest of the universe, though from within the ride seemed no different than any other. Normal space engines could then move the ship at tremendous speed. By the same token Newton's laws no longer applied — the matter was changed to the point that they became moot.

The primary drawback to this kind of travel was that it tended to degrade hull integrity over time, and in rare cases, if the fusion plants failed and released the starship from 'flux', Newton would forcefully retake the ship and send the crew of the unfortunate vessel into oblivion in a split second recovery of his lost laws.

The crew becomes a bloody stain on the wall, and that is what could happen to me. The Holy Cause is more important than myself, but I am its mortal leader. I must rely on the Gods of the Unity National to protect me from all harm.

Lord High Chancellor Bingham seemed to have a bitter line of thought nowadays. He watched the stars passing by in quick flashes, wondering how much he really weighed — literally and figuratively — in the grand scheme of things.

Such pessimism was something he hated, particularly within himself. He recited an extra prayer each day to cleanse himself of any negativity, but still it remained. Sometimes he couldn't help but wonder if it truly was doubt of the Quest...

No. No, the Gods were testing his vigilance and finding that he could hold steadfast to his religion when the world crashed down around him.

He felt like he had been traveling for two years, not two weeks. Still, destiny was upon him. No more worries about the aliens which had circled his planet. No more concerns over the protection of the Genesis colony. The Unholy Plague was by now gone from Earth, and once the planet was secured the entire human race could safely abandon the aging colony. The perils of the Larosians and Kroggs be damned into eternity.

Bingham looked up slowly from the view port in his quarters, checking the chronometer. Four more hours and they would enter the outskirts of the Sol system. A journey which had taken the Genesis founders a hundred years had taken all of two weeks for their descendants. An achievement in which to take pride.

The door chimed, catching Bingham by surprise but not leaving him unprepared. He blanked his expression, turned to face the cabin hatch, and spoke in formal tones, "I will receive you."

The door slid open and ArcGeneral Elizabeth Hastings stepped in silently, dropping courteously to one knee as the door shut behind her, "I am humbled; thank you for your most Holy audience."

"You are welcomed by the Gods. Rise now," Bingham maintained the formal attitude.

Hastings rose quietly under Bingham's scrutiny. Her face was set in a neutral expression, but something in her manner made it obvious to the Chancellor that she hated this religious tradition.

She is Navy after all, and Naval types are inferior and unfaithful. It is her opinion that on a ship of the Holy Fleet she should bow to no one. She is the chief of Naval operations, after all.

Bingham found himself almost sympathetic to her before he checked himself. The Church would never permit sympathy.

"I have come to inform you that we are an hour from Sol, Your Eminence," Hastings said frostily.

That was a surprise.

"If I recall correctly the last probe mission we sent to Sol took three additional hours. Why the difference in time? I trust you have taken no risks with our Holy Fleet while in flux drive," Bingham was careful not to sound polite. In fact, he wanted to sound annoyed — it would shield his true empathy and pride.

He succeeded.

Hastings' mouth opened, then shut quickly. Hastings was not one who enjoyed being told her job and she'd barely saved herself from a disrespectful comment to the Lord High Chancellor. After a brief moment she calmed her mild fury.

"Your Eminence, the last time a probe came this far was *twenty-four* years ago. It relied on a far less advanced flux drive. We are able to maintain higher speeds and higher safety margins with our current technology. I assure you, I would not risk our Holy Fleet for the acceleration of a few hours."

What she really wanted to say was that she was not a fool and that a few hours were so inconsequential she felt offended at my mentioning it. She still considers the fleet to be hers *and not* ours. *At least it is respectable that she silenced herself, even if her body language betrays her.*

"Very well, I will accompany you to the bridge to oversee the entering of the Holy Sol system," Bingham's tone revealed none of his thoughts.

With a deep bow Hastings led him out of his cabin and to the bridge of *Genesis*.

On the outskirts of the Sol system eight Fifth Rate frigates cruised, making a low but reasonable pace of fifty percent (adjusted) light speed — 50 pls. Squadron number 111, nearing the end of its rotation on patrol duty, was one of a dozen cruiser groups on constant lookout for the humans' return. Soon it would be returning to Earth space to continue with battle drills and war-games.

The squadron's commanding officer was a three meter tall kodiak bear, Commodore Andra Ursla. Despite always feeling a bit cramped in starships, she loved the Navy. The corridors and cabins of a frigate — exactly 3.058 meters high — were quite low for her. That didn't dampen her enthusiasm — she just learned to duck so as not to bang her head on the tops of doors and on the lower supports on the engineering deck.

At 03:00 hours she was awoken suddenly in her cabin by the alert klaxons aboard her flagship, *Cerberus*. She shot upwards, narrowly avoiding the ceiling as she recalled her location. She quickly pulled on her uniform and ducked out into the corridor. The felines, canines, and even other, smaller bears in her crew cleared out of her way as they dashed to their action stations. This was not only out of courtesy to the Commodore, but to avoid being trampled by a 600-kilogram bear.

Ursla appeared on the bridge a minute later, crashing into her chair like a falling mountain.

"What's happening?" she roared, watching the holographic displays around her.

"We've detected a large energy anomaly cruising in at 2,000 pls," the feline Captain of the ship reported softly.

Ursla's mind hit high gear as she punched up a mental image in her head. *Cerberus* cruised at 2,600 pls — it could go faster if needed. But now speed was less relevant than size...

"Put the squadron on alert status and inform Admiralty House. Send my compliments to the First Lord and request he gets the fleet out here immediately," Ursla ordered before she really thought. "This is it."

And if it's a false alarm? I just called out the fleet! Trust your instincts. Better safe than sorry.

"Squadron alert status confirmed. Message to Fleet Command sent — it'll arrive in thirty-four seconds ma'am," the Signal Officer reported excitedly.

Now we wait.

A definite disadvantage to flux drive was the gradual deceleration. The field had to slowly decrease in strength until it became nonexistent, allowing a gentle return of Newton's laws instead of a sudden, fatal one. The total time *Genesis* required to slow to such a speed was about ten minutes, during which the crew generally experienced disorientation and mild vertigo due to the shift in states of matter.

Hastings seemed totally unaffected by the process as she sternly paced the deck of *Genesis'* bridge. She was not impatient, merely cautious. To her, this was potentially hostile territory. Bingham, on the other hand, was not so accustomed to the sensation. He clung helplessly to the arms of his elevated seat in the center of the vast bridge, watching the walls spin around him in a nauseating dance.

Then it was over, ending suddenly as the ship's Artificial Intelligence shut down the flux field and engaged standard drive.

"Navigator, position please," Hastings sounded cool and collected as she returned to her chair just in front of and two feet below Bingham's own.

How can she be so calm in this situation? Prophecy is being fulfilled and yet... I too must appear so calm. I must be appearing calm right now.

"We are in the Sol system's outer region," the Navigator reported in low tones.

"I am detecting a group of unknown ships directly ahead, ma'am," the Sensor Chief added quickly. His voice was showing signs of the excitement.

With that last announcement the bridge was filled with a strange anticipation. This was a new challenge put into place as a test by the Gods to assure the Holy Fleet's commitment, Bingham was sure of it.

"They aren't Krogg or Larosian?" Hastings' voice cut sharply through the atmosphere.

"No ma'am, they're the size of Larosian Warcruisers, but they're of a completely different design... and built of different materials. They have no Krogg organic components either," the Sensor Chief was thorough despite his excitement.

Hastings turned her chair to look up at Bingham, and he found himself frozen. He had no idea what to do... surely the Kroggs would have warned them if a known species existed in this region...

"If Your Eminence would permit, I would like to hold this position until the unknowns declare themselves," she said quietly.

Bingham nodded, "I agree. These could either be hostile or friendly, and only time can tell..."

"By the Earth!" Ursla had expected a force of ships equipped to survey... to defend the surveyors... to colonize... but *this*? Two thousand, four hundred and thirteen ships, all carrying weapons... all with human bio readings! That was a third again the number of ships in the Earther Navy!

"The rest of the fleet is en route," *Cerberus'* Captain, a calm panther named

Nightclaw, said soothingly. "They should arrive in less than half an hour. The other patrol squadrons will arrive in less than ten minutes."

Hopefully the humans wouldn't become irrational and attack before half an hour then. But they could easily be disturbed by the arrival of the Earther Fleet. Ursla would have to do something to take the surprise out of the events to follow... *tell* the humans what to expect.

But as a Commodore, that wasn't *strictly* Ursla's job. She commanded the squadron that warned the Admiralty and got the fleet moving when the humans arrived... she wasn't the one who talked to them.

So this is going to be a fateful decision then.

"Stand by to broadcast a text only message to the human fleet," the bridge fell silent. It took the Signal Officer a moment to digest the order and prepare the appropriate broadcasting equipment.

"Message as follows," Ursla began smoothly, trying to maintain her calm...

"To the human ships which have just entered the Sol system, we are not hostile and are only awaiting the arrival of our commanding officers to initiate formal contact. Please do not be alarmed at the arrival of a large group of vessels with similar configuration to our own. They contain our commanding officers and are also non-hostile. We only wish to greet you with the greatest honors. We will initiate formal contact within the hour. Much Thanks. Commodore Ursla, Earther Navy," the Communications Chief read the message aloud to *Genesis'* bridge in an uneven tone. "The message came in English, ma'am."

It wasn't exactly shock that filled *Genesis'* bridge, but an unsettling feeling of surprise. Still, the apparent absence of a language barrier was irrelevant compared to the content of the text... no, no, they were equally relevant.

"Well, ArcGeneral, are you going to take this *Commodore* at her word?" Bingham demanded, secretly so anxious he felt physically sick.

"I... *think* so, Your Excellency," Hastings said curiously. "The ships seem to have gone out of their way not to startle us, though they could be trying to get us to let our guard down while a heavy force closes in. I'd recommend going to General Quarters, code yellow, so that we are ready if this arriving force proves hostile. Otherwise I'd vote to believe the message... for now."

"I concur, ArcGeneral," said Bingham, wishing he was so level-headed.

Caine was involuntarily digging his fingers into his chair arms. *Cerberus'* sensor sweeps were being piped to his flagship via energy comm, and he quickly gleaned what information he could from them. The humans had gone all out to ensure their operation was safe. Their fleet numbered just under 2,500 — the Admiralty's 'worst case scenario' estimate — and no one yet had a clue as to their technology level. The data on how they managed to enter the Sol system was still sketchy, but at least Caine knew they hadn't used technology at all similar to that of the Earther Navy — their ships were still in physical matter form upon arrival.

Earther ships traveled interstellar distances by converting their hulls from patterned forms of matter to carefully structured and maintained patterns of energy. Using Wyndhymn generators, a special type of energy reactor developed three centuries before by Egbert Wyndhymn, a ship could be completely converted into an energy field that could be propelled to speeds much faster than matter. Inside the hull of a ship, and to within a certain distance of the outer hull, nothing appeared different — even the stars remained in sight. From the outside a ship under energy drive appeared as a ball of swirling blue-yellow energy, not unlike a burst from one of *Orion's* mark XIX cannon. Even if the Wyndhymns failed midway trough a trip and dropped a ship out of the energy state, the residual energy would carry through the translation, protecting the ship from the momentum — and its crew from becoming a stain due to Newton's laws. After that energy died away, grav generators would kick in to anchor the crew smartly to the deck.

The distance was ticking down as *Orion*, under normal space drive with the Earther Fleet all around it, cruised to meet the 111th Flying Squadron on Pluto's orbital plane.

Cerberus had been tense for minutes now, like a predator wondering if it had been noticed by a herd. Its gun crews were at their stations, but its guns remained in their ports. Ursla was noisily tapping her foot on the deckplate, but nobody really heard her. Besides, what could they do about it if they did? Maybe a handful of the crew outmassed her and nobody had a mind to complain in the first place, let alone at this critical moment.

"Any response yet?" Nightclaw asked in subdued tones.

"No sir," the Signal Officer replied immediately.

Did these people get the message? Are they too thick to get it? We've all heard bad things about humans... will they answer...? Will they start shooting...? Better get our shields up...

"Tactical, start bringing up our shields. Do it slowly and drop off non-combat systems to keep our energy output fairly level. Don't give them a reason to worry," Ursla's tapping stopped as she gave the orders.

"Yes, ma'am," the coyote at tactical sounded glad to have a task to focus on.

"Coded message from the flagship, ma'am," the Signal Officer interjected abruptly. "It's going through the decoder.... got it."

The atmosphere on the bridge suddenly thickened as tension turned up several notches to become apprehension.

The message slowly scrolled up on Ursla's chair-arm screen:

To: Commodore Ursla
    Commanding Officer FlyRon 111

Andra,
We're 15 minutes out but we don't want to jump straight in on energy drive. That might disturb the humans a little too much. Keep sending updates every five minutes. If they go hostile don't try to take them on. Signal us and we'll jump in to support.
Be there soon.
Good luck
Setter

Small comfort. I wish he'd jump in, get here now to take over. I'm supposed to be rotating back for squadron war-games! Ursla's mind was screaming at her, but she shut it out.

"Ma'am! Got another message coming in… from the human fleet. Text only, but it's definitely meant for us. It's in English," the Signal Officer announced suddenly.

"Source?" Nightclaw didn't let the excitement dampen his senses.

"The biggest ship up front — about the size of a First Rate, not as big as *Orion*, but a monster all the same," the Sensor Chief answered as the message began to scroll up Ursla's screen.

To Unknown Ships,
We appreciate your advisory and await the arrival of the proper authorities. We are not hostile to you and will remain in this position until otherwise informed.

"What an odd message," Nightclaw said quietly. "Pass it on to flag."

An almost undetectable energy pulse shot out of *Cerberus'* signal buffer to *Orion*.

"Why would you call it odd, exactly?" Ursla kept her voice quiet, leaning towards her Flag Captain.

"They're rather trusting. They aren't asking any questions. It's their Holy Quest to recolonize Earth, and they find a squadron of warships in the way. Wouldn't you be suspicious if you were in their place?" Nightclaw said. "I think they're holding back."

Ursla nodded in agreement, "Good thought, but Setter probably wouldn't like it if we just started shooting. We'll wait until he arrives."

"Of course," Nightclaw sounded the slightest bit wounded at the implication.

•••

"Any response to your message, ArcGeneral?" Bingham was getting impatient. After two weeks of hard travel the final insult was being forced to wait by these unknown *Earthers*. But wait or no, he would go with Hastings' recommendation because any problems could then be blamed on her.

"No response Your Eminence, but our long range probes are picking up a large number of unknown ships of similar configuration coming out from deeper in system. More ships are joining them from around this orbital plane — groups of eight of the same class already out here."

More coming...

"Shouldn't we upgrade from yellow level to battle alert? Arm our lasers and load our tubes?" Bingham bit off the question as he asked it — it was his job to *give* the orders, not ask about them.

"Your Eminence is quite right," Hastings said heavily, obviously not pleased with the suggestion. She'd taken it as a rhetorical question, not a plea for help. "Bring up defense nets, charge lasers, load missile tubes. Activate our energy armor. Comm, signal the fleet to full battle ready," Hastings turned back to Bingham. "We will be ready to eliminate any treachery, Your Eminence."

He nodded and turned away relieved. She rolled her eyes and quietly sighed.

"Ma'am!" the Sensor Officer's voice cut across the bridge with a suddenness that made Ursla jump.

"What?"

"Massive energy spike. Looks like their entire fleet is clearing for action," the Lieutenant's voice was tense.

"By the Earth..." Nightclaw paused for a short second, "Beat to quarters! All hands to action stations. Turn to present our broadside. Shields to full."

"Advise the squadrons here to do the same and send word to *Orion*," Ursla added quickly. "No ship is to fire unless a member of this fleet is fired upon."

There was a pause as the next order, the most important order, was predicted. Nightclaw looked to Ursla, who nodded in silent agreement.

Another pause.

"Lieutenant Kirby," Nightclaw addressed himself to the First Lieutenant, "run out the guns, if you please."

"Your Eminence!" Hastings called, her head bowed over her console.

"What is it?" he managed to sound calm though he'd jumped at the abrupt warning.

"The unknowns have opened missile tubes..." Bingham's heart pounded desperately for a moment, "...wait, they seem to have pushed *cannon barrels* through them."

That was a surprise. Another surprise. Could these unknowns still be using rail guns? Even a non-military type like Bingham knew that technology was ages out of date.

Bingham held his tongue. It would probably be better to pretend he was unconcerned instead of trying to appear as someone who knew what to do. The minutes ticked by.

Ursla was making a conscious effort not to rip the arms off her chair. Her only hope of survival was the level-headedness of the human commander. She'd known there were risks when she joined the Navy, but no one had said anything about suicide missions.

The human ships hadn't budged since she'd run out the guns... they couldn't be *afraid* of her tiny squadron, could they? No, that would be too easy. They seemed to be using missile tubes — slow moving self-propelled warheads. She could probably get her squadron out of the hailstorm those ships could throw if she began powering the energy drives now...

"Orders to the squadron," Ursla's voice was calm. "Begin to charge energy drives. Just in case we have to make a break for it."

"Aye ma'am," the Signal Officer replied keenly.

Just a couple of minutes more...

Orion rippled out of a ball of energy as her drive disengaged. Caine had been monitoring the sensor data from *Cerberus*, and he'd decided not to worry about startling the humans.

The entire fleet appeared almost simultaneously, traveling in 225-odd vanguards of eight ships each, all weapons being charged and standing by for the order to run out. The 1,800 ships began to enter sensor range of the Genesis Fleet a few seconds later.

Bingham gasped despite himself, then mentally slapped his face a couple of times to regain his self control. Hastings was sitting coolly in her command chair, nodding to herself.

"The message seems to have been genuine, Your Eminence," her voice reached up to him and he felt a twinge of jealousy.

"And how have you made *that* determination ArcGeneral? They *do* have their weapons charging!" he snapped, trying to belittle her in an effort to comfort himself.

His anger bounced off her like a stray laser off a mirror. She was right and she knew it.

"Your Eminence, if they meant to destroy us they would have probably arrived all around us, not together in a single wave. And unlike the first unknowns, these haven't opened their weapon hatches," her self control nearly drove Bingham to insanity.

He could have his Crusader marines haul her into an airlock and decompress it, just to appease the Gods, but it would put *Genesis'* crew into an uproar. Even hundreds of his Crusaders couldn't handle 1,000 angry crew *and* hundreds of fleet marines... not on such short notice, at least.

And worst of all, Hastings *knew* it.

"ArcGeneral!" the Comm Chief barked abruptly. "A message is coming in! From the biggest ship out there..."

Bingham checked his own panel for the sensors' picture of the biggest ship — a huge box with rounded edges, long, more wide than tall, with over 150 of those damned weapon hatches. It was far and away the largest unknown ship, a third larger than *Genesis.*

What are these things? The Gods themselves...?

His question would be answered in a split second...

There was no point waiting. Caine intended to open communications before a misunderstanding led to an exchange of fire.

He straightened his uniform one last time, and then *Orion's* bridge holo tank glowed into life...

Bingham's shock forced his jaw open, as a sharp breath expelled itself from his lungs. A *wolve.* The ancient records of Earth showed these creatures to be senseless beasts... and near it sat a *trigar*... and a *bear*...

The beast's mouth opened, and Bingham gasped outright, along with all the bridge crew save Hastings, who looked properly fascinated.

"Good day to you, human friends," Caine had to gulp out the word 'friends' through great willpower, "and welcome to the Sol sector. You've been expected."

CHAPTER 3

It felt as though a definite chill was running through *Orion's* main launch bay, but then Caine wouldn't have been surprised if there was. At 500 meters long and 100 wide, the bay covered almost a fifth of *Orion's* lowest deck. It was hard to heat and, below the deck plates, nothing but icy space remained.

Still, the chill felt more like a portent of what was about to happen than a heat circulation issue. At the far end of the bay the massive airlock doors were open, the bay's pressure being held firm by a powerful energy field. In the distance he could pick out the red hull of the High Chancellor's approaching pinnace.

This hastily-arranged first meeting would be as significant as any other event in Earther history — not to mention the history of the planet itself. And the responsibility for whatever came of this encounter would rest squarely on Caine's shoulders.

Well, two-thirds of it anyway...

Ursla doesn't like me now I think.

It seemed the humans held their religion above all else, Navy included. Engineered into their psyche hundreds of years before, this trait meant that their religious leader — High Chancellor Bingham — was arriving on one pinnace, while their fleet's military leader was arriving on a separate shuttle in a separate bay. Thanks to the most recent laws established in quantum theory, Caine couldn't be in two places at once to welcome them both simultaneously — at least not without some difficulty and a quantum field generator.

So he'd placed a call to an old friend and gotten her to do the other job.

Commodore Andra Ursla and been caught so completely off guard by Caine's request that she welcome a military leader, she'd forgotten to argue. She and her company of marines from *Cerberus* had just made the crossing to *Orion* on an assault dropship, because it was the fastest thing she could find. It also happened to be the sleekest, and therefore the *lowest*. She'd have headaches for a while after that wonderful flight — especially after hitting her head in the same doorway four times.

And why am I here? Oh right, I had to get ambitious and send a message when the human showed up. Brilliant. No more initiative-taking for me.

Orion's second landing bay was hardly as glamorous as the first. It was a plain steel-gray chamber, without any polish or detailed paintwork, one third the size of the main bay. It had the singular redeeming quality of head room — a few dozen meters of clearance in all — making it heaven in Ursla's estimation.

The heavy airlock doors at the end of the chamber were open, and a force field was shimmering defiantly against the vacuum of space as a plain gray military pinnace approached them.

The energy barrier in the main bay let the red pinnace pass through, bonding to every contour of the craft. The vehicle, slightly smaller than a standard Earther Navy pinnace, crept slowly over the deck following the instructions of the Deck Chief and the markers flashing along the floor. Behind it the air lock doors began to close.

Caine found himself fighting a feeling of impatience. Someone fulfilling a virtual *prophecy* really shouldn't have to wait. The pinnace finally slowed to hover in the air above its larger-than-necessary landing slot, almost ceremonial in its actions. Its bows turned slowly from one side to the other, looking over Caine, with Forepaw behind him to the right, and six companies of fifty marines each standing at attention in full dress on his flanks.

It seemed as if they were being judged, appraised as to their worthiness to greet the High Chancellor. The six companies of marines — all bears of about 2.7 meters average height — held their attention poses unwaveringly, their eyes darting over to watch the human craft. They all carried energy rifles, fully charged in case the humans became... *irrational*. Caine hoped that the situation wouldn't degenerate to that degree, but the mood this blood-red ship created inspired no confidence.

If the humans did lose control Caine would probably be the first to fall. Another job perk they hadn't mentioned when they'd offered him the position, he decided wryly.

The pinnace slowly began its descent to the deck, its landing feet testing the surface cautiously before letting the ship rest.

Ursla fixed her collar for a third... *fourth* time — she had no parade of officers behind her to draw the attention from the apparent imperfections of her long-stored, seldom-worn dress uniform. Her marine company was divided in half, one side the feline platoons, the other the canine platoons. They stood on either of her flanks, at full attention with their rifle safeties on. They looked smart, not hostile. That was a plus. Bear marines — the other type of marines especially common on the larger ships with room to accommodate them — always looked intimidating, no matter what their intentions.

Since Ursla was a kodiak and *bigger* than most of those marines, she could imagine the reaction she alone would cause in a small, fragile human.

The gray pinnace began to pass through the atmospheric shield, and it looked surprisingly neutral, like so many small craft that had come and gone before. It advanced at a moderate pace — neither slowly enough to appear suspicious nor quickly enough to appear rushed. The pilot required surprisingly little instruction from the Deck Chief, following the markers to the landing slot with little ceremony. The craft hovered for a second while its landing feet lowered, and then let itself drop gracefully to the deck. The feet made a mild thud as they met the deckplates, and the coolant tanks began to vent most unceremoniously. A practical arrival.

Caine was mentally keeping his heart rate in check — his mind needed *something* to do while the menacing pinnace just sat there doing nothing. In fact, there was no sign that anyone inside had any intention of coming out. The craft seemed outright abandoned, as though it had come under its own will, just to get inside *Orion*...

Finally there was an abrupt but quiet hiss as a hatch cover slid upward into the craft's hull, and a walk ramp a mere meter wide slowly lowered to the ground. It seemed to take eons to reach the deck below, once again as though it was testing the worthiness of *Orion's* hull.

After an agonizing minute it touched down, and there was another period of inactivity. Caine sighed deeply and tried to control his impatience.

The coolant hiss faded away after a minute or so, and a hatch popped with the accustomed bang as pressure was bled off. Near the gray pinnace's front a door swung outward, and then a grated walk ramp dropped loudly to the deck.

Here we go...

Ursla straightened up and readied herself.

A sudden sense of commotion in the main bay caused the Earthers' instincts to flare. Even Caine was briefly stunned, but he composed himself quickly — his Earther instincts, remnants of his predatory past, seldom burned so strongly. Only in the presence of extreme danger had he ever felt this much sheer discomfort.

He could pick out the voices of whispering humans, speaking quietly but in unison... saying something... *praying*... being *blessed*... by the High Chancellor... and then another racket as they stood up, the fabric of their uniforms making a wisping noise as they rubbed together, and then a clicking as they punched something into what sounded like weapons.

Finally they came down the ramp, a group of the High Chancellor's marines. They wore crimson cloaks with matching hoods covering their faces below their eyes and above their foreheads. Over their eyes were black visors, on their hands red gloves, on their feet red boots, and on their shoulders flat black epaulettes.

In a display that, by Earther standards, was rather sloppy, they swept into a semi-circle around the foot of the ramp, kneeling down with their weapons leveled. And what weapons they were. They looked as though they fired *projectiles*, just like their ships. Probably self-propelled projectiles.

Their heads were turning to scan the marines on the deck, who at an order all snapped in unison to full attention and turned to face the visitors. The thunder of 600 boots being forced down by their strong bear owners was thunderous, and one of the humans in the semi-circle lost his position and flinched in fear, slipping to one side.

Caine could easily relate — the noise still disturbed him and he had lived with it for more than a century. To some unexpecting human...

There was another racket as four more humans angrily descended the ramp, and the soldier who slipped was suddenly on his feet, trembling. There was a crack louder than the boots of the marines could have made, and the human's chest exploded inside his cloak.

With the crack of the shot, the front rank of Earther marines dropped silently to one knee and took careful aim at the humans. The second rank's rifles rose, and the humans froze visibly.

Earthers would not fire unless given a reason, though in some circles of thought, the firing of a weapon at a diplomatic meeting could constitute a hostile act. But these marines waited as their Lieutenant Colonel edged slightly past Caine and held up an unnecessary hand to order a standby. It was up to the humans now...

The leader of the human group led two of the crimson-hooded soldiers as they hauled the corpse back into the pinnace. The fourth human took the dead one's place, seemingly unshaken.

It had all happened so quickly. Caine still wasn't sure he had fully processed it. He knew the history, he'd seen this Bingham fellow over the monitor, but he hadn't expected that a High Chancellor would condone such acts as this.

Caine took a somewhat calming breath and nodded to the Lieutenant Colonel who acknowledged and silently waved the marines back to attention. They snapped back to their display room poses. The humans at the ramp's foot appeared partially relieved — though by no means comfortable.

Finally Caine heard one set of footsteps, followed by what he estimated to be fifty others. Escorted by marines identical to those already at the base of the ramp, the High Chancellor slowly descended to the deck, his crimson tunic, pants, and cape fluttering as he marched. The marines at the ramp's foot leapt to their feet and snapped to attention with reasonable crispness.

They parted to let their High Chancellor pass, and he moved between them. Bingham walked slowly but determinedly towards Caine as the wolf held his position and looked the man over curiously. He looked much like the humans in the history books... maybe a little shorter than expected.

I must look as alien to him as he does to me.

The High Chancellor stopped a meter from Caine and spoke, "I am High Chancellor Bingham, of Genesis."

"I am First Lord of the Admiralty Caine, of the Earther Navy," Caine identified himself properly for the first time. The invitation to *Orion* had been brief and not terribly revealing.

The mention of *Earth* made the human party apprehensive, and though Bingham appeared outwardly calm, he wasn't. Caine could sense his nervousness and his steadfast refusal to let it surface.

"If you will come this way, High Chancellor, we will go to a meeting in which all of this will be explained," Caine continued.

Bingham paused for a second, then nodded, "Lead on, *Lord* Caine."

A human female stepped lightly but assuredly down the grated ramp in bay two. She was followed a little ways behind by half a dozen human troops, each wearing plain brown slacks and green tunics, and carrying lightweight projectile weapons.

The leader wore a green tunic with unimposing gold bars on the shoulders and a large number of medallions on the breast. She glanced around the bay with a slight nod and a half-concealed smile of approval before stepping up to Ursla.

The human stopped a couple of meters from the Commodore and looked up at the tall bear with slightly widening eyes. Ursla tried to look pleasant... and the human smiled in a friendly fashion and pushed one hand outward.

Ursla was pleasantly surprised by the human's seeming comfort in the bay — she had to admit she'd been expecting a different reaction. The handful of human troops that emerged from the ship behind her appeared equally calm, sizing up the situation around them with practiced ease. They exchanged nods with some of Ursla's own marines.

"I'm ArcGeneral Elizabeth Hastings, CO of the Genesis Fleet," the leading female in lead said in most friendly English.

Ursla's carefully manicured, formal welcome went overboard with that introduction.

"Commodore Andra Ursla, Earther Navy," Ursla's mighty hand stretched out to meet the ArcGeneral's, and she was careful not to crush every bone in the human's hand when they met.

"Well, I suppose we should go on to the meeting, Commodore," Hastings nodded slightly towards what she presumed was the door.

"Indeed," Ursla smiled carefully so as not to show too many of her teeth. "If you'll follow me."

CHAPTER 4

Ursla's expression grew cold as she led the ArcGeneral down one of *Orion's* immense corridors towards the conference room. The human marines' boots clicked loudly, complementing the low rumble of the boots of the Earther marines. The transformation from casual, pleasant beings to cold, calculating fighting troops had occurred as soon as the Church Crusaders had come into view down the hall. Ursla's expression had transformed along with her charges' moods.

Those Crusaders seemed to be the High Chancellor's instruments of terror. They certainly carried themselves with a sinister air — their crimson cloaks were cryptic, their dark patches menacing, and their demeanor was blatantly unpleasant. The plain green of Hastings' marines' uniforms and the khaki of the Earther Marine Corps stood in stark contrast, and marked the approach of the two bodies of non-religious troops on the deck.

Earther kodiaks, standing watch next to the Crusaders, offered Ursla barely visible nods of greeting. There were fewer bears than humans, but somehow that struck Ursla as unimportant. It seemed unlikely that the boldly dressed religious troops could match the large Earther professionals in any sort of engagement, let alone one in the close confines of the corridor.

Ursla raised one hand, stopping her troops and the humans a long way up the hall from the Crusaders. If the religious types became unpleasant, she'd keep her guests at a safe distance — her humans wouldn't be accidentally caught in the confusion...

My humans? Now there's an abrupt and unfounded association, if I've ever made one. I know nothing about these people, but my instincts are telling me to favor them.

So I just have to decide whether to trust my instincts or my brain...

Despite being only slightly more than half as tall as the Commodore, Hastings had kept pace as the pair moved up the hall towards the entrance to the conference room. The kodiaks snapped to attention as Ursla approached while the Crusaders glared at the ArcGeneral. When the first of the Crusaders reached a close distance, Ursla's Earther instincts, which usually remained pleasantly idle, detected an inherent danger. Maintaining self control was almost difficult.

Ursla had only felt this spike in instinct a few times in her life, and always during crises. The fact that this particular spike was occurring during what was supposed to be a diplomatic envoy was highly disturbing.

Well that inspires confidence.

Senses heightened, Ursla led the way through the hatch to where Caine and the High Chancellor awaited. Bingham was almost as tall as Hastings, his balding head rimmed with silvering hair. The baldness gave Ursla pause — she had seen plenty of bald men in old human films, but it was entirely more shocking in person.

Hastings bowed ruefully upon entry, taking Ursla so by surprise that she almost turned to see if the ArcGeneral had fallen. A silent warning from Caine passed intangibly through the air and stopped the Commodore immediately. Her instincts screamed, but Ursla forced herself to take a seat and watch as the High Chancellor appeared to deem Hastings at least somewhat worthy of his presence.

Caine's broadcast of general warning — appealing to Ursla's instincts — had not been visibly detected by the humans present. He probably wouldn't have sent the message if he thought it was discernable... so perhaps there were some latent communicative advantages on the Earther side.

Hastings was finally allowed to rise, and the Chancellor pointed her to a seat at the long table between himself and Ursla. She sat with complete stillness, appearing devoid of free will and completely under Bingham's control.

That realization caused Ursla's instincts to surge yet again. Hastings sat as though her spirit had been broken. It was a complete transformation and it disturbed Ursla deeply.

Still, she was a Commodore in a diplomatic situation, so her expression and her posture remained steady.

Caine approved of Ursla's restraint. He hoped his was as unwavering, because after sitting in a room with Bingham for only a few minutes, a feeling of dread quite unlike anything else he recalled was pounding through his blood.

It was nothing the human said... it wasn't even his visible attitude. Something about the High Chancellor seemed unstable. The man carried an air of contradiction, his arrogance acting as a mask for... doubt?

Caine knew that assessment was based purely on instinct. He also knew he couldn't fully trust that feeling in this circumstance — Earther instincts and human characteristics might not mesh properly.

But he still felt *very* uncomfortable.

As did Bingham, though the human was confident that he wasn't showing it. His stare remained fixed, an arrogant glare dominating his face as he tried to gather insights about the Earthers from the decoration of the briefing room.

It was an empty venture — everything in the room was austere and inhuman, much like its occupant. Caine, he was called, and he sat with as little expression as Bingham hoped he was showing. Bingham hated the sight of him — a beast trying to stand between the human race and the fulfillment of prophecy! How could this animal and his kind build these ships, arm those marines... even clothe themselves? How could they exist?

Unsettled feelings caused the High Chancellor's stomach to swirl, as the certainty of his own superiority was momentarily shaken. Stress and fear of being proven unworthy brought almost uncontrollable panic. His *life* was this Quest — the thought of being stopped at the hour of its fruition was cruel and damning.

It was too soon to condemn the chances of victory, Bingham reminded himself. This was only one more hurdle. The last and greatest hurdle, perhaps. Very great, as evidenced by the array of beast warriors in the landing bay, dressed in their smart khaki fatigues and hefting their weapons. Abominations... demons.

Never had he imagined a race that seemed more dangerous than the Larosians, but here was one that conveyed that impression. Bingham feared what he saw, because a place in his mind that he sought to ignore told him that they saw more of his true thoughts than even the telepathic Larosians could.

What *were* they...?

Ursla sat stiffly as the unnoticed silence grew, looking from Hastings' blank stare to Bingham's icy glare. Friendly guests, then... hopefully they were at least comfortable...

Ursla's internal sense of humor — the running commentary she allowed herself — was not as effective as usual. She liked to be lighthearted and amiable about all things, but the room was darkening in mood so quickly even her resilient ability to be an optimist was being affected. Her instincts continued to warn her that something was *wrong* here. With the humans.

Professionalism, again, forced it aside. She sent a shielded glance to Caine, and he offered similarly invisible affirmation. Time to get things moving.

"High Chancellor, I should welcome you again to *Orion*."

Bingham's mind stalled briefly as he tried to think of a reply. The simplest solution seemed best for this circumstance — he was the *High Chancellor*, and he would be as demanding as that position warranted. Uncertainty could go to the devil, he had his faith and his prophecy.

"What are you doing in this space, Lord Caine? It is ours by right."

His statement smacked of all the arrogance Bingham had ever shown his own world, and the still unmoving Hastings almost cringed at its heavy-handed use in this room.

The ArcGeneral didn't know why, but the presence of the two human-shaped beings was comforting. Even though she knew nothing about them, she felt... a *bond*. Or almost one, anyway... something that she trusted much more than she'd ever trust a Churcher.

She just wished she understood exactly where the bond came from — it was unsettling to trust like this. It was hard to trust the trust...

And now Bingham was clearly trying to browbeat the Earthers. He wanted their compliance. He wouldn't get it, of that Hastings was certain. But how far would he go? How far could these kind-seeming animals be pushed?

Just as Bingham hadn't been surprised by Caine's kind greeting, the First Lord of the Admiralty was completely prepared for the High Chancellor's arrogance. Even if it was only a mask Bingham wore to shield his doubt, it was visibly scathing.

Fortunately, Caine wasn't volatile. Earthers generally weren't, "Earth isn't *yours*, High Chancellor. We have occupied it since your race's departure."

Bingham scowled purposefully, "How kind of you. We will have it back, then. The Gods demand it."

Caine cocked an unimpressed eyebrow and looked to Ursla, who gave an almost invisible shrug. They'd hoped it would have been easier than this... even though they hadn't really expected it to be.

"The *Gods*, High Chancellor. We might be able to tell you something about your *Gods*. And your prophecies and your Quest, for that matter. We've had the opportunity to read about them, in both edited and unedited documents."

The High Chancellor's scowl deepened, "Ridiculous. Don't try to play prophet, *Lord* Caine. You will serve only to incur the wrath of the Gods."

Caine sighed thinly, "The Unity National, sir? This might be hard to accept, but the Unity was... *is*, I suppose, nothing more than a historical collection of humans. The proper name is actually *United Nations*, and it was the leading global government on Earth about seven centuries ago."

Bingham blinked. *What?* Did the beast expect such fictions and semantics to change destiny...

"There was a Holy War in those times. A Cold War of terrorism and conflicting faiths... Islam and Christianity. Crusades, High Chancellor, and they were ended once and for all with the release of what we've come to call the Omega Virus. The documents we've found call it a self-aware, intelligent disease, and it wiped out humanity."

Caine was trying to speak smoothly, but Bingham was still processing a challenge to his faith in the tidy phrases. It was as though the First Lord had read the scriptures and had somehow bastardized them to use them against the faithful. Pitiful... yes, pitiful.

"The War of the Gods, Lord Caine. It is from our scriptures, and your words do it injustice. Is that all of your fiction, or would you perhaps care to tell us how your beastly race appeared?"

Hastings stiffened and looked to Caine, but the Earther seemed outwardly calm.

Ursla saw the underlying current of increased tension. Setter Caine was a very wise Earther, but he was also one who had been a leader of his people for many years. He was nothing if not proud of their many achievements, and he was deeply offended by the slight.

But his discipline remained, and Caine clung to that as he tried to calm his breathing. His explanation continued unabated, "Well, High Chancellor, this virus wiped out most of your race, except for a colony that was sent into deep space by the United Nations. I suppose you'd call it the Genesis Exodus, because that's what they named it. They quarantined the colonists carefully, got them aboard the ship, and sent them on a century-long journey to Genesis. I presume that is your home?"

Bingham's eyes narrowed and he offered a single jerked nod. Caine knew of the Genesis Exodus... that was of the scriptures. The heretic...

"They psychologically conditioned the crew, High Chancellor. They programmed a new religion into the brains of the colonists, and developed an extensive mythos that would unite the colonists in a Quest to return to Earth. And they did it on a schedule, too, based on the projected time it would require for your people to develop the technology to return. They estimated 600 years, wrote it into your scriptures as a prophecy, and... well... here you are."

It had almost been amusing to listen to the heresy at first, but as the First Lord made his conclusions, Bingham was losing patience.

"Very clever. I'm sure you must enjoy twisting prophecy, yet you still do not explain your own damnable existence."

Caine and Ursla ground their jaws simultaneously, the purposefully abrasive High Chancellor angering them both even more thoroughly.

"*We* were likely developed to replace humanity," Caine said coolly, and Bingham snorted a laugh. The First Lord ignored him and spoke on, "Omega seems to have exhausted its food supply too quickly. With humanity gone it had nothing to feed on but for the crude primates that share your genetic characteristics. We believe it selected our order, Carnivora, and began manipulating the DNA of a single generation of offspring. It made us more human so we could serve as a food supply."

Bingham's deep scowl darkened further, "You call yourselves cattle then. And you defile scripture with heresy. I will not be swayed by stories, Lord Caine."

Caine's eyebrow arched slightly, "We grew and learned from the civilization of your ancestors, Chancellor. We discovered your people's stubborn streak, and your tendency for destruction. We had hoped your new society would have moved beyond that."

Bingham snorted a laugh, "Yet you meet us with a war fleet."

Ursla silently flagged Caine and he nodded thinly in reply. Dividing the workload here would help maintain calm... hopefully.

"I believe, High Chancellor, that our fleet was built in response to a potential threat — exactly the kind of threat your fleet has brought, in fact."

She locked eyes with Hastings as the latter looked up, recognizing the slight shift in tactics. The ArcGeneral wouldn't have expected to play a role in this theological debate, but now the Earthers were bringing Naval matters to light. Or perhaps Ursla was trying to communicate *something* to Hastings...

"We've been expecting your return for our entire existence. We've learned English to that end, and our education always includes the study of human culture. We're all somewhat humanoid, and so we predicted the... *varied* forms your return to Earth might take."

Bingham opened his mouth but Hastings spoke first, feeling as if she owed Ursla a fair answer, "Ours is a fleet built for a different war, Commodore. We have alien allies and enemies near our home — the Kroggs and Larosians. We have built this fleet with Krogg help and we have promised to assist them in return. We brought so many ships because we feared the Larosians–"

"Silence!" Bingham's fist hammered the table. "I will not have our secrets betrayed!"

Bingham was thrown off by Hastings' comments — she was not supposed to *speak*, but it was as though she'd been hypnotized by the big beast. It was her weak faith...

"We have come to take our planet back, Lord Caine. No matter what our situation is at home, we will see our Quest fulfilled," the tension in the High Chancellor's voice was more noticeable than before.

It was clear to Caine that Bingham hadn't expected Hastings to speak. The High Chancellor was trying to hold his cards close, but he wasn't as secure at home or here as he'd have liked.

"The Earther Navy will defend Earth, High Chancellor," Caine's words were simple. "There will be no unilateral occupation or conquest. We will gladly discuss terms for coexistence, but we remain senior here."

Bingham's nostrils flared, "You *beasts* have no right!"

Even as he yelled at the creature — the *Earther* — his mind was beginning to shudder. There would be a fight... and the contest would be difficult. But for all the dogma Caine had attacked, Bingham could quote thousands of verses of scripture which proved the Quest legitimate.

"Your track record with Earth's well-being has been abysmal, High Chancellor. We want the planet to remain in good order, and *habitable*. We will not simply choose to believe that your people have learned the lessons of your ancestors. Indeed, you don't even know of your ancestors," Caine's voice was cold in response to the human's anger.

"You speak of your fictions as though they *exist*, Caine. Your Earthers are the lie! Look at your animal beings! You are but scum!"

Caine's eyes hardened, "We coexist with each other and our home, High Chancellor. We do not exploit and destroy. You hardly seem qualified to judge us."

"You have *no claim*," Bingham was shouting now, his anger building to an inevitable eruption.

Hastings saw Caine's coat begin to rise, but Caine took two deep breaths to try to steady himself, "Your prophecy is a lie, High Chancellor. I understand your reluctance to accept this, so allow me to provide proof."

Hastings sat up with more interest. If Caine could *really* cut the legs out from under the Church, it might mean freedom for the Naval class...

The center of the table darkened and a three dimensional projection glowed into existence. The humans' eyes widened with surprise, and Bingham jerked back slightly in shock.

Ursla looked to Caine and tried to determine the state of his self control. His demeanor didn't inspire confidence.

"Here is the first page of your scripture book, if I'm not mistaken," Caine keyed a page to life, and it doubled and floated to Bingham and Hastings.

The ArcGeneral studied the page carefully, and Bingham scowled, "How did you get this? Did you steal it from our ships' archives?"

"This is a scan of the *original*," Ursla submitted in low tones, and Bingham glared up at her... briefly. Ursla's unimpressed expression forced his attention back to the screen.

"At the bottom is the signature of Secretary General Amy Valens. I believe she's known as the Holy Scribe in the texts," Caine's words were short now, and laced with his frustration.

"Yes yes — this changes nothing! Scripture is scripture, and no matter who has it, the meaning remains."

Caine's head tilted slightly, "Does it?"

A second page appeared next to the first, with the same signature at the bottom.

"This is the first draft of the page, High Chancellor. With commentary from government officials and Amy Valens herself in the margins."

Bingham froze. His eyes shifted between the two documents, first to the signatures on the bottoms and then to the text.

"This, the Holy Book of Genesis, known as the Scriptures, shall guide the human Quest to Earth," Bingham read the original words almost inaudibly.

"The first draft wasn't so catchy," Ursla turned to the original. "The following is the timetable for Earth recolonization under the Genesis Quest project."

The High Chancellor's head whipped up, then he glared at the opening sentence of the Earther page. The Commodore had read it directly.

And then in the margin to the side it said 'Not religious enough, Amy'.

The rest of the page was like that. The defining verses of Genesis scripture were being edited — they were different than they should have been. One spoke of 'psychological conditioning' instead of 'faith'. Reality seemed to fall away beneath the High Chancellor's feet.

They were telling the truth...? The page was by itself no evidence, but almost immediately upon his completion of its text, another pair appeared.

"We have the entire volume on file, High Chancellor. I recommend you read it."

At some point the thought struck him: his Quest, and by extension his *life*, was fiction.

He was reading bureaucratic evidence of its falsehood... evidence left by his ancestors through the Earthers...

Wait.

No, this was compelling, but it could still be false. Counterfeit. It *had* to be.

And then Hastings spoke and forced Bingham's mind back to reality, as she again acted out of place, "These seem legitimate, Lord Caine. Perhaps, though, you could release the originals for examination."

Caine let out a long-held breath, glad that the human Naval officer was level-headed. The Earthers had always been prepared to offer evidence in support of their claims, "We'd expected your interest, so we have them aboard. I'll have them sent to your–"

"*No!*" Bingham exploded to his feet, smashing his palm against the nearest keypad until the images went away.

"This is heresy!" he whirled on his ArcGeneral. "And *you*, attempting to *spread* it! I should have your head for your insolence, you contemptuous harlot!"

Caine's tension exploded through him, and Ursla bristled instantly.

Hastings shrunk down into her seat and bowed her head. She'd be dead very quickly if Bingham demanded it...

"And you heathen *Earther* beasts, trying to keep us from Earth. We will see it, and we shall have–"

Caine was on his feet in the sort of blinding motion that marked his skill on the sparring mat, "You will have to come through *us* to have your way, High Chancellor. And you will *not* win."

The First Lord seethed, and his eyes bored into Bingham. The High Chancellor felt a flicker of fear, backed suddenly by doubt, but forced it down.

"I will not be dictated to–"

Ursla needed to stop this short of war, and she knew it. Coming to her feet, she cleared her throat, "I think we should separate ourselves, perhaps consider our respective positions."

Caine blinked against his anger; Bingham's head whirled to glare at Ursla. The Commodore's eyes broke his stare, and he began to breath again.

His angry eyes turned back to Caine's, and the First Lord's muscles unconsciously tensed. He was ready to cross the table and–

"High Chancellor, we would like to offer your people an opportunity to visit Earth. Perhaps travelling to the planet will help clarify our position..."

Oh no. Ursla hadn't thought before she'd said it, but she couldn't go back on the offer. And now she had to make it work...

"Perhaps I could coordinate with the ArcGeneral to make arrangements, while you return to your ship."

Caine began to blink his brain out of the haze that was clouding it, "Yes. That's... quite right."

Bingham's breathing came in short bursts. He saw it now, the weakness in Hastings' faith had been detected, and she was being targeted by heathen. She was beyond saving.

"Have it your way. We are not finished with this, Caine. Gods help us, Earth is ours."

He stormed out, and the room was left with the darkest of atmospheres.

CHAPTER 5

Ursla wasn't sure whether to regret her quick intervention at the meeting table or not. She let the possible consequences slowly roll over in the back of her mind while she escorted Hastings through *Orion*.

Having been Captain of the First Rate during its initial trials, Ursla was familiar with the inner workings of the ship, though much time had passed since then and there had obviously been some changes.

Despite her misgivings about the meeting, she knew she had to give Caine time to collect himself after his bout with the High Chancellor. With the fleet at heightened alert, she couldn't ask Forepaw to give this tour, so it was entirely up to her. Not that Hastings seemed like bad company compared to the Chancellor. The two were nothing alike, at least from what Ursla had seen so far.

Hastings was wide-eyed as she followed Ursla through *Orion's* bulk. The corridors were more than twice as tall as those aboard *Genesis*, probably for characters such as Ursla. The plethora of officers and ratings they passed seemed uninterested in her, allowing Hastings to observe them at something of an advantage — she got to see the normal workings of the crew. And there were of so many different species!

There were smaller, white and black versions of Ursla, similar sized and multi-colored Caines, and Tirgers — *tigers* — of assorted colors as well. They were adorned in either the dark blue of the Navy or the marine khaki, and they cut sharp figures, despite their oddly humanoid forms.

Ursla picked up on the anxiousness and the quick glances given Hastings by the crew, and was glad they'd kept about their business. Hopefully Hastings hadn't noticed — there'd been no indication that humans picked up on the clues that signalled the Earthers' heightened instincts.

As the awkward pair reached an entrance to the low port gun deck they paused — partly to let Ursla introduce their location and partly to let Hastings catch her breath after a brisk walk on her shorter legs.

"Here's the local entrance to port side low gun deck. I think this might interest you."

Ursla's simple introduction coaxed a nod from the ArcGeneral, "Shouldn't this be restricted? I mean these are the weapons my esteemed leader would challenge..."

The hatch swung open as Ursla thumbed the appropriate key, cutting

Hastings off. The human stepped through followed by Ursla, "Knowing what they are and how we use them won't change the fact that they're here, ArcGeneral."

The answer, while unexpected, fit with all the Earther actions so far — they had yet to try to conceal anything from the Genesis Fleet. It was an openness entirely foreign to the human. No one opened doors they didn't have to on Genesis ships, and there was certainly no volunteering of information.

Thoughts stopped... if only for a second.

It was *enormous*.

"Big, isn't it?" Ursla asked with a hint of pride.

One of *Orion's* mark XIX energy cannon was directly in front of Hastings'... it was at least eight meters tall, with a twenty meter long barrel... Good *Gods*.

Hastings drifted slowly towards the thing as if in a dream state, assessing all of its parts and guessing at its capabilities.

It was *amazing*.

"This is a mark XIX, biggest we mount on starships. Only the First Rates get these — and not every First Rate gets them either. The smaller the ship the smaller the gun. My frigates mount thirty-eight mark XIII's. They're smaller than these by a third or so..."

The gun deck was *cavernous*.

It stretched up.

It stretched out.

"H...How *many* does *Orion* mount — of these I mean...?"

Ursla was both amused and pleased by Hastings' reaction. It was gratifying to know that *Orion* (and therefore the fleet) lived up to — and beyond — the standards of another race's Navy.

"A total of 175. That's seventy-five to a broadside, fifteen bow chasers and ten stern chasers."

Hastings kept her jaw rigidly clamped, forced her shock to dissolve a little, and blinked her brain back into working order.

Partial working order, anyway.

Holy *Gods*.

"Th...that's pretty... um... wow..."

Trying to disguise her shock would do little for her image now.

"I know, it's overwhelming at first. These guns can stop just about anything — small planets even. The thought of them being turned on a hull is a bit disturbing," Ursla's statement did little to settle Hastings. She could picture these guns shattering her fleet, but quickly dismissed the image. That wouldn't happen unless she let it happen. Unless Caine let it happen. And it seemed unlikely either of them would if there was any way to avoid it.

"So, umm... how exactly do you target and fire one of these things?"

Ursla's response came in the form of a thick finger pointing to a platform coming out of the wall about eight meters directly above them.

"Gunners' platform. Every gun has one, with a crew of five, including a Gun Captain. Perhaps you'd be interested in going aboard one?" Ursla elaborated.

"How do we get up there?"

Ursla gestured to a large red square on the gray deck and a matching one on the ceiling fifteen meters above. Hastings and Ursla stepped onto the lower square just as the ArcGeneral had decided it must be some sort of elevator.

Suddenly she was floating. Up and up and *up*.

"Energy lift, very handy for short rises without compromising pressure seals on the deck."

There was no sensation of rising — it felt like there was solid deck under her — but by looking down through meters of plain air it was obvious that she had nothing beneath her...

And then the deck of the gunners' platform surrounded her as the lift deposited her at its junction.

The gun crew snapped hastily to attention, the unexpected visitors surprising but not shaking them — until they saw the human. A tiny, quickly-hidden shudder of shock ran through the group.

"As you were," Ursla said formally, and the gunners went back to their duties, sitting down behind a pair of two-person consoles that faced out through the now visible gunport. The Gun Captain sat behind a desk-console at the platform's rear.

Ursla led the way to that position and nodded, "Lieutenant Broadpaw."

Ursla kept the relief out of that acknowledgment. Varnia Broadpaw had been the Bridge Carronade commander on *Cerberus* for a year, so was well-known to the kodiak. A friendly face in this situation was certainly helpful...

Hastings faced the gunport, then slowly looked left and right at the rows of gun platforms that seemed to stretch eternally each way. An odd thought struck her. The crew of this platform was made up entirely of canines, even the Gun Captain. The crew to her left was completely made up of felines, and to her right was a crew completely composed of bears. Discrimination...?

"Commodore," she caught Ursla's attention, "What's the point of segregating these gun crews?"

Ursla turned from her conversation with the Gun Captain and glanced quickly at the surrounding platforms as if to reorient herself. Hastings was expecting a clipped and diplomatic excuse as to why she couldn't be told that. Maybe she was even hoping it was a dark secret... a social stigma... some flaw.

"It has to do with the rate of fire and accuracy. Feline crews tend to fire at a faster rate than either of the other species, but they're less accurate. Canines are next fastest and a bit more accurate, and the bears are slowest but tend to be the most accurate of the lot. On the larger ships we stagger the crews so that the ship keeps a volume of fire up at each level, but smaller ships — my frigates for instance — tend to have mixed crews. We don't have enough guns to make the system practical."

No secrecy, no discrimination no attempt to hide the facts at all...

Is there another shoe waiting to drop here? Is this naiveté... or confidence? Could they be blamed for being confident with ships like these? Is there something to be learned from them...?

"Do your ships have similar crews?" Ursla asked softly.

The question made Hastings pause — she hadn't been asked much thus far. Her old intelligence training from the academy demanded she evade the question. It could open a door...

Or Ursla's simply curious. And she's polite. I should reciprocate, at the very least.

"No, our ships run off a central targeting AI. That's backed up by a gunner but... well, it isn't anything like *this*," Hastings didn't bother hiding her admiration.

Ursla noted a very slight shift in Hastings' demeanor; it seemed positive.

No more hiding... finally, can I meet the real being within?

"The Lieutenant has agreed to test fire her gun for your benefit," thoughts aside and back to business. "She won't actually shoot but she'll *simulate*."

Good thing... a shot now would end bloodily.

Hastings nodded in silence — not ready to contaminate the moment with some tactical observation which wouldn't serve any purpose in the first place. Ursla gestured her towards a seat near the Gun Captain's desk and she sat quietly.

Now I really get to see the efficiency of these people in action. Why am I so terrified and so comfortable at the same time? Because they could kill me and every human within light years. But they won't...?

"Targeting online," one of the gun crew barked and Hastings sat with interest.

The gun began to hum as the gunner aimed at a non-existent target — adjusting its trajectory to hit the target perfectly. A soft ping resonated through the platform as the gun tracked, and then with a deadly cold shriek the lock was made.

"We're locked on the enemy ship's engines, ma'am."

Engines? Not going for the kill...? Was that for my benefit or standard practice...?

"Gun stand by..." Broadpaw's voice was smooth as she watched her well-honed crew perform. She was proud, and Ursla could plainly see it.

Not inappropriate, that pride — the crew was acquitting itself admirably. Of course, this was *Orion*. Most of its 2,500 souls had been hand picked for their expertise and skill — one could expect a lot from these ratings.

"...*Fire*."

Although no energy erupted geyser-fashion from the barrel's mouth, the simulated force recoiled the gun along its track. That startled Hastings, and left nothing to the imagination about the remarkable firepower of the cannon. The deck tremored slightly as the bulk came rumbling back.

Ursla leaned closer to Hastings' ear, "Simulation uses grav anchors to recoil the gun — pretty dramatic really."

Gods. Could we ever stop that?

Like lightning. Gray flashes followed in quick response by white ones, surging back and forth across the padded sparring ring. The gray would halt for a second; another blur and another...

And then the agile wolf had the bulky polar bear pinned to the mat like a netted animal. Seconds later she hopped to her feet, laughing with the polar bear as he stood and dusted himself off.

"Lucky that time, Lass, but I'll have you tomorrow!" the bear boomed as they walked off.

"Not likely my friend..." she replied, but was then beyond the range of Hastings' ears.

"That... they...?"

Ursla smiled briefly in response, then shrugged. Hastings had to admit that the Commodore's presence was feeling increasingly... comfortable. *Like an old friend shaped like a giant stuffed bear. What an odd thought.*

"Those two? They're the old timers. Been sparring for ninety years now. One of these days he'll get her."

Old? Sarah Manchester mightn't be able to keep up with them... and she's the best in the fleet.

"Well, could I see some of the best you have? That was... amazing..." Hastings couldn't resist requesting it. So much wisdom and skill flinging itself together in bouts of controlled aggression piqued her interest.

"Certainly. I believe Lieutenant Tarkam and Sergeant Major Carras will be sparring next — they're the best on the ship — some of the best in the fleet," Ursla understood her guest's attention. She too enjoyed watching the bouts of skill and she was also an avid sparrer, surprisingly agile for her size.

A feline and a canine had stepped into the ring, wearing white robes and moving cautiously. Two more friends and rivals. Tarkam was a shorter southern wolf with a tan-brown coat, a very sleek physique, and certain confidence in his posture. Carras was a black panther with a shining coat and an angular face. She too was secure in her confidence.

These two must be–

It happened before Hastings finished mentally analyzing the possibilities. Carras went forward only to find Tarkam was no longer where he had been. She didn't seem surprised as she dropped into a battle stance, mirroring Tarkam who had appeared behind her. Then the brown flashed forward, a foot... or was it an arm... striking. The blow was deflected by a flicking shrug outward, and then the black moved again in a streak, followed by the brown.

They moved with precision, speed and assurance. They *knew* when an attack was coming and where it would land. By the time a blow was to connect, they were either ready to counter it or had moved away and were spiraling into their own assault. Yet neither found an advantage.

The exchange went on for what felt like hours but could only have been minutes. Ten. Twenty. At thirty minutes, Hastings could see no noticeable loss of speed in the movements, but it appeared that Ursla could. Even before the ArcGeneral could see a move, Ursla was reacting — with a nod or a bit of a chuckle — to its response.

Hastings had a feeling this wasn't an uncommon characteristic among Earthers — if the Earthers sparring on the floor were any indication, the breed of beings now guarding the Sol system operated on a physical and *instinctive* plain somewhere above the human norm. They were quicker, in all senses... of course, that was a couple of hours of observation talking, but it seemed accurate enough.

Finally, after forty minutes, a chime sounded and the match ended in a stalemate, the opponents laughing and noting flaws in the other's technique — giving tips and joking. Not noticeably out of breath... at least not to Hastings.

"That was a hard match!" Ursla was enthused. "I haven't seen the two of them training with each other for a while. Lucky thing you were here when you were!"

That depends on your perspective, I suppose.

My crews are the best... or at least the best we have to offer. But these Earthers... it's like they're on an entirely different level. They're relaxed at General Quarters, they're casual in allowing me around their flagship... they seem to know they can handle us.

They probably can...

"What is this? It's *delicious*!" Hastings jabbed savagely into the main dish with her fork.

There was little worry about volume in the abandoned wardroom in *Orion's* upper quarter. They had come for a meal and had decided on a place where they could have privacy — to keep the ArcGeneral from feeling awkward.

"Salmon. A good fish, I must say. Bears have been eating it for as long as we've been around, and the rest of the Earther population really latched onto it when they discovered it could be synthesized. I *love* it." Ursla was hunched over the table opposite Hastings, shoveling part of her gargantuan serving into her mouth with what could best be described as a mini-pitchfork.

"This is synthetic?" Hastings took another loving bite of the rich food.

Ursla nodded again, "We used to have to fish for it in our oceans, but we developed the technology to assemble 'pseudofish' from raw atoms a hundred-odd years ago. I like it better than the original, honestly — boneless too. When

I was a cub we still ate the real stuff and the bones really slowed me down."

Hastings was already nodding when something dawned on her, "When you were a *cub*... Ursla... forgive me for asking but *how old are you*?"

Ursla blinked, wondering why she could be offended by such a question.

"I'm 146, rather young for the rank I suppose..."

Hastings almost choked — luckily she'd swallowed before the answer.

"How long do you think you'll live... exactly?"

Ursla stopped shoveling food for a second, blinking, "Oh, 250 years or so. Maybe 300. Why... how old are you? I wouldn't put you a day over... 190..."

Hastings blinked, inhaling instead of swallowing some of the water she'd been sipping. She started to cough and Ursla almost stood, only to be lowered by Hastings' reassuring hand.

"*190*? I'm not a Gods-damned day over forty-five, thank you very much!"

That spawned silence in Ursla. *They haven't fixed that yet... even after seven centuries?*

As if she'd read the Commodore's thoughts, Hastings added, "I'll be *very* lucky if I see your age, my friend!"

Ursla could not contain her surprise, "Documents from the humans of Earth suggested a short life span, but we'd assumed you'd be lengthening it by the time you got back here... you know, playing with genetics and so on."

Hastings couldn't hide her shock, "The closest we have to effective treatment for short life is diet and exercise. It only works so well."

Ursla cocked an eyebrow and smiled a little, "I don't know, I think my fitness regime does me credit."

With another blink, Hastings smiled too, "You're not so bad. I mean, it's relative isn't it — if I ate with that pitchfork of yours, I'd have a stroke."

That drew a deep laugh from Ursla — and in her amusement she dropped her pitch...*fork* onto the table with a thud. The resulting shudder sloshed water over the sides of their glasses and bounced Hastings' fish off its plate.

The ArcGeneral looked from her escort to the fish and back, then inexplicably started laughing too, her face turning red as she leaned forward and tried to recapture her food.

As Ursla's brain gradually kicked her back into sanity, she took a deep breath, "Well then. There's much for us to learn, I think."

Hastings nodded with some difficulty, dropping her salmon onto her plate with limited grace, "You're not kidding."

She hadn't laughed so hard in years... what did that say about Earthers?

More importantly, what did that say about the *Church*?

Nothing she didn't already know...

CHAPTER 6

Crusader Shappa Bactule stood stiffly in the quarters of his High Chancellor. He was fiercely loyal to Bingham, to the Holy Cause, and to the absolute purification of the human race, although that ultimate goal would have to wait until after Earth had been retaken. He hated all that was not the Church's *true* way, and had a particular aversion to the *Naval* way. He would not hesitate to sacrifice his or *any* life for the Cause.

Bingham reflected on this as he accepted the leader of the Crusaders into his quarters. He was well aware that Bactule was someone he could truly trust — not a doubter like Hastings. He suppressed a shudder with that thought. The entire encounter with the Earthers had seen him weakened, and the ArcGeneral had, unsurprisingly, given him no support. Traitor. "I suppose you are wondering, Shappa, why I have asked you here."

Bactule was silent. He had been wondering, but he would not ask. Meetings with the High Chancellor were *never* held in his quarters. But upon practical analysis, it did make sense; these quarters were likely the only place aboard *Genesis* that couldn't be observed. The rest of the ship was vulnerable to the Navy and its tools of subversion.

"I *had* wondered, Your Eminence, though I had assumed you were worried about the sensitivity of the subject and wished no one else to be privy to our conversation," Bactule's voice was controlled and respectful.

Bingham smiled with shrouded relief. Where Hastings had offered his faith no support at all, this tall, dark-skinned man was truly a supporter of the Quest. And that went to the heart of the matter at hand.

He may be a pillar for my faith in this ordeal.

"Very perceptive my friend. That's exactly why you're here," Bingham paused as he gestured the Shappa to a seat, then sat opposite him.

"We must remove the Navy, Shappa. *Eliminate* them."

Bactule froze in his chair — this was excellent news, or would have been if not for the fact that the fleet was impotent without its crews. But what had brought this sudden pronouncement...?

Bingham anticipated his subordinate's confusion, "These Earthers are a corrupting band of beasts, Shappa. They lied to my face about creation... so effectively I was very nearly convinced, Gods save me. They *tempt* with plausible lies, and hide their savagery behind a mask of apparent civility... until they are angered by the Gods' truth."

The line of thought slightly confused Bactule, "But... the Navy, Your Eminence?"

With a nod, Bingham took a breath, "Hastings has already *abandoned* herself to temptation. One of theirs gravitated toward her immediately. They saw her weakness, I think. And I fear they will turn her. And then the Navy. Think of it, *I* was made to doubt..." and he still felt the uncertainty they'd instilled, though he would never admit it "...what of the faithless Navy? One encounter and they will turn on us and side with the animals."

Bactule was silent, eyes wide.

"We cannot afford the liability of the faithless, my friend. They are capable of crippling the Quest if they turn, and we cannot allow that."

The Shappa was uncertain as he frowned in reply, "What may we do, then? To eliminate them now or have them turn and be crushed... it makes no difference, Your Eminence. We will have ships with no crews."

Bingham nodded in understanding, then launched into his scheme, "I know Crusaders are not trained in the science of ship piloting, but I think we can teach them. Then we can take every ship in our Holy fleet and proceed in the best interests of our people."

Bactule's eyes narrowed thoughtfully. Such a plan had never been conceived, because it would have meant disgrace for those Holy men put behind consoles. Naval work was society's lowest vocation. But the new crisis now upon them cast 'disgrace' in an entirely different light, and the High Chancellor's plan might actually be possible. The Quest fleet was commanded by about two million Naval crew, and there were nine million Crusaders between the landing forces and shipboard contingents. Admittedly, eight million were spread out in eight Colonizers, but that still left a core on the fleet's warships.

On smaller ships — anything below a Heavy Cruiser — those Crusaders did not have a great numerical advantage, the ships didn't have enough room. But aboard the *key* units in the fleet, the truly worthwhile ships with some tonnage and punch, there were close to even numbers. There *was* a chance. But his Crusaders were trained to be rigid warriors — fearless and utterly deadly... not... well... *Naval types*.

Bingham's small but telling smile alerted the Shappa that he too had thought of this. But training men in the art of ship command would not be easy — it took the infidel Navy, whose life was devoted to the fleet business, many years to produce effective officers. Faith would have to help compensate for inexperience...

"Well, Shappa?" Bingham pried gently, and Bactule squared his shoulders — which he hadn't realized he'd slumped — and collected himself.

"We can, I think, provide the training... though I must admit I would have no idea what to do with a space fleet." He paused. "Frankly, Your Eminence, we cannot command this fleet without the Navy and that is perhaps the danger. If your inspired revelations indeed come to pass, we will be seriously disadvantaged."

Bingham nodded slowly, then spoke,

"But, can we teach your Crusaders how to carry the fleet's weight? Or more specifically, do you think we could dump the required information into their implants so they could actually utilize the knowledge?"

That thought set Bactule back a step. The High Chancellor was either very quick on his feet at the moment, or he'd planned for this contingency before setting out on the Quest.

As unbelievable as it seemed to Bingham, this was a plan he'd improvised coming back from *Orion* when he'd been a mass of rage and anger. The Gods of the Unity National had stayed with him, helped him through the struggles, and then, when the situation seemed to be most desperate, elevated him to new levels of thought. The last number of hours had been a challenge to his faith — the Earther lies were tempting in their logic, but he *had* to remain steadfast in his beliefs.

They were, after all, his life and the foundation of his people.

He'd been able to see how the Earthers had favored ArcGeneral Hastings. It was clear that she'd been tempted to side with those heathen — she was not strong in faith to begin with. Both a Naval officer and a woman, a highly contemptuous combination. Women lacked the strength to focus on the Cause, Naval officers lacked belief in the Cause entirely... Nothing of the past could be changed now. He could only gain justice...

The clarity of his thoughts astonished Bingham even more. Not even the most clever heathen could out-fox him when he was like this. The Gods were one with him! All personal issues aside, he had brooded in his pinnace, and decided that he would support a tour of Earth — he would send Bactule to appraise the Earther position, and let Hastings be further tempted. He could see how damned she was by how she, and indeed her Naval types, acted on that tour. In the meantime, he would have his loyal Crusaders learn the trade of ship flying, and all would be complete. Then damn the cursed Navy! It was a clever ploy — all from his mind. His *touched* mind, for surely now the Gods were helping him.

As Bactule waited for the Chancellor's next words, he considered the proposal of using implants to teach Crusaders how to fight warships. Crusaders were entered into the Churches' minions at the age of ten, young boys committed to the service by proud, faithful parents. They went through much hardship; almost sixty percent washed out and returned to their homes as commoners. Those who reached the level of Crusader were heralded as the Warriors of the Gods, and were ultimately given cerebral implants that allowed data to enter their brain raw from core dumps, and let the Crusaders learn much more quickly than the rest of the population.

To do what the High Chancellor proposed was actually only an adaptation of normal teaching, but...

"It is a very good plan, Your Eminence, but I can foresee a problem," Bactule was cautious about his approach to this subject — he didn't want to offend his Lord and Master. "If we take the two million we need to run the fleet and give them the core dumps, they will loose all of their ground combat skill."

Bingham raised an eyebrow.

"The human mind has a limited capacity for raw data, and the old data — and much of their own personalities for that matter — will have to be erased to accommodate the necessary information. That would still leave us six million Crusaders with which to retake Earth, but this may be a concern."

Bingham nodded. He was now more grateful than ever that he'd brought along seventy-five percent of the standing Crusader army — despite being warned that leaving only a quarter might be... *dangerous*. Another decision guided by the Gods, no doubt.

"They would be martyrs — they would have sacrificed themselves to save the Quest. They *will* understand."

The Shappa nodded.

"I will immediately begin selecting the divisions for this task. The best of the legions will stay as they are; I will choose the least skilled for this duty. They will have to be aboard our Colonizers. The presences aboard the Naval ships must remain static, lest the Earthers and the Navy attempt to act as we exchange garrisons. Trying to bring more Crusaders aboard every ship in the fleet would tip off the traitors."

Bingham smiled, "My thoughts exactly." He paused, "Now, there is a second matter for us to address. I will be sending you to Earth."

CHAPTER 7

The gray pinnace sat on the other side of the observation deck's glass, and Hastings contemplated it as though it held the answers to every question in the cosmos. To Ursla it seemed clear that the ArcGeneral didn't want to return to her command or face the High Chancellor.

Ursla was troubled by the notion of division among the humans, although she had to admit it might prove useful. If the Naval humans, who seemingly made up the majority of the ships' crews, could be convinced not to fight... well, that was a lot to expect, just now.

Bingham seemed to enjoy being a harsh, cruel dictator. He'd thoroughly raked Hastings' knuckles with virtually no provocation, and had certainly been unpleasant in his words with the Earthers.

Meanwhile, Ursla had to admit she was taking a liking to Hastings.

Even reflecting on how the two human parties came aboard, it was clear they had different values. And the fact that Bingham could attack his own officers with so little reason seemed to say something about him, and, Ursla guessed, his kind. The *Church* people, anyway. Those in pursuit of their Holy Cause were fanatics. Apparently.

"Well, the tour was great, Ursla."

Hastings turned slowly and brought herself to a chair in the landing bay's observation deck. Since this was only the secondary bay its observation deck was far from glamorous, but it was functional. Dark tinted glass, a small table with four chairs, a small holo plot — it was compact but effective.

Ursla nodded, "Thanks. Now the only thing left to talk about is the visit to Earth."

Hastings blinked. She'd temporarily forgotten about *that*. And despite the fact that she feared what Crusaders might do on Earth — or, at least, what they'd try to do before being slaughtered by the Earthers — the opportunity to send some of her own was too good to pass up.

Maybe even to see the planet myself...

"Yes, we should get right to that..."

Setter Caine centered his balance and dropped into a battle stance again. The sparring chamber, a cavernous gray room attached to his personal quarters, was a foggy and distant reality.

He *fought.*

His arms lashed out with deadly proficiency, his legs flew like well-guided battering rams. The sparring holos didn't have a hope.

He would respond to actions almost before they happened — a block to a punch just as it was being thrown — not a response but a preemption. His instincts were charged.

A sparring holo — a black-garbed one representing the master level of skill — appeared in front of him as the last blue garbed ones fell. This was his first true challenge, and he'd been sparring for three hours to reach it. The black one he could defeat, but when he faced *six* at once it was far more difficult.

And he *wanted* difficulty, because he was still seething with anger and needed an outlet. He moved swiftly, smashed into the holo with a well-placed kick, then jabbed into it again with a punch, and a kick, and an elbow strike to the throat...

The holo disappeared, dead for all intents and purposes, and the computer triggered the appearance of six more just like it. No gradual increase, no rest. The fray came fast and potent — just the way Caine liked it.

Anger was driving the First Lord to new levels of agility. The heightened instincts that clutched his mind let him strike faster, and more lethally. Even in his youth, he hadn't met attackers with such prowess.

The six moved as one, immediately striking at his throat. Predictable — but he wasn't where they had seen him, and the attack failed. Then his leg turned into a rod of iron, driven straight into one of the spines of the attackers. It vanished.

They moved again, recalculating where he was, what he was doing, and came to meet him. Again he stopped the attacks before they had been delivered — his instincts telling him where the blows would originate and what blows they would be. He intercepted them, deflected them, and then, with a single concentrated move, snapped the neck of another opponent with one hand.

As it vanished, two legs took him in the ribs. Caine had known they were coming but this time had no chance to avoid. Instead he used the momentum they provided, absorbed the shock and somersaulted backward, landing squarely before launching at the attackers, his own legs like ballistic missiles. The unfortunate holos vanished as he made contact with their throats.

The last two attacked, their strikes coming in blurs as they worked together to overwhelm his defenses. He had never gotten farther than this before, and he'd been sparring with this program for almost ninety years.

But on this occasion the holos found their attacks blocked almost as soon as they were conceived. Caine drove a deadly elbow into one's nose, driving the bone upwards. The last opponent tried to attack once, missing as Caine shifted away from it on strong feet. He drove his right arm into its neck, brought the holo back onto his knee and broke its spine.

When it vanished, Caine suddenly realized he wasn't even tired. But...

The crimson warrior holo suddenly appeared in front of him, its robe reminiscent of Bingham's. There was no higher level than crimson — to defeat *blue* showed the fighter to be expert, black showed the warrior to be a master, but only seven or eight Earthers had ever beaten crimson...

Caine was gone again as the holo attacked, and he was so absorbed that his mind became as swift and deadly as a battle computer. The crimson robe vanished, he spun without thought and engaged the six crimsons that appeared.

Ursla watched Hastings' pinnace depart and then went to see Caine. The last half hour, reserved for the planning of a trip to Earth, had been no more stressful than the tour of *Orion*, but Ursla was still left unsettled.

In two days, 200 humans would land on Earth to tour Earther civilization — with an escort of course. The thought of Hastings and her sort on Earth actually pleased Ursla, but the Crusaders...

Caine's quarters were quickly in front of her, and she rang the admittance chime. She paused for a response by the First Lord, but he made none.

He might be sparring. She'd known him long enough to know how he let off steam.

Ursla keyed the door opener and the lockless hatch slid open. She stepped in slowly, taking in her surroundings. Caine's walls showed all of his flag pennants, photos of him with his family, and a glowing holo of his first command — *ENS Indefatigable*. To one side was the entrance to his sleeping quarters, to the other the entrance to his personal sparring area — the place he used to keep himself fit and battle smart.

Judging by the sounds of combat emanating from the sparring floor, her guess had been right. She smiled slightly.

Might go help him out. Sounds like he's having a hard time.

Ursla pulled off her outer dress tunic, preferring her undershirt for hand-to-hand battle. She drifted silently to the sparring floor, but stopped to gape as she arrived.

Twelve crimsons battled Caine — and they were obviously losing. Badly. His moves were so fast, so precise that the holos winked out of existence one by one — even despite their lightning speed.

As the last of the crimson disappeared, *twenty-four* more took its place.

Twenty-four!

Caine was beginning to show visible stress in dealing with these. Ursla wouldn't stand for that; her friend would not go without help. She pounced — amazingly agile for her mass — and slammed a leg as broad as a tree trunk through three of the holos, sending them to oblivion. Caine's head came around.

Where did that come from?

Ursla also seemed to be performing at double her peak efficiency. Her arms flew to meet blows before they were thrown, her strikes were decisive and deadly. Despite the pleasant time with Hastings, much anger had buried itself in the Commodore's mind, courtesy of the High Chancellor. Now it was being vented.

Caine accepted the aid almost subconsciously, adjusting his posture and focus away from Ursla. She would cover his back, and he would cover hers. His fist caved in the face of one of the holos, and it vanished. His foot snapped one's spine and it vanished. Her massive knee snapped one's back, her elbow snapped one's neck.

And they vanished. All of them.

There was a pause filled with heavy breathing as the computer reset. It had programs for this contingency, but they were likely not well used. Ursla and Caine remained in their deep-set combat stance as they waited, slowly calming and tightening themselves.

Forty-eight crimson warriors appeared. They swept into action.

Half an hour passed without any conscious marking as Ursla and Caine continued to battle more and more holos. Nothing seemed to stand in their way. They battled tirelessly as more and more crimson warriors came and went.

And then the simulation came to an end, "Cycle complete."

Ursla was so fixed in her battle readiness it took a minute for her brain to consciously retake control; Caine took slightly longer. Their breathing had returned to its previous calm, and now they slowly stood straight, their combat stances fading.

Caine blinked, "Andra, how long ago did you arrive?"

Ursla blinked as well, "Um... I'm not entirely sure..."

Caine swirled his water around in the mug and pondered what had happened. He couldn't draw a conscious line between when he'd been thinking about his sparring and when he'd simply been fighting. It was disconcerting to think that he could release his awareness like that, but at least he had recognized Ursla as an ally when she arrived. Had he attacked her, he would have had reason to be concerned.

"You know, when humans do this they emit *sweat* from their pores to cool the body. We just breath out excess heat," Ursla remarked as she sat across from him.

"I'd heard that, actually," Caine smiled a bit at his comrade. "My granddad wrote the book on them, remember?"

Ursla shrugged, "You might have forgotten."

Caine chuckled for a moment, then took a deep breath and fell silent. What was in store for Earth and the humans now?

"So, Andra, how do you read these people? What are they, what do they *really* want?"

The question was expected but still uncomfortable. Ursla shifted in her chair for a moment and sighed.

"I get a good feeling around Hastings. She seems... reasonable. But you saw it as clearly as I did, Bingham has her under his thumb. When we were alone on the tour she seemed competent and professional — she struck me the same way any of ours would: interested in what the other fleet is like."

Caine nodded slowly and took a breath, "I am *very* curious about their fleet, Andra."

Ursla's eyes narrowed slightly, "You're thinking something."

A frown formed on Caine's face and he looked flatly at Ursla, "We stating the obvious now?"

Ursla grinned and shrugged, "I like to play narrator."

Caine's eyebrows bobbed and then he took another long sip of water, "I very much doubt a man as seemingly irrational as Bingham could command a fleet in action. He panicked when he saw that page... it doesn't seem that he's been under fire much."

"To be fair, neither have we..." Ursla leaned forward thoughtfully, "but point taken, go on."

Caine tipped his water to Ursla in acknowledgement of her point, then went on, "Hastings had her life threatened by the leader of the Quest, and kept her head. That suggests two things to me... she's got the sense or the experience to remain stable under pressure... and that somehow, she has very little respect for him. I mean, if I threatened your death, what would you do?"

Ursla cocked an eyebrow, "Get your head checked."

Caine blinked and sighed, "Bad example. All the same, it seems to me that she's used to dealing with that sort of heavy-handedness. She was certainly well practiced in staying quiet."

There was a pause, and Caine finished his water while Ursla's eyes narrowed thoughtfully, "You're thinking the segregation is that bad?"

Caine nodded slowly, "It's a hunch, and I won't say anything definite until that tour of yours is over. But it might be an opportunity."

"I was thinking as much earlier. If we could get the Navy to liberate itself somehow... use the chaos to force Bingham to peace. His Crusaders won't do him much good if we can immobilize the fleet..." Ursla leaned back and ground her jaw.

"I'm not getting too hopeful yet. When's the tour?" Caine's tone reflected his caution.

"Only forty-eight hours; they're coming in separate groups."

Caine harrumphed, "I'm sure they are. It'll be up to you to look into this, then."

Ursla nodded, "I intend to."

CHAPTER 8

"...so in forty-eight hours, 200 people will be escorted to Earth and given a full-day tour of the important sites. Then the Naval officers will stay a night on an Earther ship to examine efficiency," Hastings finished her report calmly, and flicked her eyes across to see Bingham's reaction.

The bald man was sitting at his desk, his face fixed in a cold stare that seemed designed only to make him appear more menacing.

Well he's probably planned for this already. He'll have selected his 100, while I get to choose 100 of my best. He'd never lower himself to pick from us — he wouldn't know where to begin... thank the Gods for small favors. So I'll get some leverage... Top Flight only. I'll have to comm Sarah as soon as I leave.

Bingham slowly leaned forward, "All is *well* then, ArcGeneral."

Hastings nodded shortly, keeping her shoulders well squared and her head rigidly high. She was in no mood to tolerate his arrogance.

"So, what is your opinion of these *Earthers*? How can we defeat them? Will it be a challenge?" He smiled darkly, "The Gods have put them here as a test of our faith, it seems. But to me they looked to be ignorant, arrogant, savage brutes."

Funny, I bet they're thinking the same about you...

Hastings inhaled quietly, then began, "I was given a complete tour of *Orion*, and I have to say their technology and their abilities are impressive. They have an energy drive which is similar to a highly advanced flux drive, a system of energy-based weapons which I have not yet encountered a match for — even among the Kroggs and Larosians — and an amazing regimen of physical and mental discipline. They may not be so light a challenge, Your Eminence."

Bingham didn't look at all abashed, "So you do not believe that our Holy Crusaders could withstand them?" His grave laugh filled the room, "Those savages? Ha! Are you trying to be humorous, ArcGeneral? We are obviously superior!"

Hastings fought off a snarl.

"Well, they are no match for the Crusaders of the *Church*, at least," he persisted, determined to dismiss the doubts she had — doubts a tiny part of him might acknowledge.

The degrading tone of that remark stung, and Hastings found herself on edge again.

"Though your second grade marines may not be able to match them!"

The words were meant to antagonize her. She knew that, but knowing didn't help.

"Your Eminence!" The icy razor in her tone caused Bingham to halt in his laughter. "In my opinion, the Earthers would have little trouble defeating the Kroggs and the Larosians *combined*! We are fortunate that the way in which they've evolved has made them civil enough to give us a chance to prove ourselves. You nearly threw that opportunity away but the fact that we're still in one piece is something of a testament to their honor. I have grave doubts about our ability to defeat them in battle."

Bingham gaped but Hastings persisted, "I've seen their hand-to-hand combat, High Chancellor! They could kill you, me, the Shappa, or any of our best without so much as a hesitation! Caine could have thrashed you to bits had he wavered, but he was able to control himself! He is no savage! None of them are!"

The silence in the room was sudden and awkward, Bingham's glare mixing with Hastings' determination in a cocktail of hatred.

His mind replayed important parts of her speech, dismissing or filing them. She was *serious*.

As was he.

"*You* may wish to apologize for that outburst, *ArcGeneral*. You're fortunate you are critical to this Quest, or I would have you purified!"

Her determination was still written all over her face, curse her! His doubt was starting to tug at him...

"I will consider your *military* assessments, but know that I have seen these beings. Their lies about creation are proof enough that they are evil!"

The room was silent.

Bingham began to feel rage again.

It forced his mind to pause, as he recognized that rage was becoming far more common in his day-to-day life here in Earth space. The Quest, the epitomy of his faith, was drawing from him characteristics that were most unlike him. He was accustomed to disciplining those weak in faith, but not so harshly. It felt as though he was becoming defensive.

But defensive of what? The Earthers were the liars! They had to be... but still, he could not act as though what they had said was threatening to him. He had to calm himself, because even if he was beginning to doubt what he had always known to be true, he could not show it — especially not to a member of the Navy.

"Perhaps I am being overly harsh, ArcGeneral, but the fact remains that this trip to Earth must be planned."

Hastings had braced for a death order — one which didn't come. She'd seen more than one outburst against the High Chancellor end very badly — her predecessor had been spaced.

"Of course, neither you nor I may go on this trip — we are both too important to the Quest. I will send Shappa Bactule. You may choose your own leading officer, and the people you will send."

Hastings tensed at that remark. The faint hope she'd held that she might visit Earth disappeared. It was reasonable to keep the fleet commander with her ships, but that wasn't why Bingham was restraining her. She was being held as a sort of punishment; he was staying because of his arrogance and fear.

"I agree, Eminence."

"You are dismissed. I will send to you the 100, and I will want them well transported. You are free to leave, Gods protect you."

Hastings kept the iron resolve on her face as she nodded, then backed out of the room, her head spinning.

What the hell was that?

Hastings walked the corridors of *Genesis* in silence, her mind replaying Bingham's words, actions, and body language. Was it possible that the Earthers had gotten through to him?

Doubtful. Not that she couldn't understand something of the difficulty he might be facing — his life had revolved around the Quest, as had the life of every Chancellor before him. It wouldn't be easy for him to cut loose that devotion.

He was quite afraid of life without it, but she wasn't. It made her hopeful.

Caine's words were at last sinking in and images were piecing themselves together in her mind. Many scared men and women, just like Bingham, trying to save their civilization, knowing that Holy War had already split it once...

It made sense, in its horrific, desperate sort of way. But for whatever reason, the Naval personnel, and all the other technicians of the class, had never been integrated into the new religion. That didn't make sense to her, but she might yet come to understand it.

Somehow, for the first time in her life, she was certain she *would* come to understand her society — not just live with it.

The Earthers had given her that.

Without realizing, Hastings came to a stop in the middle of the corridor. The *Earthers* gave her that? Maybe what they offered her — what they offered *every* human — was a rational explanation for existence. No dogma or fanaticism, just history.

But Hastings cautioned herself against making such a big leap of faith — Ursla had been very kind, Caine had made sense, and they both had made tempting statements. But she still had an inclination to use the Gods' names in vain — Gods help her — and the prospect of Genesis being thrown into turmoil with the unseating of the Church...

The chaos was too dramatic to think about. Cities already segregated, going to war. The planet decimated.

No, she couldn't afford to trust the Earthers, at least not yet. They had easy, sensible answers, and she wanted to believe them.

Her life would be bettered beyond measure, at least as far as she could see, if the yoke of the Church was thrown off. But only if the resulting chaos could be reined in.

Hastings never trusted hearing exactly what she wanted to hear. It could well be too good to be true... she could have been deceived.

Which was all the more reason to send Sarah. The Earthers might trick an old battered ArcGeneral, but Sarah Manchester was no one's fool.

If Sarah believed, Hastings would.

And as she began walking again, Hastings found herself hoping that Sarah Manchester was convinced by the Earthers.

The ArcGeneral desperately wanted peace.

CHAPTER 9

ArcBrigadier Sarah Manchester tugged uncomfortably at her collar. She hadn't been able to dry off properly after her shower and the damp uniform was starting to bind.

She finally let the collar rest and examined herself deftly in the mirror. Tall, trim, dark short hair and well toned, she was one of the most respected officers in the service. Most people wondered at her hard workouts and sparring sessions with the marines — few realized they were the only outlet she had to keep her substantial levels of frustration in check.

She sighed at that knowledge. She *hated* Crusaders and often found herself in the mood to kill as many of them as she could. Fortunately, her sparring kept her rage under control, and her Crusader travel companions were none the wiser.

The present situation had forced her concerns to become more immediate — they were looking down their tubes at a potentially hostile fleet. Gods only knew what'd come of it — Gods and perhaps the ArcGeneral.

Manchester's shower had been interrupted by a message from Hastings, sent through their private back channels and flagged as highly important. The clandestine route was understandable — the ArcGeneral and the ArcBrigadier were quite good friends — but it was the 'heightened importance' that was unusual. Seldom did their back-channel communications require a label of high priority.

The message itself hadn't clarified much, saying very little:

SARAH:

WE'RE FINALLY GOING IN. I NEED YOU AND 2 OFFICERS OF YOUR CHOICE (FROM YOUR SQUADRON) TO MEET ME ABOARD *GENESIS* BY 18:00 HOURS — I KNOW THAT'S ONLY 2 HOURS FROM NOW, BUT IT IS *CRITICAL*. MAKE SURE THEY'RE TOP FLIGHT, BECAUSE THEY'RE GOING INTO AN *EXTREMELY* SENSITIVE SITUATION. I'LL BE SEEING YOU.

LIZ

Top Flight, eh? What possible reason could she have for assembling them now?

Indeed, the timing was ludicrous. They were at battle stations around the clock. She'd hardly been able to steal two hours for a workout, and Hastings wanted to pull flag officers from their squadrons?

"Oh bloody well. I'll find out in two hours, I suppose," she said quietly to herself, her smooth mostly-British accent complimenting her words.

She leaned in closer to the mirror, fiddled with her collar one last time, brushed off her uniform, and then left her quarters.

The main briefing deck on the Battlecruiser *Warlock Prophet* was abandoned but for two people who were sitting in light conversation at one end. Manchester sighed, peering at her watch as her compatriot, ArcMajor Hoshi Chen, executive officer of the Battlecruiser *Paladin Saint*, paused.

"He's late again," Manchester said tightly.

Chen laughed softly, her voice echoing in the abandoned cavern, "He's always late, Sarah."

Manchester smiled at the remark — it was good to be around her friends, especially in times of stress. Away from the rank and file, her 'Top Flight' people were, in fact, her best (and sometimes *only*) friends.

As if to dispute the comment, the door on the briefing deck slid open and ArcColonel Patrick Conroy strode quickly into the room. His tall, broad frame contrasted starkly with the slighter figure of Chen, and Manchester's tall, slim physique.

"Nice of you to come," Chen heckled as he approached.

He heaved a sigh, turning out one of the chairs at the opposite end of the long table and crashing into it.

"I had a flash inspection by Shaspa Ragthar. Lovely old bastard that he is, thought I was trying to smuggle out a fleck a dust or something," his thick, almost-Irish accent cut through the room, and Chen and Manchester both snorted laughs.

The right of Crusaders to arbitrarily check ships' craft or quarters as they saw fit was certainly a huge problem for anyone who had a life beyond duty. Over time those with things to keep out of the light learned to disguise — not *hide* — them, or to keep them stockpiled in their head.

"Glad to see that 'old bastard' didn't have you shot. Out of the fire yet again," Manchester smiled as she spoke.

Conroy laughed, "Let him give it a go. I'll have him out a lock before he can put his bloody boots on!"

Manchester smiled grimly, but they all knew Pat's words were little more than bravado. A Battlecruiser the size of *Harbinger Bishop* — Pat's command — carried 150 fully-armed and armored Crusaders, while the ship's complement was only 1,000 total. Of the 850 Navy crew, only eighty were marines, fifty were lightly armed security personnel, and the last 720 were unarmed under normal circumstances. If something happened, the Crusaders would take out the armed Navy personnel and subdue the rest before *Pat* could get his boots on.

No one liked to think about that.

"Well," Chen finally spoke, "what are we doing here? Not that I hate to visit but I could be back working out crew efficiency on *Saint*."

Manchester nodded briefly, "I got a communiqué from Liz. She wants me and two of my best on *Genesis* asap. I can only guess as to her reasons, but I would surmise that she wouldn't pull good officers from ships without solid cause."

Conroy nodded, "Hell, maybe she wants us to go pay a visit to these Earther folks — check out their morals and all!"

Chen and Manchester chuckled at the remark. Manchester leaned back in her chair as she did, taking in the ArcColonel as if to appraise *his* morals. She finally gave up after a dozen seconds.

"Well, we best not keep the ArcGeneral waiting."

Hastings watched as *Genesis'* naval briefing room began to fill. Over eighty of her best were mixing, sharing jokes and laughing. The tension of the present situation was bleeding off thanks to the camaraderie of the officers present. ArcBrigadiers were talking freely with ArcEnsigns, ArcMajors with ArcColonels and ArcLieutenants.

It was relatively relaxed, yet Hastings knew that when it came down to it, there was no lack of discipline. The command structure would always work, even if the whole of the command chain were best friends, or worse, drinking buddies.

Still, Sarah had yet to arrive. Hastings sighed anxiously — forty hours to prepare and Sarah would have to be in charge. She'd have to get here soon to get the ball rolling.

Manchester was Hastings' best friend, there as support and stress relief at all times. They'd become fast friends after a chance meeting at a strategy seminar when Manchester was still a civilian and Hastings, an ArcMajor, had been presenting. Manchester had been fifteen, Hastings thirty-two. It was the most unlikely friendship, but it had worked well for over a decade now. It was one of the very few things Hastings took comfort in.

The hatch at the far end of the briefing room opened and some of the last officers entered — Manchester, Conroy, and Chen, three of the fleet's very best. As the latter two happily began to mix with the crowd, Manchester drifted up to the elevated podium where Hastings stood.

The ArcGeneral stepped down from her higher position and smiled in greeting. Manchester smiled back, "Sorry we were delayed, Pat got a flash inspection."

Hastings nodded without a change in expression — inspections were a fact of life, these days.

"Well, you won't need to worry about too much contact with Crusaders for a while. Let's get everyone sitting down and I'll explain."

●●●

Crusader Shappa Bactule was not an easy man to impress, but the congregation of 100 that knelt and bent before him made him proud. They were the elite of the elite — the so called 'Faithful' of the Church. No discipline needed to be enforced among them; they were far beyond common failures when it came to the Church.

He viewed the group for a long moment, then turned and bowed to the High Chancellor who stood elevated a meter behind him. Bingham nodded slowly.

"Holy men of the Gods, rise to hear the words of the Church!" Bingham spoke loudly, and in unison the congregation stood, neatly ordered into line by Church rank.

Bactule pushed aside his pride to focus on the High Chancellor's sermon.

"We are near fulfillment of Prophecy!" Bingham proclaimed. "Now, the Gods have sent one last, strong test to ensure our worthiness. Deep within this system lies Earth, but in our path, as you know, are these *heathen*. They call themselves *Earthers* — a defiling of the Holy name. They say they wish to 'guard' Earth, though in truth they wish to steal it from us — deny our rightful claim!

Bingham paused briefly and looked over the room before continuing, "They are the test. We have fooled them into letting you, the best of our faithful, onto the Holy world as visitors. Your duty will be to observe and learn; when the time comes, whatever knowledge we have gained will help us defeat them."

Bactule smiled at the words. The Earthers were fools, and soon, he would himself stand on Earth, ready to rule the Holy Land...

"*Us...?* Pardon me, ma'am, but what good are we going to do on Earth?" Pat Conroy gaped openly as Hastings finished describing the mission to the officers before her.

Hastings laughed lightly, as did some present, "Don't worry Pat, this isn't an attack. I'm not *that* stupid. Your job is to get there and appraise the situation. Meet the Earthers, learn about them... learn *from* them. I know the Commodore who'll be showing you around. Her name is Andra Ursla. She's three meters tall, but is the nicest creature I've met in a while. And she's wise. *All* of them seem to be."

Hastings paused a moment, drew a device from her pocket, placed it on the podium before her, and thumbed a key on its side. The two yellow lights that began to flash on its casing marked the activation of a jamming field that blocked any listening devices in the room and afforded the conference freedom of speech without worry of the Church.

"There, a bit of privacy. Everyone, listen to me. I seriously think any campaign against the Earthers... well, it's like the Larosians. We'd be better off as their *friends*. We all know how shortsighted the Church is, and I honestly believe they are wrong about the Earthers. Your job will be to confirm that statement while you're on Earth. Ask questions, be constructively critical. *Learn*. We might be able to find a way out of this without exchanging salvos."

There was an uneasy pause, then some sounds of acknowledgment from the crowd. Hastings persisted, "Ladies and gentlemen, this is deadly serious. If my impressions are right about these Earthers, it might be in our best interest to deny the Church our support if they order us to war. Refuse action."

The room stirred cautiously. To refuse the Church would be to bring the Crusaders down on every crew. Under most circumstances, that'd mean death.

"I know the risk, but trust me. Find out what you can about these Earthers. I think it'd be in the interests of our survival not to fight them. They might even want to help us."

Slowly, the room accepted her words — if somewhat reluctantly. What she was suggesting could amount to treason... no, it *was* treason against the Church. That meant certain death for all involved, and perhaps the extermination of families back home...

Not a small matter.

Hastings smiled thinly, "Now that you've all leant enthusiastic support, I should tell you that this operation will be under the command of Sarah Manchester. You'll be heading to Earth aboard *Warlock Prophet*, her flagship. Right, questions now. Anyone have any?"

Sarah raised her hand quickly, though the rush wasn't necessary since hers was the only one.

"Sarah?"

Manchester leaned forward as she spoke, "Are we going to be joined by Crusaders? I'm all for getting to know the Earthers but if we have Crusaders breathing down our necks, it'll defeat the purpose."

Hastings nodded in acknowledgment, "A hundred Crusaders are travelling aboard *Saint Steven Tennor*. Ursla assures me she's made arrangements to separate the Navy and the Church — you'll be landing at opposite geographical poles, in fact. She already recognizes the divide between us and the Church. Don't worry, you'll all get to know these Earthers, and without the Church looking over your shoulders. I think you'll really like them."

Manchester sat at a table next to Hastings and sipped at her water in a distracted fashion. The officers mess on *Genesis* was abandoned at this hour, so she and Hastings had chosen to get a quick drink before she returned to *Warlock Prophet*. The meeting had broken just ten minutes before.

Sarah Manchester was still reviewing the situation: finally reaching Earth, only to meet *Earthers*? And now the chance that they might help... might free the Navy. It was a lot to take in.

Hastings believed in these Earthers, Manchester could see that plainly, and yet Hastings had never been a very trusting person. It did make Manchester wonder.

Was this all too good to be true...?

"What's going on here, Liz? You've got more going on in the back of your mind than you're admitting," Manchester said finally.

Hastings looked up from her drink and frowned. She had hoped it wasn't obvious, but then Sarah knew her better than anyone.

"It's always been our dream to get out from under the Church's boot, hasn't it Sarah?" Hastings asked softly, waiting for Manchester's nod before going on. "I think we may have a way to do just that. Not only do the Earthers have documented proof that our Church is built on a lie, they're *better people* than the Churchers. I'd stake my career... my *life* on that. I'm just thinking that... well, if the Earthers would take us in, wouldn't we go?"

Manchester cocked a surprised eyebrow, and thought of her brother, "Liz, we've all got family back home. We can't just desert. The Church would shoot Graham as a heretic in my stead!"

"It wouldn't be permanent, Sarah. Just think of it this way: the Church will slaughter us if we refuse action, but if the Earthers will give us asylum and our people can reach their protection, we can paralyze the Church. Those bastards don't know a bulkhead from a bucket, and if we leave them the Earthers can force them to capitulate and give us *total* control of our ships. We could go back to Genesis and sink the Church's rule. We can tell our people the truth!"

Manchester leaned back and heaved a lengthy sigh, "A noble aspiration, but it depends a lot on the Earthers. Do you *really* think they can be trusted to help us? And what of the Church? I doubt Bingham would resign himself so easily."

Hastings shrugged and leaned back in her own chair, "I already trust their First Lord and Ursla, but that's why I asked you to lead our contingent to Earth. You haven't been biased by any previous contact, so I want your opinion. If you trust them, then maybe we can explore this... *notion* of mine."

Manchester pondered the words carefully — she had always trusted Hastings' judgment, and the ArcGeneral believed in these Earthers, "Right then, if I get a good impression, I'll broach the subject to whoever's in charge — tactfully, I should say. Our *notion* is useless if they won't help."

Hastings managed a smile, but she was already losing herself in the details of a mass exodus.

"Well, I'll start looking into how we could get everyone out of the fleet. I might just throw out some lines... talk to the ArcLieutenant-Generals discretely, see if they have anything to say. They'll go along I think. If you come back with a positive report, we'll get everyone to come aboard. About time the Church gets some of their abuse back."

Manchester nodded silently, but her brow creased, "What about the crews. We're sitting high and saying this, Liz, but will our people agree?"

Hastings' expression seemed to get even grimmer, "I think our people have suffered enough from the Church. If we let them know it's a temporary absence from Genesis, and that it could change... well... *everything*, they'll stand with us."

"Assuming the Earthers go along with it," Manchester noted quietly.

Hastings nodded weakly, "They will."

They must.

CHAPTER 10

Ursla went over the plan in her mind one last time, though she knew that if she discovered a problem there wouldn't be time do anything about it anyway. The human ships — a 'Battlecruiser' and a 'Dreadnought' — were already coming in.

The very classifications of those ships was a bit confusing, not nearly as simple as the rates and gun numbers of the Earther Navy. After all, to her, a 74 was a 74, not a Dreadnought. A Fifth Rate of 38 guns was a Fifth Rate of 38 guns, not a Battlecruiser...

She scolded herself for her wandering mind as the pair of ships cruised into the neat box formed by her frigate squadron. The convoy of ten turned and made for Earth, the human ships accelerating into flux drive, the Earthers into energy drive. At the speed they were making, Earth was only twenty minutes away — not enough time for her to decide this really was a bad idea.

This visit had started to seem more and more like folly as the forty-eight hours of its preparation had progressed. Earth was ready and willing to receive the humans — it had been preparing for over 600 years — but while Ursla had confidence in the Naval personnel, she had little faith in the Church. Those fanatics would likely try to kill a busload of cubs for the sake of their 'Quest'.

With that concern in mind, she'd handed over the job of escorting the Church group around Earth to a dear old friend of hers — a trick she'd learned from Caine.

General Andros Grieve stood grimly on the deck of *Cerberus'* main landing bay, pulled uncomfortably at his collar, and sighed. He was a soldier, not a washy diplomat! But Ursla was an old friend and he'd been glad to agree to do her a favor — before she told him what it was.

Oops.

Commander-in-Chief of the Earther Marine Corps — nearly 95,000 troops deployed between Earth, the Navy, and Earther outposts — he'd always enjoyed being rough around the edges. Dress uniforms disagreed with him, and from what Ursla had told him about these Church humans, he wasn't expecting to make any friends.

He sighed again in resignation and turned to look over the platoon he'd picked to accompany him. Twelve of the best marines in the service, eight bears like himself, two wolves and two cats. He had deep respect for each of them, and they all knew it.

The intercom on the ceiling of the landing bay chirped, "General, the Church pinnace is now approaching."

Grieve nodded to acknowledge the report but was unsure who he should be nodding to. His experience was almost exclusively on ground stations, most notably the Antarctic Base. He always felt far too cramped on ships, but then he found most bears did. He was descended from a species of Grizzly bear, making him about two and three-quarters meters tall. Ursla had a quarter meter on him, but somehow, despite the head room issues, she still loved the Navy.

At the far end of the bay the space doors had parted and a crimson pinnace began to float through. It was a bloated-looking thing, as if it had over-indulged at the dinner table. Grieve sighed again and waited in silence.

Ursla smiled as she watched the large, slightly boxy Naval pinnace drop to the deck with precision and finesse. Everything she saw of these Navy types drew her to them even more.

The Bosun's pipes twittered in welcome — something she'd added specifically for the Naval types after her discussions with Hastings. The squad of marines behind her came to attention.

As the pinnace hatch opened and dropped, a tall, slender figure descended the ramp with a crisp march that would match an Earther's. Stopping two meters in front of Ursla, this human came to attention.

"ArcBrigadier Sarah Manchester, Genesis Navy," she said, offering a sharp salute.

Ursla replied in kind, "Commodore Andra Ursla, Earther Navy. Welcome aboard."

The air became more casual as the salutes came down. The first of the Naval officers descended the ramp, and Ursla gestured for the marines to go forward and meet them. The officers coming to the bottom of the ramp paused as they saw the unknowns approaching, but remained calm. Ursla nodded in approval as the marines, who she'd selected for their amiable characters, began to answer questions.

Manchester had a hard time staying composed as she stood next to her behemoth counterpart — she'd thought she was ready for three meters tall. Her officers were mixing well with the Earthers, collecting into small groups of about fifteen around them. To Manchester's surprise, the marines were only carrying sidearms (though they could have been small assault rifles by human standards) belted into their holsters. The Earthers were all very close in size to her people as well — another pleasant surprise. Three *felines* and two *canines*, all about two meters tall.

Realizing that the questions about the ships would likely absorb a few minutes, Manchester decided to take the initiative, and turned to Ursla, "Commodore, may we speak for a moment?"

The question was directed into the bear's rib cage, as Manchester forgot the size difference.

From above Ursla nodded, "Certainly. If you'd like we could board the pinnace we'll be taking to the surface."

Manchester nodded and Ursla began to walk towards the appropriate craft. *Cerberus'* secondary bay was small enough to make the journey short, but long enough to give Manchester time to reflect on how soft and well-controlled the Commodore's tone was.

As the two stepped into the small craft's cabin, Ursla nodded to the pilot and gestured Manchester into a chair. The seat, to Manchester, was like a throne, with a solid foot of clearance on either side of her thighs. She smiled at the absurdity, feeling like a child, and then quickly snapped back into indifference as she remembered herself.

Ursla took a neighboring seat, and surprisingly, the larger Commodore did not squeeze into the smaller ArcBrigadier's space.

"Well, what can I help you with, ArcBrigadier?"

Manchester looked upwards at her counterpart — who was shorter in relative height while seated — and gathered her nerve, "Quite frankly, I want to know your motives here. Liz... *ArcGeneral Hastings* trusts you, but I need to get to know you myself before I can make that decision — especially when my officers are involved."

Ursla heard the question and smiled, "A prudent question. No wonder the ArcGeneral sent you."

Manchester cocked an eyebrow, "The ArcGeneral and I are friends, but that won't change the question."

Ursla kept her smile from growing to a point where it revealed bared teeth, then spoke, "Quite simply, ArcBrigadier, I am here to introduce you to the planet Earth. Since we're being frank, however, I'll also inform you that I'm responsible for evaluating how the Navy compares to the Church. Can the Earther Navy coexist better with the human Navy or the Church?"

Manchester frowned at the last question.

"However," Ursla's voice lowered, "I think we both know the answer to that, and I sincerely doubt it's the Church."

Manchester relaxed all of a sudden as pressure she hadn't even realized was building was released. She'd been wondering for the past forty hours whether or not Hastings' trust in the Earthers had been misplaced, but it was already beginning to seem like the confidence was well founded. Ursla was evidently quite atuned to the tensions between the Navy and the Church.

Obvious though those differences were, the Kroggs had never picked up on them... their alliance was with the Church of Genesis, and so long as Genesis warships continued to attack Larosian invaders, the Kroggs couldn't be bothered to look at the human society. Then again, given the Kroggs' lack of subtlety, their disinterest was probably a good thing. Nonetheless, it was pleasant to know that at least one other race sympathized with the Naval position.

"Well... then let me introduce myself," Manchester smiled, and extended her hand across the seat. "I'm Sarah Manchester. Pleased to meet you."

Grieve rubbed his forehead with premature exhaustion. He felt as if he'd been escorting these humans around for weeks already, and it had been less than ten minutes.

I'm going to get Andra for this.

The Crusader 'Shappa' — Grieve's counterpart, as near as he could tell — was smug, superior, and extremely disrespectful. His humans weren't any better. The minute they'd descended the ramp they'd demanded to know where their honor guard of 100 marines was, then where the ceremonial carpet was...

Grieve had been tempted to have his platoon run out bayonets, but the sight of the large marines waving them to a pinnace seemed to move the humans well enough, even if their displeasure was clearly etched on their faces. Now they were boarding the large passenger craft, a huge mob at the bottom of the ramp slowly climbing in order of worthiness.

Shappa Bactule separated himself from the crowd and stormed over to Grieve, who braced himself and again silently promised *not* to flatten the guest... *literally*.

"Only *one* pinnace? Our Upper Holy men need separate transport, in recognition of their greater holiness!" he snapped.

Grieve felt his muscles tense but forced himself to relax, "You all arrived in a single pinnace."

Bactule threw his arms up in the air as if despairing at Grieve, "It was *blessed* to hold both by the High Chancellor! This is a damned machine! We must balance the faith or–"

"Look," Grieve growled outright, "we have *one* pinnace slotted to take you down to Arctic Base. If a second one tries to make an unscheduled drop it'll cause a bit of a commotion and it *might* get you shot out of the sky. I trust you wouldn't *prefer* that to a bit of unholiness!"

Bactule's eyes widened and he started to draw himself up to throw another tantrum when Grieve bent over to look him squarely in the eyes. The two stared at each other for a long second, then Bactule turned on his heel and stormed off. Grieve had to consciously unclench his fists.

It was going to be a very long day.

"And you're telling me this is the secondary bay, lassie?" Conroy didn't bother to hide his astonishment.

The tan wolf marine nodded, "*Cerberus* is a Fifth Rate — I believe that's equivalent to a Battlecruiser."

"Aye," Conroy grinned as he looked up again, "but this bloody cavern's almost half again as big as *Bishop's* main flight deck."

The marine Conroy had pulled aside cocked a curious eyebrow but kept her smile, "*Bishop*, sir?"

Conroy was a bit distracted as he listened to the question, marvelling at the clean lines of the Fifth Rate's bay. Finally, he looked back down and nodded, "My Battlecruiser. *Harbinger Bishop*."

The marine nodded in understanding, then glanced at the thinning lines on the pinnace's boarding ramp. She turned to Conroy to speak but was preempted by his nod, "Aye, let's be going then."

As the two strolled to the pinnace Pat spotted Chen wringing another marine for information, but decided not to try to call her — she was obviously having her fun.

As he boarded the pinnace Pat was surprised by the magnitude and comfort of the seating cabin, and he quickly spotted Manchester at the front with the bear lady — *Commodore Ursla*. The seat next to her was empty, and though Conroy and his large frame were generally averse to window seats, he realized he'd fit into that particular one like a child in an armchair.

He excused himself and slipped in front of Ursla and Manchester, then collapsed into the seat, appreciating immediately the soft construction. He then glanced over at Manchester and smiled, "By Gods this is a beauty of a ship!"

Ursla found herself feeling gratified by the newcomer's words, "Thank you..."

Conroy looked up to the bear and smiled, sensing the lead in. He stretched his arm over Manchester's head with some difficulty, then shook Ursla's hand, "ArcColonel Patrick Conroy. Pleasure to make your acquaintance."

Ursla immediately liked the big man... he reminded her of Grieve, and was a physical human equivalent by the look of it. Heavy-set but respectably sturdy, and with *another* accent.

"Commodore Andra Ursla, nice to meet you."

Conroy smiled, "And like I was saying to Sarah here, Commodore, this is a beautiful ship!"

Ursla smiled and bowed her head, "*Cerberus* is my first flag, and her Captain is nothing short of extraordinary–"

"Commodore Ursla, comm message for you from the First Lord," the intercom chirped.

Ursla looked up at the speaker, then stood, "Excuse me a moment, please."

As Ursla stepped easily to the cockpit, Manchester turned to the grinning Irishman, a smile lightening her features, "Having fun?"

Conroy laughed, "These Earthers are my kind of folks. They really give their ships the spit polish! No bloody Crusaders either. I could do to spend time with them for sure."

Manchester laughed and rested her head against the back of the chair, "Indeed. Same old Pat..."

"You wouldn't have me any other way, would you?" Conroy chuckled, stretching his wide frame out in the chair.

"No," Manchester replied softly, "I don't think I would."

Ursla dropped heavily into the cockpit chair, her mind still occupied with the thoughts of the interesting people she was meeting when the holo-screen lit up with Caine's face.

"Problems yet, Ursla?" he asked.

Ursla frowned, "Why would there be? If it wasn't for the lack of fur they might pass for Earthers. They've got some really interesting people here, Setter."

Caine cocked an eyebrow slowly, "Really? Andros isn't enjoying the same... geniality. There's already a lot of friction with his guests."

Ursla's expression sobered, "Well, suffice it to say these Naval types are the kind of people I like to deal with. Let's just hope for Andros' sanity."

Caine nodded, "Good luck, Andra."

The screen blanked, and Ursla stood, giving the chair back to the pilot.

"Commodore, we'll be ready to launch momentarily. If you could alert our guests..." the pilot reported as he sat, and Ursla gave a brief nod in reply.

She turned and walked down the short passage, past the boarding ramp which had retracted, and into the cabin. She stopped and stood just long enough for people to quiet, then spoke, "We're about to launch, so we'd appreciate it if everyone could get seated and comfortable. We'll be landing at the Fleet Base in Antarctica for our first stop."

She nodded to the passengers and their conversations started up again. Ursla retook her seat next to a smiling Manchester and a grinning Conroy, the latter peering out the window at the deck crews in operation.

There was excitement in the air — it was impossible to miss. And it made sense that people escaping tyranny and oppression, if only temporarily, would look forward to the experience.

Ursla certainly was...

From both the main and secondary landing bays in *Cerberus*, two pinnaces emerged and made for Earth at moderate speed.

CHAPTER 11

Antarctic Base was maintained near the south pole by the Earther Navy. Its landing field covered thirty-two square kilometers on the surface and had countless kilometers of tunnel networks dug into the ice below.

Landing at the most central receiving field was the first of *Cerberus'* pinnaces which held 100 Naval officers and a light tour guide escort.

Vice Admiral Savanna Felix was accustomed to giving civilians tours of the facilities on a semi-regular basis, but those civilians were Earthers. He had no idea what to expect from the humans; in fact, he would never have expected the Admiralty to bring them down for a look.

As commander of Antarctic Base, it was his job to keep things running smoothly. He was fairly certain he wouldn't have the patience to deal with the humans as Ursla and Grieve were... at least, not the Churchers. He'd read Caine's memo about that meeting with Bingham, and it didn't inspire confidence.

Felix watched as the pinnace slowly lowered itself onto the metal-plated landing field, its feet pressing on the panels, pushing them down into the ice. It was a chilly morning for a tour — as usual on Antarctic Base — but Felix had gotten used to it. His species, the Siberian tigers, were genetically predisposed to deal with such temperatures, thanks to their natural habitat.

Felix suddenly wondered how well off the humans would be... after all, they had no fur to keep them warm.

Ah, but Ursla had doubtless considered that already.

Ursla nearly ripped off the arm of her chair when she realized the humans would be freezing in their normal uniforms on the Antarctic Plain. Earthers were generally thick-coated enough to not have a problem with temperature, but the humans...

Well, Hastings hadn't brought it up as they'd planned this tour. It hadn't occurred to Sarah during their conversation on the way down either. Everyone was, quite understandably, preoccupied with the situation. So she'd deal with this now.

As the pinnace landed she stood and asked everyone to remain seated while she went forward to the cockpit. As she arrived the pilot glanced up at her, "Need something ma'am?"

Ursla smiled and half shrugged, "Contact the tower, get them to run 100 extreme-weather uniform jackets out here, canine fit."

The pilot grinned with understanding and spoke through his comm to the tower. A minute later three field technicians came running out of the complex with boxes in their arms.

Ursla turned back to the cabin and addressed her charges, "We've landed at Antarctic Base. You lucked out to arrive when you did, it's still light down here. You'll see Arctic Base later — it's in a dark period. Since we're on the south pole of the planet and the rotational axis isn't vertical..." Ursla started to explain with gestures but realized her charges were experienced Naval officers. They hardly needed to be told how planets rotated.

"Anyway," she continued after her pause, "it's light out, but it's pretty cold... at least I *think* it's cold by *human* standards. We Earthers have fur so our duty uniforms tend to suffice in normal weather down here, but I have some of our extreme-weather coats waiting for you at the bottom of the ramp. They're cut for canines but with luck you'll all fit into them."

There were a few cocked eyebrows and puzzled faces, but general nods prevailed.

"Sorry about the inconvenience, but we were a little short-sighted about the optimum temperatures. So single file down the ramp, take a coat from one of the techs at the bottom, put it on, and stay near the pinnace."

People began to stand, organizing themselves to empty from the back first while Ursla descended the ramp to help distribute coats.

"*Why is it dark?* We are the Holiest of the Church, yet you try to hide this base from us!" Crusader Shappa Bactule snarled.

Grieve thought very briefly about hitting him, an act that surely would have killed the human.

"Well *Shappa*, we'd have liked to show you the base when it was light outside, but it would be too much trouble to change the *rotation of the planet*. Perhaps you'd like to wait for six months."

Bactule had the urge to order the heathen shot, but stopped himself. What worked with the Navy would not work with the Earthers. He already had a good idea of the defense potential of the planet, so he could afford to assert his superiority without risking the mission. But prudence demanded some control.

On the way down he'd had his recorders going and he'd been watching the planet *very* carefully. His experienced eyes had found the continents and cities as they were noted in the scriptures. To his surprise, though, the Earthers seemed to have only two Naval bases on the entire planet, including this night-clad one.

In any case, he would show the heathen General how to treat Holy men, even if it interfered with his reconnaissance. In the back of his mind one fact remained clear: with two million of his best he could easily take this planet.

• • •

The coat was obviously cut for a wider individual — a wolf, no less — so it hung loosely from Sarah's shoulders. She shivered at the bite of the cold breeze crossing the field, and pulled the straps tight, bringing the size of the coat down as far as possible. Pat stood next to her, pleased by the fact that his coat fit him near perfectly.

Sarah smiled at him, "Ask nicely and they'll probably let you keep it."

He grinned, "Just one? I'd buy a case! Fits better than any coat I've ever owned..."

Sarah laughed and then turned to inspect her surroundings, sighing in relief as the heaters in her coat began to warm her up.

The south and north geographical poles of a planet were interesting places to build fleet bases. Virtually devoid of civilians, they allowed the noisy business of a fleet to go unhindered. They also allowed response ships to reach anywhere in the globe at a reasonable clip.

The wildlife might be a factor though.

Sarah's jaw dropped as her eyes fell on the mass of about 200 black and white birds standing on a landing field further out. They certainly didn't look like Earthers... what were they doing?

As Sarah spotted Ursla she gestured to the Commodore and pointed, "What are they, exactly? Your ultimate weapon?"

Ursla chuckled at the remark, "Them? I'm surprised they've stuck around. I was sure they'd have moved on by now. They're *penguins*, the only local wildlife. They used to group around the coast, but since we moved in and dug canals out to the ocean they've been spending a lot of time near the base. They're Antarctic natives... with a few exceptions, this is their only habitat on the planet. They tend to come and go as they please, and we let them."

Pat grinned in reply, "You let them land the shuttles for you too?"

Ursla bellowed her laughter, turning a few human heads, "No, no. They don't cause us trouble, and they were here first. We just let them go about their business. They've gotten used to us and we've gotten used to them."

"And they don't interfere with efficiency?"

Ursla shrugged and raised her hand to the horizon, "We aren't running out of space just now, and we try to do our best to do as little displacing as possible. We're a bit sympathetic to their plight — we're only seven centuries apart, really."

Sarah smiled and laughed silently, turning back to observe the penguins a while longer. The day should certainly prove interesting.

"Setter, they refuse to leave the *pinnace*!"

Caine stared at Grieve through the monitor of the second *Cerberus* pinnace, and raised his eyebrows. The General tried to calm himself with a few deep breaths.

"Really? Why exactly are they refusing?" Caine asked quietly, trying to keep Grieve's anger from affecting him.

Grieve sighed deeply, collected himself, and spoke, "We landed an hour ago. Their Shappa leader claims they're being disrespected by being taken to a place that is dark. I swear, he is the most aggravating being in the cosmos..."

Shaking his head, Grieve sighed and leaned back in the pinnace's engineering seat. Caine frowned and twitched his ear slightly. He'd hoped things would go more smoothly, despite the first impressions he'd formed of Bingham and the Church. Ursla had reported fifteen minutes earlier, and the Naval officers were touring Antarctic Base. That would take at least another two hours, so sending the Crusaders there was out of the question.

He had to keep the Navy and the Church separate, or the tour would be a waste. Something productive did come of this — it was a confirmation of the opinions Caine and Ursla had held since their first meeting with the humans. Naval personnel were reasonable, the Church was illogical and fanatical.

"What's next on your schedule Andros?" Caine asked finally.

Grieve thought for a moment, "The Rockies, Washington, then London."

Caine pondered the destinations, coming up with a secondary plan almost immediately.

"Okay," he said slowly, "leave now for the Rockies... give them a tour of the glaciers up north and then take them down south. See if you can swallow up a chunk of time. If you're at a loss swing by the Amazon. That might grab their attention."

Grieve nodded ruefully at the words, "Will do. I'll contact you as soon as possible."

The General leaned forward to deactivate the transmission but Caine put up a delaying hand, "One more thing Andros. Try *not* to kill anybody."

Grieve's expression didn't change, "No promises."

Caine smiled as he disappeared, and Grieve turned to the pilot, standing to give the chair back to the pinnace's engineer.

"We'll head to the Rockies. We'll land north and tour the glaciers, then cruise south."

The pilot nodded and started running his plots for an optimum course. Grieve slowly collected himself and then turned back to the main cabin.

This was going to be painful.

Again.

Pat tugged on Sarah's elbow and pointed at the Command and Control center of Antarctic Base. They were in a corridor above, looking down at it through the hallway windows. It was perfectly coordinated and organized, though one could tell from the mess of consoles and the determined-faced Earthers that it was wrapped up in heavy affairs.

Namely our arrival, I'd wager, Sarah thought with a touch of sadness.

"That'd put Genesis HQ to shame," she whispered softly in verbal reply, and Pat nodded with a smile.

"Is it just me, or do you get the feeling the Church is trying to drag us into the deep end with them?" Chen asked from Sarah's other side.

Pat laughed lowly, "Not just drag us in, they've tied a bloody anvil to our ankles."

The trio laughed bitterly. The fact that these Earthers were quite capable of handling the Genesis Fleet was becoming painfully clear, though with the Genesis Fleet numbering 2,400 — plus the Crusaders — it would inevitably be a bloody contest. And despite her pride in her ships and crews, Sarah had to admit to growing doubts of the humans' ability to defeat the Earthers.

Just like with the Larosians and the Kroggs. And if we bleed ourselves out against the Earthers, the Larosians will have no opposition next time they probe... and the Kroggs will tighten their grip on us.

The power situation at Genesis was not good in that regard — to get to Earth on time and in strength, the Church had made commitments to the Kroggs, a race generally seen among the Navy as evil. It was an understandable association — the Kroggs demanded the Navy fight the Larosians, and that was a suicidal prospect.

Of course politically the Kroggs were embraced as friends, but anyone with any brains — including some in the Church — knew better than to believe the Kroggs were wholly benevolent. While no human had even spoken to a Larosian, there was a growing sentiment that the human race might be better off making its own peace with those aliens... But the Kroggs were useful because they volunteered technical aid in return for the support of the Genesis military. The Church remained wedded to them in order to see the Quest fulfilled

In any case, if the humans wanted to live through the clash between those titans they would need their fleet — at the *very* least — and if the Earthers could be convinced to ally with Genesis it might give them leverage against the Kroggs. With the Church running the show that would never happen.

Sarah was prodded back into reality by a light elbow in the ribs from Pat, and she clicked in to find herself inside the C&C center, where Vice Admiral Felix, a striking white feline, was explaining the details of fleet operations.

Forgetting the tumultuous political situation at home, Sarah relaxed and allowed herself to enjoy both her freedom and the new ideas the Earthers were offering. The revelation came to her sometime that day that she, and all of her Naval contemporaries, would have to somehow stop the pending conflict, or they would be facilitating the useless bloodletting of many, many good people.

The thought chilled her.

CHAPTER 12

Ursla had decided to let Grieve unload his charges first since he had been most distressed by their presence. While the Church pinnace crawled slowly to *Cerberus'* main bay — as if exhausted by its trip — the pinnace holding the Naval officers flew a holding pattern around the frigate.

Ursla had elected to stay forward in the cockpit during the trip, giving the humans time to reflect on their long, sight-filled day. She had no doubt these people would do whatever they could to stop an all out shooting war, so it would be her job to discuss the situation with Manchester.

That conversation would wait until they were aboard *Cerberus* — the Naval officers were scheduled to stay a night on the frigate and get a little more background on the Earther Fleet before they returned to their own ships, while the Church members would spend the night on their Dreadnought.

Pat whistled with amazement as he saw *Cerberus* for a second time through the pinnace's window — a simple ship but so elegant! Its ports glistened, its silver paint glowed... the ship would put *Harbinger Bishop* to shame. Somehow the rust-colored Genesis ships just didn't compare.

The ArcColonel was stoically protective of *Bishop*, and those who criticized it often found themselves in bad situations, but he had to admit this Fifth Rate was a gorgeous vessel. He turned to Sarah with the smile of a child peering through the front window of a toy store, and the ArcBrigadier laughed.

Throughout their long friendship, the two had enjoyed little time outside the grip of the Church. They seldom had much time to relax, even less to talk openly about things. Now Sarah found herself glad of the chance to refresh her friendship with the Irishman... and she enjoyed being free of the ominous Crusaders.

The only person she'd ever really been able to confide in over the years had been Hastings — owing to the latter's ability to ensure privacy for conversation. Long ago Sarah had been taken under the ArcGeneral's wing, and the rewards of discipline and judgment had helped her qualify for the rank of ArcBrig years before most fellow officers. Pat was a year older than Sarah, but he had lacked the friends to accelerate his promotions, and thus was a rank below her.

The pinnace, unbeknownst to Sarah, had begun its landing run on *Cerberus'* secondary bay, and before she could focus she was inside the ship. The cabin was emptying and her officers were being escorted to guest quarters where they could see how the Earther Navy treated its personnel.

"Sarah? Come now girl, we aren't supposed to sleep in the pinnace," Pat's voice seemed distant but it helped Sarah snap back into reality.

She slowly stood, surprised to find an empty craft but for herself and Pat. He'd managed to get past her and was standing in the aisle, offering a hand to help her up. She took it and slowly shuffled out into the space, then forward to the exit ramp.

Ursla stood at the bottom with a pleasant smile which Sarah returned.

"I have the two of you across the hall from each other in the upper end of the guest wing. Since you're the two seniors from your Navy I thought it would be best, especially if you want your privacy," the Commodore said.

Sarah blushed immediately; Pat laughed nervously.

"And what, my large friend, is *that* supposed to mean?" he asked, trying to mask his surprise.

Ursla frowned inwardly as she picked up a mix of shock and embarrassment from the two officers. Manchester seemed to be changing her skin pigment, Conroy was getting louder. What had she said?

She went back over her dialogue quickly, then tried to read implications into it... oh.

Well then.

"Ah... oh. I'm sorry. That didn't quite come out right. I didn't mean to imply a romantic interlude, really. I thought you two might want to compare thoughts on the day for your overall evaluation... I'm... sorry..." Ursla stumbled through the apology, comforted when she sensed the relief of both officers.

"This way," Ursla gestured to the door, and the three set off just a bit awkwardly.

Sarah Manchester was shocked by the magnitude of her cabin. It was almost as big as her flag cabin on *Warlock Prophet*, but it was far more luxurious and a lot less cluttered.

Stretched out on the couch in her nightclothes — a shirt and sweats wrapped in a robe which she had sent over from *Prophet* for this occasion — she was enjoying the full *cushiness* of her accommodations.

She'd decided to lie down in order to clear her head and reflect on her day — prepping for a report to Liz — but she was entirely too comfortable to focus properly. Her mind had switched tracks as soon as she sank into the soft couch, and she found herself daydreaming.

Her mind wandered to thoughts of living like the Earthers — their advanced technology, their pleasant nature... their penguins. She really didn't know all that much about the day-to-day lives of Earthers, but she got the impression that despite their Naval strength, the furry humanoids led peaceful, even utopian lives. Half of her still wondered whether it was too good to be true, but a more vocal part of her mind was being convinced that the Earthers deserved Liz's trust.

She was wondering how the penguins could stand that vicious Antarctic cold when the door chimed. The sound, though designed to be gentle, startled her. As she tried to sit up the door opened, Pat leaning his head in.

"Did you open that?" he asked cautiously.

"No, did you?" Sarah replied with equal care.

"No. Must be the odd locks on these doors... can I come in then?" Pat's tone was low and a little amused.

Sarah nodded with matching amusement, then remembered herself. She was stretched out on a comfortable couch, probably looking quite like a child.

She sat up quickly as Pat came in, and bit her tongue as he collapsed heavily into a chair across a coffee table from her. Pat's company was appreciated, but he'd want to talk business... and for the first time in ages, she was finding herself able to forget work... if only for a while.

"Thought we should take advantage of our quarters like Ursla suggested," he smiled, and Sarah blushed again, shifting uneasily. Pat chuckled. "What she actually *meant*, not what came out."

Sarah relaxed muscles she didn't know she'd tensed, glad of his candor. She released a relieved sigh and nodded.

"I was trying to organize my thoughts about today but I made the mistake of stretching out on this couch..." she said weakly.

Pat nodded with a smile, "Damned comfortable things. I got trapped in one for a while too."

Sarah cocked an eyebrow, "You?"

Pat snorted a laugh, "I may be a bullheaded man of Irish descent, but I *can* love the comfort of a couch!"

Sarah laughed in reply, then sobered.

"So," she asked a bit ominously, "what do you think about this... this mess?"

Pat heaved a sigh, his brow furrowed, and he leaned back, "I don't know," he sighed. "I really don't know."

There was an uneasy silence for a moment, Sarah not wanting to prod her friend, Pat trying to decide what to say.

Finally, he continued, "You see, I like these Earthers... they're good people. They remind me of us... just... well, a bit different looking. You know that doesn't bother me but... well." He stopped again as if troubled by what he was trying to say.

Sarah waited as he collected himself, realizing he was just trying to sort his own thoughts and impressions of the day.

"They aren't trying to coerce us," he said eventually, "they're just treating us the way we should be treated. I haven't been given this much respect outside the Navy in... no, actually, I never have. They answered my questions, they were very up front about their C&C... you must have gotten that feeling, eh? They *respected* us..."

Sarah offered a slow nod of confirmation, and Pat pressed on, "Right, so there's that. But the rest is a lot less clear. I get a good feeling around the Earthers. My skin crawls if I'm in a room with a Krogg..." he chuckled "...or a Crusader, for that matter... but Ursla... even that Felix fellow, as protective as he was of his base... anyway, I got a good feeling. The kind of feeling I get when I'm around you..."

Sarah cocked an eyebrow, "How should I take *that*?"

Pat grinned, "Not the way Ursla did, bless her. Anyway, a really good... friendly feeling, I think."

Sarah nodded, "I agree... they don't seem like an enemy to me... I just fear that it's all too good to be true."

Pat frowned, "You know, I'll have to ask Ursla, but I'd bet they don't know the meaning of the phrase."

Ursla sat heavily in the chair behind her desk and let out a well-earned sigh. From her point of view the day had been a complete success, and she was more sure than ever that the Naval personnel in the Genesis Fleet were not a threat to Earth. But Grieve...

She felt another pang of guilt for asking her old friend to show the Church personnel around the planet. He'd damned near had an aneurysm. The Church was... well... beyond description. Self-righteous, bigoted... amazingly disagreeable.

The situation the Earthers were now facing was remarkably complex. Every ship facing down the Earther Navy had two components: the good and the bad. On the good side was the Genesis Navy — solid, sensible, and perhaps not inclined to fight...

But the decision whether or not to follow the High Chancellor's order to fight rested with ArcGeneral Hastings, of whom Ursla already had a high opinion. Sarah Manchester would likely contribute to the decision.

Ursla reviewed the mental portfolio she'd assembled on the ArcBrigadier throughout the day, and smiled. Like a younger and more vibrant Hastings. She was brilliant as a tactician too, no doubt, with the keen eye Ursla had come to recognize in strategists.

The holo on Ursla's desk chirped and she keyed it, the projection glowing to life. Caine was on the other side, looking anxious and slightly worn.

"Well, what do you think?" he asked with a bit of a hurried undercurrent in his voice.

Ursla sighed, "They're completely different, just like we thought. The Church people are literally fanatical, but the Naval personnel are just as agreeable as I am. I'd swear that they come from two completely different cultures."

Caine nodded, trying, like Ursla, to understand the vast gulf between Navy and Church. It was fascinating. Despite their biological differences, Earthers all shared the common threads of a culture; humans, despite their biological uniformity, were just the opposite, or so it seemed.

"I'll try to learn about that division from Sarah or Pat tomorrow, but in the meantime, I think I'm seeing a plan developing."

Caine stared blankly at Ursla for a second, "And Sarah and Pat are...?"

Ursla smiled, "Sorry — that would be ArcBrigadier Manchester and ArcColonel Conroy. When I'm around them I get feeling they want to ask me about something, but are afraid to."

"About something good I hope," Caine's brow furrowed.

Ursla shrugged slightly, "Don't hold me to this, but I think that *maybe* — and I do mean just *maybe* — your speculation about them might be right."

Caine stared for another second, "A mutiny? A desertion, even?"

Ursla tilted her head slightly and shrugged again, "I doubt it would be that easy, but that might be what they're thinking."

Caine nodded slowly. Assessments based on Ursla's instincts, like his own, could cautiously be taken as truth. If the Genesis Navy wanted to switch sides, the Church fleet might be crippled... and shots would not have to be fired. Could the Navy take over their ships, or would they just abandon their fleet? If they just abandoned their fleet, where could the Earthers shelter them? And would there be demands made for support? And...?

"There are plenty of variables there, Andra, if they really want to consider changing sides. Taking in a fleet of refugees... that could be a bit of a logistical problem... but... do you think they can be trusted on Earth? Their track record isn't spectacular..."

Ursla paused, "We weren't around back then. And I think the Navy would listen to reason. But I'll look into all of those details tomorrow and get back to you. In the meantime, you might want to start looking for mass accommodations. We might be able to throw up some pre-fab residences on Luna... I don't know. Get some sleep and then look into it. I'll comm you tomorrow."

Caine sighed and nodded in reply. Having to take in millions of humans wasn't exactly what he'd been expecting to do, but if it spared the bloodshed, he could scarcely be happier.

"Sleep well, Ursla," he said softly, and disappeared. With a tired sigh, Ursla pushed herself up out of her chair and made way to her bunk.

"Sarah?" Pat asked quietly for the third time.

Out like a light, she was. Twenty minutes into discussing how to protect the Navy from the Church and she'd fallen into a deep sleep. Of course, she'd had a particularly busy day, and the relief of not having Crusaders around had eased everyone's tension remarkably.

Pat was impressed by her conduct today. He was also pleased that she seemed more relaxed on the tour... more like herself, maybe.

The big Irishman sighed, stood up and stepped lightly over to his friend. Shifting her into a lying position on the couch, he tossed a blanket over her and fixed her pillow.

Silently, he stepped out the door, then turned to try to lock it. He gave up on that effort after about a minute, sighed, and crossed back into his quarters.

CHAPTER 13

Sarah had been quite disoriented when she woke — talking strategy with Pat one minute, in a dreamworld the next, with no recollection of the transition. She'd shrugged off the unsettled feeling after a couple of minutes, and started to get herself ready for the morning.

Their day aboard *Cerberus* was scheduled to start with a breakfast in the guests' mess at 08:30, and it wasn't until five minutes before that she'd finally gotten herself showered and into a fresh uniform. Today would be the most interesting of all — to her at least — as she would finally get a look at the Earther Navy.

The door chimed and opened just as Sarah, still buttoning the flap of her tunic, was walking to answer it. Pat stepped in with a shrug at the lock and held his arm up to gesture to the hall.

"They've started to get the lower ranks moving, I thought you'd like to be up and about before they got to you," he explained as she finished with her tunic buttons and smiled.

The two left the cabin and walked slowly down the hall towards the Naval officers gathering at its end. One hundred people was a fair number to move, so it would take a few minutes.

"Liz got a tour of *Orion* — the flagship. She told me to expect some magnificent things... though *Orion* is reputed to be about six times the size of this ship," Sarah said quietly as the pair drifted down the hall.

"So I take it the ArcGeneral was impressed, then?" Pat replied in equally low tones.

Sarah smiled, "More like astounded."

They reached the group of human officers and moved to the front where Ursla was explaining the plan for the morning to her marines. Sarah stood back until the marines had dispersed and then stepped up to the Commodore, who looked down with a smile.

"Commodore, I'll need to speak with you before we leave this morning, perhaps at breakfast."

Ursla nodded, "I was about to suggest the same. There are a few things we need to discuss."

• • •

"The breakfast we'll be serving this morning is the general Earther favorite — salmon and potatoes. The salmon is actually a fish, but about a hundred years ago we learned how to synthetically produce its flesh without having to kill the animal. Potatoes are a native vegetable of Earth, and they are particularly favored," one of the marines was explaining the meal to the Naval officers sitting in groups in the guests' mess.

Sarah, Pat and Ursla had been left to a table of their own, allowing them privacy to discuss the pressing issues they were facing.

Ursla spoke first, "ArcBrigadier, we want to make it very clear to you that... well... we think we have a good grasp of the situation you're facing. The High Chancellor leaves no doubt that the Church is pushing for an occupation of Earth, and we have seen no evidence that he can be reasoned with. The Naval cadre of your fleet, on the other hand, seems to be quite like our own. We have no wish to kill anyone, but if the Genesis Fleet tries to press through the blockade we will have to protect our planet."

Sarah nodded slowly as she ate, trying to maintain her calm outward facade. This was very good news, but it would hardly be professional to admit to her growing excitement...

"We would be glad to have humans on Earth, but we couldn't accept them unless they agreed not to..." Ursla paused, trying to put it diplomatically.

"Institute chaos, destroy the ecological balance, and generally run amok," Pat suggested quietly in a tone that masked nerves with humor.

Ursla frowned and then nodded slowly, "Basically, yes. The First Lord and I have come to think that we would have little worry from your people in that regard... we believe any differences could be worked out. But the Church's behavior suggests no such tolerance — their treatment of you being clear evidence of that — and, if one is to interpret scripture literally, they would try to exploit the planet as well."

Sarah nodded again and leaned back in her chair, "So what you want is a bloodless way out of the vice we've put you in."

It was Ursla's turn to nod, as Sarah sighed deeply. General consensus then. The gravity of what was being discussed surfaced on her serious face.

"ArcGeneral Hastings and I," she began slowly, "are prepared to refuse action if it is demanded of us, and we're confident we have the loyalty of the fleet. If we do, though, we'll face execution for mutiny... unless we're given the opportunity to escape. If we tried to leave our fleet could we expect your protection?" Sarah's voice was level and grim.

Ursla paused for a second, looking down into the ArcBrigadier's eyes, "Yes."

The trio at the table paused uneasily, then Pat spoke up, "We know virtually everyone in the Navy has been alienated by the Crusaders — six centuries of abuse tend to draw firm lines. Gods, the whole Church treats us like the very bottom scum of the entire second class... and that's some pretty awful company in some cases. We've just never had a real chance to break away. Mutiny isn't a new idea... *defection* might make it possible."

Sarah nodded again as she chewed some of the salmon, marveling at the flavor.

"And," she said finally, "if we leave the Genesis Fleet is left sitting helpless. No fight, no casualties."

Ursla nodded, "That's what we want. We'd be able to stop this before it starts."

"One thing you need to understand, though, Andra," Sarah said quietly. "This would not be permanent. We want to re-take our fleet after the Church is forced to submit, and we want to go home. We want to let our people know what happened here — and to protect them."

Ursla considered the statement for a second, and then nodded again, "That shouldn't be a problem."

"We might need some help with that too..." Pat's voice trailed off, and Ursla slowly nodded.

"I can't promise anything firm until we're more familiar with the situation, but we'll offer you whatever help we may."

Caine wouldn't have a problem with the humans going home, and the humans on Genesis had to be considered.

Sarah, having finished her serving, wiped her lips with her napkin and took a sip of the water accompanying the meal. She felt better about the promise of Earther *help* than she ever had about Churchers... so she nodded, "I'll give the ArcGeneral my recommendation to go ahead."

The heavy topics of the breakfast conversation, important though they were, had been somewhat tempered by the awe every human Naval officer felt while walking though *Cerberus*. Most ships in the Genesis Navy were so computer-dependent that the crews never got to see their nuts and bolts, but Earther design philosophy called for personnel to have open access to all systems.

Operating doctrines like that allowed the guests to see all of *Cerberus*, right up to her modest gun deck — something unheard of for Genesis vessels, whose computer cores were jealously guarded against any tampering. Though not nearly as massive as the gun deck Liz had described from *Orion*, it was still breathtaking. The guns were huge, their four-person crews so... honed.

As Sarah stood on the massive deck, images of these very guns smashing into the enemy filled her, and the resolution to preempt conflict became more and more justified. The Earthers were, in a way, quite a contradiction. They had an incredible ability to make war and a stalwart determination never to have to.

After the gun deck the human officers were led to the training gym, where a large group of marines were positioned around several sparring mats, practicing hand-to-hand combat. They were all canines and felines — it seemed the bear marines Hastings had mentioned were kept to larger ships. The sparring was of particular interest to Sarah — after all, that was how she kept in shape.

While the officers were left to drift around and observe, she went to the mats almost immediately, Pat following her with some interest.

Sarah stopped a few meters from the nearest mat to watch the two marines spar, and found herself gasping with amazement at their skill. It was as if they were dancing across the floor, their bodies blurring as they moved quickly, their limbs striking out and deflecting at a speed that seemed impossible.

Ursla came up quietly beside her — a feat that seemed remarkable given the Commodore's size, "The ArcGeneral mentioned you were skilled in hand-to-hand. If you'd like to try out the mats, feel free."

Sarah snorted a laugh, "I'd be no match for one of them..."

Ursla smiled, "I wouldn't be so sure. They look fast but you might just have the skill to hold your own. Don't know until you try..."

Sarah bit her tongue as the Commodore spoke, and her heart rate increased. The temptation was strong — she could really get a sense of how formidable these Earthers were...

The mat cleared from the last match, the victory gone unnoticed by the ArcBrig due to her preoccupation. One of the marine Sergeants addressed the humans, "Would any of our guests like to have a first-hand demonstration?"

There was a pause as all those in earshot slowly drifted over, then an officer called out, "Sarah, why don't you have a go?"

She took a deep breath and raised her hand enough to grab the Sergeant's attention, and he nodded to her in acknowledgement. Unbuttoning her tunic slowly as she reached the center mat, she quickly became convinced that this was insane.

She nearly stopped at the sight of the large gray wolf, but pressed on. She had to put on a good show for the Navy — both Navies. Ursla had shown nothing but respect for the human party, but they needed to prove their mettle to everyone.

She slipped off her tunic, then adjusted her undershirt and pants so they wouldn't restrict movement. She kicked off her uniform boots, laid them with the tunic at the side of the mat, and then walked slowly to its center. Her heart rate was rising quickly.

This wolf, undoubtedly a nice person outside the ring, must have been able to lift 200 pounds easily, and probably weighed eighty pounds more than Sarah. And if he was anything like the Earthers she'd seen sparring, he was fast.

She, by comparison, was just a gifted amateur.

Oh well done, Sarah...

The Sergeant smiled and nodded to her, stepped forward and bowed, "Sergeant Major Beckett Lupus."

Sarah bowed in reply, "ArcBrigadier Sarah Manchester."

The wolf frowned for a second, then nodded, probably trying to place how high up on the rank scale she was... or how easy he should go on her. She couldn't look too dangerous.

Without a second's notice the Sergeant dropped into a martial stance, and out of instinct Sarah responded. In her mind, there was little question of who looked the more formidable.

And *no*, it wasn't her.

They circled each other for a moment, Sarah determined to let the Sergeant move first. She had little hope of victory so she wanted to get the first look at capabilities. An attack on her part would be foolhardy and–

Lupus was before her immediately, his arm coming over — much to Sarah's shock. She barely evaded the blow, hopped back a few paces and tried to focus herself. She *had* to concentrate...

The Sergeant came in fast, this time leading with a kick. Sarah swung aside, and as the leg reached where she should've been she clutched and rolled it. The Sergeant flipped and landed on the mat, leaping to his feet with a grin.

"My apologies for underestimating you, ArcBrigadier," he said with a nod, and Sarah suddenly felt nervous.

She had nearly lost and he was just toying with her–

He came again, faster this time, his arms driving outward too quickly to avoid. She blocked the first, deflected the second, but was too tied up to respond. She swung her leg around, trying to take out the Sergeant's legs with a solid kick, but he was already gone. Behind her.

She turned quickly, arms already up to block the incoming blows, while she edged backward. They stood about three meters apart and circled for a time, Sarah focused solely on the Sergeant.

Finally Lupus came forward, his leg swinging around in a heavy roundhouse kick. She dodged it evenly, her own leg coming out as his missed, striking at the leg supporting his weight. He stumbled but was able to drop his other leg in time to regain himself, his expression becoming resolute as he did.

Determined not to wait any longer Sarah let herself go, her body slamming forward with a complex series of blows matched with kicks, and for the first time in minutes, the Earther seemed to be off the attack.

From the sidelines Ursla smiled — Beckett Lupus was being very politic today.

He continued to repel Sarah for nearly a minute until she accidentally overextended her kick, and he used it to flip her as she'd done him, sending her face first to the mat. Before she could fall her arms were out to push her back up, and bare milliseconds after landing she was back in stance three meters from him.

She analyzed the situation in a split second. He was strong and relied on heavy attacks. How could that be used against him... inertia.

She slowly changed stances, trying successfully to look awkward, and the Sergeant, sensing an advantage, came forward. By the time he was half way across the mat Sarah had returned to her previous stance and sidestepped. His first blow lanced past her, and she grabbed his striking arm in both hands and levered him over onto his back, her knee coming down to rest lightly on his chest as she did. She was breathing heavily, sweating, and there was a hush in the room. She only then recognized her seeming victory, and leaned herself back and stood, helping to pull up the Sergeant who smiled as he stood.

"I must say, you are quite the fighter, ma'am," he noted in a friendly tone.

"Thank you, Sergeant," she smiled with a little nod and then turned back to her pile of clothing.

The humans cheered her respectfully, some coming to pat her on the back. As the crowd cleared Lupus turned and, catching Ursla's eye, offered a knowing smile. He hadn't thrown the match so much as he'd diplomatically chosen *not* to win.

Nobody downed Beckett Lupus, but the humans didn't need to know that just now.

Sarah picked up her jacket and walked to the bench that sat along the wall of the training gym, Pat following her closely. Most of the officers drifted behind, letting her finish dressing before congratulating her.

"My God, Sarah, you took that poor fellow apart!" Pat said lowly to her ear, and she laughed and shook her head.

"Hardly, I lucked out and found a weakness, that's all."

Pat snorted a laugh, "That's all? That's the mark of a good strategist — not to mention martial artist guru! Didn't you know how fast you were moving, woman?"

As Manchester sat to pull on her boots she frowned at her friend, "Not a clue. Why, was I going fast?"

Pat stabbed a finger at the mat where two marines were sparring again, "As fast as that, at least."

Sarah stopped struggling with her boots briefly. *That* fast?

"Well, I suppose I perform well under stress."

Pat laughed again, "Yeah, just remind me never to annoy you, eh?"

Sarah smiled back innocently, "Why Pat, I'd never hurt *you*..."

The two chuckled while she pulled her tunic back on and dried her face with a towel, ready to see the rest of *Cerberus*.

CHAPTER 14

"How long do we have, Pat?" Sarah asked, as she walked briskly through another of *Cerberus'* long, uniform corridors.

Pat glanced at his watch absently, "An hour and a half — there's no need to rush, Sarah. We'll be out of here in plenty of time."

Sarah nodded more in acknowledgement than agreement. She needed to shower before she returned to the Genesis Fleet — her sparring match with Lupus had made her feel sticky and uncomfortable, despite the towels on hand.

It had seemed simple enough to leave the main group of tourists and say she was going to shower, but as it turned out, *Cerberus'* network of passageways had baffled her. Pat, tagging along just to make certain she reached her destination, hadn't helped matters.

Earthers passed the pair without noticeable reaction, going about their duties with what seemed to be casual disregard, and Pat maintained that they should just ask someone which way to go.

Sarah, of course, didn't want to ask.

"I think I remember this corridor!" she said triumphantly as they rounded a corner. "Yes, just down here and to the left..."

The pair walked briskly down the hall and made a left turn, emerging into the gym. The tour group was still there, the Earthers still sparring.

"I shouldn't have doubted you, Sarah. Your sense of direction is *nothing* to laugh at!" Pat teased cheerfully and patted her on the back. Sarah turned on him with a murderous expression.

Raising two hands in mock fear, he waved to Ursla as she noticed the arrival of the pair. The huge Commodore approached quickly, wondering why they'd returned.

"Back already?" she asked as she slowed before the two humans.

Sarah bit her lip and flushed a bright red, "We were... a bit misdirected."

Ursla smiled at the comment, "*Cerberus* is surprisingly complex, I know. It's easy to lose your way, especially if it's your first time navigating."

Sarah nodded, color slowly fading from her face. Pat grinned.

"If you need to get to your quarters, head back down the hall you just came from, key the lift at the end, and go to Level Six Guest Quarters," Ursla swung a massive arm over to show the general direction for the trip, and Sarah took careful mental note.

"Thank you, Commodore," Sarah said stiffly, then turned to Pat. "*You* stay here this time."

With that, she set off for her quarters.

Pat smiled after her, then turned back to Ursla, "She's stubborn when it comes to things like directions. Typical, I suppose."

Ursla chuckled, "Indeed."

The pair turned back to the gym, where further demonstrations of Earther skill were taking place. Sparring pairs were leaping back and forth across padded floors, blurs of action.

"ArcColonel, while I have you here, could you answer some questions for me?" Ursla asked in low tones, and the big human looked up at the Commodore.

"It's still Pat to you, Andra, and I'd be glad to. What do you want to know?"

Ursla gestured to one of the benches at the side of the gym. Pat marched to it and sat down. Ursla gently let herself down next to him, making the bench shift noticeably.

"I'm just... well, your entire fleet is ready to mutiny? Just like that..." Ursla's voice trailed off, and Pat's smile slowly faded.

"Probably sounds as convenient to you as you lot seem to us. Too good to be true? Well, Commodore, we talk to our crews about it quite often. And usually we're trying to keep them from mutiny against the Church because we haven't anywhere to go. You know about things like segregation? The Church keeps its loyal families in one half of a city, and only lets others in the area to do the work. As far as I know, it's been like that since... well, the beginning."

Ursla cocked an eyebrow, and Pat nodded.

"When the old ship landed after the Exodus, there were two types of people on it — the really faithful folks who wanted to return to Earth more than anything else, and the level-headed types who knew how to run the machines. Based on what I've heard about your version of the story, the level-heads must've been technicians or something... I don't know."

Pat paused as a two-and-a-half meter tall bear squared off against a lean, white tiger, and Ursla could sense the animosity he felt for the Church as he watched silently.

"Some of what I've read on the subject might confirm that. The original plan was for the non-conditioned technical workers to be assimilated into the Church over time — at least that's the way the mission planners laid it out in their proposal," Ursla said quietly.

The original UN reports had mentioned exactly what Pat had said — the technicians, pilots, and other operating personnel couldn't undergo any type of mental conditioning since it could have interfered with their technical abilities. If they hadn't been assimilated into the Church as originally planned, that could explain quite a bit...

"Aye, the technicians were discriminated against as soon as the ship made planet-fall. They were treated like scum by every Church member who got near them — whole families were segregated because they didn't share the Church's view."

Ursla twitched her ear thoughtfully, and Pat continued, "For centuries, the technicians have been discriminated against, Andra. The best profession left for us is the regular Navy — under the boots of the Crusaders every day, and arbitrarily ordered to fight battles against good races just to keep alliances with bad ones..."

Ursla listened in silence. Human history on Earth had plenty of examples of discrimination of the sort Pat was mentioning — from slavery to racism, it was an unfortunately common phenomena. Records had shown that many humans had divided themselves for no reasonable purpose, and ended up killing each other. Late in the twentieth century and early in the twenty-first, the discrimination had been slowly fading, but then the species had been all but destroyed.

And the only surviving humans had decided to revive *that* particular habit.

"You and Sarah sound like you have specific Earth cultural backgrounds," Ursla commented as Pat watched the bear quickly topple the tiger.

"The Church doesn't like it, but some non-committed... that is to say, non-*Church* families go out of their way to keep Earth culture alive. We've been more inclined to remember Earth, I suppose... Church doesn't like that too much, but we think of it as a bit of home. Sarah's family is one of hundreds that still have British accents — or at least we *think* they're British — and mine is one of hundreds from Ireland. I call myself an Irishman all the time... though I suppose if I met a real one he'd knock my teeth out for it."

Ursla grinned, "Doubt that'd be a problem for me, so I'll indulge..."

Pat smiled and shrugged, nodding a bit more jovially, "There are Chinese, Japanese, Germans, Americans, Swiss, Italians, Australians, South Africans, Brazilians, Indians, Dutch... they all speak English now, but their cultures are in good shape. The Navy isn't just a broken band of assimilated people. Each group tries to keep our bit of culture alive. Half to remind us of Earth, half to annoy the Church, I suppose."

Ursla nodded quietly. Having seen numerous old human movies, she decided Sarah was speaking in a British accent, and that Pat's was certainly Irish. In any case, his point made things far clearer to the Ursla. The Genesis colony was indeed made up of two separate cultures.

"Don't you worry yourself, Andra. There is no way the Church will get wind of this. Our spacers have been wanting a way to get away from the Church for too long. Once we're all over here with you, the Church'll be completely impotent... a lot like now, I suppose..." Pat let a grim smile return to his face.

Ursla nodded, then noticed someone waving to her from the door.

"Sarah! Oh, Gods wept, can't you find anything?" Pat barked, standing with a laugh to try and help his ArcBrigadier find her room.

Ursla sat sedately as the duo disappeared into the corridor again. Humanity wasn't a very logical race... but if everything that was good was also logical, then Earther instinct couldn't be said to be positive either.

And it clearly was.

CHAPTER 15

Hastings tapped her foot anxiously for a moment, then continued to pace the deck. Where was Sarah? She looked up at the chronometer on the wall of *Genesis'* main flight bay and sighed wearily.

Saint Steven Tennor and *Warlock Prophet* had rejoined the fleet an hour and a half ago, and she'd sent a message to Sarah to shuttle over to the flagship almost immediately. Unfortunately, the younger ArcBrig didn't appear to be rushing.

Finally, after another five minutes, the huge space doors at the end of the flight deck opened and the pinnace glided in, passing through the force field set to keep space out and atmosphere in.

It followed landing lights to its ordained slot next to other Naval pinnaces, a ramp dropping as its feet connected with the ground. Manchester descended evenly, her calm, professional shield well established.

Hastings walked hurriedly to meet her, and the ArcBrigadier stopped to offer a salute which the ArcGeneral returned hastily, "Well? What happened?"

Manchester shrugged then said quietly, "We should talk in private."

Even Hastings' quarters didn't live up to the luxury of the Earthers', Manchester reflected silently as Hastings brought her a glass of water and sat down opposite her in a chair.

Manchester sipped the water, then looked up at her mentor, "Well, you were right."

Hastings leaned back and sighed, "In what part, exactly?"

"The Earthers aren't the bad guys. Hell, I think we should be allying ourselves with them against the Kroggs..." Manchester paused at the notion of allying to fight an 'ally', but Hastings nodded in agreement.

"The Kroggs aren't our friends, Sarah. We know that. But you agree that the Earthers are not the ones we should be shooting at?"

Manchester nodded in reply, "Me and every other Naval officer on that trip. Commodore Ursla — she is quite friendly, as you said — told me plainly that if the Naval personnel wanted asylum they'd get it. She told me that more than anything else, the Earthers want a bloodless solution."

Hastings released a relieved sigh, "So it's decided then. If we refuse action, the Church can't fight. Of course, surviving will be the hard part... if Bingham gets wind of this, he'll have us spaced and leave our crews without a way to escape. Force them to fight under Crusader leadership, and get everyone killed. We'll all have to leave — *all* of us, as we discussed. And somehow, we have to keep a mass evacuation secret and get all our people to the Earther Fleet. I've been toying with ideas, and I think we could start by sounding a decompression alert — fleet wide — which would make running crews seem perfectly natural. Crusaders would run to the security of their fortified barracks, confusion would be rampant. We could lock down ship systems under intruder protocol and seal off the AIs. Then, we all pile into small craft and run like hell towards the Earthers, leaving the Church gutted."

Manchester drained the last of her glass, "Yes, true, we could get out that way. But I still think we could save some of our lighter ships... Battlecruisers and lower... if we could surprise the Crusaders. Think about it, the ratio of Crusaders to marines on those ships is a lot closer, so we could capture a good part of the fleet's escort force."

Hastings paused and her eyes narrowed, "I'd leave that to each CO's discretion — if an ArcColonel thinks it'd be too dangerous then forget it, but if it's possible, then by all means. In any case, I'm going to start sending out orders. I'll brief the Task Force commanders face to face... they can brief squadron commanders, who'll brief ArcColonels, and their staffs. We can call it personnel rotation."

Manchester nodded briefly.

"I think, Sarah, this'll be happening very soon. Bingham's up to something. Bactule went straight into a meeting with him. I've got a very bad feeling, because he did it in the Chancellor's *personal* cabin. Bad signs."

Manchester's face darkened further, "I've got a tight-beam comm frequency so we can get in touch with Andra. You two can work out a timetable... soon, I should think."

Hastings nodded in agreement and took a long swig of her own drink. Any option they had of changing their minds was quickly shrinking.

Well, they might be leaving the fleet, but Sarah wasn't about to lose her squadron in the process...

"Just one more thing, Liz," she said softly, "I can save most of my squadron and probably other ships too. I've been thinking about it a lot. All I need is twenty minutes warning before the signal to move goes out. I'll stage an insurrection on *Prophet*. Bingham will want to crush it decisively, but to do that he'll need a lot of Crusaders to shuttle in from other ships..."

"Making them easier for us to take," Hastings paused at the statement. It took a lot on... well, faith, for lack of a better word. But if Sarah wanted to try... "Alright. But get yourself out alive. I'll move your squadron to the front of the fleet, and I want you to start tight-beaming signals to Ursla as well. She has to be ready and waiting for us when we show up."

"She'll be ready," Manchester assured. "We're depending on it."

• • •

Crusader Shappa Bactule sat rigidly in the chair before his High Chancellor's desk and waited for the leader to return. He had gone to get the pair some blessed brandy — to celebrate a successful mission.

As Bingham re-entered the room he slowly slid into the chair behind his desk and laid one of the two glasses he was carrying before his Shappa. The Crusader took it and sipped, "Thank you, Your Eminence."

"So, your mission was as successful as we hoped?" Bingham began softly, and Bactule nodded.

"We have, Your Eminence, identified the Naval types as being soft towards the Cause, and I have selected the best places to land our six million warriors for the capture of the planet," Bactule's voice was as level as usual, Bingham noticed with satisfaction.

"And the conversion of our Crusaders to starship controllers?" Bingham pressed.

"Two colonizers of Crusaders have been selected for the duty, and the conversions have begun. It will take some days, Your Eminence, but it will be done. We will be able to eliminate the Navy altogether now, and the Earthers will fold."

Bingham cocked an eyebrow, "The heathen I met seemed determined to stop us."

Bactule's smile was hungry, "Your Eminence, the heathen I met were very imposing in appearance, but had little stomach to act in conflict."

Bingham sipped his brandy, "I trust, then, that we will defeat them."

It wasn't a question.

Bactule nodded, "With a certainty. The test may be a difficult one, but our faith will prove us to the Gods. By my estimates, we will be ready to initiate takeover of the fleet in two days, and a day after that we can engage the Earthers."

Bingham forced a smile. He knew he should be happy. Yes... he *was* happy... he had to be. So he would be.

This was a test of the Gods; they were trying to help him strengthen his faith, not to allow himself to be weakened by the stories of the Earthers, no matter how plausible. Even though a piece of him might be inclined to make peace, there would be no surrender. Instead, he would fight, if only to remain secure in his values. He would focus on the victory of this Quest.

Manchester sat in her briefing room aboard *Warlock Prophet*, the weary ArcColonels of her twelve Battlecruisers sitting around the table. Aside from Conroy, none of them knew what was about to be said.

She was confident that the preparations would be made swiftly and silently, and the plan she had set for this squadron alone would save most of its ships.

Manchester had sent tight-beam laser messages to *Cerberus* and *Orion* several times already, updating the Earthers on the current situation. Now it was time to lay the ground work.

Thumbing a transmission scrambler to ensure privacy, she began, "We're going to mutiny."

Those words resonated around the room and caused instant attention. Before their meaning processed and questions arose, she pressed on.

"All of us. The whole fleet. It'll be tricky but it *has* to be done. It'll be very soon too, I'm talking twenty-four to forty-eight hours. The general goal for the fleet is to get its personnel into small craft and over to the Earther Navy, where the Church can't reach them."

She let the silence settle around the table until, finally ArcColonel Ed Jeffries spoke up tenuously, "Um... ma'am. Don't you think evacuating two million people will catch the Crusaders' attention? In small craft we'd be sitting ducks."

Manchester nodded briefly as some of her own doubts were spoken, "It's a risk, I know. I brought that same point up with the ArcGeneral when she told me, but what we're looking at doing is activating decompression alarms to confuse the Crusaders and then initiate intruder lockdowns. The Church doesn't have the codes or the knowledge to override them, nor do they have the ability to fly ships anyway."

"Ahem," Conroy cleared his throat and was given attention. "Do you mean we're abandoning all of our ships, ArcBrigadier? I may have said *Cerberus* was a beauty, but I still do love my dear *Bishop*."

Conroy knew that the fleet general order was for crews to abandon their ships, but he had asked anyway, probably to help lead the briefing where she needed it to go — the issue of her squadron.

"Not quite, Pat," Manchester said slowly, and then dove into her plan. "We'll be doing something different for this squadron. Instead of evacuating like most ships, we'll get rid of the Crusaders and then escape from the fleet. What I intend to do is stage a preemptive mutiny aboard *Prophet*. If Bingham does what he should, Crusaders will start shuttling from all of your ships to reinforce the Crusaders here. Our dear High Chancellor will want to make an example of us to the rest of the fleet, and while we evacuate *Prophet* in small craft you'll have time to take over your ships."

There was dead — and entirely understandable — silence. Such a plan called for heavy casualties among the rebelling crew of *Warlock Prophet*, but their sacrifice would lure at least some of the Crusaders away from the rest of the squadron's ships, improving their chances for survival. Naval marines could hit any Crusaders who remained behind, and eleven of the Genesis Fleet's Battlecruisers would get away.

"Before we leave, we can rig *Prophet* to self destruct. That'll wipe out the

Crusaders, and we can get away."

Manchester's voice was grim as she detailed the plan, and now she leaned back to accept the suggestions and questions she knew would come.

"Ma'am, if the whole two million officers and crew of our fleet are going to evacuate, preparations are going to have to be made... well, the Crusaders aren't entirely stupid. They'll notice, or someone will talk..." ArcColonel James Stanton said cautiously, and Conroy barked a laughed.

"Man, have you ever seen a Navy man and a Crusader talking? These bastards have pushed themselves so far apart no one would ever tell them. It'll be your job to assure your crews this is what has to be done, but that shouldn't be too hard!"

Manchester picked up after her friend, "And the Crusaders don't know enough about Naval operations to realize what's happening. Basically, with the exceptions of some, we'll be abandoning ship. The crews must know what's going on, but we won't need to rehearse it."

There were grudging nods of agreement.

"I realize there is a *lot* that can go wrong, but can you honestly tell me you want to stay with the Church to fight the Earthers? I've seen the Earther Navy. I've seen our fleet through their gunports. I can tell you plainly, if we fight, they'll slaughter us. This is our chance — our *only* chance — to go home on our own terms."

"But they want us as company?" Jeffries asked again, his tone weighed down by skepticism.

Manchester sighed, thinking about the difficulties so many squadron commanders must be having trying to give the same briefing. It wasn't an easy subject.

"They're a lot like us, lad," Pat answered, recognizing the weariness that threatened to overwhelm Manchester. "They're plain folks, just like us. They want to find a way out of this which doesn't require a whole lot of blood. They're offering asylum because they believe it'll lead to a peaceful resolution. I don't trust easily, and you all know it... but I trust them."

That statement, at least, gave the Earthers credibility. Throughout the past Pat Conroy had trusted very few people, but he was willing to lay down his word for the Earthers.

"We go soon. Maybe tomorrow. Get back to your ships and get ready. Silence any leaks. If the Crusaders get nosy, lie," Manchester heaved the words, and the officers in the room stood and left.

Elizabeth Hastings tapped her fingers nervously on her desk as she reviewed the fleet status grid on her monitor. The readiness reports had started to come in very slowly at first, but the trickle had begun to flow like a tide. Almost 2,100 of the fleet's ships had prepared for the insurrection, but 300 were yet to report.

And it only took one clever Crusader to end it all...

She turned away from the screen, her eyes sore from the glare, and looked at the chronometer. It was already around 20:00 hours, and she'd been staring at the monitor for almost three hours. She had a nagging fear about the plan already. It was far too large scale for someone not to talk, for one Crusader not to notice. But this was their only chance. Otherwise the Crusaders would find a way to start a fight, even if the Naval officers were forced at gun point. Eventually some would cooperate, and it'd become a bloodbath.

No, their only hope of escape and survival lay with the Earthers, no matter how risky that hope turned out to be.

Turning back to her monitor, Hastings keyed up a small window to display how many ships would be taken over in the mutiny. So far, 102 ArcColonels thought they could successfully take control of their ships from the Crusaders. Mainly they were Destroyers and Light Cruisers, but there were a few Heavy Cruisers and even a Dreadnought. Sarah intended to get eleven of her twelve Battlecruisers out.

If her plan to draw the Crusaders in brought a different reaction than expected — like a Crusader lockdown throughout the squadron — the operation would be paralyzed. It was a risk, but it was one that seemed worth taking. In the end, it all came down to the spacers, the Petty Officers, and the ordinary crew. It was their mutiny more than anyone else's, and Hastings suddenly had a pang of fear that they wouldn't want to go, even though they'd expressed exactly that desire for years.

Time would tell.

ArcGeneral Elizabeth Hastings leaned back in her chair and rubbed her eyes in a bid to keep them from shutting. She prayed to the Gods that she'd made the right decision.

She prayed the Crusaders wouldn't catch on.

And for half a second she wondered what she was doing *praying*, but the irrelevant question was put out of her head.

She needed assurances...

Leaning forward, Hastings took a breath and keyed her comm, which buzzed active.

"Communications, Chief Gails here..."

CHAPTER 16

"It is hard to explain, Your Eminence. It just... *feels* as if they are up to something," Shappa Bactule's words were frustrated, mirroring the man's general attitude.

The High Chancellor's cabin was dark, the late evening lights aboard *Genesis* having dimmed the room to simulate a night. Bingham sat at his desk and considered his Shappa's words silently. He had learned long ago to respect the 'feelings' of the Crusader leader, but there had been no word from Crusaders aboard the ships of the Genesis Fleet that something was stirring.

In fact, the Navy seemed to have calmed from its normally rambunctious attitude to a demeanor of silent respect. That was disconcerting, but perhaps it was legitimate.

Not likely.

"Shappa, I have nothing but respect for your opinion, but there is a lack of evidence..." Bingham's voice trailed off for a moment, as thoughts held him again.

He hadn't wanted to take over the fleet until he could crew it with Crusaders, but the conversions were only about half complete. If he took over the fleet now it would take hours to successfully re-crew any of its ships, and even then only half the fleet would be crewed. To move now would make no sense, unless the Navy was going to try something themselves.

Bingham's mind wrapped around that kernel of thought. What could the Navy really do? Taking over the fleet was out of the question — he had the advantage of trained, well-armed soldiers on every ship. What then? A refusal to fight? That would be of no consequence in the end — his 'Navy' Crusaders would come to replace them eventually. Then what?

A mass exodus? Over to the heathen? That would be unthinkable! The commotion of preparing such a thing would be impossible to miss.

"Shappa," Bingham asked gently, "how long until the conversion of our Crusaders is finished?"

Bactule thought for a second before replying, "I would expect the process to be completed by this time tomorrow evening."

Bingham nodded absently and dove back into his thoughts. If the Navy was planning something they could probably try it by that time. But... if the Crusaders began to take over their ships tomorrow at noon, then they could have the ships empty of the Navy and awaiting faithful crews that evening.

Yes, attack at noon, leave the rest of the day to weed out any resistance and begin re-crewing, and then finish crewing the fleet at night. Then, by the next morning, they could attack the Earthers in earnest.

Keeping everything well coordinated to that extent would make for a delicate operation, but it could be done. It *had* to be done.

"Shappa, here is what I intend," Bingham spoke with renewed confidence as he spelled out his plan to his trusted Shappa.

Bactule stepped out of the High Chancellor's cabin, a grim smile on his face. He walked determinedly to the barracks of Crusaders on *Genesis*. It would be a glorious takeover, and it would prove, once and for all, that the Church was worthy of the Holy Quest. Success would only come from a very well-coordinated plan, and the ships of the Genesis Fleet would be taken into the sole ownership of the Church.

As the Shappa marched down the corridor into the Crusader section of the Superdreadnought, he noticed a pair of Navy technicians working quietly over an open panel in the wall.

"What do you think you are doing here, scum?" he demanded, and the pair looked up with a jolt of shock.

One of them was a woman, Bactule noted with distaste. He — and the whole Church — were of the opinion that women had no place in the Quest. The fact that the fleet commander was a woman did little to change that belief.

"We're repairing a damaged intercom line, sir," the man said humbly, laying his tool on the deck and standing.

"Who gave authorization? Non-believers have no place in this part of the ship!" Bactule snarled, and the technician shrunk.

"The authorization came from the ArcColonel, sir. He wanted to make sure no loss of communication reached this section," the woman said cautiously.

Bactule shook his head as if he was giving up, "You have five minutes. If you are here after that you will die."

With that, he stormed past the two shaken technicians and to the Crusader barracks where he would brief his Shaspas of their plan.

"Gods, I thought we were dead," the male technician sighed, kneeling again and picking up his tool.

The woman nodded, "We'll be out of here in a minute anyway. Give me the bug."

In silence, the two proceeded to link Crusader communications into the ArcGeneral's personal comm net, and then retreated from the Crusader wing of the ship with desperate haste, not willing to chance the return of the unstable Shappa.

•••

"The plan is this!" Bactule said dramatically to the Crusader Shaspas and soldiers in the huge barracks aboard *Genesis*. "We have trained two million of our Holy warriors in the way of flying these great ships. The Navy scum are no longer necessary!"

The Shappa paused as he peered out over the room's 400 occupants and pondered what was about to take place.

"It will be our purpose, and that of every Crusader on every ship of this fleet, to take control of each vessel! The Naval heathen may be killed by whatever means is convenient, but the key is that we capture every ship of the fleet so that our loyal warriors can take control!"

The room, of course, was completely silent. Crusaders didn't give any reply or make any suggestions to their leaders, for that would make it seem as if they doubted the Divine Grace held by those superiors.

"We will have to act swiftly, and prepare this night. Tomorrow, at noon, we will attack simultaneously. The Navy will not know what is happening until it is far too late, and we will win the fleet in the name of the Quest.

"By the morning of the day after tomorrow, we will have control of this fleet, and then we will force the Earther heathen from our path and achieve the goals of prophecy!"

"Prophecy," Hastings spat the word with venom as it piped over her comm channel. The bastards had planned to wipe out her people all along, and somehow they'd trained replacements.

The original reason for abandoning had been replaced deftly by another. They had to go. And before noon tomorrow.

With this vital information in hand, the ArcGeneral cut the feed from the barracks intercom and heaved a sigh. If they intended to attack at noon, the Crusaders would be arming themselves and getting ready as early as 09:00 hours. And that meant they'd be ready to stop the escape.

Hastings glanced again at her wall chronometer and pursed her lips. It was currently 22:45. They could go early in the morning, after the Crusaders went to bed but before they roused... around 02:00 maybe. Yes, that'd catch them asleep and without much cohesion. With luck, they'd be overconfident too — after all, they expected to be in a position to kill all the Naval personnel that day.

That was it then. Two o'clock in the morning. She'd have to alert the fleet quickly — send the word down the chain of command through tight-beam lasers. The Earthers would also have to be warned.

She'd already adjusted fleet deployments so all the ships capable of taking control could have an easier escape, but almost fifty were still held up in the main echelons. They'd have to deal with the situation on their own — there was nothing more she could do for them now.

Turning to her console, Hastings opened a tight-beam secured channel to Sarah, the screen brightening after only a second to show a tired but uniformed ArcBrigadier on the other side.

"Liz?" Manchester asked softly, a neutral expression on her face.

"They've managed to train Crusaders to fight our ships. They planned to kill us all tomorrow at noon and take over," Hastings said grimly.

Manchester's eyes widened, then she blinked and assessed the situation, "Going at 02:00, then?"

Despite herself, Hastings grinned, "How'd you know?"

"You like even numbers," Manchester managed a smile as her mind began to wrap around the logistical implications of the situation. They'd been waiting scarcely two hours and there'd only be four more before the time came to move... "My little mutiny will start at quarter past one. I'll alert the Earthers; you get the fleet ready."

Hastings laughed gruffly, "Yes ma'am!"

Sarah released a short chuckle, smiled sadly, and cut the comm link.

And so it begins... Gods help us all.

CHAPTER 17

The high shrill of fleet comm brought Ursla suddenly from her sleep, but she managed to keep from shooting upwards to bang her head. She swung heavily out of bed, stumbled — crashed really — over to her desk and dropped into the chair like a ton of bricks.

Her squadron — as well as twelve other frigate and sloop squadrons — were now sitting front and center, a screen between the patiently waiting Earther Navy and the Genesis Fleet. The 104 ships of this new Task Force were exclusively under Ursla's command, and it was her job to guard the abandoning humans as they escaped.

It wasn't a huge force to fill the role, but the ships were light and fast, allowing them to get between any Church broadsides and small craft. Of course, their orders were not to fire on the Church when the time came, but there were no guarantees as to how agreeable Bingham would be about the situation.

Ursla still doubted that her force — dubbed the "Exodus Battle Group" — would be needed. The Church would be incapable of operating their fleet when the Naval personnel left. But nothing could be left to chance.

Ursla yawned as she keyed up her holo tank for the message, and soon saw Caine staring at her from the other side. He had a deep frown across his brow.

"They've trained Crusaders to fly their fleet, Andra."

It was hardly a good greeting. Ursla barely kept her shock in check as the words sunk in. That meant the entire plan was shot... there'd be a battle, regardless of the Navy. Hastings' people still had to be saved... but so much blood would be spilled.

"The Crusaders are planning to kill all the Navy personnel and take over the fleet tomorrow at noon. Hastings has decided to go at 02:00, and Manchester will start her decoy at 01:15, their relative time," Caine continued.

Glancing at her own clock, Ursla did the math... carry the four... it was 03:25 Earther standard time now, giving her just over two hours.

"I'll be ready," she said solemnly.

"I know," Caine nodded, and the link cut.

Ursla turned to her intercom panel and keyed the bridge, "Officer of the watch?"

"Lieutenant Merrimac here, ma'am," the answer came promptly.

"Beat to quarters. Get the crew to an early breakfast. I'll be up shortly."

The battle alarms sounded on *Cerberus*, then throughout the rest of the Exodus Battle Group as the message was passed on. The ships' crews raced to their posts and their guns and shields began to charge.

Caine leaned back in his desk chair and focused his mind on the task at hand. The undertaking was gargantuan, to say the very least.

The First Lord looked at the picture of his family sitting on the corner of his desk. They'd just commed it to him and he'd printed it and framed it as soon as it arrived. His wife and young son were smiling as they walked the grounds of the family estate hand-in-hand.

He hadn't seen them in ages... and now battle was inevitable. He was confident the Church wouldn't make it to Earth to do any harm to his family — he would *not* let them — but they could still kill many Earthers before they fell.

Trying to clear his head of the images of what he would face, Caine turned away from his family photo and back to his holo plot where the squadron formations of both fleets were displayed. The positions hadn't changed much in the past days — the Earthers were content to let the humans reflect on the situation. But things would change drastically, and very soon.

Caine would have to be ready to reply to anything after the Naval personnel evacuated, though it would likely take time for the Crusaders to get all the ships manned. The Earthers would have very little breathing room.

The biggest threat Caine could see were the Colonizers — massive ships twice the size of *Orion*, each carrying a million Crusaders and an armament to match their bulk. If they got near enough to Earth to drop troops... eight million infantry hitting Earth's soil when the Earther Marine Corps maxed out at 95,000.

No, six million. Two million Crusaders would have to stay with the Genesis Fleet. Still, six *million*... Those ships would have to be intercepted. Frigates wouldn't be enough. No, it must be ships of the line. Second Rates at least. Even 74s couldn't hope to match that might... *Orion's* 175 guns could hardly do so. Well, the decision had to wait a little while, until he had more information. That information would arrive with the Naval officers. And they'd be here in two hours.

"Battle group reports all ships are standing by," *Cerberus'* Signal Officer announced, and Ursla nodded.

From sitting at standby to battle ready in scarcely six minutes — a time any task force in the Earther Navy could envy. There was still no sign of movement in the Genesis Fleet, but then there wouldn't be — there were two hours to go before anything should *start* happening.

Ursla's battle group would be ready to deploy as soon as the first ships began to move, and now was the time to iron out any wrinkles in the inter-ship signalling network which allowed the battle group to operate as a perfectly coordinated entity.

This would be their first *real* action after all.

Ursla watched her chair monitor silently as it brought up a visual of the Genesis Fleet, and sighed at that force's bulk. Traveling from one side of that fleet to the other would take twenty-five minutes in a small craft, so escapees coming from the rear of the formation would have a hard time getting through. Nonetheless, they had to.

The Exodus Battle Group would have to be there to interpose itself between anything coming from the fleet's far side and the Church ships — any active vessels at least. But now they also might have to guard the Earther Navy's front door against immediate attack, and that was too much for 104 cruisers.

Keying up fleet comm she signaled Caine, who appeared immediately on her small screen.

"What's up, Andra?" his tone revealed his stress.

Ursla shrugged her broad shoulders tiredly, "If the Church fleet goes active, I won't have enough ships to escort the small craft *and* screen for our main body."

Caine nodded slowly in understanding, "Right..." he paused in thought, "I'll bring up the 144th, 145th, and 146th. They'll hold the door open. Your battle group has to get those small craft out safely."

Three squadrons more — 74s no less. Setter wasn't playing, and Ursla felt a surge of relief, "We'll do our best."

With a last, somewhat sympathetic nod, Caine disappeared. Now it was just a matter of time.

CHAPTER 18

Warlock Prophet was silent at 01:15. To Crusader Shaspa Raganath, it felt like the calm before the storm. He slept comfortably if intermittently, having fully briefed his loyal Holy warriors the night before. His cabin was next to the Crusader barracks, in the private section reserved for the specific use of the Church troops.

Then gunfire shattered the silence.

A Crusader sentry slammed the alarm key on his comm unit just before his chest exploded, and suddenly all the Crusaders were on their feet, putting on armor and loading rifles. The response of a well-trained force, but a response which was treacherously slow when a ready enemy was just outside the door.

Raganath was in his uniform less than a minute after the alarm, and he swept stealthily out into the corridor to see what was happening. The three other sentries were kneeling, their rifles barking repeatedly, rounds clinking into the deck around them. At the far side of the hall, two dozen Navy marines in their own armor knelt to reply.

Without thought the Shaspa sprinted back into his quarters and thumbed the emergency line to Shappa Bactule. Despite the early hour, the Shappa answered immediately, looking only somewhat disheveled.

"Yes, Shaspa?" the commander-in-chief said roughly.

"Insurrection aboard the Battlecruiser *Warlock Prophet* sir. We will fight to the last but they have hit us at night, confined us. It will take time to counter effectively," Raganath reported hurriedly.

The Shappa's eyes widened and he nodded. Nothing needed to be said. If this was an isolated incident, help would promptly arrive from nearby ships. If not, then the Holy Cause was being tested yet again.

Raganath took his heavy pistol and returned to the hall. The number of Navy marines had doubled on the deck's far side, and the near side was a dead end. A single entrance, simplifying both offense and defense, and theoretically making the former much more dangerous than the latter. Now it was a death zone.

Raganath reflected on the estimated fifty Naval marines firing at his Crusaders — the ship carried only eighty such marines, so chances were the rest were in reserve. His 150 Crusaders, which could have normally wiped the heathen from the ship, were trapped and their potency diluted by this secretive attack. Despite that, they swept into the hall, almost a dozen falling, beginning to deploy their portable sheet-titanium breastworks to cover the corridor.

If help did not come, they could lose this fight. But if the other nearby ships sent Crusader detachments they would win decisively. With that thought in mind the Shaspa returned to his cabin, marched to his desk and keyed in a code on the console.

"Ready for orders," the computer AI replied in its cool, shrill voice.

"Initiate Crusader Lockdown Faithful. Alert the flag and then lock down all ship's systems!"

With that, every major system — from defense to navigation — stopped accepting non-Church orders aboard *Warlock Prophet*.

Bactule rushed into *Genesis'* Church briefing room, stopping to bow to a less than pristine High Chancellor.

"*What is happening?!*" Bingham demanded.

"An isolated attempt by the Navy to take over a Battlecruiser sir: *Warlock Prophet*. So far the ship's garrison has locked down all major systems but it will not survive without reinforcements," Bactule's tone had a sharp edge, marking his anger.

Bingham sighed deeply, "The only attempt, you say?"

Bactule nodded hurriedly, "The only one, all other Navy crews seem to be subdued. The ArcBrigadier on *Warlock Prophet* went on the Earth trip. I think she influenced the crew."

"A *lot* of officers went on that trip... still, if they were planning to try to take over they hardly would have gone one at a time..." thought consumed the High Chancellor for a moment, and he stared intently at the wall.

Bactule stirred uncomfortably, then spoke, "Your Eminence, I recommend we send Crusader boarding parties from the rest of the ships in that squadron to crush the attempt. A swift and decisive defeat will show the Navy they have no hope of resistance."

That had already occurred to Bingham. In fact, if the defeat was decisive enough the Navy would be terrified into submission, making tomorrow's work easier.

"Send seventy-five Crusaders from each ship in that squadron... no, 100. That will be most impressive," the High Chancellor finally ordered.

The Shappa hesitated at the command, "Sir, the whole squadron is made up of Battlecruisers. They carry only 150 Crusaders each... there will barely even be room for those 1,100 warriors on *Prophet*! It might be tactically unwise..."

"Damnit! Holy work is not a hostage of tactics! It will be a display of our power! They won't dare resist when they realize how much might will fall on them. We can demoralize them this morning and kill them at noon!"

• • •

"That's it, they've implemented their lockdown."

The report didn't sound defeated — it actually came across as amused.

ArcBrigadier Manchester nodded silently at the Executive Officer's report, and strummed her fingers on the arm of her chair on *Prophet*'s bridge. As soon as passive sensors read incoming Crusader landing craft, they would have to get their weapons back online.

Manchester reached to the keypad on her chair arm and tapped in a combination, "Computer, initiate intruder alert lockdown. All command functions routed to flag officer voice command."

"Acknowledged," the AI said in a monotone.

There was no visible difference in the operation of the ship — or more specifically, the lack of operation. The change, however, was decisive. The Crusaders weren't aware that their special lockdown subroutines were superseded by the intruder alert lockdown subroutines, so they would have no idea of what was happening. The primary difference came in who held control of *Warlock Prophet* — namely ArcBrigadier Sarah Manchester, the only flag officer aboard.

"Computer, activate point defense systems. Designate any small craft not using a Naval transponder code as hostile and prepare for incoming assault shuttles," Manchester said after another pause.

"Acknowledged," the AI affirmed.

The Artificial Intelligence's job was to run ship systems with the minimum number of required personnel, but it was by no means sophisticated enough to differentiate between the loyalties of the officers giving it orders. As far as it was concerned, Naval priority was greater than Crusader, as Naval matters directly involved more of its systems. So now, all that mattered to the computer was that Naval command had deemed the situation dire, and that if a small craft wasn't flying a Naval pennant on its transponder code, it was hostile.

The limits placed on its targeting ability by the Crusader lockdown wouldn't allow it much fire control of its own, but the Navy's gunnery crew in auxiliary control had agreed to stay on long enough to manually target the incoming Crusader assault ships.

"Now we hope the Crusaders take the bait," Manchester said quietly.

ArcColonel Patrick Conroy watched with a grin as the pair of Crusader assault ships, each carrying fifty Crusaders, left the main hangar deck of *Harbinger Bishop*. The main monitor showed them angling away from his ship and making for *Prophet* at a good clip.

The Crusaders had taken the bait — hook, line, and dynamite, as the old saying went. Now, only fifty of the bastards remained on his ship, and even though they were awake and on alert, they wouldn't have a hope when his marines swept in. One-to-one was too much for the Churchers — that's why they worked so hard to outnumber the Naval troops at all times.

Conroy keyed the intercom line to his marine CO, "Gill, you ready lass?"

"Don't call me 'lass', Pat. We're ready," the voice of Captain Gillian Hodge replied.

"Well then go, girl! I'm locking down comm now," Pat half laughed.

The link shut and the Comm Officer locked down the communication nets around the ship. No Crusader would be able to send a warning about what was really happening — *Bishop* was now effectively cut off from the rest of the Genesis Fleet.

Captain Hodge was the sixth person to enter the Crusader barracks aboard *Bishop*, but most of the hard work was already done by the time she reached her kneeling position to the right of the doorway. Two of hers were down, but that was a trade for *thirty-eight* of the Crusaders. The fanatics hadn't known what was happening until the grenades went off. The last dozen were behind cover, spraying rounds towards the door in panic.

Crusaders were usually very disciplined, with most of their strength coming from numbers and organization. Now they were broken and trapped...

Another Naval marine hit the deck hard, but the next one pitched a shrapnel grenade, and another nine of the Crusaders stopped firing. The last three, stunned by the amazing losses, leaned over their cover to watch their dying comrades.

Their chests exploded in reply, and in the space of six minutes, *Harbinger Bishop* was liberated.

The first Crusader shuttle hit *Prophet*'s flight deck hard, skittering to a screeching halt and releasing its 100 charges. It was the only one that would make it. Thirty marines and a hundred-odd volunteers from the Battlecruiser's crew sprayed the Crusaders with fire as they tried to descend its ramp, and an energy tractor built into the deck for guiding incoming shuttles grabbed hold of the assault craft and swung it out through the energy field.

The shuttle's disembarkment hatch was still open, and as it lost pressure the remaining twelve crew and Crusaders on the ship died horribly. Its weapons couldn't be used against the Naval marines.

The first assault craft had been allowed entry specifically to draw the rest into range. Twenty-one such craft carrying Crusaders from the rest of the squadron were inside point defense weapons range, and the ones with the easiest escape were targeted first.

As the last Crusaders to survive the landing were cut down by the crew, *Prophet*'s anti-missile grid opened fire. Dozens of light lasers swung into automatic fire, pulses slashing out into the bewildered assault craft. Those systems *should* have been under Church control, but none of the approaching craft had time to consider that fact.

Thanks to the gunner's programming, the AI blasted away eighteen of the craft with brutal efficiency. The last three swung in close to the hull of the Battlecruiser, linking into the closest maintenance airlocks to empty the fifty Crusaders they each held.

Manchester watched all this from the bridge monitors with a healthy amount of detachment, and then punched another sequence into her keypad.

"Self-destruct activated. Silent alarms, there will be no warnings," the AI said mechanically. "Timer set at twenty minutes."

Satisfied, Manchester looked at the chronometer: 01:40. The timing was bang on. Now all she had to do was grab her personal kit and get to the landing bay.

With that in mind she keyed the intercom, "ArcBrigadier to all hands, retreat to point B and stand by to initiate the Exodus maneuver."

With that cryptic message broadcast for all to hear, she drew her heavy autopistol and joined the bridge crew as they abandoned their consoles.

"Somehow they got their point defense online! Only 150 made it through, but they report they have forced the crew into a defensive pocket. They are unsure of how long it will take to secure our victory," Bactule reported to Bingham, trying to maintain calm even after the disgrace.

The High Chancellor nodded, "Have them deactivate the point defense then. Send 1,000 more Crusaders — take them from wherever is closest!"

Bactule nodded in agreement. He had no desire to send more to die needlessly, but the Navy had to be demoralized, or exterminating them would prove highly difficult. Replacements could be drawn from the Colonizers after the fight.

Walking quickly down one of *Prophet*'s corridors, the command staff carried their small personal kits and their sidearm autopistols. Crew members were flocking to the landing deck, hundreds of Naval personnel moving there with all haste to take the ship's large numbers of small craft to safety. If each of *Prophet*'s small craft took on unsafe loads, the entire crew could escape to the other ships of Sarah's squadron.

Then they just had to wait until the rest of the fleet made its–

The ArcLieutenant in front of Manchester exploded. Blood and parts spattered the ArcBrigadier as instinct forced her to dive to the side of the hall. A squad of Crusaders appeared at the next intersection, firing viciously at the command staff. They were cut off.

Manchester leveled her pistol and began to fire automatic bursts, her mind already trying to decide how to get around the Crusaders. From behind her the Executive Officer was cut down by a second squad. She glanced back between shots, seeing another squad of Crusaders behind her. The other seven bridge crew took cover in locked-down doorways and frantically returned fire.

They were trapped.

Come on Sarah, get out of there!

Harbinger Bishop was the closest ship to *Prophet*, and it would be the one taking the bulk of the latter's crew to safety. The time was 01:54, so the pinnaces from the fleet would start launching in about five minutes. That last stretch of time was murder on Pat Conroy.

Crusader reinforcements were headed to *Prophet* from the nearest squadron of Heavy Cruisers, giving those ships a chance to escape in earnest when the hour came. But those reinforcements wouldn't reach *Prophet* for ten minutes, and by then he could shoot them down without jeopardizing the fleet's secret plans.

Still, these last six minutes would be crucial to the crew of *Prophet*, especially since the ship was going to self destruct...

Four bridge officers remained alive, though two had critical injuries. ArcColonel Tom Forrest, Manchester's Flag ArcColonel, was missing his left foot. The tactical officer had lost an arm. Only she and the helm officer stayed fully functional, a condition which wouldn't last long at this rate. If the Crusaders didn't get them, the exploding ship would.

And you, Sarah dear girl, got yourself into the thick of it.

The irony of the situation grabbed the ArcBrigadier for the first time, and she smiled, then laughed outright. The Helm Officer glanced her way nervously, leaning out to make sure the ArcBrigadier was still okay. He was knocked off his feet as he did so.

Sarah Manchester watched the lifeless body fall to the deck and was overcome by rage. She leaned out from her perch and sprayed fire one way, while the ArcColonel, still clutching his pistol, sprayed bullets the other way.

And, surprisingly, the Crusaders all fell.

From behind them armed crewman appeared, brandishing sidearms and rifles. They sprinted up to their officers and helped them up. Manchester waved off their assistance, then helped the ArcColonel hobble along on his single foot. She glanced at her chronometer. It was 01:56.

As the last of the crew reached *Prophet*'s landing bay they were quickly ushered to pinnaces. The time was ticking by, and the Crusaders were pressing in on the defensive pocket. Soon, they'd take control of the flight deck. It was only 01:58. But waiting two minutes for the fleet to mutiny would be too risky for the eight pinnaces sitting on the deck.

Manchester was in the cockpit of the lightest pinnace, staring from the chrono to the view port and back.

"Is everyone set and aboard?" she asked calmly, and the pilot repeated the question quickly through his headset. The pilots of each of the other pinnaces acknowledged, and then he turned and nodded to the ArcBrigadier.

With a deep breath, Sarah Manchester took a last look at her Battlecruiser's flight deck. Then she nodded.

"All pinnaces launch immediately."

At 01:59 eight pinnaces rippled from *Prophet* at full speed, and Pat prayed silently that Sarah was aboard one of them. The small ships sped away from the Battlecruiser, running at their maximum velocity for *Bishop*.

As the chronometer switch flipped to the hour of 02:00, *Warlock Prophet* erupted into an expanding ball of flame.

The rest of the Genesis Fleet collapsed into chaos.

CHAPTER 19

As 01:58 arrived, ArcGeneral Elizabeth Hastings was sitting nervously at her desk, watching the sensor scans from ships near *Warlock Prophet* for any sign of the crew getting out.

Audacious as it was, Sarah's plan had worked. It took advantage of the Crusaders' predominating arrogance and swung it against them, and as a result freed eleven Battlecruisers from the Church's hands. That it still might cost the lives of *Prophet's* crew, including Sarah herself, was something that Hastings was refusing to think about.

The clock hit 01:59 and the buzzer in her desk computer went off, alerting her that it was time.

She turned away from the sensor displays, pulled her autopistol off her desk and hung it from her belt in its holster. Standing shakily, she turned a last time to look over her quarters, picked up her kit off the bed, and hit the flashing key on her desk. Immediately, the intercom klaxon sounded on every ship in the Genesis Fleet — it was a familiar sound, heard before any ArcGeneral made a fleet-wide address.

"All officers and crew of the fleet, this is ArcGeneral Hastings. I have just witnessed one of the most remarkable events in this fleet's history. Now, I have but one thing to say. The time is now."

"...the time is now."

Bingham was looking up at the ceiling speakers in the Crusader briefing room as if he could gain a greater understanding of the message from visual aid.

Shappa Bactule, who was at the room's far side communicating with his troops through the visual monitor, turned to face his High Chancellor in confusion.

"Time for what?" Bingham snapped.

Are they denouncing us... or the mutineers?

Suddenly, a screaming alarm blared through the ship and every screen in the Crusader briefing room went dark. The normally white lights changed to red, and the AI began to chant.

"Intruder alert. Systems lockdown. Decompression alert. Deploying emergency bulkheads."

•••

At exactly 05:31, Earther standard time, Andra Ursla watched the power readings of almost every human ship fall off drastically. Some small craft were already in space, though for the most part the Genesis Navy seemed dead.

"That's it. Flag to Exodus Group, all ships to advance by squadron at 25 pls. Battle divisions, stand by for independent escort deployment."

The orders were rerouted from *Cerberus'* signal station to the rest of the frigates and sloops in the Exodus force. Every Captain in the group already knew exactly what he or she should be doing, as they'd been briefed and also had order packages on their ships. Signals from the Flag served only to simplify the process, keeping all ships coordinated in their efforts.

The ships of the battle group started forward as a single entity, their systems fully charged, their hope still that they could avoid getting embroiled in a fight. The orders were to get between the defectors and the Church ships — assuming any were active — but *not* to engage the Church, unless there was unavoidable incoming fire.

Ursla, like Caine, hoped they could still come through this encounter peacefully, though such an outcome looked increasingly unlikely. After the Navy personnel were safe the Genesis Fleet would be a concern, but not until then.

"All ships advancing, ma'am," the Signal Officer reported, and Ursla nodded grimly.

Off to war for the first time.

Hastings' marine escort was waiting just outside her door, and she joined it as soon as the command lockdowns had gone into place. The Crusaders aboard *Genesis* had been locked into their sections by emergency bulkheads. However, because they had plenty of firepower behind those bulkheads, punching through might take only minutes.

And the Crusaders would soon override the AI safeguards, if they could figure out how. There were always unprotected overrides put in place in case an AI locked up, and those simply couldn't be deactivated. She couldn't set the self destruct on *Genesis* — that could have ended the Church Crusade rather swiftly — because one could only push a flagship AI so far without it asking the ranking Church officer for permission.

It also might make her own survival... difficult.

The dozen marines around Hastings were moving swiftly down the corridor to the nearest lifts. They'd be heading immediately to the landing bay to get aboard a pinnace, but the Crusader section was between them and the flight deck. If even one bulkhead gave out...

The crew was moving all around Hastings' detail, some armed, some not, but for the most part simply ignoring them as they went about their own pressing business. Things seemed to be moving smoothly, at least here on *Genesis*.

For now, Hastings realized darkly, what happened on *Genesis* would be the only thing that mattered to her. She silently hoped that somewhere Sarah Manchester was safe, and thinking fondly of her friend, Hastings pressed down the corridor.

"Get the explosives on that bulkhead!" Bactule roared, and his Crusaders, already moving quickly, ran up to the pressure door and set their highest-power explosives against it.

Only a few Crusader detachments carried these trillium bicobalt shaped charges, so not too many Holy units would be able to escape this sort of situation with such speed.

But Bactule had made sure the *Genesis* detachment had them — he was always most comfortable knowing he could destroy anything, even an emergency bulkhead. The Crusaders were quick but careful in their deployment of the TBS charges, a testament to their long (and brutal) training in the Crusader temples.

Still, the work was maddeningly slow, so the Shappa returned to the briefing room and entered slowly. The High Chancellor was sitting, perfectly motionless, staring at the wall.

"Your Eminence, we are about to break through," Bactule said quietly.

Bingham nodded, then waved him away. The Shappa left uneasily — the situation seemed to be spiraling out of control...

Bingham was nearing a nervous breakdown. They had plotted against him. They had somehow immobilized him and presumably the *whole* fleet. The Quest would be vulnerable to the Earthers for hours! Of course, he had his Colonizers' crews, but there was no way to communicate with them.

Hopefully, Shappa Frastrar, the commander of the Colonizers, would see what was going on and dispatch the crews anyway, but still, the Navy had dealt a crippling blow.

If the Navy stayed in space long enough and his forces could activate the fleet soon enough the Quest would be safe and the traitors would pay. But if not... What was even stopping those accursed Earthers from killing them all now? Some misguided sense of honor? No, the Earthers were waiting to get their fellow heathen out before they attacked.

No. No, no, no... *no*!

He wouldn't let the Gods-damned scum have their evil victory. It was that simple. His mind tackled the problems he was facing... a command lockout of all systems on *Genesis* was the main hurdle. If control was established, he could get everything else moving.

"Computer, can I take control of the ship?" Bingham asked with renewed vigor.

"No," the AI said, "command override may only be overridden by Naval personnel or by emergency protocol five."

Bingham blinked, "What is protocol five?"

The AI, oblivious to the consequences of its words, explained, "Protocol five is used when intruder alert is found to be an insufficient solution to the problem, and the ship must be evacuated. It is initialized by the palm print and voice code of two officers. Initiation must be from the bridge or from the engineering deck. The subroutines—"

"Can the officers be Crusader?" Bingham demanded gruffly.

"Yes."

With that the High Chancellor was on his feet and heading for the door. Just as he reached the hatch an explosion roared in the corridor, and the sound of small-arms fire cracked out unevenly. They had broken through.

Bingham stepped nervously into the hall, then walked over to the Shappa who was standing behind his men with a rifle, unconsciously beginning to crouch in response to the sound of fire beyond.

"We can take back this ship," Bingham said grimly. "Just get me to the bridge."

There was gunfire ahead, and Hastings instinctively drew her heavy pistol. The marines around her slowed their pace, ten of them forming a loose pack forward while the last two stood on her flanks. Easing ahead, she sighted a firefight brewing in the corridor to the Crusaders' section.

They were breaking through.

Another dozen Naval marines had been assigned to guard the access bulkhead, the single entry point. Evidently the Crusaders had managed to keep some heavy explosives without putting them on the Navy manifests.

The explosion that had knocked out the bulkhead had killed half of the defending marines, and only three remained after the short firefight. Some crew and officers had joined the Naval troops, snatching up rifles from the dead or using their sidearms, but they weren't trained or equipped to fight like the marines.

Of some dozen volunteers who had joined the action, there remained only seven. And the Crusaders were pushing hard.

"You ten, get in there and help pin them in. Hold as long as you can and then break for the flight de—" Hastings was just giving the orders when the grenade went off.

She hadn't even seen it come through the hole in the bulkhead. The ten defenders struggled for the grenade but it was on a detonator control. As they dove some cunning Crusader blew it, the explosion and shards killing the whole defense group.

Already, Hastings' escort was sprinting for cover to pin down the exiting Crusaders, and for the first time Hastings wondered why only a dozen marines had been slotted to hold the point. Still, not much could be done about that now. They had to give *Genesis'* crew five more minutes to get off the ship, and if there were only twelve defenders, so be it.

Or thirteen.

Hastings holstered her pistol, tossed her bag down the hall, and picked up a rifle which had been thrown towards her by the blast. She took cover behind some portable breastworks laid down by the initial defenders, two marines kneeling next to her. Leveling her rifle, she aimed at the door, and as the first Crusader came through, she fired.

The marine detail had not stayed close to the bulkhead, but had deployed up the hall so no grenades could easily get them. A group of passing crew suddenly joined them, some sporting rifles, others pistols. The number holding the breach was up to sixteen. The Crusaders still had 400 behind that bulkhead...

Where were the rest of the marines?

Bactule swore as he saw the first dozen through the hatch cut to ribbons. It seemed that fresh Navy troops had arrived at the breach, and they were too far away and behind too much cover to neutralize with grenades.

He turned to his Crimson Guard, the personal warriors he had selected for his escort, and spoke, "Get breastworks and go through that door. Let us get a platoon through."

The casualties with those twelve would be total, a shame to be sure, but only the best could do what needed doing.

Bactule turned back to the breach, clutched his rifle, and waited.

The first Crusader of the next rush was dropped by seven rounds to his chest. The second, however, managed to dive through. He was carrying a breastworks rig, which he promptly set up, and the titanium sheet on support struts gave him cover while the next two out died.

Even with the massed fire coming at them, the Crusaders were making progress, and they were setting up a perimeter... Hastings swore quietly as she slapped a mag into her rifle. She had two more mags of 100 rounds, both pulled from the dead. Her belt held four fifty-round pistol mags, plus the mag in the gun. Plenty of ammo — for now.

A grenade flew out from behind the Crusader breastworks, and the marines' heads went down. The shrapnel grenade exploded just ahead of the foremost breastworks, and one marine collapsed back, his face gone.

More Crusaders poured from the breach through the smoke, and Hastings bit back her fear that the Churchers were going to win. A grenade soared back at the Crusaders, going off just in front of the breach, knocking down a half dozen. But still more came.

Then a hailstorm of grenades flew over the marine position, one landing right next to Hastings. She turned violently away from it, but she knew it was too late. The explosions all sounded at once, a body hurling itself in front of the ArcGeneral as they did. A piece of shrapnel tore into her leg, another sliced her neck, but the brunt was taken by the unarmored crewman who was now dead on the ground in front of her.

Shocked at the sacrifice and in excruciating pain, Hastings clung to her senses for a few haggard seconds, then descended into unconsciousness.

The grenade volley had torn apart the defenders. Four marines and a crew-woman remained, but they had no illusions that they could hold. The crew-woman and a marine picked up the ArcGeneral and started dragging her down the corridor.

The other three marines picked up a breastworks and bolted down the hall after them. Stopping every ten meters, these marines would lay down the breastworks with its magnetic clamps, duck and spray fire into the Crusaders, then run again before the grenades started to fly.

The flight deck was almost empty when the ArcGeneral was carried in. Only two pinnaces remained, a dozen marines standing watch around them. Most of the crew had already been through, now the remainder were clustering in the bay — those who could leave, at least. They kept in contact by ship intercom, and only twenty were left outside the bay.

As the ArcGeneral was loaded into a pinnace the first Crusaders reached the deck, and the lone survivor of the Navy's running defense joined the fresh marines as they sprayed fire into the hall.

Within a minute, ten of the stragglers had reached the flight deck, and they boarded the pinnace with their ArcGeneral. As soon as they got aboard the pinnace rocketed out of the bay, leaving one craft for whoever was left.

Bingham stepped onto *Genesis'* bridge and immediately spoke, "This is High Chancellor Bingham. Activate protocol five!"

"Please provide palm scan. Please provide second officer," the AI said in its robotic tone.

"This is Shappa Bactule. Activate protocol five!"

"Palm prints are needed to–"

"Where?" Bingham demanded impatiently.

"Command console."

The High Chancellor, technically the commanding officer of all forces of the Genesis colony, and Shappa Bactule, walked hurriedly over to the command console sitting before the ArcColonel's chair. They put their hands down on the two palm scanners

"Protocol five initiated. Ships functions reactivated. All personnel evacuate ship. All personnel evac–"

"Stop evacuation signal. Arm weapons and destroy all small craft!" Bingham snarled.

"Cannot comply without gunner to support."

Bingham blinked, then swore violently. None of the reeducated Crusader crews were aboard, and no one could fight.

"Link me to all ships that can reply by comm net," Bingham said in a slightly subdued tone. "I will have those heathen yet."

Pinnaces slashed frantically out of the ships of the human fleet, and the last one to exit *Genesis* was the craft carrying the wounded ArcGeneral. In the Superdreadnought's flight bay, the remaining beleaguered marines were cut down in a crossfire when Crusaders erupted from another exit. Their pinnace tried to launch but was hit by massed rifle fire, tearing into its pilot and engines. Any survivors were killed.

Genesis, like its namesake colony, now belonged to the Church.

CHAPTER 20

Sarah felt shaky as she took a step down onto the deck of *Harbinger Bishop*. Her pinnace was the last to land and she could feel the slight shift as the Battlecruiser turned hard and accelerated for the Earther Fleet.

She glanced around the deck. Only three of *Prophet's* pinnaces had ultimately landed here, the rest had gone to the other ships in the squadron. The flight bay was slowly emptying of people — some of *Bishop's* crew had been waiting for the guests and were set to usher them off to the ship's extra berths.

Sarah just stood in the middle of the flight deck and watched. She felt as if an immense, horrid weight had been lifted from her, but a new one had dropped on to replace it. So many had died... so many would die. But she had no choice but to press on. She may no longer belong to the Genesis Navy, but the Earthers would likely need her help. Or Liz would. She had to get as many ships to safety as she could, and hope the small craft still coming in would bring Liz and the rest of the officers who outranked her.

"Sarah!" the call came across the now-empty bay as Pat stormed in through the far door. "Good Gods, you gave me a scare! Thought you'd not made it!"

Sarah blinked, looked at her approaching friend, and smiled weakly, "Well, I'm here. Just thinking."

"Well then let's think on the way to the bridge. I need you to help me straighten this whole bloody thing out!" Pat turned back to the door and Sarah fell into step next to him, her mind regaining its composure.

"Any idea how many ships we've got out yet?" she asked, and Pat shook his head.

"We can see about a dozen moving out now, but it's only 02:14. A lot of ships are still working on it."

Sarah blinked. She'd survived something she'd been half-certain was suicidal. She mentally scolded herself... this was no time for excessive self pity. People had died, but those still struggling to live would need their flag officer.

"Right, and the small craft?"

"So far," Pat noted with a bit of a frown at Sarah's exhausted tone, "enough for about 500 ships. Not too bad for fifteen minutes."

Sarah nodded as they exited the flight deck and started down the corridor towards the bridge. *Harbinger Bishop* was of the same class as *Prophet* had been, so Sarah was familiar with its decks.

As they reached the bridge Sarah sat in the secondary seat next to Pat and started to review the sensor data that was blitzing in. The fleet was a ways behind now, but telemetry continued to stream to *Bishop*.

Sarah's squadron, all eleven survivors of it, was cruising towards the Earther Fleet at a low .25 cee — or 25 pls, as the Earthers had called it. Ursla's battle group was going to meet them in about two minutes. They'd likely proceed right through to the rear of the Earther Navy — for the time being at least.

Other than her squadron, a dozen other ships were moving. They were storeships, the craft which kept the fleet supplied with weapons and provisions. The fleet had sixty or so, though they weren't armed and were generally not counted when totaling the number of ships in a fleet.

Sarah recognized those ships as the whole 449th Supply Squadron — the only formation not carrying a full Crusader unit, just an advisor and some guards, because of the smaller size of the ships. They were about three-quarters the size of standard ammunition haulers but with equal cargo space — too cramped for a full unit of Crusaders.

Despite their less than spacious accommodation, the missiles the 449th carried would be gladly accepted. They held enough to keep 144 capital ships and escorts armed and ready. Other than that squadron, however, nothing was moving.

A hundred-odd ships had hoped to get away, but they would have a harder time of it than Sarah's squadron. It would likely take them half an hour at least–

Three new icons came onto the screen, two Destroyers and a Heavy Cruiser, all boosting hard for the Earthers. They were in the middle range of the fleet, not right on the edge as *Bishop* and *Prophet* had been, so theirs was a much less pleasant cruise.

The tide was beginning to flow.

Ursla watched the ships coming towards her with a mental nod of respect. Sarah Manchester had sacrificed her own ship and risked her own life to get her ships to safety. And she'd probably scrambled the Crusaders so much that they'd had no concept of what was happening until it was too late. So far, the only ships moving were using Naval transponders — IFF signals that distinguished them from Church vessels. The idea had been Hastings' and it had been quickly implemented after they realized the Church would have the ability to crew the ships.

And now the Church ships were sitting helplessly before the guns of the Earther Fleet, shielded first by the Navy trying to escape them, and second by the Earther hope for a peaceful resolution. A slaughter went too much against the Earther character — they still had to try for peace.

In the holo plot, Ursla observed the movements to the rear of the Earther

Navy, where a small fleet of transport craft had arrived to house and move the Navy personnel to a temporary berth on the Lunar Base. There was now plenty of room set up for them, and the domed base had one of the nicest climates in the system.

The transports were hovering and waiting, even as the first pinnaces began to pass the frigates and sloops of the Exodus Battle Group.

"The Church has ordered its crews to be distributed. *Genesis* is taking on crew, but it'll take hours to get them aboard. It seems the last pinnace on the line exploded and took out the flight deck," Pat's report wasn't as bad as it could have been.

Sarah nodded. With an efficiently running flight deck, it would take two or three hours just to get the crew aboard a Superdreadnought. Moving from airlocks alone because of the damaged deck would double that time. She was more worried about marauding Battlecruisers and Heavy Cruisers.

Hell, *any* fighting ships the Church could get flying would swat the pinnaces from the sky like mosquitoes. And there was only so much Ursla could do to protect them.

"It looks like they're focusing on the ships nearest the Colonizers. About four Dreadnoughts, fifteen Battlecruisers, about twenty Heavies, and twenty Lights and Destroyers," Pat continued, and Sarah nodded again.

Essentially, the last three categories were the threat. Crewing Dreadnoughts was hard, though not as hard as Superdreadnoughts. Cruisers and Destroyers could run with far fewer crew members and had bigger flight decks relative to their size. Dealing with those would be critical... and perhaps one or two Dreadnoughts as well.

"We're passing the Earther screen," *Bishop's* Tactical Officer reported, his tone slightly nervous.

"Signal coming in from the Earther flag," the Comm Officer added.

"On forward screen," Pat said, and Ursla appeared to *Bishop's* bridge.

"Good to see you Sarah, Pat," she said softly.

"Glad as all hell to see you!" Pat grinned.

Ursla grunted a short laugh, then sobered, "If you could form your ships behind our fleet, please, ArcBrigadier. We'll deploy them properly later, but for now just get them there. If the Church comes after you and your pinnaces, the Earther Navy will be in the way."

Sarah nodded, a bit of relief almost surfacing, "We'll form as best we can, thank you Commodore."

Ursla paused for a second, looking rather uncomfortable, then asked hesitantly, "Do you have any word of ArcGeneral Hastings?"

Sarah was slightly surprised by the question, or more particularly, by the sincerity with which it was posed. But then, she remembered, Ursla and Hastings had already become friends.

Sarah shook her head slowly, "Sorry, Andra, nothing yet. We do know that the last pinnace trying to leave *Genesis'* bay blew up inside, crippling its flight capability."

Ursla looked grim at that news, but nodded, "I hope she got out."

"So do I," Sarah said softly.

There was another pause as the two squadron commanders, one Earther and one human, took in the information. Finally Sarah spoke, feeling inexplicably awkward.

"Good luck, Andra."

Ursla tilted her head slightly, appreciating the human's consideration, then nodded, "And to you Sarah. We'll get your people home."

With that the line went dead, and the bridge was silent as everyone took solace in the giant Commodore's words. For many, she was the first Earther they'd ever seen.

There was a chime from the sensor console, and she looked up, "Ma'am, some of Genesis Fleet's point defense is coming on line!"

Sarah spun to the Sensor Chief, "How many ships?"

The ArcLieutenant paused, "About 150... throughout the fleet... *Genesis* included."

Damn. The chances of getting everyone home just disappeared.

The first pinnaces winked out of existence on Sarah's display. The rest ran desperately towards salvation and the guns of the Earther Navy.

CHAPTER 21

"*Scipio, Psyche, Agile,* detach and escort the pinnaces to starboard," Ursla ordered, and the commands were passed to the three frigates.

The ships detached, turning and accelerating towards a large mass of Navy small craft just emerging from the fleet. A single ship's point defense systems could turn all those pinnaces to smoldering wrecks...

But three of the Earther Navy's 28-gun Sixth Rates rushed to them, their shield configuration designed to give the maximum coverage of space around the human ships.

Ursla's original battle group of 104 was down to twenty-four, the rest having been detached in small groups or individually to protect the incoming ships. Now if the Church got anything online to hunt down the running Navy, her reduced force would be far less capable of performing its protective duty.

Caine was holding the other 1,700 ships of the fleet together for safety — for the sake of both the Earthers and the Navy they now guarded. There was no telling how quickly the Church would turn around, and the Earthers couldn't afford to get caught in the open against the superior numbers of the Genesis Fleet.

"More ships to port," the Sensor Chief reported. "Commander Magnus sends his compliments. *Flame* and *Match*, detaching to escort."

"How many ships do we have?" High Chancellor Bingham demanded of the face on his screen — Crusader Shaspa Sagraso.

The Shaspa, unused to dealing directly with his religious leader, let alone bearing his anger, visibly shivered. Finally, he collected his nerves and spoke, "Four Dreadnoughts, fourteen Battlecruisers, twenty-one Heavy Cruisers, and seven Light Cruisers. We ignored Destroyers for their lack of size."

Bingham nodded gruffly, trying to ease his frustration with the juvenile Shaspa. Sagraso was the only Crusader officer currently available with familiarity in the workings of the Navy — no officers with greater understanding were reachable thanks to the Navy's treachery. Sagraso had served as liaison to an ArcGeneral for a few years before the Quest's outset, and unfortunately that granted him the impromptu and temporary title of Naval expert.

Evidently, he was not the best officer ever to wear the Holy garment of the Crusaders — he was painfully young, commanding the Crusader detachment aboard a Heavy Cruiser. Given the option, Bingham would have swiftly removed this responsibility from him. But there was no choice.

And besides, only an utter fool could lose with the odds Sagraso had in his favor.

"Alright, Shaspa. I want you to collect your force and start hunting down the heathen. Look for ships they are trying to steal, pay less heed to the small craft," Bingham ordered finally, trying to soften his voice for Sagraso's benefit.

"Yes, Your Eminence."

"And, Sagraso, do *not* engage the Earthers, under any circumstances! With only your ships active, we can scarcely afford to fight... yet."

"Yes, Your Eminence."

With that, the young Shaspa vanished from the bridge monitor on *Genesis*. The AI had been able to establish a good sensor map of the fleet, identifying all ships flying those special Navy transponder codes as hostile.

The purpose of those codes must be to tell the Earthers whose side they're on... they are our primary targets.

ArcColonel Bill Wallace sat very quietly in the command chair of his Heavy Cruiser, *Darymanis City*. Somehow, he'd been given command of an entire flotilla... a flotilla stuck behind the Genesis Fleet.

Thirty-two ships made up this flotilla — two Heavy Cruisers including *Darymanis City*, twelve Light Cruisers, and eighteen Destroyers. Not the most potent force ever assembled, and hardly a match for what the Church was likely to throw at it.

He cursed uncomfortably. They were pinned! As the mutinies had started, the Crusaders on these thirty-two ships had held out the longest, and most had been to the rear of the 2,400-ship formation. Now they were trapped — some Destroyers and cruisers had run through the fleet to escape, but when point defense systems came online that became suicide.

As a rule, point defense lasers weren't too powerful, but at the close range into which the escaping Destroyers were forced and the slow speeds at which they had to move, the beams would carve them up.

Wallace had coordinated with ArcColonel Audrey DeBrooke, commander of *Grendelsbane City*, *Darymanis City*'s sister ship, to break out of the fleet together. Unfortunately, as they slowly drew back, other ships started to congeal around them — survivors of those who'd been destroyed or other ships unwilling to try to run alone.

While either of the *Citys* could have gotten through, these smaller ships couldn't. So the thirty-two ships had stayed, and now, as they hovered nervously, it became clear that they had few options. The 449th Ammunition Squadron had been near the rear of the formation, and thanks to the immobilization of the now mostly-Church fleet, the defection of those storeships left a gap in which the *Darymanis* and its consorts were hiding. Point defense lasers couldn't reach them as they huddled in the center of the rift... but they couldn't maneuver.

So far, none of the Church ships could move to attack them, but Wallace's plot showed forty-six ships — most bigger than anything he had — slowly gathering and turning to meet him.

So what was there to do?

"Alright, all ships turn to the rear and prepare to blast our way out the back. We'll try to hit flux as soon as we get free!"

Ursla was preoccupied with the unending tides of pinnaces when the bleep in the main holo tank caught her attention. She'd detached all but eleven ships — eight of those from her own squadron. Others were starting to return from previous duty, slowly refilling her stocks.

But that bleep...

It was hard to see exactly what the computer was calling to her attention because of the mess of ships hurrying through the Genesis Fleet, but as she magnified it became grimly clear. Thirty-two ships with allied transponders were getting squeezed by forty-six enemy ships... including capital ships.

The weight of broadside was in favor of the Church by almost five to one.

But what could she do? That was on the other side of the Genesis Fleet and she could hardly go to energy drive through the human formation to reach them.

But she could go *over*.

"Dran, signal *Sybille* to take over the battle group. Orders to 111th: form line ahead and stand by to accelerate to 175 pls."

Going any faster so close to other ships would be asking for disaster, even at energy drive. Traveling at 175 pls was a crawl for interstellar travel, a sprint for in-system travel, and tricky business altogether. They'd have to go up and over the Genesis Fleet, and even at 175 pls the trip would take a minute... and then they'd have to drop out of energy drive and maneuver into place under normal engines... two minutes. And then eight ships would have to shield thirty-two against forty-six...

"Ships ready," Nightclaw reported softly.

"Go."

It wasn't happening fast enough!

Wallace crossed his fingers as if the act would save his flotilla, but knew their chances were brutally low. The Heavy Cruisers were going through first, clearing a channel for the lighter ships to follow. Any Church vessels able to fire at the escapees were getting full vollies of missiles from the two *Citys*, and with their armor offline that was more than enough to atomize them.

But, it was taking too long to clear a route. And they'd still have to accelerate to flux for escape. With this much traffic and coming from such a low velocity, that'd take almost five minutes. It didn't look good, but they had to try.

"How far away are the Church ships?" he asked in a low tone.

There was a pause, "About five minutes behind us... closing."

The Churchers didn't have to worry about clearing a path. In open space the bigger Church ships would have been slower, but *Darymanis* and its consorts were being delayed substantially by the fire of stationary vessels in their path.

"How many left to take out before we can run?"

"Sixteen."

Wallace nodded grimly. Two Heavy Cruisers couldn't clear that in less than five minutes. Damn. They'd have to run for it... sprint and pray.

"Alright, send to all ships, get moving as fast as you can. Try to swamp the point defense lasers and clear the other side."

With that, thirty-two smaller ships attached to *Darymanis City* accelerated fast, trying to outrun the AIs and ill-trained crews on the ships firing point defense lasers at them.

Shaspa Sagraso was getting nervous. If he failed, it would be to the pits of Hell's gulags. He mustn't fail.

So far, it didn't look like he would. He was just under five minutes behind the traitorous ships, and even this mad dash they were making wouldn't save them. If they kept up this speed they would clear the fleet in two minutes, then have to cycle up their drives to escape.

He would be on them after only four minutes, and their slower speed for entering flux would end them. If they tried to run under normal drive he could take a short cut through the fleet and hit them, or, if they ran away from the system, not towards the Earthers, he would simply send out his cruisers to catch them.

Yes, like an easily solved problem in mathematics, this battle was coming together. Nothing — not Navy, not Earther, not the devils themselves, could halt the Holy ships now.

The 111th Flying Squadron of the Earther Navy dropped out of energy drive beyond and above the Genesis Fleet. The unit had overshot its intended exit point, but it could hardly be faulted for the error. Trying to go so fast in such a small relative area was incredibly tricky, and it was an amazing enough feat that the frigates hadn't shot completely out of the system.

Turning, the eight *Hades*-class Fifth Rate frigates, each carrying thirty-eight cannon plus their carronades, accelerated madly towards the rear of the human fleet. They were a minute away, and the Naval ships were just breaking out. Their numbers were down to thirty-one — the humans had lost a Destroyer in their attempt to escape.

Behind them, Church vessels were coming fast. At the speed the newly-crewed Genesis ships were making, they would be clear of the rest of the fleet in only three minutes... free to fire on the Naval escapees.

"ETA?" Ursla asked anxiously.

"We'll be in range in... four minutes," the Sensor Chief reported.

Only a minute's difference... but perhaps there was another way to save the humans. The thirty-one ships were slowing now, beginning to cycle up their flux drives. From what Ursla understood, it would take them five minutes to accelerate away. That gave the Church ships two minutes to attack, Ursla only one to defend. Unless...

"Orders to squadron, adjust course..." she paused as she read the coordinates from her monitor. "Seven degrees to starboard, down angle twenty-two. Roll forty-nine degrees to starboard. Hold course for one minute, then level off relative and maintain. Come to stop after additional ninety seconds."

There was mild surprise on some of the faces around her — they were no longer making directly for the Naval ships. Instead they were running parallel and above, trying to position themselves between the two forces of Genesis ships about forty seconds faster than would otherwise have been the case. But they wouldn't actually be between them — they'd be relatively above the humans and they'd need thirty seconds more to be able to interpose.

It was a perfect maneuver if one intended to present their broadside and engage... Nightclaw, who had been pondering this, blinked and glanced at Ursla. She had something in mind... he hoped.

CHAPTER 22

Shaspa Sagraso was basking in the victory, though he hadn't achieved it just yet. The Church flotilla was about to leave the fleet. Its missiles would lash out, and the pathetic Naval traitors would be caught while readying to jump into flux.

Earthers were coming in parallel to his base course, probably aiming to get between him and the traitors, but he would have a volley free before they could get in the way. Maybe even two. No, the Earthers were too late, and their heathen comrades would die.

"Squadron now at all stop," *Cerberus'* Sensor Chief announced calmly.

Ursla nodded, watching her sensor plot as the Church force approached its exit point from the rear of the Genesis Fleet. Those Church ships would fire as soon as they got out, but she was confident they wouldn't be ready for what she planned to do.

"All ships, charge canister and run out the starboard broadside. Port broadside to stand by, all ships initiate 180 degree starboard roll after firing and continue rolling broadsides until otherwise ordered," Ursla commanded, and the orders were transmitted.

"Mister Carrian, load canister and run out the starboard broadside. Master stand by..." Nightclaw repeated the orders to the bridge even though they'd already heard them from their Commodore. He then leaned over to Ursla, "What are we targeting?"

Ursla smiled, "You'll see."

ArcColonel Wallace wondered what the hell the Earthers were doing. They were too far above to render assistance or shield him, and now they had their weapons armed. So far, they had refused to engage the Church ships, so what was happening?

"Time until flux?" he turned to his Helm Officer.

"Two minutes, fourteen seconds."

We have to survive that long...

Ursla watched as the Church ships emerged from the Genesis Fleet and began to come together. Their formation had no order — that was clear. The four Dreadnoughts were cramped together in the middle, the rest of the ships clouded around them uneasily. In a fight, they'd have been ripped to shreds. Luckily for them, this wasn't a real battle.

The starboard broadsides of her eight frigates — a total of 128 guns — were aiming down on the Church's path, each charged with canister.

Canister fire was made up of energy that hadn't been fully locked into a tight burst, and its relative lack of striking power made it the least-used type of charge employed by the Earther Navy. Most of the time Earther ships would fire their guns with energy well held together so it would do more damage when it struck the target, but canister had no such effect. The energy simply cascaded out, and wasn't nearly heavy enough to break shields or cause serious damage to hulls.

Ursla had thought of firing canister directly at the Church ships, but her orders expressly forbade such an action. No, the ships couldn't be fired upon. However, her orders said nothing about Church *missiles*.

It might have been splitting hairs, but the fact was that as long as she didn't attack the Church ships, the projectiles were fair game. Canister may not have a lot of effect on heavy ship hulls, but small, fragile weapons like missiles could probably be detonated on contact. And the detonations would detonate others... and others... and others.

Well, that was Ursla's theory, anyway.

If it did work, Ursla would nullify the opening broadsides, buying a single critical minute for the Naval flotilla. After that she'd get between the Church and the Navy, and any missile that came near would be shot down. She couldn't stay at this range forever — eventually the Church would get too close to the Navy. No, she'd interpose before they closed the range... buy the escaping ships the last minute they needed.

"Detecting spike from the Church ships... they're firing!" the Sensor Chief barked.

"All ships," Ursla ordered coolly, "target those missiles and fire."

Earthers were unaccustomed to the fact that they could destroy enemy weapons with such ease. The shot from any of the Earther Fleet's guns — save the smaller carronades — could only be stopped by a direct, head-on hit by another energy shot of similar strength. That was one of the main purposes of those short range carronades. Using canister to wipe out an enemy's weapons as they cruised was a completely foreign concept... but it would work. It *had* to.

As the first broadside from the 111th rippled out the squadron began to roll, readying to bring port side guns to bear. Ursla watched in the main battle tank as the first broadside raced away. It appeared more like a cloud than anything else — a departure from the ordinarily rigid wall of energy that accented standard Earther broadsides.

And just as she'd hoped, the hailstorm of missiles crashed right into it.

...

Shaspa Sagraso's face twisted in horror as the Earthers fired their mighty cloud down on his missiles. He had never thought salvoes could be swatted away at such range — in a missile duel, warheads would actually have to hit each other to be destroyed, and that was no easy task when they were so small and space so large.

But this terrible blanket of energy from the Earthers... it was as though a devil had thrown a cape over his missiles, making them all vanish. None seemed to get through the huge storm of energy released by the flawless Earther gunnery.

Damn them!

The second flight of missiles vomited from the Church force's tubes, but the Earthers replied in kind. Another cloud of energy, just as large as the first, hurtled down. Those missiles would not survive either...

"Hold fire — all ships to emergency acceleration! We must reach beam range with the traitors!"

The Church had stopped firing and had started to accelerate even more quickly towards the Naval ships. But the 111th was already on its way to the Naval flotilla, and it was faster.

Wallace was in total shock as he watched the volleys — about a thousand missiles each — simply vanish into the swirling energy clouds the Earthers produced. He was suddenly very, very glad they hadn't elected to fight them.

The Church ships had to be advancing fast. The explosions of the missiles were clouding Wallace's view of the enemy, but he knew that the Church commander, no matter how foolish, had to realize that his missiles weren't getting through. Because beam weapons couldn't be shot down, they would be his only option.

"Time to flux?" Wallace asked, a plan forming.

"One minute, four seconds."

Wallace judged the distance the Earthers and the Church had to cover. The Earthers would be in place in about thirty seconds, the Church would be in beam range in about twenty. The Earthers were probably expecting to shoot down more missiles, but there was nothing they could do about beams... except get between them and the flotilla. Unless they wanted to invite slaughter, the Church couldn't fire once the Earthers were in place.

So he needed ten more seconds.

"All ships, turn on the 180, flush your tubes into those Church *bastards*!"

Ursla had not expected to see the flotilla turn. It was a quick maneuver performed by small, agile ships, and it brought their tubes to bear on the advancing enemy.

About 400 missiles erupted from the small flotilla. Compared to the thousands put forward by the Church it seemed pitiful, but the Church couldn't see them coming. The previous explosions were only now dying out, clearing the mess on their screens.

The Church's loose, open formation would make it so much worse. It was standard practice, in the Earther Navy at least, for ships to stay together to coordinate defense. Carronades could prioritize incoming threats and sweep them away, and broadsides could be coordinated to systematically intercept targets.

In a missile duel, cooperation would be even more important, as without it some missiles could inevitably slip through anti-missile point defense fire. But the Church ships were far apart, and as they saw the missiles cruise in, their countermeasures came online too late and with too little intensity. A well-ordered battle group could have taken at least a third, maybe half the missiles out of action before the rest hit, but only a few dozen went down to this unit's defensive fire.

The rest struck home, and the Church saw some retribution from the Navy it had maligned so badly.

A Dreadnought was swallowed, as was a Battlecruiser, three Heavy Cruisers and one Light. Ships took evasive action, avoiding some missiles only to slam into others. The formation, if it could have been called that, split completely apart. A dozen more ships were mauled, but the rest still tried to press in, decelerating now so as not to overshoot the flotilla. Ten seconds were bought.

The 111th suddenly dropped into place between the Naval flotilla and the Church battle group. The flotilla was rushing to escape, its engines flaring, twenty seconds from pushing all of the matter in the ships to a state of flux. The Earther shields reshaped to form a wall against the Church, and the broadsides were run out to deter them from attempting intervention.

The battle group came to a harsh stop before the wall of frigates, and behind the Fifth Rates, the flotilla accelerated to light speed, turning towards the Earther Navy just two minutes away.

Pride swelled in Ursla's mind, but she was already pushing it onto a mental back burner. There was still much to do, and she'd only bought a little time with this stunt.

"Squadron to energy drive; 150 pls. Let's go escort the rest of the pinnaces in," Ursla said it as if what she'd just managed was somehow average.

Everyone on the bridge knew it wasn't.

Bingham was wide-eyed, mouth hanging open, his mind a mix of anger and shock. He had watched from *Genesis* as the Earthers had stopped 2,000 missiles with their broadsides, and seen how they'd let the traitor ships not only escape, but fire in reply.

Saint Bernard Corbett, Shaspa Sagraso's command ship, had been blown to pieces, as had half a dozen other ships. It was a nightmare. And now, the ships loyal to the Church were all the way to the rear, so they couldn't help hunt anything escaping far forward for at least twenty minutes!

It was absolutely insane.

Bingham slammed his fists into the arms of his chair, turned to Bactule and spoke, "We will have our revenge for that!"

Bactule nodded angrily, "A certainty, Your Eminence."

CHAPTER 23

The last pinnaces had reached the safety of the Earther Navy. Over 800 lost in the flight — nearly 80,000 dead, Sarah calculated ruefully. But from two million, that number was... statistically acceptable. It was inevitable that a massive expedition such as the defection would cost lives, and at least the number had been relatively low.

That was small comfort for Sarah Manchester... none at all for the dead.

She was aboard one of *Harbinger Bishop*'s pinnaces, cruising to meet with the First Lord. That was usually Liz's job, but she was... indisposed.

Sarah cringed as she remembered the amount of blood the ArcGeneral had been oozing when the medics had rushed her from *Bishop*'s flight deck to its sick bay. She would not soon forget the sight.

In any case, the Naval personnel's rank and file was still being organized. For now it was her duty, as senior officer with Earther experience, to meet with Caine. Eventually, one of the ArcLieutenant-Generals would arrive and take command, or barring one of them, a more senior ArcBrigadier.

Orion loomed large in the windows of the pinnace's passenger compartment — a massive, elegant ship, with three rows of gun ports and dozens of small carronades on its hull for point defense. It was a good size larger than *Genesis*, but somehow it looked faster... and a lot friendlier.

As the huge main landing deck appeared, the pinnace turned to face it, leaving Sarah to view the rest of the fleet. Naval pinnaces were still cruising through it like wasps, all heading back to the waiting transports and the liberated ships of the Genesis Fleet.

Suddenly the view was cut into by the sides of the landing bay, and Sarah watched without interest as the pinnace found its slot and landed gently. She was preoccupied as she stood and went to the ramp at the rear of the small vessel, not even noting the clatter as the ramp dropped.

She walked lightly down to the deck, peering around to see who was waiting. No honor guard had been turned out, she noted with as much pleasure as she could muster. There were no formalities to observe.

A lone wolf stood a dozen meters away, hands behind his back, a polite smile on his face, a weary look in his eyes. Sarah walked slowly towards him, trying to discern who he was, if he was — the First Lord or just an escort. The gold tabs on the collar of his navy blue uniform made her think the former.

As she approached the slightly taller officer she stopped and delivered a crisp salute, which he returned, "ArcBrigadier Sarah Manchester, sir."

The wolf nodded with a slightly broadening smile, "First Lord Setter Caine. Glad to make your acquaintance."

The First Lord stepped back and waved his hand to the door at the landing bay's far side, and Sarah fell into step next to him.

"I take it by your arrival that ArcGeneral Hastings is... unavailable..." Sarah could almost feel the concern in Caine's voice, and she nodded grimly in reply.

"She lost her leg. A piece of shrapnel from a grenade got lodged in her shin — stuck in one side and out the other. If they'd tried to pull it out they'd have split her leg in two. She was losing so much blood and the wound was already showing some sort of blood poisoning from some of the shrapnel. They had to amputate with an emergency med kit on the bloody pinnace..." Sarah's voice trailed off as the pair emerged from the landing bay and walked to a lift just beyond.

Caine led her into the lift, "Level fifteen." There was silence for a moment as the lift began to move, then Caine spoke up, "It's never easy."

Sarah raised a tired eyebrow at the comment — the sad, understanding tone — then glanced at the First Lord, "Sir?"

"Losing a limb... being badly injured. But I know she'll pull through. Andra knew the ArcGeneral far better than I did, but I could tell she was strong the moment I met her."

Sarah heaved a sigh and nodded without commitment, "I suppose so, sir. It's just... well, no one can really hope for active service with one leg. She'll be most unhappy that she can't command her fleet from the front."

As the lift doors opened onto a new deck Caine gestured for the ArcBrigadier to go first, then followed and fell into step with her, "One leg?"

Sarah shook her head with another sigh. She was so tired... "Well, sir, prosthetics are never right. They take concentration to operate and she can't be focusing on that if she's running a battle or–"

"Prosthetics?" Caine's voice reflected his confusion. He had no idea what she was talking about, Sarah realized. The Earthers probably had no need of such things.

"Yes sir, artificial limbs."

Caine stopped in the hall, and after a few steps Sarah turned to face him, "Sir?"

"By the Earth, ArcBrigadier, we don't need prosthetics!" Caine extended his left leg. "I lost this in an accident a century ago. I got in the way of rather large crocodile. My wife had a new one ready for me in two weeks, I was walking properly again after four."

Sarah blinked, "...How?"

Caine smiled and then continued walking, "Genetic imprints were taken, they grew a new leg based on my DNA coding, and then attached it. It's as if I never lost it. We can probably manage a similar treatment for humans."

Sarah blinked twice and Caine nodded assuringly.

She fell into step again, suddenly feeling better. Knowing Liz was down had drained more from her than she'd realized. What few doubts about the Earthers had survived now vanished, and she realized just how bloody *tired* she was...

Only then did her mind alert her to the fact that they were in a section which appeared to be for crew quarters, not conference rooms. If *Cerberus* was anything like *Orion*, these doors led to personal cabins. Caine turned a corner ahead of her and stood next to a door which opened. He gestured inside.

"Where are we?" Sarah asked cautiously.

"My quarters. Pardon my comment, but you look like the last thing you need right now is an official setting," he replied.

Sarah was unsure whether her sigh was in hesitation or relief. She was about to be entertained by the military commander-in-chief of her new allies... somehow her exhaustion was overpowering her will to worry.

She walked into the bright, spacious quarters, noting three doors to other rooms off this main area, and turned as Caine followed her.

"Sit down," he gestured to the couch. "Can I get you something?"

"Um...water. Please."

Caine smiled and nodded, leaving through one of the doors. Sarah flopped onto the couch. Realizing with terror that it was one of the intoxicating couches she'd dealt with on *Cerberus*, she vowed not to fall asleep during the meeting. But Gods, she was tired.

The walls around her were decorated with holos of ships, pennants, and all sorts of other memorabilia that were a testament to the First Lord's career. On his desk was a picture of a wolf and a little wolf... cub. They were probably Caine's family, the wife who'd grown him a new leg and his son... or daughter?

Caine returned with a bottle of water and handed it to Sarah before he sat down in the chair that usually faced his desk. He had worried as soon as he'd seen the drawn and exhausted ArcBrigadier. Ursla had told him many good things about Manchester, and he believed them. But the events of the past few hours — and, to be fair, the past days — had obviously taken their toll.

He had originally planned to meet in the briefing room, but this seemed more to the benefit of the ArcBrigadier. She'd just accomplished an amazing feat, after all. She deserved a break.

"So, sir," she began finally, "your wife is a surgeon?"

Caine nodded, "One of the best in the field. She can regenerate just about anything."

Sarah nodded, trying to make small talk but coming up with nothing to say. She took a long gulp of icy water which helped to restore her senses, if only marginally.

"Don't worry, ArcBrigadier, I can't make small talk either," Caine said quite plainly, and Sarah laughed.

Caine cocked an eyebrow as the ArcBrigadier chuckled, not fully understanding the humor but not disapproving of it.

Sarah sobered and, seeing no smile on the First Lord's face, realized she was probably acting inappropriately. Too much stress and not enough sleep. She'd be herself after a good eight hours, but not before, "Sorry, sir... just a bit..."

Caine smiled, "Please don't worry. You've been through a lot today. What I need to know is how your remaining ships and crew are faring, what kind of organization they'll have, and what help we can give."

Sarah sighed briefly, then spoke, "We've had no word from any of the ArcLieutenant-Generals as of yet. They're just below Liz... I mean ArcGeneral Hastings... and they command our four fleets. I'm not sure if any made it out — the Crusaders aboard each ship would've been determined to kill them, and we lost a lot of pinnaces on the way over."

Sarah paused briefly, closed her eyes, and then opened them again, "Until ArcGeneral Hastings is back on her feet... foot... well, is active again, fleet command will fall to whoever's senior. Right now that's me, but that's probably going to change. Other than that, we have a fleet of exactly one Dreadnought, seventeen Battlecruisers, eighteen Heavy Cruisers, eleven Light Cruisers and thirty-seven Destroyers. We also have a squadron of twelve supply ships to keep us armed. We can go wherever you need us."

Caine offered a simple nod in reply.

"As for help... just get anyone who doesn't have a ship a bunk somewhere. We can't ask for more... you've given us so much already..."

Sarah stopped to take another gulp of water.

"We're more grateful to you, ArcBrigadier. If you hadn't abandoned we'd be in a great deal more trouble. Quite frankly, I wouldn't want to have to face you over a broadside," Caine said softly.

Sarah nodded politely and smiled, "Thank you, sir."

"Well, ArcBrigadier, I'll get you some guest quarters so you can get some sleep. Then you can head back to your fleet."

Sarah stood quickly and began to object, but Caine put up his hand, "No, ArcBrigadier, you've done enough to deserve a good rest. I understand you saved your whole squadron from the Church — and that you sacrificed your flagship to do it. I also know for a fact that you've been coordinating every action your people have made for the past ten hours. You need sleep, and the universe can get by for eight hours without you."

Sarah sighed again, secretly thanking the First Lord but feeling as if she should object.

Caine smiled, "You're welcome. Trust me, I know exactly how you're feeling. A long time ago it took a good Flag Captain named Ursla to sit her Commodore down and tell him to go to sleep."

Sarah smiled, "I imagine you listened, sir? Arguing with Andra would be... *counterproductive* I think."

Caine laughed, "Well, the crocodile that ate my leg would have had a lot more of me if not for her."

Sarah nodded with a smile, paused in question, then gave up. Caine led her out of his quarters and down the hall to a guest cabin a couple of hundred meters away.

"On the topic of hand-to-hand combat, I heard you put Sergeant Lupus down a couple of days ago," Caine's voice revealed more of his pleasant mood with the comment.

"I was lucky," Sarah nodded.

Caine laughed again, "No one gets lucky against Lupus. You either beat him, or you don't. He's one of the best in the fleet."

Sarah blinked in surprise at that — somehow she'd handled one of the best in the fleet. That was something to take pride in... and something which helped make her think of the Earthers more as equals. She had been putting them on pedestals, she realized, certain they were superior. Now, after chatting with Caine, she was beginning to feel they were not above her. They weren't giants, they were just good... *people*.

Except for ones like Ursla... they were *giant* good people.

The guest quarters Caine had brought Sarah to had one of those wonderful couches, and she flopped onto it, letting the exhaustion be swallowed up by dreams.

Caine walked thoughtfully back to his quarters. The humans seemed to be very resilient and very determined. ArcBrigadier Manchester was a most interesting human as well — highly skilled and fiercely determined to do her duty, even despite her youth. Beckett Lupus had even been complimentary of her sparring, as any teacher might be of a student.

He wondered if Hastings and Manchester were good indications of all the Naval personnel. He was counting on the good nature of the Naval officers and crew — they'd all just taken a huge risk on his word.

But he was trusting his instincts, and he could live with that.

The Church was sitting a few million kilometers away, crewing and preparing for a fight. Hopes of settling this whole mess peacefully were fading, and if it did come to a battle, thousands... hundreds of thousands would die.

If... *when* it did come to a fight, Caine was certain the Earthers would win. They had to — if they didn't Earth would be exploited. Destroyed beyond the brink, and maybe the next Omega Virus would wipe out *everything*.

Setter Caine shivered at that thought as he entered his quarters. He sank into his desk chair again, and looked longingly at the picture of his family. The chances of them... of all civilians being dragged into this was growing steadily. He hoped that no Crusaders ever set foot on Earth.

And if any did, he would have to kill them to protect his own. That was his responsibility, and he'd long ago resigned himself to it.

CHAPTER 24

High Chancellor Bingham leaned back in his desk chair and tried to make sense of the world. Nothing seemed as it should any more — the Navy had escaped justice, the Crusaders were no longer merely warriors, a fleet they had never thought to pilot was now theirs...

As his anger had faded, one thing had become very clear to Bingham: things were not as they should have been.

For the first time he regretted the mistreatment of the Navy by the Church. It had been seeded in the original colony — those who ran the machines were unholy non-believers. But he couldn't shake the feeling that if he had chosen to have them well treated, all or at least *some* of them would have stayed.

The doubts he'd felt before based solely on what the Earthers had told him were now magnified beyond all scope of understanding. The Navy had accepted the Earther tale, and he could see what had tempted them... what had tempted *him*. Of course he did not give in — his Church demanded the supreme Quest be fulfilled, and nothing else could count. Since he had been a young boy he'd been taught as much by his father, the previous High Chancellor.

Now that he was getting older, over fifty, and he was beginning to see other things as important. But he could not allow that to happen. It was his duty to see the Quest through to the end, crisis of faith or not.

Shappa Bactule was his only pillar of faith, though Bingham could recall no other ever existing. He had always been Harvey Bingham, the beacon of faith helping others against the unfaithful world.

But what was the situation now?

Bactule supporting Bingham in a fight for the cause of humanity? The Gods of the Unity National? The heathen Earthers... or just the Earthers?

The thought that everything he'd ever done, ever lived for, was in the name of a lie was more terrifying than he could bear. His theology could not have been constructed by a flawed, desperate people determined to win the last hand. But the story Caine had presented was all too plausible, knowing the nature of humanity.

No... it could *not* be. Things had to be the way the Gods, not *Caine*, said they were. This duel of faith could simply be credited to the recent deception and trauma he had faced. Couldn't it?

A chime from his cabin door returned Bingham to reality. His mind desperately blocked off any further thoughts of his deceived life, as he regained his composure and spoke, "Enter."

Shappa Bactule slowly entered the room, bowed his head, and then stood at attention.

"Sit down, Elias," Bingham said softly, and the Shappa looked down with puzzlement. The Lord High Chancellor never used his first name.

Bactule obeyed the order rigidly, sitting nervously in the chair before Bingham's desk. He examined the drawn and worn face of his leader. It was as if the High Chancellor had been drained of his energy.

"Elias, I need to speak with you as... a friend," Bingham said quietly.

Bactule bowed his head to the side and answered, "As you wish, Your Eminence."

"Not Your Eminence, Elias, I need to talk to you as another human. For now, I am Harvey Bingham. I need you to be equal with me, if only for a little while," Bingham corrected, and Bactule looked up.

This was definitely unusual. The High Chancellor had never asked to be addressed in such a way before. What was making him change? Exhaustion? Wisdom? Crisis of faith? The latter was almost beyond the Shappa's comprehension — the most holy human alive could not be faltering... could he?

"What... ah... what do you need... sir?" Bactule struggled with the lack of title, and Bingham sighed.

It wasn't total equality, but it was enough, "I am... finding myself unsure. Of what... I am... *unsure*. Elias, I am having a crisis of faith," he croaked. "Somehow the Gods didn't stop the Navy from escaping, the Earthers took them to safety. And that is something... something... I cannot understand..."

Bactule suppressed a shudder. The High Chancellor was faltering... he needed someone to help him back onto the path from which the traitors had pushed him.

"Sir... *Your Eminence*, the Gods are still with us! They allowed the traitors to run to their fellow heathen so that when we fight the Earthers, we can eliminate the unholy Navy as well. One fell swoop will end all opposition," Bactule paused, then his earnest words persisted.

"I know this time has been trying... especially for you... but you must keep the faith. You *must*. This is just the final test. The Gods are waiting to see how you handle the powers aligned against you, and already you have distinguished yourself!"

Bingham's eyes seemed locked on his desk.

"You have not backed down, or given into the lies of the heathen, or conceded any part of our Quest to their scrutiny! You have carried out prophecy to the letter, and the Gods must — *must* — be pleased with you for that!"

Bingham took a breath.

Yes... but do the Gods see into my mind... my doubt?

Bactule paused in silence, watching as his words pressed into the High Chancellor. Bingham mused over the testament Bactule had given, and wondered if he could go on.

So many were depending on him, so many were waiting for him to lead them to Earth. He could not let them down. If for no other reason than that, he had to continue.

He leaned forward, his face filling with more determination and faith than he recalled feeling in many days. Even if it was just a gesture to prove to himself he was sane, he would take his people to Earth.

Bactule felt utter relief at the apparent return of his High Chancellor. The crisis was understandable, and a lesser man might have been lost to it. Now it was just a matter of going through the motions of war, and the Gods would bring divine victory.

"So, Shappa," Bingham said finally, his old control returning to his voice, "what did you wish to see me about?"

Bactule straightened his posture, which had slumped forward unnoticed during his conversation with Harvey Bingham, "Your Eminence, I wished to report on the status of our Genesis Fleet."

Bingham spoke without emotion, "Well, Shappa, by all means, inform me of our status. How long until we may deliver our ultimatum to the Earthers?"

Bactule smiled briefly, "Within the next seven hours all of our ships will be crewed and ready."

Bingham nodded, "Good. See to our readiness, Shappa. I will prepare the message."

Bactule stood, bowed with well-hidden relief, and left the High Chancellor's quarters silently.

Bingham had resurrected his confidence and he found himself wording the ultimatum in his mind even as he turned back to his monitor. The Earthers would soon understand that they could not withhold the planet Earth.

No longer would they be allowed to stand in the path of destiny. The Church was in full possession of the Genesis Fleet, and in the skilled hands of the Crusaders it would bring the greatest victory the Holy Cause had ever witnessed.

In seven hours.

CHAPTER 25

Sarah tapped her foot lightly on the floor. *Harbinger Bishop*'s flight bay was a busy place, what with the Battlecruiser being the current flagship and the nexus of activity in the new Naval force. It had been a long morning, and since she'd left *Orion* at 06:00 hours, she'd been trying to pull the captured Naval ships together into a coherent formation. Not *too* bad on less than six hours sleep.

Now, other matters were drawing her attention.

Ursla was on her way over with the Earthers' leading expert in the field of genetic regeneration procedures, who was coming to take a look at Liz's injury. They hoped to be able to fix her up with a brand new leg, exactly the same as the old one, but there were concerns regarding the DNA makeup.

In the time since the humans had arrived, no Earther had thought to ask for genetic samples — it was quite possible that the regen treatments would be incompatible with the humans. But there was only one way to find out...

Sarah crossed her arms in front of her and waited impatiently, wondering when the Earther pinnace would land.

Ursla slumped in her chair aboard *Cerberus'* command pinnace. It had been a long stretch of hours — little sleep and a lot of action. Add to that the worries about ArcGeneral Hastings, the Crusaders... she was glad she'd have a little down time before the Church came back on the offensive.

Some of that time was slotted for the groundwork for the first inter-species medical examination in human-Earther history.

Sitting silently next to Ursla, medical kit on her lap, was Doctor Elandra Caine, the First Lord's wife and Ursla's friend. The leading specialist in the field of genetic regeneration treatments, she'd come out from Earth aboard a sloop specifically to assess the genetic similarities between humans and Earthers.

Setter, as Ursla had predicted, wasn't entirely pleased with having his wife so near the front, even if just for a few hours. Their son was at home with friends for the day, so concern for young Phealan, at least, wasn't an issue.

"Commodore, we're approaching *Harbinger Bishop*," the pilot reported over the intercom.

Ursla didn't need to reply, it was a simple alert to make sure she was prepared. Or awake, as the situation might be. Ursla squared herself and glanced over at Elandra.

"Ready, El?" she asked quietly.

The brown-coated wolf, wearing a lab jumpsuit with light synthetic jacket, smiled, "I think so, Andra. I'm rather looking forward to meeting a human."

Andra smiled in reply, "They're full of surprises, but we seem to have a lot in common. You should get along well with them."

Elandra nodded and watched through the pinnace's small porthole as *Harbinger Bishop* grew. Even though a Dreadnought had been salvaged during the defection, the most senior officer currently in the human fleet flew her flag from the Battlecruiser, and so the small human task force was clustering around this vessel.

The ship ahead grew slowly, the other small craft coming and going around its flight deck increasingly visible. *Cerberus'* pinnace was the only Earther one in sight so far. There were many more to the rear, helping to transfer humans to the Earther transports for travel to the lunar bases, but one could hardly hope to see them at this range.

The pinnace finally passed through the human atmospheric shield at the end of the bay, cruising ahead slowly over the strange flight deck as it looked for its parking slot.

This was the first time a human flight deck would see an Earther pinnace, Ursla realized. The Earthers had hosted all the meetings thus far, and head room hadn't been a big problem...

The size of the Earther pinnace meant that it had to take up one and a half of the available guest slots on the flight deck, and the pilot skillfully guided it to the position and lowered it gently to the deck.

Ursla stood, watching her head, and let Elandra go forward ahead of her. The co-pilot was standing at the disembarkment ramp door, and he swung it open and released the ramp as the pair came forward. He saluted Ursla, then returned to his seat in the cockpit.

Ursla was first to descend the ramp, mostly because she had greater experience with the humans. Elandra was virtually on her heels, but kept a bit behind and to the side of the massive Commodore as she observed the humans awaiting them with some wonder.

Sarah stood at the front of *Bishop's* full complement of marines, assembled for this honor guard, and snapped to attention. Ursla stopped at the end of the ramp, snapping a sharp salute in reply.

Elandra, having been married to Setter for a century, was well experienced with such drills, but still found them fascinating. The variety of humans displayed in this particular array added much to the experience — as did the promise of getting a look at live human DNA.

She descended the ramp and stood next to Ursla, bag in hand as she watched the commanding human, a woman with short hair, approach with a sad smile.

Sarah walked up to Ursla and extended a hand, "How are you, Andra?"

Taking her hand, Ursla looked down with a slightly tilted head and shrugged, "Tired, but glad to see you. How are you doing?"

Sarah sighed and raised an eyebrow, "I've been more well rested, but I'll survive. No choice really."

Ursla nodded in understanding, then turned to Elandra, "ArcBrigadier Sarah Manchester, this is Doctor Elandra Caine."

Sarah smiled a little more brightly and stepped over to the wolf, "Glad to meet you. You're the First Lord's wife?"

Elandra nodded with a polite smile at the human, "I'm glad to meet you as well, ArcBrigadier, and yes, I'm Setter's wife. A century now."

Sarah's eyebrow arched higher, her smile broadened, "I'd forgotten about that aging detail. I hope you can help us with that particular issue of genetics, but for now I think you need to see Liz."

With a sweeping gesture, Sarah pointed out a hatch on the far side of the deck. The formation of marines was dismissed and dissolved as the trio paced over the floor. Only then did everyone present realize one of the problems Ursla was going to have on *Bishop* — the hatch was a full meter too short for the Commodore.

"I could wait here," Ursla suggested, but Sarah was already ordering a member of the deck crew off of his ordnance cart.

"Here, if you sit you can get through our corridors," she said gesturing Ursla onto the back.

Sarah and Elandra climbed in front, noticing but ignoring the pronounced tilt as Ursla sat. The corridor hatch opened and the small cart, fortunately built for heavy loads, rolled into the wide hall.

"We have reserve magazines for our landing craft in the belly of the ship, so we built the halls wide enough for these little carts," Sarah explained as they sped by surprised crew.

Ursla nodded, amused by the surprised looks she was getting. It wasn't every day you'd see a giant bear riding on the cargo end of an ammo cart, whipping past you at a neat clip.

Finally the cart came to a stop next to the door of the medical bay. Ursla slid off the cargo platform, crouching while Sarah and Elandra climbed out. The ArcBrigadier was first through the wide door, with Elandra and Ursla close behind.

Several orderlies gaped in shock at the arrival of the Earthers. With so much going on, the staffers hadn't been warned of the arrival of the visitors, and they could hardly have prepared for Ursla's mass even if they had been.

A doctor approached, his expression carefully controlled. Ursla could tell he was nervous, and he looked unpleasantly pale.

"This is Doctor Bradley Kyle, our surgeon," Sarah gestured to the tallish man, and then turned to the Earthers. "Brad, this is Commodore Andra Ursla and Doctor Elandra Caine."

The three exchanged nods and then Kyle led them to the small wing of the sick bay where ArcGeneral Hastings lay with a mask over her eyes, evidently trying to sleep.

"What now, Brad?" she asked impatiently, then some instinct told her to lift the mask.

She smiled in obvious pleasure at her company, then waved Kyle back. Ursla walked over to the wall next to Hastings' bed and sat on the floor, leaning back against the armor alloy and causing an unsettling creak. Sarah marched to the ArcGeneral's other side, Elandra moving with her.

No one commented on the ArcGeneral's evident lack of a left leg below the knee.

"Liz, this is Doctor Elandra Caine," Sarah made the introductions, and Hastings extended her hand to shake Elandra's.

"Are you related to the First Lord?" Hastings asked as they shook hands.

Elandra smiled, "Setter's my husband, actually."

Hastings smiled, but from the other side of the bed Ursla could detect the energy she was exhausting to keep up the facade. The ArcGeneral was in a *lot* of pain, and the only thing keeping her at all animated was a dogged sense of duty.

"So," Hastings said matter-of-factly, "you're here to look at my leg?"

Ursla immediately detected the desperate plea hidden in that calm question.

Elandra nodded, "Yes. I'll take some samples of your genetic structure to see if it's compatible with what we do, and if it is then we'll see about the procedure."

"Could it be done aboard ship?" Hastings asked quietly, as Elandra pulled the sheet back to reveal the stump of the ArcGeneral's left leg.

"No," Elandra said absently as she opened her case, "we'd have to take you back to Earth, but you'd be able to return to duty within a few months."

"With a new leg just like the old one?" Hastings asked, trying not to wince as she tugged at her sheets.

Elandra nodded and began to frown as she ran a hand-held scanner over the leg. She looked up at Doctor Kyle with a curious expression, "Did you put her nerve endings into stasis?"

Kyle stared blankly for a second, stepped forward nervously, and raised his eyebrows, "Stasis?"

Elandra drew a small patch about the size of her palm from her kit and raised it for the humans to see, "This patch can put any specific part of the anatomy into stasis. It's pretty standard — to us. Have anything like it?"

Kyle examined the device thoughtfully, shaking his head, "We can only put a whole body into stasis."

Elandra cocked an eyebrow, "Then you might want a few of these."

Gently, she applied the patch to Hastings' leg just above the kneecap, and it began humming. Pain suddenly ceased to exist in the area, and Hastings sat up slowly in surprise.

"It puts your nerve endings in that area into stasis. You can't feel anything because the nerve impulses are locked down. We've found these quite useful for major injuries like this," Elandra explained, and Kyle watched in amazement.

"Now, the samples," Elandra drew another tool from her kit.

To Sarah's eyes it seemed to be little more than a fancy cylinder, but Kyle seemed more impressed with it. Slowly, Elandra ran the device over the ArcGeneral's leg, her eyes focused on its tiny screen.

Finally, she pulled the device back and read something from the display. She smiled delightedly, and everyone looked at her.

"It seems that your DNA is *very* compatible with the regeneration treatment. It looks like human DNA actually contains *more* of the appropriate sequences for the procedure than ours," Elandra announced happily.

Hastings' eyebrow climbed, "So when do I get my leg back?"

Elandra was refilling her kit under Kyle's scrutiny, and she shrugged, "I'd say a week for attachment, then therapy. We should get you back to Earth as soon as possible to begin treatment."

Hastings nodded, then looked over at Kyle, "Brad, why don't you show Doctor Caine some more of the sick bay. I need to discuss some things with the ArcBrig and the Commodore."

Having shed his nervousness, Kyle looked positively giddy at the chance to see more Earther healing tech in action, and he led Elandra out of the small wing to the rest of *Bishop*'s sickbay.

"This is amazing, Sarah. I don't feel a bit of pain from this!" Hastings pointed at the stump.

Ursla nodded in understanding, "They're very useful, those patches. We've only had them for seventy years or so, and I can say from experience they sure beat painkillers and letting wounds sit."

"First hand experience?" Sarah looked over at her counterpart.

Ursla smiled knowingly, "Quite literally, actually, since this is my *second* right hand," the Commodore raised one arm. "Put it this way, when Setter lost his leg to the reptile, I was the one who pried it off him... and the thing kept a large portion of my arm. That was a couple of years before we developed these patches, and painkillers didn't... do the pain justice."

Sarah smiled, barely recalling that part of Caine's story from yesterday, then explained it briefly to Hastings. The ArcGeneral's confidence began to grow; to the Earthers, it seemed, losing limbs wasn't too uncommon.

"Well, what I need to know, Sarah, Andra, is the state of things outside these walls. Kyle wants me in an information vacuum, but with you here Andra, he's got to give me some leeway," Hastings' words were heavy as she leaned back up against the head of the bed.

Sarah and Ursla traded a short glance. The ArcGeneral had been completely isolated from Fleet Ops by Kyle's orders. Now seemed as good a time as any to break the silence, "Well, the current force under our command is eighty-four ships — one Dreadnought, seventeen Battlecruisers, eighteen Heavy Cruisers, eleven Light Cruisers and thirty-seven Destroyers. They're all pretty much ready to fight. We've also got the 449th fully loaded with arms and service equipment."

"A Dreadnought?" Hastings asked. *"Saint Alistar?"*

Sarah nodded. *Saint Alistar Drake* was the only capital ship to escape. Its ArcColonel had actually poisoned the Crusader Shaspa, dropped emergency bulkheads around the Crusader section, and then blown the section's airlock. It was an entirely ruthless but effective solution to the problem.

"As for officers, to date I've seen no sign of the other ArcGenerals. About 170 ArcBrigs have checked in so far. I think the Crusaders were really gunning for our flag officers. We lost about 80,000 people on the flight in. All things considered, the losses could have been worse, but that's still *80,000*. Right now, I've got fleet command, and I'm flying the flag from here."

Hastings nodded slowly, digesting the reports in silence. Then she turned to Ursla, "And the Earthers?"

Ursla tilted her head, "Well, we didn't take any casualties in the action. The Church seemed to be under orders not to engage. We have 1,821 ships, about half of them of the line. The Church hasn't come online yet."

"And you're not going to take them out while they can't fight back?" Hastings asked coolly, and Ursla slowly let her eyes rise.

"I'm sorry, ArcGeneral, but we have very little interest in a bloody slaughter. There's still a chance that this can end without violence — we won't give up on that hope until we have to."

Hastings sat in silence, brooding over the words. She wanted desperately to be a part of this... her anger at being knocked out of the fight was only being dampened now by exhaustion. She wanted to crush the Church. Now.

But it seemed perfectly in character for these Earthers not to oblige her — noble and fair. Damned near too good to be true.

The determination in Ursla's eyes changed the ArcGeneral's opinion. Whatever these Earthers were saying... well, they were willing to back it.

"Very well," she said quietly, nodding.

"I'm afraid we'll end up spilling more blood in the end, though, than if we crushed the Church now," Sarah noted quietly.

Ursla nodded, "We fear as much, but we've made our decision."

Sarah turned to Hastings, "We estimate the Church will have their fleet back online in about three hours. I'll be going to see Caine when Ursla leaves, to set up our defensive preparations. In the meantime, you should get shuttled back with Doctor Caine for treatment."

Hastings ground her jaw. She hated to be kept out of a fight like this, but knew that, even if she was at full strength — which she most certainly wasn't — taking command with just one leg would be far too difficult. No walking to the sensor plot, no looking over the gunner's shoulder.

No running to an escape pod.

So Hastings looked to Ursla, "Commodore, is there room on your pinnace for both the ArcGeneral and I?"

Ursla started to nod, then stopped and frowned for a second. Sarah stared blankly, and Hastings shook her head and chuckled, "That was my subtle and exquisitely timed announcement of your promotion, Sarah. I'm glad everybody got it."

Sarah froze uncertainly, "Oh."

Hastings looked from the new ArcGeneral to Ursla, who shrugged.

"Well... I suppose you couldn't have an ArcBrig in charge of this little fleet," Sarah swallowed.

"Congratulations, *ArcGeneral*," Ursla smiled at Sarah, who nodded back.

"Don't all thank me at once!" Hastings snorted.

Sarah paused and tried to process the... *promotion*, then cocked her eyebrow, "Right... um... thanks."

She paused again, as her mind caught up, then things began to occur to her.

"I'll have a few promotions of my own to make before we leave," she said with a bit of a smile.

CHAPTER 26

ArcBrigadier Patrick Conroy absently brushed his uniform. It was clean, but he was convinced it was dusty, and the extra braid and round tabs which had been hastily added to his dress greens felt odd on his shoulders.

He was now a flag officer.

Him. Patrick Stephen Conroy. His mother would be very proud, his father appalled that the situation had become so dire...

He smiled to himself and chuckled.

Harbinger Bishop was now commanded by his old ArcMajor exec, and the whole squadron — one of the most potent elements of their small fleet — belonged to him. Sarah would be transferring her flag to *Saint Alistar* when they returned from this strategy briefing — very much against Pat's advice. The Dreadnought would be a bigger target than *Bishop* in the coming battle.

But more than that, he'd miss having Sarah aboard ship. He had very few friends, and she was the only one he'd count as a *good* friend. Her presence was to some degree comforting; now he'd have to worry about her well-being on that big capital-ship-sized target.

The Earther pinnace from *Bishop* had left just an hour after it arrived, taking himself, Sarah, and ArcGeneral Hastings with it. Liz had then departed with the Earther doctor when they reached *Orion*, heading back for Earth to begin treatment for a new leg.

Now, with about an hour and a half before the Church would be able to restore control, officers were assembling in *Orion*'s massive main briefing room. Pat and Sarah were the only two humans present, and they were repeatedly introducing themselves to members of the Earther Navy's flag officer cadre.

Almost twenty Earthers were present. With the exception of Ursla, they were all canine and feline. This was probably an issue of practicality — being so tall, Ursla had to have a hard time walking around aboard ship.

Finally, after about ten minutes, the door opened to reveal Caine. Jovial greetings were exchanged — there was obviously a deep respect between everyone in the room, and it resulted in a level of ease and comfort unmatched by any human command Pat could recall.

It took Caine a couple of minutes to get through the greetings from the officers and to the holographic battle plot. The whole feeling in the room changed as everyone gathered in the seats around the impressively advanced display floating in the glowing blue holo tank.

The projection intrigued Sarah — it displayed the Sol system in *three* dimensions. The Church Fleet was marked by gray dots, the Earther Navy by white, red and blue, and her small force by green. Sarah reflected on the three Earther colors — probably representative of three separate Earther Fleets.

"Well, everyone, this is the situation," Caine began, as all eyes turned either to the First Lord or the plot. "We're guessing the Church will have its fleet back in about an hour, so we should keep this short. We need a way to stop these Colonizers..." Caine pointed at the larger dots in the gray area "...from getting to Earth, while we neutralize the rest of the fleet. ArcGeneral Manchester, do you have any suggestions as to Church strategy here?"

Sarah took a breath, feeling as if all eyes shifted to her, then leaned in towards the holo, "I suspect High Chancellor Bingham will separate these six Colonizers — a million Crusaders each, plus about twice the armament of a Superdreadnought — and have them heavily escorted in an end run."

Relieved when the Earthers nodded, she pressed on.

"He'll probably start his larger attack first. His goal will be to tie up your fleet and destroy it, while he swings around a heavily armed force to run at flux to Earth. He can't go more than 1.25 cee... 125 *pls*... in system. I personally wouldn't go past light speed, but he probably doesn't know any better. If he can land his six million troops, the battle goes to him."

Everyone around the plot nodded grimly, and as someone near a control panel tapped a few keys, the holos shifted to show what she was talking about.

"An end run," one of the canine Earthers, an Admiral named Varnon Broadpaw, remarked dryly.

"We could pull back to Earth, hold there with orbital and lunar support," another, Rear Admiral Jax Furgus, put in.

"I'd worry a bit about the collateral damage to the planet," Pat observed. "Overshot missiles, debris... the consequences could be quite unpleasant."

Ursla cleared her throat conspicuously, and everyone looked to the massive Commodore — the lowest ranked Earther present, "Well, I could use the Exodus Battle Group again. Station us at Io and we could dog them all the way up to the asteroid belt, pick them off while they're in there."

Sarah had seen how Ursla handled her frigates. The big Commodore could probably pull it off but she would need backup.

"I think that'd work," Sarah said thoughtfully. "If you put my ships off..." she examined the name under a small red planet, "*Mars*. I'd say you should leave most of the Earther Fleet because the Church ships *will* be fighting hard."

Caine watched the plot move the markers around as he tabbed a few keys. If Bingham acted as expected, he'd send only big ships with his Colonizers. They'd get picked apart one at a time in the belt by the Exodus Battle Group, and whatever got through would be hit by the humans...

But if the High Chancellor did send only big ships, whatever got through would outgun Sarah's force. Especially those Colonizers. The Earthers would have to commit some heavy ships to deal with those... First or Second Rates. No, even standard First Rates would be too small.

Only ships like *Orion*, the massively oversized First Rates, would be able to handle Colonizers.

Recognizing this, Caine spoke, "Alright, that sounds like a plan. I'll just add one element — I want a force of First Rates with your ships, ArcGeneral. The Church will probably be sending a lot of capital ships with their attack, and your force only has one. Even with Ursla there for support, I think you'll be heavily outgunned."

There were collective nods as Caine continued.

"What worries me most are the Colonizers. It'll take some heavy ships to handle them, so I'm going to order back *Agamemnon*, *Algenon*, *Endymion*, *Poseidon*, and *Lycaeon*. *Orion* will fall back to you under energy drive as soon as the battle begins. That'll give us six ships with 125 guns or better to match their six Colonizers."

There was silence around the plot, then Admiral Broadpaw spoke again, "I guess we'll all be transferring our flags to other ships for the battle then... or since you'll be taking *Algenon*, you could take me too..."

Caine smiled dryly, "Sorry Varnon. I'll command the squadron personally. Kella Felar will have fleet command."

Broadpaw grinned, "You know I had to ask."

Sarah became extra thoughtful. She'd be fighting alongside the First Lord.

"Good, we should get moving then. We only have an hour, and I'll want our forces to be in position within forty-five minutes."

There was a final pause as the commanders exchanged nods, then eyes turned back to Caine.

"I don't need to tell you all the importance of this... I doubt anything I say will seem profound enough in the history books. But there *will* be history books — *Earther* history books. We're going to win this fight."

There were solemn nods from around the table, the mood darkening a bit. But Broadpaw grinned, "See everyone, no worries. He's already planning his retirement!"

A surge of laughter broke the tension, and with a smile Caine nodded, "Good luck to you. I'll see you all soon."

High Chancellor Bingham impatiently tapped his fingers on the desk as the Crusader Shappas and Shaspas around him tried to plan an attack. They were hardly Naval officers, just Crusaders who had worked enough with Naval officers to gain some knowledge on the subject.

Of course, none of them could agree about what to do in the current situation. Some thought they should try to outmaneuver the Earthers, some demanded a duel of missiles... or guns... or *whatever*. Still others wanted to split the force in a bid to flank the heathen forces.

Finally, fed up with the unintelligent suggestions he was hearing, Bingham rapped the table with his knuckles, "I will not have more of this useless conjecture! We have a Quest to complete, and I believe I have the means by which to complete it.

"Now is not the time for intricate maneuvers for which we were never trained. It is the time for direct, blunt action, and that is what I intend to use. You see, the fate of our ships comes second to the retaking of Earth.

"Shappa Bactule assures me that if even *half* our army reaches Earth soil, he will have the planet subdued in a matter of days. If we have the planet, we can force the Earthers to surrender! Our goal is not to destroy the Earther Fleet — we would risk the fate of the whole Quest if we tried something so totally ridiculous! We are blessed, but we are neither immortal nor invulnerable."

There were several slight nods around the table.

"No, a large battle should be nothing more than a distraction. What we must do is separate our Colonizers, put them under heavy escort — at least 100 of our most powerful ships — and send them past the Earther Fleet while it is busy fighting. When the Colonizers reach Earth, the planet's defenses will be crushed by our superior force. We will land our Crusaders, and we will win."

Bingham was unsure where the words and ideas had come from. By nature he was not a tactician, so perhaps a divine power had touched him, given him the knowledge to complete the Quest. It instilled him with a feeling of incredible power — this knowledge had been granted him by the Gods... it *had* to be.

The table, in the meantime, had fallen silent at his words. Shaspas and Shappas watched him with reverence and awe, recognizing immediately the wisdom behind the words.

"Very well, we must develop the force we wish to use in this expedition. What ships? What types? Speak your minds, faithful warriors. We need all the knowledge you have to offer!"

Shappa Bactule had never seen such charisma from the High Chancellor. It was as if Bingham had been touched by the Gods themselves — and perhaps he had been. Whatever the case, the plan he had designed seemed more efficient than any Bactule had been able to come up with.

Now, he stood aboard the Colonizer *Benadict the Savior*, and watched as the ship readied itself to move. The million Crusaders aboard had to be ready to drop, but could not interfere with normal ship operations.

The comm unit chimed behind Bactule, and he turned to key it. The High Chancellor appeared with a triumphant smile.

"We will be ready any moment now, Your Eminence," Bactule reported.

Bingham bobbed his head shortly, "I have every confidence in you, Shappa. We will give you all the cover you need."

Bactule bowed towards the monitor, but Bingham was looking away — something else had drawn his attention.

"Shappa, I am afraid I must go. May the Gods be with you today!"

With that, the screen winked out, and Bactule turned back to the bridge where the Crusaders were bustling around.

"Reporting. Comm Officer. Signal detected between Earther flagship and *Genesis*. Orders?"

Bactule, not used to receiving such lifeless reports as those from the monotone, personality-vacant Crusader crew, took a second to reply, "Display their exchange on the main monitor."

First Lord Caine's face appeared.

CHAPTER 27

Caine had been anxious about this last attempt at peace. He dreaded the prospect of dealing with Bingham again, but there were many lives at stake, and despite his doubts, he was obliged to try to save as many as possible.

He sat rigidly in his chair, watching the main holo tank and waiting a moment as the Signal Officer spun up his transmitter. The few seconds between the order and the signal running across space to *Genesis* were mercilessly short.

"Message being received," the Signal Officer reported. "Stand by... reply incoming."

High Chancellor Bingham appeared in the holo tank. He looked even less stable than when Caine had last seen him, and his expression was in no way conciliatory.

Disturbing, to say the very least.

"High Chancellor, this is First Lord Caine," it was a predictable introduction.

Bingham eyed him cautiously, "I can see that, *First Lord*. Just what is it you want now?"

Caine took a deep breath, trying to remain calm and controlled despite Bingham's mocking tone.

"I wish to end this conflict without bloodshed, High Chancellor."

On *Saint Alistar*, Sarah watched the expression on Bingham's face fold into a frown, and compared it to Caine's neutral visage. Everyone watching or participating knew there wouldn't be any peace.

Tapping the signal at this range provided a lag time of a few seconds, so it was tricky to judge what she was seeing and how its timing compared to the fleet positions now glowing on her screen. She'd be a minute late in realizing the battle had begun because of that. Still, her eyes went back to the exchange, just as Bingham's face twisted on *Saint Alistar's* screen.

"No bloodshed?" Bingham's eyes widened. "You suborn treachery and steal from us our Navy personnel, you block the *Quest* and defile its prophecies and foundations... and then you expect to escape without blood being spilled?"

Sarah wasn't sure, but it looked as though Caine nearly bared his teeth. He stopped himself, of course, and his face remained a cool slate.

Her own hand, which had been resting easily on the arm of her chair, was balled into a fist.

...

"Now, *High Chancellor*, stop this righteous talk. We know what you intended to do to the Naval personnel yesterday. You say we *defiled* the name of your Holy Quest? We explained the truth of it to you! We are not here because we thirst for blood! We want to protect our planet from people who cannot be trusted to respect it. And we won't shed blood if we don't have to!"

Caine snapped the words harshly, and he regretted his tone as soon as he spoke. Bingham's face twisted with anger, and his expression made him appear to be a man possessed.

Finally, he opened his mouth, "You, *Caine*, have ten minutes to surrender all your fleets, bases, and the planet Earth. If you don't give the planet to us, we will take it from you!"

That's it, then.

Ursla watched the transmission blink out of existence, then turned to her bridge crew aboard *Cerberus*.

"Here we go," she said grimly. "Signal Officer, send to battle group, all ships clear for action. Stand by for full acceleration."

"Beat to quarters," Nightclaw was simultaneously addressing his orders to *Cerberus'* First Lieutenant. "Master, bring engines to ready."

The bridge came alive with acknowledgements as the Fifth Rate made final preparations for combat.

Ursla leaned back in her chair, tapping her fingers on the arms in a futile bid to relieve some of the anxious energy building up within her massive frame. This wouldn't be a fancy action like the one she'd used to pull the human flotilla out. This would be brutal — a stand-up broadside fight.

Those were the bloodiest kind.

Sarah leaned back in her command chair. She wasn't yet accustomed to the bridge on *Saint Alistar*, so the movement didn't bring the comfort she'd hoped it would. This was the Navy's only Dreadnought right now... and that meant *Saint Alistar* would get a lot of attention from the Church.

That's what they pay me for, I suppose. But we'll show everyone what a well-handled Genesis capital ship can do. Gods know the Church won't...

"Signal all ships, start up offensive systems. Charge armor, flood tubes, and load missiles. Stand by to accelerate. Sensor Chief, keep an eye out for the Church's flank force. Comm station, keep in touch with the Exodus Battle Group."

The orders were coming from instinct, Sarah's thought processes having quickly switched to auto-pilot. And that was a good thing, because Sarah Manchester's mind was one of the best in the Genesis Fleet.

...

Bingham's anger cooled, letting him think more clearly. The First Lord had done nothing to dissuade him from his plan — instead the Earther's words had incensed the High Chancellor. Caine had so much audacity, acting as if he was *right*.

But now what had he done? Ten minutes to surrender? Of course Caine would never give up. If the Earther had meant to surrender, he would have done so long ago. It would be a fight — one which the Church would win.

Waiting ten minutes made no sense, he realized. The Quest was on the verge of completion. While the Earthers were sitting, waiting, he could hit them by surprise...

"All ships, prepare to attack," Bingham said darkly.

The Shappa put in command of fleet operations turned to him, "Your Eminence? I thought it would be another ten minutes."

Bingham smiled, "A promise to heathen need *not* be honored."

And now, divine prophecy would be fulfilled.

Caine had steadied himself, and now he sat waiting. Bingham had said ten minutes, but he somehow doubted the High Chancellor would act with honor and allow that much time to pass.

The human was being fueled either by some notion of divine intervention, or fear that no such intervention truly existed. He seemed a madman to Caine, and he was wielding a massive fleet in a fanatical way.

That was precisely the sort of situation the Earther Navy had been built to deal with.

So here we go.

"Sir, I'm reading power surges in the Church Fleet," the Sensor Chief reported, and Caine looked down at his console.

Things were happening — the fleet was charging its energy armor, opening the doors to the tubes that would belch their missiles, swinging light energy mounts around as if testing them. Their engines were gathering power.

So Bingham wasn't waiting.

"All ships, load with canister — first broadside for each quarter only. Open ports, stand by for flank acceleration," Caine delivered the orders to the Signal Officer, then turned to *Orion's* Captain. "We'll pull back after the first broadsides."

Lab Forepaw nodded in silent reply.

"Sir, their tubes are loading," the Sensor Chief chimed.

"Fleet, hard to port. Run out starboard broadside. Stand by to roll port to present the second broadside after firing."

Orders rippled out from *Orion*, and the two massive fleets assumed their attack postures.

The 1,700 ships in the Earther formation turned to present their starboard broadsides in near unison, guns being run out even as they turned.

Opposite them, the Genesis Fleet, tubes mounted for forward firing, aimed straight at the Earthers. The spearhead-shaped ships looked menacing, but their order was loose and there was no sign that they so much as understood the concept of fighting as a unified fleet. Still, no one could look laughingly at 2,300 ships of war.

Earthers watched their foes through open gunports. Crusaders stood blankly at their stations.

And then, for the first time, the Superdreadnought *Genesis* launched missiles in anger.

CHAPTER 28

Genesis put 100 missiles into space, and the rest of the ships of the human fleet fired after their flagship. Almost 100,000 missiles lanced out at .8 cee. The tubes began to cycle, each taking eighteen seconds to load the next missile into its launch position.

Caine watched with the heightened awareness that had helped make him an outstanding officer, and elevated him above his peers to the position of First Lord. An alarming number of missiles were just a minute from him.

No, he almost smiled, an inviting number of *targets*.

"All ships, target missiles. Fire as you bear."

Ursla had demonstrated the usefulness of canister against the missiles in her earlier engagement, and now 35,000 Earther guns fired in unison, spraying space with loosely bonded energy. Moving at light speed, the energy cloud would strike the missiles almost exactly midway between the Earther and human ships.

Already, the Earther Navy was rolling. It was an old drill — fire one broadside, then roll along your axis and present the second. The unison of the port broadsides didn't match that of the starboard ones — ships rolling faster fired sooner. Still, just as the second flight of missiles left human tubes, two Earther broadsides were in space to meet them.

"All ships, advance by squadron!" Caine ordered smoothly, and the Earther Navy swung around and chased their own broadsides at a solid 95 pls.

"Lab," he turned to Forepaw, "I believe we have a rendezvous to make. Signal Officer, inform Admiral Felar she has the fleet... and wish her good luck."

Genesis vomited its second volley of missiles before Bingham saw the energy cloud the Earthers had produced. That cloud would doubtless swallow all of his warheads...

"Cease fire!" he barked, but already some ships had let go their salvoes. No matter. "All ships advance at .2 cee."

It was a crawl, but his ships needed to stay closer together or their firepower would lose a good deal of its potency. Besides, Bingham knew the Earthers would probably take the cowardly way and try to stand off and fight them. The Holy Fleet would have to get too close for those big Earther guns to make a difference.

The Genesis Fleet lurched ahead slowly, the missile fire fading into nonexistence. It would take them a few minutes to reach the Earthers.

"Send to our Lancer Task Force, detach immediately!" Bingham ordered.

That was the key to this plan. If he could keep the cowardly heathen busy, his ships on their way to Earth would meet no real challenge. Just to make sure, he and *Genesis* would join them after some of the fighting was done.

Bingham watched the screen as the group of approximately 100 ships — six Colonizers and nothing smaller than a Battlecruiser — slipped away from the fleet on an oblique angle that would take them well clear of the battle. Their flux drives were already charged, making it a simple matter for them to start moving.

They jumped into flux, moving at 150 percent of light speed — a crawl for deep space, but necessary because of the smallness of the planetary system. Bingham turned his attention back to the Earther Fleet. The existing energy cloud had grown thicker as a second broadside joined it, and as he predicted, all the missiles his fleet had fired were eliminated.

So the first broadsides ended in a stalemate. Very well then. Prophecy would be decided on the Church's superior terms, while the Earthers stood off and...

The ships of the Earther Navy rippled through the cloud of energy in a tide. Their chase guns fired into the crawling Genesis ships, and as they turned over to port, their broadsides roared with concentrated shot instead of the canister they had used before.

Then the humans began to respond. As the Earthers started to roll again, their port broadsides coming up, a ragged volley tore away from the Church ships. Some of the missiles slammed into the shot of the first Earther broadside, but to the terror of the humans, most of the energy bursts hit by missiles *kept coming*, despite destroying warheads.

And as for the rest of the flight of missiles, the second Earther broadside had been again set for canister. Almost the entire flight of missiles was wiped out, the rest either bouncing harmlessly off shields or being shot down by swift-firing, turreted carronades.

When the broadside from the Earther cannon roared in, it was entirely too much for the humans. First, the light salvo — only six or seven thousand chase-gun bursts — slashed into the Church ships, though the armor mostly absorbed it. A handful of ships were crippled, only three Destroyers taken completely out of action.

The human fleet's armor had been weakened.

Thirty-five thousand tight balls of energy slammed home in the second broadside, and they were the devastating blow. Almost the entire first line of human ships vanished in fireballs, the second and third lines receiving massive damage. Beyond them, the later lines received moderate damage.

Two hundred and four ships were taken out of action by that single salvo, hundreds more damaged to varying degrees.

And then, like the predators that had been their ancestors, the Earthers swept in. The human formation came apart, some charging madly at the Earthers, others trying to fall back. Some just held their course in a stupor.

No longer fighting as their singular, massive formation, the Earthers broke into their squadrons, then sometimes broke down even further. Frigates charged deep into the enemy fleet, rolling constantly, sending out walls of energy. Capital ships — First, Second and Third Rates — brought their mighty broadsides around and poured fire into the human fleet.

No responding fire lanced back to meet them.

Bingham roared the order to return fire, slamming his fist furiously into the console before him. Unlike what he'd come to expect of the Navy, this fleet of his was moving without coordination, without swiftness. Crusaders with operations manuals downloaded into their brains simply came up short when compared to the finely honed crews that had previously commanded these ships.

But they could still *fire*!

The key to this plan was to hold the Earthers in the fight long enough for the Lancer Task Force to reach Earth.

After what seemed an interminable delay, missiles began to cruise back at the Earthers. This time, there was no massed cloud of energy to tear them apart, and some found their targets. Daring frigates were torn open by the heavy fusion warheads, slower moving capital ships were being hammered. The real battle was beginning.

Genesis had been in the rearmost ranks of the fleet — a position ideal to moving around the battle and on to Earth. That placement had protected it from the massive blows the Earthers had thrown, but now frigates and Fourth Rates were coming in.

Individually, these ships simply didn't have the weight in fire to hurt the massive Superdreadnought, but attacking like a pack of wolves they could do very considerable harm. And Bingham needed to survive the battle so he could help Bactule on Earth.

"Create a defensive perimeter around the flagship!" he snarled the orders, and they were mechanically obeyed.

Ships in the ranks ahead of and behind *Genesis*, as well as above and below, shrunk back into a protective sphere around their flagship. They poured out missiles as fast as they could, taking a great deal of heat from practiced Earther gunners.

No wolf pack would be reckless enough to charge a circle of elephants, no matter how careless the behemoths might be. The Earthers swooped around the outside of the sphere, moving fast and dodging with impressive agility, while their gunners methodically destroyed or disabled one ship at a time.

Four squadrons of frigates and Fourth Rates engaged this defensive sphere — thirty-two against twice that many Church ships. Had there been experienced Naval crews aboard the human ships, these Earthers would have been harder pressed by the action.

But the Crusader crews weren't experienced.

Admiral Felar did not enjoy the slaughter, but she took comfort in the relatively low numbers of Earther casualties as the figures scrolled through her holo tank. She'd held her capital ships back from the fighting as long as possible, but now, seeing the success of her frigates, she decided to slowly pour them into the melee.

First, the workhorse Third Rates. Mounting, on average, 74 guns each, these ships were the most plentiful — over 500 in all. They cruised in from the front, their heavy shields shrugging off most blows. Some were knocked back by missiles in the advance, but the rest bore in, and at point blank range they brought their titanic batteries to bear. Ships simply came apart under the fire of a 74.

Carronades, the range close enough for them to be used, cut savage gashes in human ships, while the replying energy fire was far less impressive. In close quarters, though, the human missile worked like a hyper-kinetic weapon. When set to point blank range, the missile would move just a shade under light speed, giving it far less endurance but a great deal of punch.

Seventy-fours began to feel the melee as those fast missiles began to drive in, but they were still giving far better than they got. They pressed further and further, some alone, others clumped in twos or threes. The human ships tried to turn their forward-mounted weapons back on their attackers, but just as they did, Felar sent in the First and Second Rates.

There were only about 400 of those two classes combined, but they were even tougher than the 74s. They savagely mauled the unprotected rears of human ships, while the missiles seemed to bounce harmlessly away from their heavy shielding.

The Church simply broke.

Felar was not a violent lion; she considered herself quite a life-loving person, but these humans had to be stopped. Earth was at stake, and that left nothing to debate.

Bingham gaped in horror as the Genesis Fleet's losses rose past 800, compared to only a few hundred for the Earthers.

"Order whatever Superdreadnoughts are near to follow us — set course to join the Lancer group, 1.5 cee!" he snapped.

The monotone, personality-vacant Crusader at communications confirmed his orders, as did the one at the helm. Slowly, *Genesis*, with another thirteen Superdreadnoughts, eased back away from the battle. As the distance began to open they turned their backs, accelerated upwards and outward, just as a group of 74s and Second Rates arrived to smash the defensive sphere.

The battle on the Pluto Orbital Plane began to slow. The First and Second Rates fanned out, neutralizing resistance, with sloops and frigates clustering around them to act as screens. An attempt by the Church to regroup in the far corner of their formation was stopped with the broadsides of a mixed group of 74s, frigates, and other ships.

It would have been a crushing and humiliating defeat for the Church, but the Quest still had a strong hope.

The Lancer Task Force hurtled towards Earth.

CHAPTER 29

Ursla watched grimly as Admiral Felar methodically blasted the Church fleet apart. She tried not to think about how many of the crews were dying — the Earthers did their best to simply take ships out of action without destruction, but casualties and fatalities were unavoidable.

She knew the Crusaders on those ships had no personalties remaining and remembered nothing of their pasts — Sarah had explained the method of 'training' rather thoroughly — but personality or not, the fact remained that they were dying.

In the fleet, the Earthers had lost only 150 ships outright, and there were hundreds of escape pod transponders indicating survivors, but that was still another fountain of blood.

Ursla shook off her grim thoughts and focused on the separate group of human ships screaming towards Earth. The fools were running at 150 pls. They'd hit the belt in only a few minutes, and some of them would probably slam right into asteroids.

The Exodus Battle Group was under energy drive at 115 pls, coming out obliquely from Jupiter so they could cut across the human flight path, then double back. What she was about to do was right out of the textbooks.

But it seemed unlikely that the Earthers and the humans were reading the same books, and that put the latter group at a major disadvantage.

Bactule gaped at the sensor monitors in horror as the Genesis Fleet disappeared. He had expected a pitched battle, but this was virtually a one-sided slaughter. The Earthers fought like the demons they were, and the Church crumbled.

But his was the key role in the Quest, and so far it looked as if the Earthers had not bothered to protect the approaches to their precious home. They would pay for that...

"Time to Earth?" he demanded of the brain-wiped Crusader at helm.

"Eleven minutes, present speed. However, we must decelerate and stop to pass around the system's asteroid belt. Total time approximately fifteen minutes."

Bactule grunted at the thought of a delay, but it seemed as though he was safe, they were safe...

For now.

...

"Stand by to drop out of energy drive — prepare for crash re-entry," Ursla ordered calmly, and the Signal Officer distributed the orders to the 100 frigates and sloops under the Commodore's command.

Ahead of the detached human force by about thirty seconds, the Exodus Battle Group prepared to drop out of energy drive. It was a delicate maneuver: drop out of and re-enter energy drive before the humans literally ran into them — and leave an unpleasant wall of energy in the Church's way...

But, as the exodus had proved, Ursla's crews were well trained. The Navy's mandate was to succeed this day. There would be — *could* be — no failure.

"Drop out in... five... four... three... two... one..."

Frigates and sloops suddenly dropped back into normal matter, their port broadsides running out as they did. Ursla didn't need to give specific orders — this maneuver would rely on her crews' expertise, not her commands. Her words would have been too slow.

The first broadside roared, the rest following quickly, and then 100 ships jumped back into energy drive.

Bactule was still gaping at the loss of the Genesis Fleet when the alarm screamed. He had just enough time to swing his head around when the screening Superdreadnoughts were ripped open like cans.

Energy shot slashed into the fast moving human group at light speed, multiplying in force thanks to the 1.5 cee Bactule's force was making on its flight. The bursts sliced through the fluxed ships like knives through tinfoil, leaving massive gouges in hulls.

But that wasn't the worst part.

Ships in flux had effectively no mass so when something fast and powerful slammed into them, they tore and *stopped*. The energy bursts acted like battering rams, stopping several large ships as they sliced into them.

And as a ship stopped its flux generators would cut off under fail-safe — if a ship was being stopped a flux drive could overload from the strain. Unfortunately, the crews of those ships died terribly as Newton coldly reapplied his laws.

Debris scattered before the force, chunks of hull doing further damage as they slammed into fast moving ships.

Bactule cursed the Earthers, but they were already gone. He couldn't fire in flux drive — the missiles wouldn't be able to get beyond the tube before the ship slammed into them from behind.

"We are beginning deceleration for the asteroid belt," the Crusader at helm said, as if nothing had happened.

Bactule didn't acknowledge. He sat silently, the shock washing over him. Damage reports were coming to him now — thirteen ships destroyed or disabled, a dozen more damaged. Most of those were his big Superdreadnoughts

— the ones he'd ordered out front.

At least his Colonizers remained intact.

The Earthers might be demons with unimaginable abilities, but they had no chance against six million of his best Crusaders. He was out of his element in space, but on the ground he was unstoppable.

The Lancer Force cautiously began its deceleration, wondering what waited for it beyond.

Ursla had elected to abandon a second pass on the Crusader ships. They were moving far too rapidly for another attempt. Instead, she'd brought her ships up to 200 pls — a dangerous speed, even for her crews — and then re-entered normal state just above the asteroid belt.

The Church formations would be decelerating, their cruder flux drives taking longer to cycle down.

Ursla would have the last punch before the Mars Battle Group engaged the advancing Church formation. She had taken out a dozen of the big ships so far, but they were still coming.

As was to be expected.

"All ships, get into the asteroid belt. Target at your discretion — do as much harm as you can, then join the Mars Battle Group," Ursla ordered, and the Exodus Battle Group scattered expertly into the mess of asteroids.

"Deceleration complete."

Two Dreadnoughts and a Battlecruiser slammed right into asteroids, blowing up as their deceleration failed. The rest of the Lancer Force stopped just short, one Dreadnought within a hundred meters of a large rock.

The casualties were steadily mounting, Bactule realized grimly. But still, they were getting through. Not much farther and–

A scouting Battlecruiser exploded, and Bactule suddenly realized the trap. He should have known what was going to happen, but he hadn't been thinking clearly...

"Get big ships forward! There are ships in that belt we have to destroy!"

Ursla watched with sad surprise as the Church sent a squadron of Dreadnoughts ahead of them. Her ships could easily outrun those hulking vessels, even though frigate fire wouldn't be enough to crack them quickly. Battlecruisers should have been deployed to knock out her ships, but the Church commander was ignorant of that fact.

The Exodus Battle Group swarmed around the big ships as they entered the belt — wolves harrying prey. The heavy missile batteries mounted on the Dreadnoughts were useless in such tight quarters, and as energy broadsides tore in there was no way to avoid them.

Two sloops were hit and destroyed by lucky volleys, their escape pods fleeing as the ships spiraled off to explode. The rest of the Exodus Group was untouched.

It was only when the Church Battlecruisers came forward that the real contest began.

Even with inexperienced crews, the differences were clear between the success of the Dreadnoughts and the success of the Battlecruisers. The lighter ships were able to maneuver away from broadsides and put missiles to space with far more agility. There were only thirty or forty, but with the Exodus Group split up they were effective. The first Dreadnought exploded, followed by two more.

"Good enough. All ships, get out of here!" Ursla ordered quickly, and the Exodus Battle Group turned to run. Three frigates were blasted to pieces as they turned, as well as five more sloops.

Then, with agility and speed the Battlecruisers couldn't match, the Earthers left the field.

Bactule viciously hammered his fist into the arm of his chair as his force regrouped. He'd lost nineteen ships, many of them his big guns. And the Earthers were probably waiting on the other side of the asteroid belt!

"Sir, fourteen Superdreadnoughts decelerating astern, flagship included," the Sensor Chief reported lifelessly.

Suddenly Bactule remembered the High Chancellor's promise of support. It had come! It did not quite make good his losses, but it was adequate — and something the Earthers would not expect. And if all he had to face were those small Earther ships then nothing could stop him.

"Message incoming from *Genesis*," the communications Crusader reported.

Bingham appeared on *Benadict the Savior*'s monitor, his face drawn, shocked. They still had a chance to win, but their great fleet had done nothing more to aide the goal than buy time with its utter destruction. Many Holy men had died.

"Ambush, Shappa?" Bingham asked grimly.

Bactule nodded.

"Very well. We go over this Gods-forsaken asteroid belt and rush through whatever waits until we reach Earth."

Caine watched as the humans began to climb over the asteroid belt. His small fleet was sitting in open space, waiting for them slightly beyond the belt. He would pin the lumbering ships against the floating rocks and then destroy them.

The squadron of oversized First Rates was arrayed in line abreast formation off *Orion's* port beam, its ships' massive hulls dwarfing the smaller units of the

Exodus Battle Group and the Allied human force.

The only other capital ship on hand — ArcGeneral Manchester's *Saint Alistar Drake* — was floating at the end of the First Rate line, seeming only half the size of its partner, the 150-gun *Agamemnon*.

The powerful Church force came over the asteroid belt and presented itself to the Earther-Allied formation.

The two enemies now faced each other in space.

CHAPTER 30

Genesis slowly dropped over the edge of the asteroid belt, and Bingham watched the last defenders standing between him and Earth. A half squadron of Earther capital ships, a hundred-odd Earther light escorts, and the eighty traitor ships.

His 100 capital ships would easily smash them to bits.

"All ships, engage at will."

Caine grimly studied the force before him. It was more than he'd expected to see — additional Superdreadnoughts had joined it, despite the fury of the battle *Orion* had left behind.

The main targets for his mighty First Rates were the Colonizers, everything else had to be stopped by the rest of the Allied force. It was not an easy proposition — even Ursla and Sarah would be hard pressed to stand against that escort force.

Caine glanced once more towards the solar system map and saw that Felar was sending him six full squadrons of 74s — taken together, more than a match for the Church ships.

Unfortunately, they were almost ten minutes away, and far too much could happen in that time.

Caine watched as the Church ships began to move ahead in a surge, and missiles rained outward.

"All ships, break and attack!"

As *Saint Alistar* leapt forward launching its missiles, Sarah turned to its ArcColonel, "Target *Genesis*. It's their biggest Superdreadnought, and the First Rates are tied up."

The ArcColonel blinked, "Ma'am, they've got twenty more tubes and a hell of a lot more armor than we do."

Sarah nodded absently, already watching the ships start to come together in space.

"We have to pull our weight, ArcColonel."

Ursla watched the Exodus Battle Group split into its 100 lethal single-ship units and swarm angrily into the Church force. The Allied ships flung themselves in behind their Earther comrades, rapid fire missile tubes filling space with metal.

Cerberus was near the front of the surging Allied force, and a Church Battlecruiser charged straight in to meet it. Nightclaw watched the incoming challenger with a cocked eyebrow.

"On my mark turn ninety degrees to port and engage with starboard broadside," he ordered smoothly, his deep voice relaxed.

Ursla let her Captains do their jobs — there was no point giving obvious orders now. Unless something broke through unnoticed, there was nothing for her to do but watch the months and years of training pay off. Her squadron's ships fought in pairs or threes, without formal orders or structure, and they did very well...

"Mark."

It was such a simple word, but so much happened when Nightclaw said it. *Cerberus* handled swiftly, its bow swung over fast, and the fifteen cannon of its starboard broadside ran out to face the charging Battlecruiser.

The Church ship fired a volley, fifty missiles flying from its tubes. Nightclaw barked an order and *Cerberus'* broadside replied almost immediately. Some of the Battlecruiser's missiles were torn from space by the swirling balls of energy, but forty bore in.

"Up angle seventy-five degrees, 95 pls, execute port 180 roll," Nightclaw's orders continued to flow easily, and *Cerberus* rippled 'upwards' relative to the Battlecruiser.

Twenty confused missiles missed the frigate, the rest turned upwards after it. Carronades swung into action, their long lancing beams slashing into the incoming flight, shooting down ten more.

"Over the top, skipper," the Cruising Master reported.

"Swing us back and bring the port broadside to bear on that Battlecruiser," Nightclaw said the words with finality. *Cerberus* eased over, upside down, then rolled to port so that broadside could fire down on the top of the Battlecruiser.

Only then did the first broadside smash into the Church ship's forward armor, three bursts getting cleanly through and tearing at its hull. The unprotected top was being ravaged.

Earther practice in such a situation would have been to roll and present a broadside to the enemy, but the forward mounted tubes forced the Battlecruiser to try to turn upward to face its foe.

All too late.

The second broadside given by *Cerberus* got no reply, and it smashed through the lighter armor of the upper hull like a battering ram. The Battlecruiser's engines gave out, and burning on the inside, it coasted away.

Two of the unfortunate Church ship's initial missiles got through *Cerberus'* carronade screen and slammed into the aft shields, but no major damage was done. In barely a minute, the Fifth Rate had smashed a contemporary counterpart, and it sped off to repeat the duel.

Orion stayed in the First Rate line until the first Battlecruisers swung to engage it. Massive carronade mounts blew those ships backward without a significant response. Several missiles hit the shields but they did no damage.

Superdreadnoughts raced out to meet the oncoming Earther behemoths but Allied escorts simply swamped them with targets. Any fire that reached the six First Rates was inconsequential. They pressed through the clouds of swirling warships, their tough construction saving them from any serious harm.

Then they fell upon the massive Colonizers with no intention to give quarter.

The Colonizers had recognized the incoming threat, but they had nothing near the maneuverability of the Earther ships, so their bows came upwards far too slowly.

Endymion released its 65-gun broadside first, followed by its twin, *Agamemnon*. *Algenon* and *Lycaeon* added their forty-five guns to the fight, then came *Poseidon*'s forty-five. Finally, the crash of *Orion*'s 75-gun broadside rippled through space, and the Earthers split apart to engage separate ships.

The first reply began to come from the huge Colonizers, 200 missiles leaving the tubes of each. The one *Orion* turned on sent its massive weight of metal almost directly onto the First Rate's port broadside.

Captain Labrador Forepaw, fortunately, had foreseen the threat, and the 75 port-side cannon sprayed canister to meet the missiles, while *Orion* climbed at full speed. The First Rate rolled fast, its starboard 75, freshly recharged, bearing on the huge Colonizer.

Again the ponderous Church vessel came around, this time abandoning missiles for its huge lasers. Though not as powerful as an Earther cannon at close quarters, these weapons were potent.

Fortunately, their gunnery lacked skill.

The beams tried to track the First Rate. A couple of the dozen hit *Orion*'s heavily shielded aft quarter, but only one managed to burn through the shielding, cutting into the hull to leave a deep scar.

The ship shook and some of the secondary landing bay was now open to space, but the damage was trivial. The Earther ship, ever fast, rolled again, and even as the second broadside tore through the Colonizer's armor, the third rippled out in its wake.

Fire from the Church ship slackened all of a sudden, and then a magazine detonated from within, the explosion blowing out a central part of the vessel. From there the hull began to warp, being forced outward but holding desperately to the welding and bolts until the pressure was too much.

The ship exploded as *Orion* raced away. One down, five to go.

hoped that the harlot Hastings was aboard. This Dreadnought needed to be destroyed before *Genesis* could go to Earth... it was a point of Holy honor.

In the tradition of many battles in many places, no one interfered with the showdown between rivals. *Genesis* fired first, but *Saint Alistar's* missiles followed immediately. The Dreadnought, slightly faster and handier at the helm, dodged downward and to the starboard side, forcing some of the missiles to miss it altogether.

Many of *Genesis'* remaining missiles were cut down by experienced point defense teams, but some got through. The ship bucked as fusion warheads tore into its flank.

On the bridge a thunderous crash sounded, and the ship's commanding officer turned to see what it was. A bulkhead behind him seemed to shatter, shards cutting him apart like so many daggers. The Sensor and Security Chiefs joined him on the casualty list, while the shards sliced and wounded the Helm Officer and the Comm Chief.

Sarah, remarkably untouched, ignored the death around her. She could be sick, appalled and horrified later.

The ArcMajor exec turned to her, and she nodded, "Up angle by twenty points! Stand by beam weapons."

The missiles which slammed into *Genesis'* armor were far more numerous than the ones which had hit *Saint Alistar*, but the damage was only equivalent thanks to the Superdreadnought's far tougher protection.

Acceleration dropped off sharply, and half its tubes vanished. But it could still fight.

It was trying to turn after the Dreadnought when *Saint Alistar* swung around to meet it, and the beam weapons came lashing out from the smaller ship.

Reply was delayed, and two of *Genesis'* heavy lasers had been sliced apart, but danger remained from the heavily armed vessel. Lasers passed each other in space, the entire front half of *Genesis* getting carved open, the whole of *Saint Alistar* being ravaged. The smaller ship's power plant was hit, and suddenly every system on the ship shut off.

Emergency power snapped on, but the lasers had no energy to fire with, and all but six tubes had been torn to shreds. The bigger ship, still with weapons and power, had won. It drifted forward under emergency thrusters, its sights set on the crippled Dreadnought.

But none on *Genesis* were paying attention to the rest of the battle. That was quite a mistake.

Ursla had peeled *Cerberus* out of the 111th, sending the rest of the squadron to engage the crippled enemy capital ships. *Genesis* was a very vulnerable target under the frigate's sights, now that it was so focused on a final kill.

The Fifth Rate appeared fast, port broadside firing... then the ship rolled and the starboard guns loosed their salvoes as well. The cannon fire met unshielded hull and tore in savagely, the entire front half of the Superdreadnought being lopped off in a spew of jagged splinters and debris. With the power for both halves cut, the darkened hulls simply drifted away.

It all happened so quickly that Sarah had little time to comprehend it. She was out of the fight, but she'd been saved from death. *Again*.

The comm line chirped, and the Comm Officer, cradling her limp arm, spoke up, "ArcBrigadier Conroy for you, ma'am."

The transmission appeared on Sarah's screen, and she looked indifferent as Pat appeared.

"Thought you might want to transfer your flag, Sarah. Your ship looks... a bit rough."

Caine watched the last Superdreadnought lose power and tumble off, and he glanced at his sensor panel to decide how well his force was faring.

The Allied fleet was regrouping, having lost less than 100 of its number, but there was nothing left to face. On sensors he could see the six reinforcement squadrons of Third Rates coming over the belt, but everything had been destroyed.

Except for one important target...

You fool... you've let it through.

Speeding away at 300 pls — far past any safe regulations for in system travel — the massive ship ran, a Superdreadnought tagging with it. He'd missed it in the melee, and now...

"Signal General Grieve on Earth," Caine barked. "Incoming, one Colonizer. Prepare ground defenses! All ships set pursuit course, 400 pls!"

It was incredibly dangerous to go that fast, but the Earthers *had* to intercept those Crusaders... a million soldiers on Earth could do unimaginable harm.

The humans had such a large head start that even at 400 pls, the Earthers would arrive too late...

In a desperate maneuver, the First Rates and frigates of the Earther Navy, as well as their reinforcement squadrons of 74s, jumped into energy drive.

CHAPTER 31

A day before the battle in space had started, General Andros Grieve, only recently returning to his usual amiable mood after his long day with Crusader Shappa Bactule, had discussed Earth's defense with Commandant Michael Falkner.

"Common human strategy," the humans' Naval marine commander had explained, "is to take both poles at once, then work your way outward. When you have both poles, you can go just about everywhere. Bactule basically wrote the rule book on that one, so if anything does get through the blockade you can bet that's what he'll try."

That wasn't such good news to Grieve — his active marine forces planetside numbered 50,000. On Luna there were 5,000, in the fleet an additional 40,000. But even one Colonizer brought more than *ten times* that number. If the humans hit both poles he could only make a serious stand at one.

Falkner had assured Grieve that his 25,000 humans — those previously of the Genesis Fleet, and literally just settled in Lunar barracks — would help defend Earth, and Grieve didn't doubt the tall, wiry human. Still, that gave him only 120,000 troops in total — and that was only if he could get all the troops from the fleet.

Falkner had made further recommendations on how to defeat the tactically rigid Shappa. His best suggestion had been to abandon the bases on the poles, and when Bactule tried to get his forces camped out and entrenched, hit him. That was the only way the Earthers could control the Church deployment.

Bactule could easily get overconfident if the bases fell, and would construct his defenses slowly. Both Earth's poles were inhospitable and any encampments would be hard to set up. That would leave the Crusaders vulnerable for a while — busy digging in, not watching the plains as carefully as they should because they thought they'd already won. Grieve had agreed with Falkner, and so the decision was to attack the Crusaders once they'd captured — but not secured — one of the polar facilities.

His garrisons at both the Arctic and Antarctic Bases had been pulled back across the plains, occupying hastily-built reserve compounds out of range of base scanners and camouflaged against air observation. The Earther Navy would have air superiority once the Crusaders got to ground.

All base personnel had been evacuated, with the exception of 250 volunteer troops who would retreat quickly while appearing to put up as much fire as a division when they fell back. The Crusaders would get their 'easy victory', and since they'd refused to see the base on their tour of Earth, none of their officers could possibly recognize the anomaly in force counts.

But Grieve had still hoped they wouldn't get a chance to land. He wasn't afraid of them as much as he was aware of the threat they posed, and of how many of his marines might die when then reached the ground.

From his command center on the Antarctic Plain, with 30,000 of his troops camped around him, he had witnessed the exchange between Caine and Bingham through his large holo tank, knowing that no diplomatic solution could be reached.

He had faith in officers like Andra Ursla, but the humans enjoyed a serious numerical advantage, and if just one of their Colonizers got through...

The small battle at the Asteroid Belt had drawn his interest even more. He watched the holos of the mighty, much-heralded First Rates slamming into the humans like sledge hammers.

And he'd watched in silence as one Colonizer and its escort raced away unchallenged. It was quite clear in his holo tank... why hadn't Caine seen it? A couple of human light ships tried valiantly to stop the Church advance, but their firepower was shrugged off and they were wiped away.

Now, those two ships were speeding in, leaving Grieve in a position he had hoped to avoid. He contacted Orbital Defense Command — the Admiralty office commanding the eight heavily-armed stations that made up Earth's last line of space defense — and confirmed his observation with them. Then he called in the Lieutenant Generals of his force on the Antarctic Plain, linking in those on the Arctic plain by comm net, and began to review the defensive plan.

After the Antarctic Base was evacuated, Vice Admiral Felix found himself displaced — no force to command, no base. So he had decided to transfer up to the orbital forts. He knew that would be the scene of any fight in local space.

"The Superdreadnought's coming in first sir, looks as though it'll try to draw our fire," a Lieutenant reported, and Felix nodded slowly.

Neither Church ship could do much harm to the forts — each station could double the firepower of a Second Rate — but that wasn't the Colonizer's intention. The Naval defectors had explained the Colonizer-class vessel very carefully: massive ships, half their outer hull committed solely to launching dropships.

Dropships. It was clear what the humans would do. The Superdreadnought would draw fire from the platforms while the Colonizer swept in and let go its 1,000 dropships, putting a million troops planetside. Neither ship would survive in the withering crossfire, but their troops might land safely.

Felix watched the icons on his sensor panel tell him the locations of the two human ships. Four minutes before his station would be in firing range.

"Orders to all forts, focus your fire on the dropships first. The ships can wait, we can't let those troops planet side."

Earther gun crews sat at their mighty cannon.

Bactule was the last one onto the special dropship. He had silently supervised the loading of the troops onto the landing craft, then found his own — the most advanced and best armored lander in the fleet.

It was critical that he got to the planet.

His was the only landing craft to sport energy armor and upgraded engines — added at his order to improve his chances of survival.

He was predicting significant casualties amongst his assault force... maybe up to thirty percent. Well, he would fight with whatever got through. He had changed his orders for the invasion in the past minutes — with but a million Crusaders, he was unwilling to divide between two poles. Instead, he had ordered *Benedict the Savior* to emerge over Earth's south pole, and had ordered his Shaspas to adjust their trajectories to land at the Antarctic Base. Striking in daylight, he hoped, would help them avoid Earther trickery.

Instead of being unsure about taking two poles, he would be guaranteed one. Silently, Shappa Bactule climbed aboard the landing craft and stood by to launch.

The two human ships began their quick deceleration, slowing to normal speed just out of Earth's orbit. Both ships flushed their tubes at the nearest station, but the carronades and canister from the fort stopped the fire.

The Superdreadnought raced out ahead, fire from its lasers and tubes grazing surprisingly unresponsive forts, while the Colonizer closed into orbit. The nearest two stations put broadsides into the big ship, but it kept coming.

The advance elements of the Earther Navy erupted from energy drive behind the humans. Both *Cerberus* and *Orion* were part of the group, along with two other First Rates and the rest of Ursla's 111th.

Their first broadsides were in space before their momentum had worn off, but it was too late.

The Colonizer's hull seemed to flake away, and a thousand flat, arrowhead-shaped landing craft flocked outward, their course adjusting so it would bring them to the Antarctic Plain.

The platforms had done as ordered, holding their broadsides back for this moment. Behind *Orion* and the lead elements, the reinforcement 74s erupted from energy drive and brought their guns to bear as well. A tidal energy broadside filled space.

No pretenses were made about targeting — there were so many ships dropping from space that the honed Earther gunners couldn't miss. Massive batteries ripped through the clouds of descending ships, hundreds of them evaporating with the first barrage. The Colonizer exploded as it was caught in that tidal crossfire, and the Superdreadnought was blasted from orbit. The landing ships continued their drop, each carrying 1,000 Crusaders.

Guns cycled through recharge, fifteen seconds passing — an excruciatingly long fifteen seconds. The ships coming in behind the 74s ran out their guns to join the thunderous broadside that was about to be delivered, and gunners targeted the areas of highest density among the dropship formations.

Orion fired first, rolled and fired a second time.

Between the two broadsides of the mighty First Rate, the entire Earther force let loose its energy. Like a hurricane of shot, it swept down onto the helpless dropships, and they began to disintegrate.

Caine watched from *Orion's* bridge, silent and very aware of the number of deaths this action was bringing. He did understand the grim necessity of it — this whole campaign, and 600 years of preparation, had been in the interests of protecting Earth from the humans. But he'd live with the guilt for the rest of his life... though he couldn't concern himself with that now.

The dropships were being smeared from space by the mighty broadsides, the survivors cruising across the sky at breakneck speeds while local air defense gunships and anti-aircraft batteries spat fire into them. A couple tried to return fire with their light armaments, but no damage was done.

And yet the Crusaders still dropped from the sky, the gunships lagging behind. Defensive batteries fell away into the distance, and the dropships crossed onto the Antarctic Plains free of attack. Only 114 dropships remained now.

The Earther ships in orbit began to crash-launch their marine detachments in assault craft, directing them to land near the south pole.

From the hundred-plus Earther ships in orbit, almost 200 small craft departed. Caine had prepared the crews for this eventuality even though he'd hoped it wouldn't be necessary, and now they needed no order. He wished that he could join his soldiers on this mission, but he had to stay above, and make sure the Navy wasn't surprised by some clever counter-move no one had foreseen.

More transports began lifting off the lunar pads, diving past the arriving squadrons of 74s towards Earth's atmosphere at speeds which would normally be unthinkable. They carried the human marines and Earther marine detachments, and had waited to join whatever Earther force was taking the brunt of the assault.

Grieve had watched the human dropships cruise past overhead, knowing that the Navy had inflicted over eighty percent casualties. That still left over 100,000 troops for him to deal with. The forces of the Arctic Base were loading up to join him and the Navy was dropping all the shipboard detachments it could muster. The humans and lunar garrison were racing down from the moon.

It was just a matter of time.

Bactule stumbled down the ramp of his maimed dropship, clutching his rifle to his chest. The Crusaders had already swept forward towards the Antarctic Base, and he could hear fire fights rattling in the distance. He looked around — the landing fields of the base were devoid of activity, except for the off-loading of the survivors of his attack force. From eight million troops when the Genesis Fleet launched, he now commanded scarcely a hundred thousand warriors. Two million had been lost to postings in the fleet, and five million more had died in their Colonizers.

And he'd sustained ninety percent casualties on that murderous drop.

But they were Crusaders still, and somehow they would find a way to take this planet.

Gods' will.

CHAPTER 32

Debris from two huge human ships slid lazily into Earth's atmosphere, orange-red fields forming around them as they began to disintegrate. An Earther Navy task force floated above.

Caine looked down on the blue-white globe with controlled anxiety. He *had* failed. Not as badly as he could have, admittedly, but badly enough. A hundred thousand, all on the Antarctic Base...

Reinforcements were pouring into Grieve's position even now, and the humans still hadn't secured the Navy base from its scant defenders, but that was just a small favor for the Earthers. They would have time to deploy unnoticed, but deploy *what*? Of the 95,000 Earther marines in the service, 40,000 were in ships or facilities that weren't close enough to aide. Five thousand more were reserve troops, and were stationed around major cities in case Bactule tried an unexpected feint. All told, the Earthers could field only 50,000 regulars in Antarctica.

By Earth standards, 50,000 was a vast count. From what Caine had learned about the humans, it was miniscule to them. The Crusaders believed in fielding at least a million troops at any given time, using that number to overwhelm anything that tried to stop them. That was apparently only theory though, because the Crusaders, like the Earthers, had never before fought a major ground battle.

In any case, Bactule had only 114,000 at his disposal.

Only?

That was virtually two-to-one odds against the Earthers, even with the help of the human allies. And since they were at the Antarctic Plain, full orbital strikes would be out of the question — they'd endanger the ice packs.

Despite that, he wanted a Naval liaison officer planetside. As unlikely as it seemed, the fleet might still play a role in the coming battle. Only a Naval officer on the ground could properly coordinate orbital reconnaissance, and perhaps even reinforcement drops as more ships sent the marine detachments to Earth's aide. Grieve had only a limited familiarity with such things — someone who commanded a squadron would better know how to judge such opportunities in battle.

Caine would have liked to go himself, but that was impossible. He had to stay with the fleet — if there was an unforeseen complication, he'd have to be there to counter it. No, he'd have to delegate the task to the much-overworked Commodore who knew how to handle herself on the ground.

Ursla felt she should have been frustrated by the request to go planetside, but she wasn't. She wanted to see this thing through to the end — the fight was far from over, and her duty was to be at the front.

And beneath that, she suspected, was an urge to see real combat. Face to face. Being to being. As it had been so long ago. They had prepared for so long, and there was a will to actually *perform* — to fight and to finally defeat the threat that had hung over their heads for centuries.

Admittedly, too, there was some connection with the hunting ways of their ancestors. The Earthers were no longer hunters, but something of that lineage still lay within them. A certain satisfaction flooded Ursla's instincts as she thought of facing Crusaders directly, and forcing them to capitulate. It was both a familiar and an alien desire.

The pinnace that departed from *Cerberus'* main bay was escorted by three others, each with their shields up and turret pulsars ready for any sneak attack.

The descent began easily, nothing that would cause discomfort to any passengers or the ship, and the pinnace swung lower and lower into the atmosphere. The Antarctic Plain was four minutes away from their drop area — they had come down over southern India, so they had to do a little flying before they could reach the continent and, more importantly, the base upon it.

Ursla watched in silence, the ocean below her rushing past at a blurring speed, the clouds swallowing up the escort only to free it again as they cruised on. Finally, far ahead, the glacial continent came into view. White ice cliffs rose from the sea, and white land suddenly appeared beneath the racing pinnace.

The small craft slowed drastically, dropping low to the ground to avoid any possible detection by enemy scans while it rose and fell over the jagged surface of the plain.

Ursla spotted the familiar mass of penguins off in the distance. They were moving on their bellies towards the coast, having been convinced by loud kodiaks that the base wouldn't be safe.

Ahead now was the sprawling Earther camp. From horizon to horizon, it seemed, the temporary shelters and defense perimeters appeared.

Forty-five thousand Earther marines were waiting in those shelters, their weapons being checked, double checked, and then charged.

Ursla was suddenly very confident of their victory. On paper, the numbers were against the Earther force, but numbers, contrary to many clichés, *did* lie. No number could make up for their resolve, skill and training. Sarah Manchester had been able to survive against Sergeant Major Lupus, one of the most skilled at sparring in the fleet. But Sarah, Ursla knew, was an *uncommon* type of human.

No, these Crusaders didn't know what was coming for them. They'd probably put up a blind struggle, and cause thousands of deaths before they succumbed.

The thought made Ursla shudder as the pinnace slowly began its final deceleration over the hastily-laid and harshly over-crowded landing platforms at the Earther temporary base.

"Damnit Sarah, you cannot go down *there!*" Pat snapped, stabbing a finger at the planet visible through the window.

Sarah was caught completely off guard by the harsh words. Pat had not taken her decision to join the Earth-side contingent well, though he'd given no visible indications of that a moment ago in the conference room when a handful of other Naval officers had been present.

At the end of the meeting, he'd come up to her quietly and asked to see her in her day cabin on *Harbinger Bishop's* flag deck. The door had hardly closed behind the pair when he'd exploded.

"I beg your pardon, ArcBrigadier?" the fact that *Pat* of all people was on the other end of the harsh words disconcerted her, so she decided to politely put him in his place before trying to–

"Don't try to pull rank, Sarah! You and I both bloody know that is *not* the place for the fleet CO to be!" he persisted as forcefully as before, and Sarah sighed and turned to look out the window.

"And that is your judgment then, is it Pat?"

His tone softened a bit, but remained firm enough to allay any suspicions that he'd been put down, "It is. I've been watching your back for days now. You've always been in the thick of the worst of it — the *Prophet* mutiny, that damned charge you tried to pull with *Saint Alistar*... it's like you're trying to get yourself killed! No way am I going to let you get into another fight like that!"

Sarah sighed. He had a point, and he wasn't afraid to tell her so.

"I'm going, Pat. But I promise I won't lead the charge or do anything crazy."

Patrick Conroy took a breath as if he was about to speak, then stopped himself. She was as determined to go as he was to stop her. For whatever reason, she wanted to be on the front line... *again.* Sarah seemed to enjoy being in harm's way.

"And what about our fleet? Hmm? They just sit here while the brain is off on parade?" he asked finally, his tone grim but far less forceful.

Sarah sighed heavily, her eyes sweeping from the planet above to the ships floating in mixed order around her.

"Only forty-three of ours left, Pat. The Earthers have over 100 in orbit. If there's trouble, I doubt our cruisers would have much of an impact, but if they're needed, Caine will take command of them. Make sure our ships are looked after."

Pat ground his teeth together and nodded slowly, "Fine. Just be careful down there."

He turned and left the room in a rush before she could say anything else. She watched the planet circle above her for a moment, then headed for the flight bay.

The pinnace carrying Sarah and two dropships cruised out of *Harbinger Bishop*'s bay. The dropships weren't the behemoth Colonizer models, but far smaller assault versions, each carrying 150 Naval marines. They swept into the atmosphere at high speed as Sarah clamped her fingers around the arms of her chair.

The entry into the atmosphere slammed into her ship like a wall, but the craft continued its hard acceleration. The ride on the two dropships was far rougher, as they crash-accelerated out ahead to get to the action sooner.

Not that a few minutes would likely matter in the clash to come.

They had managed to come down close to the Antarctic continent — Sarah had tried successfully to keep *Harbinger Bishop*'s orbit in check so that ships leaving could go straight 'down' to the plain.

The pinnace was over the ocean now, air-breathing turbines roaring to keep it in the sky, its swept-back wings had edged out to help with the handling. It cruised low, the dropships out ahead of it and gaining distance until the cliffs of the glacier appeared.

Above and to the flanks of Sarah's pinnace, more human and Earther dropships began to sweep in, arriving from the moon and dashing madly to reinforce Grieve's position.

Sarah leaned back in her chair, took as deep a breath as she could, and waited.

Grieve stood next to — and a bit below — Ursla as the human reinforcement ships, a few Earthers mixed in with them, came roaring up to the temporary base. Their air turbines made them thunderous compared to the quieter Earther boosters, but the noise was still ignored by the two Earthers as they examined the situation.

Besides, the din, which had persisted for almost half an hour, meant 25,000 more troops were arriving.

"Well, that'll be just about all of the reinforcements we're going to get for a while," the General said after a moment.

Ursla nodded silently, watching as the ramps descended from the dropships and Naval marines scrambled down. They lacked the finesse of the Earther troops in deployment, but they still carried themselves like the professional infantry they were.

Immediately, human ranks began to form — companies and platoons linking up with their units, waiting for orders.

Several dozen Earthers rushed to them, finding officers and showing them where to bring their troops. A whole section of the base had been reserved for the Allied marines, and they headed towards it swiftly.

Grieve turned briefly to Ursla, "I'll send a squad to find their CO. We'll meet and plan our attack."

Pat suddenly had a new respect for every marine. The dropship ride — one he wasn't actually supposed to be on — had nearly killed him. Lots of turbulence, way too many gees pulled, and a lot of noise.

He pulled his jacket collar up higher around his neck, the chill of the icy Antarctic wind bouncing off his coat. His rifle was slung uncomfortably over his shoulder.

Knees still a little weak, he started to check for *Harbinger Bishop*'s pinnace. He hadn't expected such a big landing area! All he could see around him were marines.

He began a trek in a random direction, hoping to find something, but just found more marines. Disembarking 25,000 men and women was a big affair, but it was a lot more harrowing when one was lost in the middle.

"Sir?" a voice called from behind him, and he turned to see a squad of Earther marines, all canines, looking at him.

He turned in their direction, noting the hover truck parked behind them. It hadn't been there a second before.

"Ahh, glad to see you!" Pat said as he approached the Sergeant leading the squad.

The wolf looked familiar...

"Sergeant Major Lupus, isn't it?" Pat came to a stop, and the Earther nodded with a smile.

"Straight from *Cerberus*, ArcBrigadier. I'm out here to collect officers for a briefing, but you're the only one I've found."

Pat smiled, "Well, ArcGeneral Manchester's down here somewhere, let's go find her!"

CHAPTER 33

"I don't know, Shappa. They gave this base up so easily..."

Bactule ignored the concerned words of the Shaspa. This victory had been *decisive* and proved beyond doubt that Crusaders were the superior warriors on the planet.

He did not dispute that the Earthers had struggled well, but the fact was they'd lost. The Antarctic Base belonged to the Crusaders and now the only question was what to do with it.

The Earthers controlled air and space beyond the base, but this area was completely isolated from every Earther population. Bactule would have to search through the base file system to determine Earth's weaknesses while his Crusaders fortified this position.

So he would hear no doomsayers now. The Gods were with them. Prophecy's penultimate moment was almost at hand. The Gods willed its fruition.

Bactule shut out the triumphant thoughts that threatened to fill his mind and looked over the base. He was standing in the central building — high above the ice — from which he could see the whole area.

To the arbitrary south, east, and west was open plain. To the north, where the buildings were built, a ridge that reached up to be level with the top of their roofs ran east to west. The compound extended to that ridge, and at its base the Earther bunkers were located.

The vast landing fields had hastily been covered with troop shelters and tents, while the 100-odd dropships that had come down lay at intervals around the new perimeter.

Bactule reflected silently on the situation. The Earther base was open to attack on all sides but the north. Fortifying properly would take days, but for now he could use the dropships as mini-forts threaded around the perimeter. Supplemented by portable breastworks, they could provide enough cover for an emergency defense. Their heavy mass driver turrets would add to the fire of his Crusaders as well, while maintaining air cover around the base at the same time.

Half his Crusaders were scrambling, laying down lines of breastworks with petons, digging pits for the light field guns they'd brought, and setting up unit positions. The rest of the Holy warriors were either sweeping the underground complex that was carved into the glacier or organizing the surface camp.

The Earthers *had* done a remarkable job with the base, digging an underground complex with kilometers of tunnel and five separate levels stretching far down into the ice.

Eventually it would make a good position from which to move, somewhere virtually impenetrable by any means Bactule could think of.

"Send out scouting platoons in all directions. Post a company up on the ridge-line as picket. Gamma and Omega Legions may stand down, the rest must stay at active status. The Earthers will not likely be able to respond quickly, but when they come we must be ready."

Sarah watched the Earther truck approach with a sigh of relief. She had never experienced a marine drop of such magnitude, and she'd found herself swept up in it with little understanding of where she should be.

The landing fields, titanium sheets laid over the ice and anchored down, were awash with Naval marines and Earthers, and she couldn't see any sign of a headquarters.

But the truck was coming, and it looked as though it was angling directly for her. She watched curiously, wondering how its performance would compare to a human-model hovercraft.

Tinted windows, a long, open back, and a glow of energy beneath the chassis, it would probably run circles around anything humans could have built on Genesis.

The truck came to a stop a few meters in front of Sarah, and she stepped briskly toward it, a cold gust of wind causing her to pull her collar up tightly around her neck. The jacket deflected a good deal of the sharp breeze, but she still felt a chill.

A Sergeant Major who looked quite familiar hopped from the truck.

"ArcGeneral!" he came towards her, then turned to match her stride, as she continued towards the vehicle.

"Sergeant Lupus, isn't it? Glad to see you," she replied with a smile.

"We've got orders to bring you to HQ. The General is looking to brief all the officers at once. We've only been able to find one other, I suppose the rest are finding their own way," Lupus explained as he led Sarah to the truck.

"Yes," Sarah nodded, "the marine officers would head immediately for headquarters... I thought I was the only displaced soul in this mess."

Lupus directed Sarah to the back door of the truck as he leapt up onto the open back, "No ma'am, the ArcBrigadier was lost too."

ArcBrigadier?

Sarah swung open the door to the truck and climbed in, slamming it after her.

"Glad we found you, Sarah," Pat said from the other side of the back seat, absently blowing on his hands to warm them up.

Sarah was too surprised to speak. Her mouth opened and started to move as if it were speaking, but no sound came out.

Pat looked at her with a grin.

"Ah, Sarah dear. You never did order me *not* to come down. I hitched a ride with the marines," Pat explained in a low tone, and Sarah shut her mouth.

She had been so wrapped up in not letting him win the argument that she *had* neglected to order him to stay in space...

"You know I meant to keep you up there! What if there's an emergency?" she finally replied, and Pat grinned devilishly.

"You said so yourself, if there's trouble, Caine can handle it. Never leave an Irishman — such as myself — a loophole, eh Sarah?"

Sarah tried not to smile at the comment as the truck turned and floated towards the base headquarters.

The medium-sized, pre-fab dome headquarters was far more spartan than Antarctic Base's strategic ops center. And, Ursla noted, the ceiling was lower.

She sat in a chair at the large battle plot in the room's center, looking over a computer-generated composite of the area. The real-time movements of the Crusaders, detected by orbiting Earther sloops, were revealed on the map.

It seemed as though Shappa Bactule — assuming he was the one in charge of the base — was making all the 'right' moves.

Grieve sat next to the Commodore, his conclusion basically the same. The Shappa, frustrating though he was, knew how to field an army... at least, he wasn't an *idiot* about it.

Andros Grieve had worked for a long time in his profession — over 100 years — and though his army had never actually had to face an enemy, he knew they were far more capable than the humans.

Grieve had spent decades perfecting his abilities as a strategist — seventy years in which he had learned attacks, counterattacks, and how to read his troops. No human to date could boast that advantage as they simply didn't live long enough.

A Crusader company on the ridge. That was the only picket to the north. A hundred troops, out in the cold with no windbreaks. They'd be uncomfortable, digging foxholes in the snow, and trying more to keep warm than to keep eyes open for the enemy.

A platoon of his best canines and felines could silence those Crusaders without allowing a single alarm to reach the base, and then he could hold the ridge... but below were the bunkers.

Ursla was already deciding that those bunkers were a different sort of challenge — a nearly impregnable one. Designed to protect the base personnel against any kind of blast, including orbital strikes, they were sturdily armored and even floated in case some sort of high-temperature weapon melted the ice.

Overwhelming them wasn't an option — only flanking maneuvers might work.

The entrances to those bunkers were south-facing. If there was a large-scale attack on the south side, it might catch the Crusaders from the wrong flank and give a move from the north... wait, *north*?

Ursla cleared her throat, "Um, Andros. Just looking at the map here... we're so close to the south pole — are you sure that every direction isn't north?"

Grieve looked up and blinked twice thoughtfully, "I just follow the big red 'north' arrow. You Navy types ask too many questions."

With an amused smile Ursla shrugged and went back to pondering.

"Sir, ma'am, the Allied officers are all here now for the briefing," a Lieutenant announced from the far side of the room, drawing both Ursla and Grieve back to the present.

"Show them in," Grieve responded slowly, and the feline nodded and turned outside where she gestured for the humans to enter the command center.

Sarah entered first, walking silently to the map table and sitting opposite Ursla with Pat on her right side. Ursla hid her surprise at their presence.

Commandant Falkner, Gillian Hodge, and two other marine officers followed, filling up the rest of the seats around the map. All eyes turned to Grieve for the beginning of the briefing.

"We don't have a lot of time here. We have to hit the Crusaders before they can dig in, or the casualties on our side will be far too great. Right now I think a two-pronged attack would be in order, but I am *very* open to advice. Commandant Falkner?"

The dark-skinned human eyed the map intently for a moment, checking the deployments and formulating his response. Finally, he spoke, "I think our best course of action would be to split our force and make a two-pronged attack, like you said General. We could use one larger part of our force to attack the lines they're throwing up, the smaller section should take the ridge and pour fire down into them. When the bunkers get flanked the whole force can sweep in and pin them."

Grieve was nodding as Falkner spoke. It was exactly what he would have done, "I agree Commandant. This is our best way to take the base, so the only question that remains is who does what."

There was silence around the table for a moment, then Falkner picked up again, "The casualties with those attacking the camp from the ground will be high — an open approach like that..."

Grieve continued to nod, eyeing the open, flat, coverless plains. He pondered the map for a few seconds, then looked around the table.

"I'll lead my 50,000 Earthers against their lines. Commandant Falkner, I think your troops should serve on the ridge — you'll have a good deal more cover up there."

Falkner ground his teeth, "Are you sure? You'll take casualties..."

Grieve raised a large hand, "We've got a few tools that will minimize casualties, but I haven't had time to brief you on them yet. Besides, the enemy is familiar with your troops, so they will know what to expect from you. I'm counting on the difference between Earthers and Crusaders to help throw them off their game. I have to make sure you can take that ridge successfully — do you need any help with the pickets?"

Falkner shook his head, then spoke, "We've got it covered. They won't get a chance to make a sound." It was a simple, *practical* statement, and Grieve appreciated that. Sarah stirred in her chair as she listened and Pat leaned back uncomfortably. The ground was hardly as detached as space when it came to fighting...

"I'd like to make a request of you, General Grieve," Sarah said without thinking. "I'd like to accompany the Earther troops — I'd appreciate the opportunity to see you in action."

Grieve was surprised by the request, and he exchanged a quick glance with Ursla. Positive instincts confirmed her request, so he nodded. Of course, that gave the Commodore an opportunity to mirror the gesture...

"Commandant Falkner, mind if I join your force for this action?" Ursla asked immediately, and the human looked the bear over once before nodding.

"Just keep your head *down*."

CHAPTER 34

They didn't deploy as quickly as Earther troops, but the human Naval marines were still quite professional. They moved in loose tactical columns, weapons at the ready, spread out in case of land mines, automatic weapons, explosives, or satellite strikes.

Far out ahead, a unit of 'Commando' marines was taking care of the Crusaders on the hill, and even to Ursla's keen ears they were doing their job silently. She walked with Commandant Falkner, carrying an Earther rifle in hand and three shields on her belt. Compared to the small humans, she looked like some sort of giant.

"So we'll take the ridge and wait for General Grieve's signal," Ursla was confirming, and the Commandant nodded.

"I'm confident it'll all work out, Commodore. The General and I are very much alike. Two warriors who know what needs doing and how to do it. And I have every confidence in our integrated force," Falkner replied, rifle held close and aimed down.

Ursla nodded in understanding. Despite the glaring physical differences, these humans still struck her as Earther-like in many ways. Omega could probably be credited for that — it was designed mainly to attack the human brain so it rebuilt Earthers to have similar mental pathways to humans in order to feed off them. Though the series of chemicals or patterns — whatever it was — that caused the human compunction for distrust and deceit seemed to have been left out.

In any case, the humans were working with the Earthers on this mission, and that felt right to Ursla.

They'd been marching for almost an hour now, and had only half an hour to go before Grieve would move the Earthers out. The timing would be close, but Falkner seemed confident that his 25,000 would be on the ridge long before Grieve arrived.

"First, Third, Ninth, and Twelfth Divisions! Shoulder arms!" Grieve delivered his orders with a surprisingly understated tone. His headset carried the words to his marines. "At the double quick! *Advance!*"

It was quite a spectacle.

Sarah had never seen so many troops execute a drill as perfectly as these ones did. The 40,000 Earthers formed a line 10,000 long and four deep, then set off at a blindingly quick march. She stood speechless, Pat equally silent at her shoulder, and watched them move rapidly away.

Grieve turned back to the two humans who'd joined his command, now standing virtually alone on the cold Antarctic Plain.

"You trained to fight like this?" Pat asked quietly.

The General smiled — it was a pertinent question. Had the Earthers borrowed their infantry methods from the same history as their Naval methods? If they did advance in line and fire by order only, machine guns would slice them apart — size and discipline would be irrelevant.

Grieve's smile prompted a cocked eyebrow from Sarah, "Well, General?"

Grieve shook his head, "This? No, *this* we usually save for the parade ground. Right now I'm using it for the intimidation factor. I understand that a company coming to attention aboard *Orion* was enough to disconcert the High Chancellor's guard, so I'm hoping this display can cause some of the Crusaders we're facing to lose their resolve."

"But the casualties..." Sarah's voice drifted off as she watched the Earthers march away.

"You know the belt packs we gave you?" Grieve gestured to a belt he was wearing.

Sarah and Pat nodded. The thick belts with little consoles on the clips had seemed awkward to the two humans, but they'd strapped them on anyway. Pat's fit neatly, his wide frame supporting the same kind of size that a canine's might. Sarah's belt, even though it was the smallest size, was loose and had slid down from her waist to rest on her hips.

"These are personal force field generators," Grieve continued as he reached down and keyed his clip.

A blue shimmer of light surrounded the General for a second, then vanished. Sarah and Pat watched with surprise, and then the General picked up a piece of ice from beneath his feet and pitched it high into the air. The ice came straight down toward his head, then hit a suddenly-present shimmering blue field and bounced away harmlessly.

"It'll stop just about everything — bullets and energy bursts. Its power isn't infinite — it drops slightly with every hit — but it will protect us for long enough. When we read on the monitor systems that someone is down to twenty percent strength, we'll halt and dig in," Grieve explained.

Sarah was only half listening as she hunched over to look down at her own belt. She didn't even bother to ask how the digging in would be done.

"I have to get up with the troops," Grieve added. "I realize our marching might be a bit much for you, so the truck and squad you were with before is waiting to bring you up. They're just back there," Grieve pointed across the open plain to where the vehicle sat, eight troops including Lupus standing at ease around it. "I'm off. See you at the front."

With that, the two and a half meter tall bear turned and jogged after his troops. Sarah and Pat took a second to collect their thoughts and then walked towards the truck.

Ursla kept low, her well-toned muscles holding her torso barely a centimeter from the icy ridge as she seemed to hover along. She found a nice crater and stopped, unslinging her rifle from over her shoulder. She made an effort to ignore the seemingly loud — but humanly silent — sounds of Naval marines hauling away the dead men only recently of the Crusader picket. These 'Commandos' knew their business.

Falkner had kept pace with the Commodore, initially worrying she might attract unwanted attention, but then realizing she was far less likely to than *he* was — the Earthers had instincts and skills that no human could quite comprehend. Now, the duo peered over the edge of the crater down towards the five large bunkers. The activity in the base reminded Ursla of an ant hill, but it was clear the Crusader defenses were very, very rudimentary.

The mass drivers on those dropships *would* cause problems to personal shields — they were ship-to-ship type weapons after all. Grieve would have to be careful.

The Naval marines began lining the long ridge, eight or ten deep all the way along, waiting for the men in the bunkers to get distracted before trying to break down the slope. It wouldn't be easy...

And then Ursla saw the trench line. It wasn't very deep — it looked as if it was a series of crevices and blast craters and nothing more — but at least 100 Crusaders were moving around within it.

So Bactule had decided to add more guards to the ridge. Logical, but most annoying. Ursla turned her attention from the ragged Crusaders sitting half way down the ridge to the bunkers, wondering how much supporting fire would come from them.

They were empty.

That is, the firing ports were vacant, and in the dim light within Ursla could not make out the shapes of moving Crusaders. Perhaps Bactule thought there would be ample warning to get his troops into those bunkers, so he'd sent them in to rest.

"Looks like they've thrown out a picket and sent the bunker troops to rest. He probably thinks they'll get plenty of warning from the ridge. We can rush them if we hit before the Earthers show up — as soon as they do the guards will come to alert," Falkner said.

Ursla nodded, "We'd have to take both the bunkers and the picket line at the same time. If you can get those Commandos of yours down to the bunkers, we could take them without the picket noticing..."

Falkner looked down the ridge at the Earther bunkers, "We'll need a diversion to cover the Commandos as they go down — something that'll get the pickets' attention... but nothing apparently dangerous enough to get them to mobilize a large force..."

Ursla's ear twitched as a thought popped into her head. How many shield belts did Grieve give her? Three... hmm... it would be a bloody fight but she could take a good number of the Crusaders in that trench line before she would have to pull out...

"How about one insane Earther attacking their trench? I'm in a Navy uniform so they'd probably figure I was out on a walk when they took the base."

Falkner looked at the kodiak with a deep frown, "You'd be killed! And why would you be carrying a rifle on a walk?"

"To protect myself from the local wildlife of course. I can take care of myself Commandant. If we get those bunkers then it's worth the risk," Ursla spoke in a low voice, then she tapped one of her shield belts. "And I'll be fine. Trust me."

Falkner grudgingly conceded, "I'll get a company into the dead Crusaders' uniforms. They can fire in your direction so the Churchers think you managed to get past the picket up here. It'll add to the authenticity, I think. Our Commandos can go around the side."

Ursla nodded silently, drawing her rifle to her, "Get the troops ready then, Commandant."

The first patrols sent out by the Crusaders walked into a wall of Earthers four deep, fronted by a line of bears at least two and a half meters high. They didn't even try to fire as the front rank of the Earther line was ordered to stop them.

The whole front line leveled its guns, those marines with shots taking them. The patrols did not get back to base. Their comatose bodies collapsed to the ice, guaranteed to remain out of action for at least a day, probably longer.

Grieve had foreseen this and had ordered Second 'Heavy' Division — the only force that wasn't marching with the Napoleonic version of his army — to pick up those Crusaders and care for them.

Though its vaunted Guards Brigade would participate in the attack, most of the Second Division would set up a provisional base wherever the Earthers finally dug in, and provide the ultimate reserve if things went wrong.

Grieve walked on, a few steps ahead of the fast moving Earther line, wondering where Ursla was.

"We're ready Commodore. Are you still certain you want to do this?" Falkner gave her a last chance to give up on her mad dash, but she turned it down.

"I'll go. Now who is it I'm supposed to disable before I get down the ridge?" she asked quietly.

The plan had gotten a bit complex. The company selected to impersonate Crusaders would line the ridge and keep firing at her, but a platoon — a *whole* platoon — had been set aside to play victims to mad Ursla's charge. They would try to catch her, and she would *deal* with them. Some would get 'shot', others she would carefully put down by hand. Between them, these imposters would attempt to lull the Crusaders into feeling secure, allowing Ursla to distract them without having them raise the alarm. The Naval 'casualties' would be collected after the skirmish.

A platoon now wearing overcoats and carrying rifles taken from the dead Crusaders stepped forward from the company. The original owners lay coatless in the snow.

"Alright, I'll need a couple of you to look like you're putting up a serious fight — not too much, because I wouldn't want to have to really hurt you," Ursla instructed uneasily. "But be convincing."

There were a few nods from the sixteen troops, and Ursla forced a smile that she hoped was reassuring.

"Alright, let's go then."

CHAPTER 35

Ursla erupted over the crest of the ridge and released a mighty roar that gained everyone's attention. The Crusaders in the bunkers stood, weaponless, to watch the lone berserker try to reach them while the Commandos — invisible because of their camouflage — slipped down the slope on the flanks.

The massive kodiak began to sprint, and a loose company of humans appeared on the ridgeline, firing at the bear. Crusaders watched in terrified awe as the great creature continually outmaneuvered the bullets, and as the squad descended the slope she turned hastily to face it.

It was quite a convincing show.

Her rifle hummed twice, and two Crusaders dropped, collapsing into the snow. The other squad members tried to stop and fire at the lumbering mammal but the beast was already upon them.

From the base of the ridge Church soldiers watched in shock as the bear's arms blurred, legs snapped around, and war cries erupted. The six other squad members went down, and then another squad took up position half way between the Earther and the rest of the company. The three-meter tall officer was faster. Four were shot as they got into good firing positions; the rest fell victim to the Earther's rifle after only seconds.

Ignoring the enemy behind her, the berserker turned and roared down the ridge slope towards the trench line. Crusaders, who had been gaping open mouthed at the spectacle, were suddenly struggling to raise their big auto-rifles.

Coming down the slope hard, Ursla heard the thick shells from the disguised Naval marines slamming into the snow behind her and was suddenly very thankful that none had hit her force field. She wanted all three of her charges full when she hit that trench.

The first shots from the trench were wide, missing by meters, but soon proper marksmen came up to look for the target. They wouldn't miss, no matter how fast the Earther was running.

The first of these swung his rifle up after carefully checking his scope. For a millisecond he didn't realize how close Ursla was, and then a foot came down to smash his rifle and an energy burst put him into a coma.

Ursla jumped down into the central position on the trench line and her rifle hummed out a stream of energy that struck down more than a dozen. The members of the other two Crusader platoons, however, turned and fired.

The first shield went down to four percent with the barrage, but Ursla was already activating the second and charging. It would get very bloody from here, as the closer range demanded hand-to-hand combat. The first field died but the second picked up where it left off, and every Crusader in the trench stopped in shock. Thirty men had poured fire into that beast and it wasn't even fazed!

Ursla swept into them, turning on her bayonet, an energy lance half a meter long that jutted out the front end of her heavy rifle. She tried to make sure her hits were incapacitating and not fatal, but in such close quarters nothing could be certain.

The Crusaders had bayonets fixed to their rifles but, despite the longer length of their weapons, they had a disadvantage in height and reach.

As red cloaks began swirling around the roaring Commodore, the first Commandos slid to silent stops at the sides of the bunkers, and waited.

Ursla's second shield barely lost any power over the next few minutes. The Crusaders abandoned their firing spots and poured towards the mighty warrior as she fought in the central dugout, and unconscious bodies piled up around her. She erupted into a clearing every half minute, and when she left a dugout it would be laden with injured Crusaders.

The Church soldiers were too shocked to coordinate and mass their fire. The officers were unconscious in the central dugout, and Ursla preempted any actions the soldiers tried to take.

Reinforcements began to spill from the bunkers. They were far down the slope and, despite their better organization, it would take them a few minutes to get into effective range against Ursla.

As the bunkers emptied, Commandos began slipping in, silently killing any who remained. Behind Ursla, the 'Crusader' company rippled down the hill to help in the fight, and some of the Crusaders who had survived the trench action tried to run to relative safety with them. If Ursla did not stop those who tried — mysterious shots from above did.

Finally, with over fifty of their comrades incapacitated, the Crusader picket dropped back down the slope to regroup with the bunker-based reinforcements. They'd leave the berserker to the company from atop the slope that had let it get through in the first place.

But as that company swept into the trenches it didn't throw itself at the Earther. In fact, the Earther turned away from it and started a slow, methodical volume of fire which cut down nearly a dozen of the Crusaders now climbing the ridge. As soon as the disguised Naval company could get cover, it joined in the barrage. The crimson coats were shed, and the deception was clear to the vulnerable Crusaders ascending the slope.

Fire poured after them as they tried to turn and run back to the bunkers, and the cacophony summoned the rest of Falkner's 25,000 over the crest and into a run down the hill. Crusaders tried to get back to their bunkers but realized with terror that somehow they'd been flanked.

Legs were cut out from under the running Church soldiers, the Earther-built energy guns mounted along the firing steps inside the bunkers sending them into comas. The Commandos in the fortifications had barricaded the south-facing doors and were laying down heavy cover fire.

Ursla led the company of 'Crusaders' down the slope now, and the company commander, *Harbinger Bishop's* Gillian Hodge, started splitting up her troops between the bunkers. As her marines rushed to deploy, she found herself next to the Commodore.

After the intensity of the battle, Ursla's uniform should have been soaked in her victims' blood. Some were undoubtedly dead after that fight — human medics would have to give her the count later. But the shield had stopped the blood from reaching her uniform, so it was clean and only a little disheveled.

Captain Hodge was surprised by the sight. She'd seen the Crusaders on *Bishop* crack under fire a few days before, but today's display had proven the Holy warriors even less formidable than she'd thought. One Earther, admittedly a large one with impeccable fighting skills, had stopped a company in its tracks and had taken out fifty Crusaders, two thirds of them hand-to-hand.

Hodge saluted the Commodore, and Ursla absently bobbed her head in reply, "How did we do, Captain?"

"No fatalities ma'am. It looks like about 100 Crusaders are dead, 300 or so injured or comatose..."

Commandant Falkner, slightly out of breath from his rapid descent, stopped next to the two officers, the rest of his force now sweeping in to join the bunker garrisons through the north-facing firing ports. He would put a regiment in each of those massive bunkers — 1,000 each instead of the hundred or so the Crusaders had deployed. The bunkers were certainly big enough.

Right now though, Falkner was in shock at what he'd just witnessed.

"Commodore," he stammered as Captain Hodge stepped back, "that was... *amazing.*"

Ursla was very much aware of what she'd just done, and she shook her head, "Not amazing. Unfortunate. And necessary."

There was silence as both the Captain and Commandant processed what the Commodore had done, and how much she'd disliked it. Ursla may have felt a certain satisfaction in facing her foe personally, but she had no hunger for death. A good trait.

"We're deploying our breastworks between the bunkers now," Falkner said finally. "I've got 5,000 marines still up on the ridge. They'll be able to cut off any flank attacks and keep anybody in those buildings from getting gutsy. We can't hold against a real hit from the Crusaders, but we've got them reeling. When the Earthers arrive they'll find a seriously weakened..."

Naval marines had stopped all around the trio and were watching the eastward horizon. Ursla, with a naturally better vantage point thanks to her height, turned to see what was happening.

So the timing *had* been perfect.

A bullet bounced off Ursla's shield as she watched, a sniper on the roof of one of the buildings being cut down by a counterpart as soon as the shot was fired. Ursla ignored both as she watched the Earther marine divisions march into view. It was a positively chilling sight.

Crusaders who had been shocked and terrified by the spectacle on the north side of the base were nearly driven mad by the arrival. They let weapons drop and stood frozen. For a minute no one spoke or moved — the base was silent except for the loud, even rhythm of the Earther march.

Finally, the Church soldiers got their wits about them enough to sound the alarm, but unthinking Crusaders spilled out into the line of fire of the human marines who did not hesitate to target them.

This play at psychological warfare had paid off.

The whole Earther army could have been fifty ranks deep from what Ursla could see, and it looked as though it was made up of thousands of bears. Considering the demonstration she'd just given, the numbers alone had to be terrifying. And they came in tight order too, not as a horde of beasts but as a disciplined line that marched to the beat of a nonexistent drum.

The Crusaders saw *hell* marching towards them and some turned to run. The first dozen to try were shot by their officers, so the rest ground their teeth together and got to the eastern ramparts. Some began talking about how effective their machine guns would be against such tightly packed lines, and how the mass drivers would be murderous.

Ursla watched as the Naval marines finished their deployment, a Crusader line of portable breastworks being hastily thrown up opposite them. A heavy barrage erupted, trying to hold the Crusaders in check, but the desperate Church position solidified in front of Ursla nonetheless. The higher pitched cracks of Naval rifles were clearly audible, but the lower thud of the Crusader guns was non-existent. They were saving every shot they had...

"When Grieve attacks the east front we have to be attacking from the north," Ursla said, professional indifference forcing her to forget, at least for the time being, bloody melee and death.

"We'll be ready. That line the poor bastards are throwing up will fold pretty quickly. We won't have a problem punching through it and getting around their flank. We'll pin them and wipe them out," Falkner agreed.

Ursla silently looked over the Crusader lines and raised an eyebrow, "If they get to retreat 300 meters they'll all be able to dive underground. It'd cost dearly to dig them out. We'll have to get to that place and hold it."

Falkner looked towards the area to which Ursla was referring — a group of low bunker-like entrances to the underground complex. All of the buildings had connections to the underground as well, but they would be a lot harder to get to for running infantry.

Beyond the base, the Earthers kept a steady pace, the front rank with weapons leveled in perfect precision. A call came from a bear out front — Grieve, no doubt. There was a sudden flash of light from the leading rank as their bayonets were run out, and without a pause in the march they pressed on.

CHAPTER 36

Sarah hopped hurriedly from the hover truck and watched the Earther line advance half a kilometer ahead of her. They were getting right into the range of the base's guns, but there was no sign that the Earthers were slowing to exchange fire.

Pat stepped down next to her and whistled his awe at the sight, "Gods wept! They're still marching in that bloody line!"

Sarah nodded, cautiously hefting the big rifle Lupus had supplied. Like her belt, it was too large for her, despite it being the smallest Earther model. Pat's was a perfect fit, but there were very few healthy Earthers with a body type similar to Sarah's.

Lupus and his squad of seven had formed with the two humans, and they too were watching the line advance. Around them, Second Division was setting up a camp and deploying reserve regiments to buffer any counterattack. The commotion was growing.

"I'd like to get up to that line, Sergeant," Sarah said softly with a short glance back to Lupus.

The wolf nodded, "Well, we either go on foot or pile back into the truck. They've got a kilometer to go now, so we could fall behind quite a bit."

It was true that humans seemed to lack the legs and the stamina for the Earther pace, but somehow the thought of arriving at the Earther lines in a truck didn't appeal to Sarah.

"I think Pat and I can handle a bit of a jog," she said finally, and Lupus nodded.

Pat didn't even get a chance to open his mouth in objection — the small unit began to move out after the advance line of Earthers at a very brisk pace.

Grieve let the line advance past him and then paced behind it with the officer monitoring shields. Colonel Lion, the one charged with that duty, held his portable panel and watched it religiously. It told him the current lowest and highest shield power status among the troops.

The Earthers had transmitters built into their belts for just this purpose. Usually, the belts would transmit to the local Sergeant allowing him to pull back those with the weakest shields, but in this massive line all the data was flowing back to Lion.

"As soon as the lowest gets down to twenty percent I want the order given. We're not going to lose anyone to these Crusaders yet," Grieve explained coolly as they advanced, and the Colonel nodded.

The line moved on, and Grieve shifted ahead again, going through to take his place at the front. The base was plainly visible now, as were the scrambling Crusaders. And he could hear many gunshots.

Turning his eyes to the ridge, he realized it was vacant of crimson. In the open space on the ridge and up to the bunkers he could see the dark shapes of the Naval marines — Ursla must have had an opportunity to storm the bunkers. That opened up the north and put the Crusaders in a crossfire.

The defenders began their rifle fire, but their mass drivers and small artillery pieces remained silent. Probably waiting for a more optimum firing range, Grieve reflected, but all things considered, they'd be far wiser if they opened fire immediately. His luck might hold out a little while longer.

"Skirmishers! Forward!" Grieve ordered into his headest microphone, the words carrying down the line through the marines' ear pieces.

The 'skirmishers' rushed out ahead of the divisions — a group from the front line which weren't actually skirmishers in the old sense of the word. In point of fact, they were engineers. Grieve was counting on their appearance itself to distract Bactule — make him underestimate them.

They moved ahead now, almost a thousand along the entire line, rifle fire sweeping at them. They were drawing fire away from the main line which was still moving steadily, and Grieve heard the loud report of a field gun. A geyser of ice showered up near some of the skirmishers but they were moving far too quickly to be touched.

Mass drivers started to spit at them — the Crusaders might have mistaken the line of engineers for a full-fledged charge. The fire from the big guns was blatantly missing, the fast moving bears evading it without difficulty. Rifle shots, on the other hand, were starting to tell.

"Two shields down to fifty percent," Colonel Lion said quietly, the words carrying to Grieve's ear piece.

The line continued forward, the skirmishers now within 500 meters of the base.

"Thirty percent," Lion chimed.

The fire roared louder as the skirmishers got closer and closer, and the shields began to drain faster.

"Twenty!" Lion called, and Grieve was already roaring.

"*Now!*"

The skirmishers, who had managed to hold a ragged line throughout their charge, dropped to the ground as the orders reached their ear pieces. Their primary shields were draining fast, but they were carrying secondaries instead of extra charges for their guns. They reached back to their packs now, pulling out silver box-like devices half a meter long and thirty centimeters thick. These devices were propped upright like the human portable breastworks but instead of serving as deflection shields, they began to hum.

Crusader artillery and mass drivers saw the evenly spaced line of small walls go up and immediately turned on the new targets. The first to fire was near one of the boxes... but the shot never reached its target.

An energy wall had spread up and to the sides of each device, angling back towards the Earther line and forming a barrier across the eastern face of the base. Shots struck the shield inconsequentially, as the fields from each generator linked together and interlaced.

This was the Earther version of digging in. The long, sloping force field was virtually impenetrable except by ship-mounted cannon, leaving it more than a match for the mass drivers on the human dropships.

The large Earther line broke ranks immediately, platoons and companies moving as single clouds, abandoning the parade ground nonsense. They moved fast and hard to reach the shelter of the line before the artillery started lobbing shells over its slope and onto them.

The Crusaders suddenly realized their mistake, but there was nothing they could do about it. The enemy had managed to secure a line 350 meters from their outer ramparts.

Sarah had slowed in surprise as the yellow-blue curtain of energy raised and angled back like a roof towards the line she was chasing. It looked as though the Earthers had raised a shield the size of a Superdreadnought's to protect their troops, and now it was deflecting Crusader fire.

She sped up again, watching as the orderly Earthers suddenly split apart, their small units rushing to the shelter. Shells would be on their way over that shield soon, and the squad she was with was right out in the open.

"Come on!" Lupus growled, lifting his feet to a steady run. The Earther squad followed effortlessly, gliding across the ice without difficulty.

Sarah and Pat moved as fast as they could, not with the swift movements of the Earthers but with a laboring gait hampered by their rifles. The line was only a few hundred meters away. Pat, already out of breath, began to gasp audibly.

A shell rose over the shield and exploded a dozen meters to the right, another fifty meters to the left. Lupus was slowing his squad to keep them in time with their charges, but Sarah barked at him not to wait. He refused at first, but she roared in a voice almost befitting an Earther and he nodded silently.

The squad sprinted ahead, leaving the two officers behind.

"Bloody damned Crusaders!" Pat rasped between pants. "I won't give them the satisfaction to see me run!"

He slowed his pace, breathing heavily but walking tall.

Sarah stopped and turned to look at him, "Are you insane?"

"Just walk, Sarah! Set a good example... let me bloody catch my breath..." he replied, and she decided it would be a waste of time to order him.

The pair walked evenly across the last stretch, the line looming closer with every step. Crusader gunners were filling the air with shells, and they seemed to be getting closer...

A shell slammed into the plain just a meter in front of Pat, exploding as it drove down under the ice. The explosion viciously hurled the pair forward and showered them in ice shards.

They came down hard, their shields absorbing a good deal of the trauma, and saving them from the falling blades of ice that would have killed them. Sarah's shield dropped to barely three percent in the spill, but she hardly noticed.

She couldn't say she'd ever stood a meter above an exploding artillery shell before — it was a strange sensation. The remarkable part was that she was unscathed. The shield she'd turned on during their jog had literally saved her life.

She stood shakily, picked up her rifle from where it had skittered across the ice, and turned to look for Pat.

"Bloody damned hellish sons of bloody damned bastards!" he was by no means subtle as he kicked himself out from under a small hill of ice.

She hurried over to him, slinging her big rifle over her shoulder, "You alright, Pat?"

The Irishman struggled to his feet with a wince of pain, "I had a bloody shell explode under me, what do you think?"

His right leg was bloodstained — his shield had run out of power after the pounding, allowing an ice dagger to cut into him. Sarah gave the big man the aide of a shoulder and the pair hobbled into the shelter of the tall energy curtain.

"Next time we run, Pat," Sarah said with an ironic smile.

"I spend my days commanding from a comfortable bloody chair. Be damned if I'm seen running anywhere!" Pat's loud comment drew some glances from the nearby Earther marines. Pat grinned at them all.

Lupus and his squad were already forming around them, and then the pair hobbled to an Earther with a red cross on his pack.

Grieve was proud of his troops — they'd deployed with the same precision they'd rehearsed so many times before. Of course, their strong defense would do little good when they had to make the assault.

The Earthers had to cross 350 meters of open plain before they hit the first ramparts. They'd have to get over those breastworks and then face the reserve lines with thousands of Crusaders beyond. He'd have to order all the troops to add their second shield to their belts — a measure that would likely restrict their movement.

They'd have to attack in a rush — not stoically marching to a drum with neat ranks this time. Covering fire and fast troops slamming into the enemy. Platoons were being detailed to targets now, the one-way force field letting their energy rifles spray the Crusader lines with vicious fire. No damage was being done to the Crusader infantry — they were too well covered — but the dropships were starting to draw attention.

"Take out the dropships and any artillery you can, reset guns to full charge for that and then go back to standard for the advance," Grieve paced along the line, platoons around him already deploying on their own, moving to obey his orders.

The Earthers operated like that — independent but as a single entity. Earthers all heard the orders, and the higher officers didn't have to detail off work. It was a simple system, but it worked.

Platoons began to move to face the dropships, and mass driver rounds ricocheted harmlessly off the shield as they did. The Earthers set their guns to unleash the full, uncontrolled charge that would vaporize living tissue, and opened fire.

The dropships were heavily armored, so it took a lot of fire to damage one, but there were plenty of Earthers firing. The first ship went up in a violent explosion, belching a thick smoke into the air.

"Let's get ready to rush them as soon as the big guns are gone," Grieve found a place to stand and observe, and the Earther marines, in their first real battle, prepared themselves to charge the enemy guns.

CHAPTER 37

Bactule was shocked.

He was in one of the complex's centrally-located and well-protected buildings, and it had plenty of windows from which to watch both fronts. He'd seen the entire episode unfold.

Those Earthers were *devils*!

Another dropship exploded into the air, the seventh to go from the east front, and the rest were under fire, unable to reply!

Damn those Earthers, and the Navy traitors who had joined them! Those traitors were in secure possession of the north side of the base, with bunkers and breastworks allowing them to fire into the flanks of his troops. He had 30,000 in the way of their advance, but he knew that if Earthers came over the east ramparts and the traitors came from the north he would be smashed.

He'd have to go underground, and that would be horribly costly. The battle would degenerate to skirmishes in the depths of a dark complex.

At least when the Earthers did come he'd have almost a minute to fire on them before they could get to the ramparts. After all, 350 meters wasn't a small distance for heavily-laden infantry to cover over on open plain...

Sarah had left Pat to the medics for the time being, but they had told her he'd be up in an hour. By the looks of the massing Earthers that would be too late to see the battle.

She approached Grieve, who nodded to her as she entered his peripheral vision, "How are you, ArcGeneral? You took a hard hit, from what I saw."

No patronizing or teasing because of the shell, she noted. Human marines probably would have been howling at her stupidity.

"I'm fine, and Pat will be. So how are we going to get in there?" Sarah got straight to the point, something Grieve appreciated just now.

He glanced at her and then looked back to the enemy ramparts, "It'll have to be a rush. We can't hope to get the engineers to lead out again — the Crusader's will be waiting for them. And we can't move our shields forward without deactivating them. No, we'll have to go straight across the gap. It'll take my troops twenty-five seconds or so to get across the plain — they're wearing second shields so that'll slow them down a bit. We'll lay down a lot of cover fire from the Twelfth and then send everybody else across. There's no time for special soldiering. We just go. When we get into bayonet range we'll have the upper hand."

It was a grim but accurate appraisal of the situation.

"I'll have to hope your marines on the far side can take the access points to the underground tunnels — it'll become a long hunt if we let the Crusaders get down there. Ursla will probably see to it that we hold the bunkers..."

Grieve let his voice fade as another dropship exploded under angry fire.

"I'll want to be part of the attack, General," Sarah said quietly, and Grieve looked at her again.

"Not at the front, ArcGeneral. After we secure the outer ramparts feel free, but don't get... *overzealous*. You're a fleet commander. You don't get to charge the guns," he said sternly.

Sarah smiled, "I'm not *that* bold, General."

Grieve cocked an eyebrow and politely bit his tongue... "Well, you *are* down here, *ArcGeneral*."

He turned away before she could reply.

"Alright, when the Earther marines hit that east wall we have to break through the Crusaders," Ursla announced, looking around the assembled human officers. "Our job is to get to those entrances to the subterranean complex. If the Crusaders get down into the tunnels it will be far too bloody to dig them out."

The officers nodded in acceptance. They understood the kind of fighting they would face underground, and like Ursla, wanted to avoid it.

"The plan is simple, when the attack comes we lay down a lot of covering fire and make a run for the entrances. We'll go in a single thrust on the right flank of the Crusaders, break through and get to the entrances. We'll set up defenses and stop anyone who tries to get down there."

There were more nods and without further discussion the officers split apart. Ursla contemplated the five subterranean entrances, thinking silently of how hard the 400 meter trek to them would be.

Grieve looked slowly up and down the line, stepped up to the edge of the force field and raised his arm. Futile bullets slapped the shield in an attempt to hit him. He took in a deep breath, then keyed his shields with his other hand.

"*Now!*"

Once again, no additional orders were needed. Every troop under his command had heard the explanation of what they were doing via their voicecomms, so they were positioned and waiting.

The soldiers of the Twelfth Division — 10,000 reservist marines — had gotten onto the tops of trucks, ice blocks, anything to allow them to fire over the heads of the advancing Earthers. Now, they started their barrage.

The First 'Light' Division, along with the Third, Ninth, and Guards Brigade of the Second, massed behind the shield and watched the thick fire erupt, slamming into the enemy ramparts. Crusaders dove for cover as the massive volley continued. A few were caught by its strikes, but not enough.

The sky was virtually blackened by the thick smoke from the burning dropships, putridly choking off the sun. The three Earther divisions rushed from their shelter, and the Crusaders who witnessed the beasts coming toward them suddenly thought they'd been drawn into hell itself.

Desperately, machine guns and rifles roared, spraying the impossibly fast Earthers as they sprinted. The Twelfth's fire slackened so its gunners wouldn't hit their own, and they hopped down from their perches and got ready to reinforce the charge.

Grieve led from one of the foremost platoons. As shields failed, marines began to fall with bloody, vicious wounds from rifle and machine gun fire, but the Earthers continued to close fast.

The Crusaders were waiting for their enemy with fixed bayonets, yet Grieve knew that his troops would have the advantage in close combat. The humans could not possibly withstand this...

The leading platoons sprayed the ramparts ahead of them with fire as they switched on their energy bayonets. Crusaders gave up firing, bracing themselves in the last few seconds, before the Earthers slammed into them.

"Come on, move!" Captain Hodge demanded harshly, but her company was already driving fast.

The Crusaders facing them were expecting a charge, but they were waiting for one that would come across the whole width of the front. Instead, 15,000 marines were launching themselves in a column at only one flank of the line, and the Crusaders' overwhelming firepower was misplaced to deal with it.

The Crusader reserves were trying to slow the numerous marines but they were cut to pieces by the running Allies. Ursla led them from the front, shooting every moving patch of red she saw, creating a fast pace that would let them break through.

The Crusader left flank started to move out of position to try to cut off the column, but the Earthers coming from the east pinned them with bayonets. Suddenly, 20,000 Crusaders found themselves stuck with the Earthers and the Naval marines on either of their flanks, and any hope of stopping the charge evaporated. Instead the Church warriors flung themselves at their foes senselessly.

Ursla realized the flaw in her strategy when she looked back at the column behind her. Crusaders by the thousands were sweeping into the running mass, locking them in bloody bayonet fighting. The charge's tail was cut off, leaving her perhaps 3,000 humans with whom to hold the bunkers.

It would have do.

•••

Grieve was in a frenzy.

He stabbed and swung and shot and stabbed and swung and hit. Crusaders madly thrust bayonets at him but he slapped them away. They tried to hit him with the butts of their rifles, but he deflected. In the end, he always won. No human could match him.

All along the eastern ramparts Earthers spilled over. Shields were virtually gone, so it came down to a match of martial skill. Rifles fired and Earthers fell, energy lanced out and crippled Crusaders. Blood spread and mixed from both sides and the butchering continued.

The Twelfth followed fast in the wake of the previous three divisions, and with intact shields it rammed through the melee with the specific goal of taking the buildings and setting up sniping parties.

Each building was defended by a regiment of Crusaders, but the Twelfth slammed into them as the fighting became even more vicious. Hallway to hallway they fought, and as the Earthers pushed harder, the Crusaders buckled under the strain.

Bactule heard the shots outside his door and realized the buildings were being forced. He had seen the 10,000 Earthers slam through the melee that was the eastern ramparts, but it hadn't occurred to him that they would be trying to take the buildings immediately — he would have sought to defeat the enemy troops first.

But now it was too late.

He had ordered the troops on the southern and western fronts — perhaps 10,000 — into the fight, but they were scattered and the fresh Earthers ripped them apart. This was a losing battle, and it was coming to a brutal end... but at least he could force the Earthers to bleed!

Bactule's door swung open. A group of Crusaders rushed in to escort him to safety, but several were shot from behind. The survivors turned back to the hall and opened fire again. He would have no guard.

Shappa Bactule picked up his rifle and sprinted out of the room, the guards sent to protect him firing desperately as the Earthers pushed at them. Energy pulses careened through the air around him, but he ignored them and ran down the hall in the opposite direction.

The building elevators were around a corner, and he reached them just as Earthers began to rush through his defenders in pursuit. A squad of Crusaders made a stand as he entered an elevator and keyed 'Sub-Level 1'. The lift began to descend just as gunshots echoed in the hall beyond.

The Shappa raised his comm unit and keyed general broadcast, "All Crusaders, retreat to subterranean complex!"

•••

Ursla watched with grim pride as the humans set up their portable breastworks between the cluster of subterranean entrances. A few machine gun crews set up positions amongst the rubble that was strewn about, but for the most part the Naval marines stayed behind their sheet-titanium defenses.

Three thousand was a large number to be holding such a small area, but Ursla had decided against expanding their perimeter after she'd been cut off. No, they'd make their stand where it really counted.

When the whole Crusader army turned from the melee with the Earthers and headed towards her, it became clear that 3,000 was a preciously small number for the defense.

The marines mercilessly poured fire into the tide of Crusaders, but tens of thousands were rushing towards the tiny unit from all sides. The well-fortified Allied marines were more threatened by swamping than by enemy bullets, but the former was as deadly as the latter.

Ursla methodically fired with her own rifle time and again, stunning what seemed like hundreds. The retreat was desperate, but the Earthers and other Allied marines were able to collect themselves quickly.

Grieve saw this taking place as he pushed to the head of a battalion of Earthers, "Open *fire!*"

Pulses from the Third came first, then the rest of the four Earther divisions opened fire. Nearly 10,000 running Crusaders fell into comas. Some of the Church soldiers changed their tack and headed for buildings through which they could get below the surface, but many found themselves blocked by the marines of the Twelfth.

That realization and their desperation made them vicious again.

Fire started to hammer into Ursla's small force, and their breastworks were the only things that saved them. Fire poured back and caused hundreds... *thousands* of casualties, but the Crusaders were so numerous none of it seemed to matter.

Ursla ground her jaw, winced, and kept firing.

"Third and Light Divisions, pull back. Ninth, go south and try and restore some order. Guards from the Second, we have to take pressure off Ursla right now! Where's the Twelfth? Get into it. Come up from the west and reinforce the defenses!"

Grieve was bellowing orders quickly. The Crusaders were running exactly where he had expected, and Ursla was trying to stop them. But the Crusaders were so vast in number that they were hammering the small area...

"Get good firing positions and start putting them down!"

Commandant Falkner had 10,000 of his troops with him, and he was using them to menace the flank of the mass of Crusaders. His troops aimed low, cutting the legs out from under the enemy as they moved towards the buildings.

He had to relieve the garrison at the center of that mass of Crusaders, but there were too many to punch through.

The Crusaders suddenly paid attention to the Naval marines, and their terror and rage manifested itself in the fire that poured into the unshielded Allied troops. Thousands of rifles opened fire on Commandant Falkner's force, and out in the open as it was, virtually all of its men and women fell.

Ursla continued to fire when the first signs of the abating tide showed. The ranks mowed down by her troops were being refilled less quickly and less completely.

Torrents of energy fire erupted from the west as the Twelfth Division slammed back into the Crusaders with their guns, forcing the mass of Crusaders back from that side. The First, Third, and Ninth ploughed in from the East

Ursla watched as thousands of energy rifles knocked down the Crusaders. The few humans still standing dropped their weapons and raised their hands in surrender.

Lowering her rifle, Ursla slowly sat back against the wall of one of the subterranean access points.

It was over.

She breathed.

CHAPTER 38

The ground around the base was carpeted with bodies — it was even worse than the battles Grieve had read about from the human World Wars.

Modern weapons and close quarters mixed a terrible brew.

Unlike those ancient battles, though, most of those on the ground were alive and they would probably make a complete recovery. Medics from the Heavy Division were guessing that 95,000 of the Crusaders were still alive and either wounded or in comas. That was still nearly 20,000 dead on their side, but the casualty list could have been far more extensive.

The Allied humans had almost 100 percent casualties — 1,000 dead, most of the rest wounded. Again, for the scale of the battle, the number of fatalities could have been far higher.

And yet the cost was still dear to the Earthers — 4,000 dead, almost 20,000 wounded.

The numbers weren't entirely unexpected, but they were horrific. And though the cost was great it *had* saved the planet.

Second Division had set up triage centers equipped for 250,000, and that would take care of all the wounded. They'd be healthy again in a few weeks...

But almost fifty Crusaders had managed to make their way underground. Whether armed or unarmed, they would have to be forced out. Some platoons were down and searching, but the complex below was vast. It would take time.

Until then... Grieve picked up a wounded Crusader and brought him to a nearby medical tent.

Sarah had been appalled at the scale of the battle — at the savagery and the death — but she had participated anyway. She and her escort had moved with Twelfth Division, and now they were underneath the base looking for Bactule.

Sarah desperately wanted to find that man, to confront him... for all he and his people had done. And she did not expect him to walk away from the confrontation.

The squad was spread around her as they moved cautiously through the corridors of the base, but there seemed to be no sign of the Crusaders.

Ahead of her the troops were moving slowly, and as they came to a corner one marine would duck around while another moved swiftly to cover him from the opposite side. They were set to receive fire, but none seemed to be coming.

Lupus dropped back to walk next to Sarah, and she looked at him silently.

"We could search for days and not find them," the Sergeant said in quiet tones.

Sarah nodded, "I just can't figure where Bactule would go. They've checked all the critical areas, so we know he's not in the major sections. Not C&C, not the armories. Not the mess or the conference rooms..."

Pausing, Sarah turned to read the sign on the wall to her left. It was put in place to help newcomers find important areas of the base, and a list of locations was displayed.

'Gymnasium and Workout Room' was one of the locations listed, and a colored line stretched down the hall they had just covered.

For some reason Sarah's mind gravitated towards that destination in particular.

"Sergeant, I think I know where Bactule is."

The forty Crusaders knelt on the gym mats and prayed for redemption. Bactule knelt with them, yet despite his usual devoutness, found he was less focused on prayer than on what he could possibly do next.

He knew the Earthers would start by searching critical areas first, then work their way through the less important sections. This gym was out of the way and hardly a major area. It was unlikely they would be found for a while yet.

Ordinarily, the poor condition of his men would have shocked him and forced him to take disciplinary action, but he had greater concerns. Of his handful of troops, only seventeen were armed, and ammunition was in very short supply. He could scrounge perhaps twenty rounds per rifle — hardly enough for a minute of battle.

The Earthers had emptied their armories before evacuating, leaving him nothing to use for firepower. Any Earther party to find them would likely be able to overpower them.

He finally understood the trap he had fallen into. The Earthers had all but given him the base only to snare him and destroy him. They were superior.

He shuddered.

The Quest had failed.

He had failed.

Prophecy had failed.

Space was filled with the debris of Prophecy.

Frigates were dispatching search and rescue teams to sift through the wreckage of ships that filled space around the asteroid belt. The same duty was being performed by 74s on the Pluto Orbital Plane, but further in-system the frigates were the only ships available.

One such frigate, *Hydra*, floated up to the burnt-out husk of *Genesis*. The forward half of the Superdreadnought was open to space, with no signs of life at all. However, the aft half, including the flag bridge, still had some atmosphere.

A group of four armed Earthers and two medics boarded this part of the ship and began to sweep it for survivors. It seemed that many of those on board who might have otherwise survived had been killed by exposure to the cold or radiation from the fractured engines.

Indeed, in a trick of what one might previously have called the Gods' grace, only one human aboard the whole of the massive ship remained alive. An unconscious, average height, bald-headed, red-adorned man named Harvey Bingham.

Sarah and her escort were still around the corner and out of sight when they heard the prayers being said in the gym.

"You should call in support, Lupus," Sarah said quietly, and the Sergeant began relaying news of their discovery to other platoons nearby. It would take time for reinforcements to arrive, but Sarah had the urge to rush in now.

Of course, the urge had to be restrained. Flag officers had no business going into rooms filled with the enemy. They stood back, oversaw the situation, gave orders, and maintained control. The universe would be a chaotic place otherwise.

Sarah congratulated herself on formulating an excellent argument as she paced into the gym, rifle leveled.

"She's *where*?!" Pat snapped at General Grieve, and the big bear looked with surprise at the ArcBrigadier. If any human had a hope of intimidating the General, it was the burly Pat Conroy.

"She took her squad down to look for the Crusaders. Sergeant Lupus just called in and said they've found them," Grieve said slowly, as Pat's face twisted with anger.

"Oh for Gods' sake, man! She'll go struttin' in there like the bloody Queen and order the buggers to surrender! I'm going down there! Right now!"

Before Grieve could object, the furious Irishman had stormed off towards the entrances to the subterranean complex.

"They're in the gymnasium!" Grieve roared after him, and Pat raised his hand in a wave without turning back.

Lupus was shocked to see the ArcGeneral go straight in, but he followed anyway. She had the sort of charisma that convinced him to follow, despite the unpleasant odds they faced. And realistically, he didn't expect the Crusaders to pose much of a threat after that sound defeat.

"Everyone put your hands on your heads! Get over to the wall! No tricks, we've got the better part of a company just waiting for you to try something!"

Sarah's voice echoed across the gym.

The Crusaders were all suddenly on their feet, terrified by the Earthers that followed Sarah. The battle had taught the Crusaders a new respect for Earth's natives, and none of them so much as twitched a finger, let alone reached for their guns.

Slowly, silently, they obeyed Sarah's words, and the squad fanned out to check them for weapons. All the Crusaders were subdued before Sarah realized Bactule was nowhere in sight.

But he certainly wouldn't have stayed above ground in the thick of that battle...

"*What? Traitors!*" Bactule emerged from the exercise room — he must have been praying in solitude.

Despite his unarmed state, he maintained his defiant attitude even as Lupus and another marine leveled their guns at him.

"Shappa!" Sarah's voice was loud and crisp. "Surrender yourself!"

Bactule stared with an anger-twisted face at the ArcGeneral, "To you? Harlot of Satan! No, if it is the last thing I do, I will die fighting!"

Sarah ignored the lack of cohesion in the statement and took a step forward, her own rifle leveled.

"Shappa, we can stun you and take you prisoner rather easily," she said.

Her anger had seemingly disappeared along with the Crusaders' resolve to fight. Intense weariness was finally beginning to clutch at the base of her mind, and all she wanted was to find one of those seductive Earther couches and sleep.

"*Never!*"

The marines expected a desperate final charge, but instead Shappa Bactule ran back the way he came, ducking and weaving to avoid their shots. Sarah and Lupus chased, and Sarah's closer proximity allowed her to reach the workout room first.

The door slammed shut behind her, and as it did she recognized that she'd been baited. Her rifle swung around but Bactule's leg knocked it from her hands. She abandoned the weapon and evaded his blows, retreating through the room filled with weightlifting equipment and various aerobic machines.

Quickly shedding her outdoor coat, she went for the pistol slung at her side, but Bactule knocked it away as soon as she was able to grab it.

"Gym... gym... hmm..." Pat stared at the halls around him and sighed. There wasn't a 'gym' on any of the signs, but one did say 'workout room'.

"Close enough," he muttered, and started to follow the colored line.

Sarah tried to break past the Shappa and exit through the workout room's outer door, but he stopped her. Now she was committed, no way out and very little room to maneuver.

Bactule was surprisingly good at hand-to-hand combat, and as she began to block his hammering blows it became clear that he wasn't a weak man either. Sarah evaded strikes as they came, blocked others, and sent back her own.

The squad was trying to get through the door, but it was locked and of solid Earther construction. She was on her own.

All because you got impetuous. Had something to prove. Just bloody wonderful.

Bactule drove a kick at Sarah, and she dodged. Her mind focused on fighting. A second kick came, which she was able to grab, but as she began to flip the Shappa off his feet, he hopped up and slammed his other foot into her shoulder.

She staggered back, tumbling into the gap between two treadmills. Bactule was already on his feet, a murderous rage evident on his face. Sarah suddenly realized that her arm... shoulder... *something* was broken from that kick. She was down an arm and fighting a crazed but skilled zealot.

Realizing she couldn't hope to beat him physically, she pushed herself to her feet and spotted her rifle. She made a dash for the weapon, but Bactule had already anticipated the move, and a twenty-five pound disc-shaped weight normally put on the end of a barbell slammed into the back of her calf. She crumpled in an explosion of pain.

Bactule picked up Sarah's lost autopistol as the ArcGeneral collapsed a few meters short of her goal. She tried to crawl forward to the rifle but Bactule came up behind her.

"Now heretic, you join the damned!" he snarled.

Sarah rolled to look at the Shappa and released a sigh. It was a shame she wouldn't get to see Pat again–

"Oh, Gods wept man! That is the worst bloody exclamation I've ever heard!"

Sarah's head snapped around as Pat came in the far door, his autopistol sidearm in hand. Bactule spun to fire but Sarah's good foot slammed into his shin. He staggered, squeezing the trigger desperately.

Bullets ricocheted harmlessly off the wall, and then Pat fired. The Irishman wasn't the fleet's best shooter, but the situation seemed to help sharpen his sights. Shells from his gun ploughed into the Shappa from his waist up to his neck, knocking him back into the wall.

The great Crusader leader fell.

Sighing heavily, Pat holstered his gun, and started ranting, "Damn your eyes, Sarah! I can't leave you alone for an hour without you going off to pick a fight with some fellow twice your size!"

The door to the gym exploded suddenly, and three Earthers rushed in with leveled guns, "On the ground!"

They slowed as they recognized the Naval humans, and Pat reinforced the sentiment, "Thanks for the thought, but I already shot him!"

Sarah groaned, one hand clasping her injured shoulder and drawing a wince.

Lupus cocked an eyebrow, and as the marines lowered their guns and helped Sarah to her feet, he leaned in next to Pat and spoke quietly, "She do this often?"

Pat shrugged with a smile, "Just a bad day. I hope..."

Lupus grinned and they left the gym.

CHAPTER 39

Ursla walked slowly through the halls of Fengate Hospital. The Earther medical facility was built for as many as 650 patients and it was full after the recent action. Wounded from every race had been brought here, many to benefit from the presence of top-line regeneration facilities and the care of Elandra Caine.

Every room had an occupant, and Ursla glanced through each door as she slowly walked by. She had gotten past the disconnected feeling she had experienced after the terrorizing fights of the battle, and now her only concern was for the wounded. Finally satisfied that she'd seen much of what she wanted to see, she set out in search of several specific humans.

Caine met Ursla a few minutes later in one of the corridors, his slow and measured stride revealing his fatigue. The past week had been infinitely draining for all concerned. In silence, the pair paced through the halls looking for Sarah Manchester's and Liz Hastings' rooms. Those were the humans they knew and worried most about, but they'd neglected to check room numbers at the reception desk, and were satisfied to search for themselves.

Pat Conroy leaned back in the comfortable, oversized chair and propped his feet up on Sarah's queen-sized bed. Though the ArcGeneral hated being laid up, Elandra Caine had informed her that the regeneration of her shoulder and wounded leg would not put up with too much abuse, so she was confined. And at present, she was napping happily.

The Irishman had decided to keep her company — there were more senior ArcBrigs in orbit to supervise cleanup, and the Earthers had the situation well in hand. Now he turned the pages of his book and read silently.

"What are you reading, Pat?" Sarah asked groggily as she stirred and sat up in bed, favoring her shoulder and wincing at the pain in her leg.

Pat looked up and smiled, tilting the book up so Sarah could see the cover, *A History of the Pre-Omega World*, by Alpha Caine. Old book it seems — the First Lord gave it to me. Said the first Earther wrote it years ago."

Sarah cocked an eyebrow and cleared her eyes with her left hand, "Is it any good?"

Pat nodded, "Apparently, for a good piece of time the Irish and the British were less than friendly. They had a bit or a war going on and it was resolved only a few years before the virus. So, my dear, you and I might just have to have a fight or two for old time's sake!"

Sarah chuckled, "To hell with 'old times' Pat. I've had enough fighting for a while. Has Elandra stopped by to say how soon I can leave?"

Pat shook his head, already diving back into the history book.

"Good morning Sarah," a voice called from the hall and Ursla stepped into the room.

Sarah sat up straighter at the sight of the huge Earther with Caine behind her. Pat closed the book and was getting to his feet when Caine silently gestured him back down.

"Thought we'd check in on the ArcGeneral," Caine smiled. "How are you?"

Sarah shrugged lopsidedly, "I've been better, but I have to say the worst thing now is the boredom. Your wife is determined to keep me in this bed — I can't leave the room at all. Just me, Pat, and the eight-legged 'spider' in the bathroom. And I'm not too fond of that one. Has a red back."

Ursla frowned at the mention of a spider and ducked into the small bathroom attached to Sarah's room. She reemerged with an Australian redback spider, one of the less pleasant arachnids on the continent, on her finger.

"Good thing you didn't bother him," Ursla said as she observed the creature. "I think I read that these could be fatal to humans. They don't cause us much bother, so we just let them be. I'll have to remind the hospital administrations to watch for human-lethal creatures in their facilities."

Ursla walked over to the window and opened it, letting the redback out onto the sun-baked side of the hospital. The view beyond showed Sydney, with the coast just beyond and a rebuilt version of the famous opera house not too far off.

"Well, we'll have to be a bit careful, eh Sarah?" Pat smiled nervously, eyes scanning the room for other such creatures.

"So how are the prisoners?" Sarah changed the subject dutifully, her features becoming more serious.

Caine tilted his head thoughtfully, "The Crusaders we captured are spread out in hospitals from here to Alaska and no one has caused trouble yet. They seem to be enjoying the comforts they've been offered. We've got marine platoons at every hospital, just in case. Though frankly, I think a few doctors and orderlies could handle them in their current state."

Sarah nodded. The Crusaders had been forced to live in spartan, harsh conditions for most of their lives. Now, the unconditional comforts of the Earther hospitals and the fact they were alive and well on Earth might have subdued them.

"Hello all!" a familiar voice called as a hoverchair floated in the door.

ArcGeneral Liz Hastings smiled as the vehicle brought her up to the foot of the bed and stopped. Pat started to his feet again, only to be waved down by the robed ArcGeneral.

"Liz! Good to see you!" Sarah offered a bright smile, and Pat nodded in agreement.

"I'm glad to hear your treatments are going well, Liz," Ursla chimed in as she sat in a chair opposite Pat.

Hastings nodded, gently lifting up her new left leg and propping it on the bed for all to see, "I can't use it yet — only the superstructure's done, not the proper nerves at the bottom. It'll be a while. And how are you both doing today?"

Sarah smiled and blushed, Pat grinned and chuckled. Ursla and Caine watched silently as Pat explained what he was reading and how Sarah was suffering through the boredom of her recovery.

Caine was still too tired to participate fully in any conversation. He was exhausted — it felt as though the life had been drained from him. In the back of his mind he was thinking about turning the fleet over to the Second Lord and taking some time to rest. He would be able to do that soon — go home and spend time with Elandra and Phealan.

Now he watched as the trio of humans told stories and laughed, just like he, Ursla, Grieve, Felix and the others did when they got together. Earthers in another skin, perhaps. It wasn't easy to understand how a race could be so varied as to contain both the Crusaders and these people...

Millions had died, some on the ground but most under his guns in space. The scope of that tragedy was clutching Caine's mind from deep within; he hated having had to kill so many, and was tortured by regret even though he knew that it had been essential to the survival of both Earthers and Earth. He could also feel that same regret in Ursla, and after spending time with Elandra again, he could feel her pain at seeing his anguish.

It was true that millions had been saved with the defection of the Naval officers, and the search and rescue teams had saved almost 750,000 more from space, but the losses were still horrid. In yet another tragic twist, some of the survivors lacked any personality because of the core dumps given to them by Bactule, and now Earther neurotechnicians were laboring around the clock to find a way to retrieve the lost people.

Of course, Earthers had died as well.

Odd, he realized, how what was closest to home was last on his list of things to think about. His conscience with the Earthers was eased by knowing that every last one of those who had died had known exactly what he or she was signing on for, and that they hadn't died in futility. Not nearly as many Earthers had fallen as humans, but there were still almost 20,000 dead.

The losses in this whole encounter had been far too high.

The room had dropped into silence as the stories finished, and eyes turned to the First Lord. He smiled, his mind recalling the tales his subconscious had tuned into during the human conversation.

Well, he could top theirs.

"I do have a bit of a story for you folks, if you don't mind..." Caine began, and the humans nodded with smiles. "It involves Ursla and me, and goes back... oh, ninety or a hundred years."

"If it's the one I think it is, it was 106," Ursla added as she glanced at Caine.

"The two of us were on safari in Africa, out in the savanna with a group from North America. This was my fourth time on the trip, but Ursla's first. I was playing tour guide when I decided to go get a little water from a nearby river.

"I was happily filling my canteen at the river... must've been a couple of hundred meters wide... and I didn't see this big crocodile start coming towards me. Ursla started calling me and waving and coming my way, and I turned and started telling her to quiet down..."

"You were worried *I* might stir up the crocodiles, I think," Ursla put in.

"Right, well, when I turned to see Ursla this big lizard jumped out of the water and grabbed my leg. I got pulled in yelling and screaming as Ursla came running up."

"I was coming for water actually," Ursla interrupted, "and warning him that there was a hungry-looking pride of lionesses about. When I got to him I got into a fist fight with the croc. Most mismatched thing I've ever been in. He wasn't half my size but he had plenty of teeth. I gave him a few pops and he backed off."

"With my left leg," Caine added with a grin.

Pat's eyebrows were up, Sarah laughed and Hastings smiled.

"So I'm hauling him out of the river and then one of the croc's friends shows up to take a piece of me," Ursla put it. "I start hitting him and then he grabs my arm and makes off with it."

The group laughed at the tale, but to the humans it was more than simply amusing. For all their hardship, these Earthers had an uncanny ability to rebound, and to restore themselves. Humans might have been scarred by such a run-in, and yet Caine and Ursla, in no small part thanks to Earther technology, were able to joke about it.

"Telling old war stories again, Setter?" Elandra breezed into the room in her white doctor's coat and put an arm around her husband. "What both of these valiant warriors forgot to tell you was that the one who got them the new limbs was me. Quite frankly, I think I'm the hero of the story!"

Everyone chuckled, and Caine smiled at his wife, "How are you?"

"I'm managing," she said quietly. "Just came from Harvey Bingham's room."

"Who?"

Elandra turned to see that Hastings had moved to face her.

"Harvey Bingham. He's directly above us..."

The air in the room darkened immediately, and the tension among the humans was palpable.

"The *High Chancellor* is *alive?*" Hastings' voice quivered as she grew more anxious, and both Pat and Sarah were fully upright with grim, somewhat shocked expressions.

"High Chancellor?" Elandra looked to Caine who nodded. "No one told me his rank... he's signed in under a triage number at the desk..."

"What is his condition, doctor?" Sarah cut in formally.

Elandra glanced around the faces in the room and sighed, "He's physically in pretty good shape. Mentally though... he doesn't seem to know exactly who... *what* he is. It looks like an energy burst hit quite a few of his neural pathways..."

"I'm going to see him," Hastings said flatly. Before anyone could object she was hovering away.

Harvey Bingham looked out his window at the warm, friendly city of Sydney and marveled at the Pacific Ocean. He didn't recall seeing anything so beautiful before, but then there were other things he didn't remember that he'd prefer to know first.

He sighed, arms behind his back as he stood peering, and wished he could have some company. The wolf lady, Elandra, was very nice to him. She wasn't a human, he'd gathered, nor were the cats and bears he'd seen walking around. He had seen humans coming and going outside his room as well, but they didn't seem to want anything to do with him. It was all so very confusing...

His life, until only a day before, was little more than a haze to him. Most of his memories seemed lost, and something about his current state seemed very wrong. But there was nothing to do about that — he had to wait, according to Elandra, and hope that things mended themselves.

Harvey heard a hum as a hoverchair entered his room. He turned to address his visitor, hopeful that the newcomer was someone to talk to.

The person who turned to look at Hastings was not quite the Bingham she knew. He lacked the drawn expression and upturned face Bingham had so often preferred, and his clothing was plain and unimpressive... he looked like a gentle older man.

"Hello," the High Chancellor said hesitantly, as if searching for words. "Do I know you?"

Hastings' eyebrow rose and she tried to decide how to address the situation. He was claiming stupidity, but it could be an act. She met his curious expression with a scowl.

"You don't know who you are?" she asked dryly, and he shifted his weight from foot to foot uneasily.

"I'm Harvey, Harvey Bingham. That's about all I know, though... I just don't know who I am... who I was I suppose. The doctors tell me I suffered some kind of psychological breakdown combined with head trauma... they say my mind is likely refusing my past..." he sighed in frustration and looked uneasily down at his hands.

Hastings had meant to be dispassionate, but this person she was meeting was hardly the cold bastard she had come to know.

But appearances were easily deceiving, and she wasn't ready to let his innocent act grip her. The hatred she nurtured for this man, and for everything he represented, should have been more than enough to let her turn away from a pleading man's eyes...

And yet she began to feel pity.

"*Did* we know each other?" Harvey asked softly, sitting on the bed and watching his visitor anxiously.

Hastings started to snap back a harsh reply but checked herself. This was difficult — Bingham had caused her so much anguish...

"We were acquainted. We worked together, I suppose you'd say," she replied quietly, and Bingham's face noticeably brightened.

"Really? Then you can help me figure out who I am! Were we friends? Do I have any family...?" he let the questions pause as he became aware of Hastings' grim expression.

He had hoped he was a good person — his extremely limited memory indicated something to that effect. But from the impression this lady was giving him, his hopes were starting to wane.

"I wasn't a good person, was I?" his voice became frank and defeated.

Hastings was surprised by the question — it almost sounded as if he cared. She shook her head weakly, a confused mind trying to understand the mixed images she was seeing. He was *still* Bingham...

"You were the High Chancellor... we all thought you were an oppressive, fanatical, violent zealot," she said quietly, and Bingham froze.

A... zealot?

Disparate mental images started to jostle for his attention — not many, just scattered memories of him praying alone in a cabin on a ship... a crimson uniform and acts of homage to the Gods...

He was crestfallen. He swallowed and turned again to look out his window, contemplating the question of identity.

Hastings suddenly felt a pang of guilt. It was as though she'd destroyed any hope this person had of becoming whole again. In Bingham's case that might seem to hardly qualify as redemption, but some instinct was telling her differently. This wasn't High Chancellor Bingham anymore. This was Harvey Bingham, an aging man with no recollection of who he had been...

"Why was I a zealot?" Harvey asked quietly, depression lacing his tone.

Hastings changed her approach to the whole encounter, "I don't think it was your fault... *Harvey*. The Church dominated your life from birth, you never got to be a person, you see." Part of her couldn't believe what she was saying, but she continued anyway. "Quite frankly, you seem like a nice man. It's just that you were so consumed by the duty demanded of you that you never had a chance to be yourself. You became an avatar of the Church."

The kinder words gave Harvey hope. While he had obviously been this 'High Chancellor', perhaps this stranger was right.

Harvey turned back to face the newcomer, "Well... I have to assume that I wasn't very... polite with you. Let me apologize now for whatever I did... I'm very sorry."

Hastings was frozen by the apology. Who *was* this man? Surely the Church couldn't have done that much brainwashing — to turn a nice person like this into the Bingham she'd known.

Was it an act?

"I don't even know your name," Harvey said weakly.

Not an act?

"Elizabeth Hastings. I suppose I'm... *pleased* to meet you, Harvey Bingham." She wasn't sure if she believed herself.

Caine had avoided thinking of Bingham, at least until rest helped him decide what to do about the Chancellor. The way that man had infuriated him was not something he was proud of, so he'd stood back until he could get some more sleep and work up his self-control before seeking him out.

He hadn't even realized Bingham was one of Elandra's patients — he'd assumed the High Chancellor would have been objecting loudly and spouting his importance, demanding something or the other. Instead, he was being perfectly polite...

Hastings was silent when she hovered back into Sarah's room, still shocked by her short conversation with her old archrival. Sarah looked at her friend with a concerned expression.

"How bad?" she asked quietly.

Hastings looked up at the room's occupants.

"He doesn't seem to remember anything. In fact, he seems like a tired, gentle old man... and he seems bothered by the possibility that he's caused harm. I don't know exactly what to think... he seems almost innocent now."

Her tone lacked conviction, and the humans in the room exchanged skeptical glances.

Caine looked to Ursla and wondered silently. Could a human as abrasive as Harvey Bingham simply vanish?

He sighed and turned his mind away from the question, waiting for happy conversation to resume.

CHAPTER 40

The Caine estate was large — ten acres in the woods on an island known as Newfoundland. Bordered by a cove on the east side, it was surrounded by forest in the other directions. The only indication that the area was inhabited was a rather large house near the coast. No clear-cutting, no fences, not even markers to indicate the perimeter of the property. Animals came and went as they pleased; the area was ruggedly scenic.

A week after the final battle on the Antarctic Plain, Caine had taken some leave and come home to this estate. Now, two days later, he and Elandra were hosting their first-ever human guests.

Ursla, Hastings, Sarah and Pat had been invited to have an evening picnic and to enjoy a rare opportunity to spend time together without having to worry about duty. Sarah and Pat had chosen to explore the coast before eating, while Caine, Elandra, Ursla and Hastings sat in the backyard of the house, sipped drinks and talked.

"So you actually have wolves around here?" Hastings asked, taking a sip of her cool, positively delicious fruit juice.

She had been walking with crutches for a few days now, and was glad to be putting her feet up between regen treatments. The wind coming off the Atlantic was chilly, but her sweater was enough to keep her warm.

Caine nodded, "They weren't common to this area before the virus struck, but when it did they seem to have crossed a half-finished human bridge from the mainland. We're still not sure how or why, but my ancestors started here. There are only a couple of packs on the island now, but they do stop by from time to time."

Hastings was still trying to grasp certain Earther concepts — including their obvious 'oneness' with nature. Not all wolves had been turned into the Earthers when the virus attacked. In fact, only a small percentage of each species' population had been changed.

Now, the Earthers had a special relationship with the animals of order Carnivora, and they were able to coexist peacefully. Hastings wasn't sure whether she would want to sit down with a wolf pack — from what she'd read about the local wildlife, they weren't the most cuddly creatures...

"Phealan really gets along well with them," Elandra commented and Hastings recalled the name as that of the couple's son.

She had yet to meet the toddler — he was off on the estate exploring, and Caine and Elandra were obviously confident he would be safe. A human would have called their lack of attention irresponsible, but Hastings already knew the First Lord well enough to know he would never neglect his son. No, if they had any concerns for Phealan's safety, he wouldn't be allowed to explore. And if he called they'd be at his side in a minute or less.

"They visit often?" Hastings cocked an eyebrow, and Caine shrugged.

"It's almost as though they recognize us as family, which I suppose makes some sense."

"Well the Equatorial doesn't hold a tide to this monstrosity!" Pat remarked as he paced along the rocky beach, comparing the Atlantic Ocean to the old Equatorial Sea back on Genesis.

This ocean was actually frigid, something unheard of on the jungle world humanity had adopted.

"Indeed," Sarah nodded, walking ahead of him along the shore.

She'd never imagined Earth could be this beautiful, nor did she ever expect to feel so at home with a cool breeze and the salty air. Britain, she'd discovered, had been a maritime nation on this same ocean. Somehow that knowledge helped her find comfort in the roaring waves — she felt oddly familiar with them.

Sarah had been out of proper uniform for four days now, and the change felt wonderful. She lived in her uniform while on Genesis, so had little else to wear. Earther auto-tailors had managed to produce a sweater and some 'jeans' for her that fit remarkably well. Pat had assembled a whole new wardrobe by way of the handy machines.

The Irishman bent over and picked up a rock, examined it closely, and then tossed it into a building wave, "Never seen so many rocks in one place! I hear they've got sandy beaches around this ocean somewhere, but these rocky ones are a marvel!"

Sarah smiled and turned to pick up a rock when her eye detected movement. She stopped after crouching, and turned only her eyes to examine the treeline a dozen meters away.

"Pat, didn't Ursla mention there were some wolves around here?" she asked quietly, trying not to look at the treeline now.

Pat turned to look at her, "As I recall..."

Both humans fell silent as Pat saw the pack of wolves standing quietly in the shade of the pines. He could certainly see the family resemblance between these creatures and Caine... hopefully they shared the First Lord's pleasant personality...

"Did she mention what to do if we got a visit?" Sarah's voice was low, and Pat barely picked it up over a crashing wave.

"Um. No."

Sarah stopped to think as the leading wolf came fully out of the brush and watched the pair. He didn't look hostile, but then Sarah had never before tried to gauge the mood of a wolf.

The leader's ear suddenly turned back to the woods, and a few of the wolves at the treeline twisted to look and see what was happening.

"I thought I saw you!" a small voice called from the forest, and for a moment Sarah thought someone was talking to her.

A small wolf, about the size of a human five-year-old, came out of the forest on two legs and wandered into the middle of the wolves. Sarah tensed and prepared to leap to the little one's aide, but quickly realized that the wolves were of no threat to the youngster.

The pack's alpha male instead began to sniff the short Earther, almost as if he were a parent checking up on a child. The rest of the pack happily welcomed their small guest, and the little Earther sat himself down on a rock and started petting them all.

Sarah relaxed enough to stand up, and the movement brought the wolves' attention back to her. She slowly drifted towards Pat, but a few of the wolves came forward to check her progress. The pack seemed to put themselves between the humans and the little Earther.

"Hi," the little wolf said, hopping to his feet, "I'm Phealan Caine. Are you some of daddy's friends?"

The wolves stopped their advances as Phealan approached the strangers.

"So we are, little fellow," Pat said, reaching down to shake the small wolf's hand. "I'm Pat and this is Sarah."

"Hello," Sarah added, and Phealan smiled.

"Hi! I've never met humans before! You guys are pretty strange... is that all the hair you have? Well you look like the pictures I've seen," Phealan spoke cheerfully as he started back towards the wolves who moved to lie amongst the underbrush and lazily enjoy the sea breeze. "Have you met the pack yet? They didn't look like they knew you. Come on, I'll introduce you!"

Sarah looked from the toddler Earther to Pat and then shrugged, stepping forward to be introduced to her first wild animal.

The wolf pack appeared in the Caine backyard an hour later, with Phealan and the two surprised humans in tow. Caine and Elandra went to welcome their new guests in a manner that baffled Hastings, and Sarah and Pat drifted over to the picnic table where the ArcGeneral sat.

"Gods, that wasn't quite what I expected..." Pat said quietly as he sat.

Ursla smiled across at him, "Met Phealan and the pack, eh?"

Sarah widened her eyes and took a glass of water from the center of the table, "For a minute there I thought we were actually on the menu."

Ursla laughed, "I'll go pay my respects."

Phealan was recounting the tales of his morning exploration to his parents, who were listening with a mixture of enthusiasm and pride.

The wolves lay around silently, seeming tense at the presence of unknown humans. Occasionally Sarah would notice one of those creatures give Setter or Elandra a questioning glance, as if sharing a connection and deciding things were safe.

Ursla was obviously quite familiar with the pack, and despite her wildly different appearance, she moved between them slowly, petting them softly, and seemingly paying her respects. Sarah watched with unhidden surprise as the pack's leading female introduced the big Commodore to young cubs, and Ursla greeted each of the smaller canines by lifting them in one hand and rubbing them softly. Neither the Earthers nor the wolves seemed at all uncomfortable mingling so closely.

It was Caine who had fostered this close relationship, because these wolves were a direct tie to his past. As far as any Earther scientists — including his wife — had been able to tell, this pack was descended from the uninfected members of Alpha Caine's family, and had originated over six centuries earlier.

Even if science was uncertain of the bond, the wolves weren't. They trusted the Caines, and the friends of the Caines, and seemed to know all Earthers as particularly odd versions of themselves. Upright and unnaturally verbal though Earthers were, the pack understood them, and felt instinctive bonds with them.

It was Caine's extended family.

Ursla marveled at the pack's new litter for a while, then gave the alpha female a reassuring pat on the back and returned to the table of onlookers.

"Sometime I'll have to introduce you to a couple of the local bears," she said with a smile.

Pat smiled a bit nervously at that, "Aye... well as long as they're as pleasant as you, I won't mind."

With a grin, Ursla shrugged, "Well, they generally seem to have very good taste in people."

The three humans paused, exchanged slightly worried glances, and Ursla laughed.

EPILOGUE

Eight months after the end of fighting, Admiral Andra Ursla stepped onto the deck of *Agamemnon*. It was her first time on this ship since she'd attended a briefing on the great First Rate years before. Now, it was her flagship.

Caine had decided, with the approval of the entire Admiralty, that the once Commodore deserved to lead the expedition to Genesis, since she had the most experience with humans. Her achievements in recent actions had helped smooth the selection process, so now she was an Admiral, three ranks above her previous appointment, and in command of the entire Second Fleet. Six hundred and three ships of war, plus the 900-odd human ships the Earthers had managed to put back into fighting order, would be her charge.

As the honor guard performed its standard drill on *Agamemnon*'s landing bay deck, she played the role expected of her. Her new adventures were about to begin.

On the bridge of the repaired Superdreadnought *Pope Joseph Barron*, ArcGeneral Sarah Manchester spoke with ArcBrigadier Pat Conroy via the comm.

"So are you ready yet, Pat?"

The ArcBrigadier had been given three squadrons of Battlecruisers, and he would be screening ahead of the combined fleet as it neared Genesis.

Pat shrugged on the monitor, "I think so. I've got the last marines coming on board now, courtesy of Commandant Hodge."

Falkner had died on the line at Antarctica, and now Gillian Hodge was the senior marine Commandant, one of the many promotions that came in the wake of the fighting.

"Well, Ursla says she'll be ready in about an hour, so start spinning up the drives."

Pat nodded with a smile, and then disappeared.

Sarah sighed and leaned back in her chair, reflecting on the number of changes they'd seen in the past months. Liz was staying on Earth for now to serve as leader for the millions of humans who remained behind.

Bingham, still coping with the restoration of his mind, was in no way ready to lead humanity. Hastings would have had serious doubts about his motives if he'd suggested otherwise, but he hadn't. Harvey had become a recluse —

perhaps in time he could right his wrongs.

So it would be up to Ursla and Sarah to lead the expedition. They'd go back to Genesis and tell the Church to stand down, tell the Kroggs to go to hell — in harsher terms, if possible — and apologize profusely to the Larosians for the problems humanity had caused. If there was trouble, Sarah's 900 Earther-tweaked ships and Ursla's 600 would end the argument.

It would be quite a trip.

Ursla was standing in her new observation lounge, appreciating the higher ceilings of the 150-gun First Rate when Caine walked in. He'd felt it was his duty to see Ursla off — he'd be staying at home with the First and Third fleets, so the responsibility of dealing with whatever happened in Genesis would fall on Ursla's shoulders.

"Ready, Andra?" Caine asked quietly, walking up to face the Admiral.

Ursla nodded, glancing back out the observation window at the grand fleet they'd put together, "We're set. Quite a step up from a squadron of frigates, eh?"

Caine snorted a laugh and nodded, "A big step. You've got a lot riding on your decisions, old friend. But I have confidence in you."

Ursla nodded in silent thanks, the responsibility appealing to her more than she wanted to admit.

"We've bound ourselves to the humans now, you realize. There's no turning back — and we could be in for some rough encounters," she said after a moment's pause. Caine's smile faded.

"The Larosians and Kroggs," he nodded slowly. "Well, we've given our word to Liz and to the Navy. We'll help them shake off the Church... help free the humans of Genesis."

Looking out into space, Ursla ground her jaw briefly, "Even if it gets us mixed up in an interstellar war?"

Caine looked up at her, and as he did she realized she didn't need an answer. They'd promised to help Liz, Sarah, Pat, and the Navy humans, and that was exactly what the Second Fleet would do.

"I don't think I was really asking," her voice picked up after a moment, "just making sure I'm not... *wrong*. There really isn't a way we could have broken our word anyway, was there?"

Caine smiled again, and shook his head, "No."

He turned back to the glass and looked out at the swirling fleets, his hands behind his back.

"I'm not worried about Kroggs or Larosians, Andra. We'll deal with them. And I trust that Sarah and the Navy will remain true to our Alliance, and to our friendship, because we trust each other..."

Ursla nodded briefly, then paused again, "But you're not sure about the rest of the humans. On Genesis, I mean."

Caine's head tilted down very slightly, "They may not trust us. They may think we're 'too good to be true', just as the Navy did at first. You'll have to earn their trust, Andra... somehow."

It was a solemn admission, and Ursla acknowledged it with a long breath, "They aren't quick to trust, are they? They're so divided, spend so much time at each others' throats, and they seem to expect everything else to operate the same way they do. The Church and the Navy... even Harvey Bingham... some of them are a lot like us, but so many are angry and jaded. The only thing they seem to have in common is their cynicism."

Caine allowed himself a thin smile, "They're not easy to grasp, you're right. All the divisions and the anger... and yet some of them do seem like us. There's no absolute human identity, perhaps... they're much more fluid than that, each one being shaped by the variables of their life, their class, their experiences. Not free to make choices and find understanding the way we do, but not completely locked into the templates their society demands either. It's like a formula, Andra, and each human — Church or Navy — has his or her own."

"I never liked math," Ursla's remark came with a smile.

With a soft laugh, Caine shrugged, "Well, you might need to brush up on it. Might come in handy for... the..."

His voice trailed off as he thought, then he spoke up again.

"The human equation."

APPENDIX A: CHARACTERS

The following pages will help sort out the characters found in this novel, and those who grow in importance in the books to come.

Bactule, Elias – Crusader Shappa
Cold and brutal, Bactule qualifies as human only in the biological sense of the word. A ruthless and efficient ground commander, he is rather limited in his understanding of tactics, but is quite expert in driving his Crusaders to suicide attacks. With little concern for human life in general, he focuses on supporting the Church and protecting his High Chancellor, and thus by extension, on completing the Holy Quest.

Bingham, Harvey – High Chancellor
Leading his people in the Holy Quest across the stars, this man is determined to fulfill prophecy. He has led the Genesis Colony through many complicated situations during his three decades as Chancellor and is perpetually plagued by the unfaithful Navy. He also finds himself in possession of the slightest of doubts about his Cause when the Earthers present their case to him after his arrival in Sol.

Broadpaw, Varnon – Admiral
One of the Earther Navy's most colorful flag officers, Broadpaw serves as commander of the Earther Third Fleet. Steady in action, this wolf's irreverent sense of humor makes him especially popular among crews and fellow officers. His ability to run an efficient Naval unit has put him on the Admiralty track, though he is in no rush to leave his ship, *ENS Algenon.*

Caine, Elandra – Medical Doctor
One of Earth's leading geneticists, Elandra Caine leads a professional life which is entirely separate from that of her husband, the First Lord. Constantly improving regeneration treatment techniques, and with a persistent curiosity about the origins of the Earther race, her expertise is unquestionable, and her contributions to medical science on par with the contributions of her husband to the military. Her practice is based in a hospital in Sydney, Australia.

Caine, Phealan
Young, curious, adventurous, and friendly, Phealan Caine joined Elandra and Setter's family only a few years before the arrival of the humans. The young wolf has a keen interest in what his father does for a living, though even at his young age, he doesn't dream of being First Lord of the Admiralty. Instead he imagines himself involved in the other traditional Caine vocation: historian. Phealan spends many days with his mother at work, and prefers exploring the forests of his Newfoundland home to any other playtime activity. He is a good friend of the local wolves.

Caine, Setter – First Lord of the Earther Admiralty
Commanding the Earther Fleet from *ENS Orion*, Setter Caine is unquestionably the most important officer in the entire military. A veteran within the Navy, and highly moral fellow, he is deeply devoted to his family and conscious of his responsibilities as a leader. He is persistently calm and thoughtful, though he can be rattled on very rare occasions, leading to potentially unfortunate circumstances. It will be his guidance that helps the Earthers face whatever is to come.

Conroy, Patrick – ArcColonel, ArcBrigadier
A self-proclaimed Irishman, Pat Conroy is the most colorful human involved in the Quest — and one of the most reluctant to have to involve himself. An exceptional cruiser commander, he leads first *Harbinger Bishop* and then a squadron of Battlecruisers with skill that would do Earthers proud. One of Sarah Manchester's most trusted friends, he has a taste for Earth history, and a desire to bring it to the attention of the Genesis Colony.

Falkner, Michael – Commandant
Commanding the Genesis Fleet Marines, Falkner is a competent and enthusiastic field officer. Aiding his new allies in any way he can, he capably finds work for his troops in the action on the Antarctic Plain, and proves his prudence in his attack on the bunkers. His misfortune that day not withstanding, he is an excellent commander, and is well-liked by the men and women under his orders.

Felar, Kella – Admiral
The First Fleet's commanding officer, Felar is another of the Earther Navy's consistent performers. Commanding usually from *ENS Endymion*, this cat has the ability to smoothly maneuver 600 warships through vicious combat, and as such she is well suited to the command she receives for the battle on Pluto's Orbital Plane. Reserved but personable, she is a well-respected line officer, not likely to be removed to the Admiralty for some time.

Felix, Savanna – Vice Admiral
A formidable administrator, Felix commands the Earther Navy's busiest and most critical installation, Antarctic Base. He is generally quite cool under pressure, owing in part to his Siberian tiger heritage, though he sometimes has a tendency to over-think issues. Perceiving limits to his talents, he has elected to avoid ship commands altogether, and dreads the day when Naval policy will compel him to join simulated wargames — he much prefers paperwork.

Forepaw, Labrador – Captain
One of Caine's most trusted friends, Forepaw is a quiet but highly competent officer, who commands *ENS Orion*, the fleet flagship. Having refused promotion to retain the post as Flag Captain of the fleet, this canine is very highly regarded within the Navy, and is sometimes pointed to as a future First Lord in his own right. With an almost paternalistic style of command, he maintains *Orion*'s reputation as the fleet's most formidable vessel, and his crew holds him in the highest regard.

Grieve, Andros – General
A grizzly (pardon the pun) old bear, Grieve is commander-in-chief of the Earther Marine Corps, and he believes in leading from the front. His service on the Antarctic Plain can be classed as exemplary, and his self control during the Earth tour with the Church party can be regarded as an example of his formidable discipline. Generally a no-nonsense sort of warrior, he will continue to lead his troops from the front, and to face new foes as the Earthers move into even messier interstellar affairs.

Hastings, Elizabeth – ArcGeneral
The matriarch of the Genesis Navy, Hastings led the movement that professionalized a dangerously amateurish fleet only decades before the Quest. Accustomed to the Genesis Navy's perpetual state of subjugation, her concern for the well-being of her personnel is commendable. An exceptional line officer, she has a record of relatively successful actions against the Larosians, and as such, her experience could prove most useful as the Allies return to Genesis.

Hodge, Gillian – Captain of Marines, Commandant
One of the Genesis Marine Corps' most reliable up-and-comers, Hodge is both a formidable fighter and a clever combat commander. Leading the marines aboard *Harbinger Bishop*, her subsequent service on the Antarctic Plain deserves recognition as an excellent example of soldiering.

Lupus, Beckett – Sergeant Major
Perhaps the best sparrer in the Earther Navy, Lupus and his elite recon squad can be relied on to deal with the most unfortunate of combat circumstances on the ground. Currently attached to *Cerberus*, this wolf is quite reserved and committed to his duty, though rumors abound that he has an excellent sense of humor. While low in rank, he will doubtless surface again as the Earthers encounter new situations demanding elite responses.

Manchester, Sarah – ArcBrigadier, ArcGeneral
Regarded as a brilliant tactician and an excellent commander, Manchester tends to lead dangerously from the front. She continually takes risks as she seeks to complete her missions and protect fellow Naval personnel, and this dedication has allowed her to rise quickly through the ranks of the Genesis Navy. Having played such an integral role in the actions around Earth, including her actions at Antarctic Base, she will move to the fore in human Naval affairs as the Genesis Fleet prepares to return home.

Nightclaw, Dran – Captain
The commanding officer of *ENS Cerberus*, Nightclaw has earned an excellent reputation within the fleet. He is as cool as any other panther when under stress, and handles his ship in action with great ease. The unrivaled efficiency of *Cerberus'* crew is a testament to his reserved but familiar style of command. Though he was Ursla's Flag Captain for only eight months, he definitively earned his promotion to Commodore to replace her as head of the 111th. He will be called into action many times in the future.

Ursla, Andra – Commodore
One of the leading frigate officers in the Earther Navy, Ursla is already on the fast-track to promotion when the humans arrive. Commanding the elite 111th Flying Squadron from her 38-gun frigate *ENS Cerberus*, this three-meter tall bear is the first Earther officer to make contact with humans. Her subsequent service displays her prowess in complex tactical situations, and her performance on the Antarctic Plain leaves little doubt of her combat ability. Good natured and generally optimistic, her promotion to Admiral will see her responsible for Earther foreign policy in the near future.

APPENDIX B: MILITARY STRUCTURES

When I read books like this — with big ships and lots of them — I always try to understand the operating doctrine for the military services involved. Often that means piecing things together based on clues dropped here and there by the author, but for *The Human Equation* — and the series — I want the doctrine to be accessible to everyone.

NAVAL SERVICES
Both the Earther and Genesis Fleets have two primary types of combat vessels: capital ships and cruisers.

Capital Ships
The capital ships are the big guns — *Orion, Genesis,* 74s and Colonizers, for example. The Earthers split them by rates, First through Fourth, based on nominal number of guns:

First Rate: 98+ guns
Second Rate: 80-98 guns
Third Rate: 70-78 guns
Fourth Rate: 60-68 guns

The Genesis Navy has fewer capital ship types, with only Dreadnoughts and Superdreadnoughts, classification based on number of missile tubes and, more importantly, size of missiles. While Earther ships have varying gun sizes, the missile calibres of the Genesis Fleet are definitive — whether a ship has 80, 90, or 100 tubes, it is size and not quantity that counts.

Cruisers
Cruisers are small, fast vessels that tend to close fast and strike hard. *Cerberus* and *Harbinger Bishop* are demonstrative of the class; they aren't heavily armed nor are they large. They work well in squadrons, and they rely on their maneuverability to stay out of the path of heavier warships.

Interestingly enough, the Genesis Fleet maintains more cruiser types than the Earther Navy. With only Fifth and Sixth Rate frigates and unrated sloops, each type smaller than the last, the Earthers have fewer technical classifications of cruisers than capital ships. This is offset, however, by the flexibility of the ships of the line — *Orion*, for instance, is often fought like a frigate in action, as that First Rate has the necessary speed and agility. The official Earther cruiser dispositions are:

    Fifth Rate: 30-48 guns
    Sixth Rate: 24-28 guns
    Sloop: fewer than 20 guns

The Genesis Fleet maintains four classes of cruiser: Battlecruisers, Heavy Cruisers, Light Cruisers, and Destroyers, each based again on missile size and firepower. Battlecruisers are the most powerful of the group, Destroyers the quickest, and the two middle classes are designed to take on tasks that fall in the gray area between. The versatility of the cruiser classes in the Genesis Navy helps offset its capital ships' lack of relative flexibility, though ultimately, the Earther Fleet is better equipped.

Discussion of deployment, tactics, and combat effectiveness of ships will come in a later Appendix.

MARINE SERVICES

Only a few notes on these, mainly to do with the Divisional Organization of the Earther Marine Corps. As we see on the plains, each marine division is made up of 10,000 combat and support personnel — though all marines are combat-ready in times of crisis. Each division is commanded by a Lieutenant General, and is broken into five Brigades of 2,000 each, with a full Brigadier General heading them. Each Brigade is in turn composed of two 1,000-marine regiments, each commanded by a full Colonel. Each regiment maintains two Battalions of 500, the first Battalion being commanded by the Regimental Colonel and the second being led by a Lieutenant Colonel. Confused yet? It goes further into companies... but I'll leave those to the imagination for now.

I should note the Crusaders' structure in brief. The smallest effective unit of maneuver in the Crusader book is the Legion — a unit of 25,000. There are subdivisions based on local control of the formation, but they are seldom detached. In the history of Genesis, nothing smaller than a Legion has been fielded by the Holy Church — it gives them a lot of punch, but it's very rigid and by no means flexible. Then again, when you plan on landing an army of eight million, that still means 320 Legions to coordinate.

The Antarctica and Pluto Orbital Plane battles were big, but bigger ones are on the way. Stick with the Earthers — they'll see you through alright!

THE
QUEST

KENNETH TAM

PROLOGUE

"The Gods have called us together, brothers, to bring Holy justice against a blasphemer."

ArcColonel Audrey DeBrooke winced as she listened to those words. She stood silently, with her jaw locked and her eyes fixed forward, refusing to show any sort of emotion. If only ArcMajor Justin Webb had done the same... if only he'd watched what he'd been saying.

"Justin Webb, an ArcMajor of the Holy Genesis Navy, and the executive officer of this ship, *Grendelsbane City*, has spoken against the gods, and his faith has been proven weak."

All he did was speak his mind... Audrey tried to keep herself from thinking things like that. Thinking them was the first step towards saying them. Saying them in the wrong company brought about this turn of events.

Audrey was the commanding officer of *Grendelsbane City*, one of the Heavy Cruisers of the new Quest fleet, and her ship was now on its way to Earth. It was a ridiculous mission, steeped in ancient prophecy and leaving Genesis, her home planet, completely defenseless against attacks from the hostile Larosians.

Justin Webb, her second in command, had said as much to one of his junior officers while they walked through the corridors of the ship.

A Crusader, one of the soldiers of the Holy Church of Genesis, had overheard that comment, and had detained him on the spot.

Twelve hours later, he was on a drumhead trial, and if Audrey knew her ship's Shaspa, he would be executed.

"There can be no defense against the charge of blasphemy that has been made this morning," the speaker was Shaspa Frederick Charters, the commander of the Church Crusader contingent on *Grendelsbane City*. Aside from commanding those red-cloaked soldiers, it was his job to ensure faith aboard the ship was maintained. The Naval crew could not be allowed to doubt the sanctity of this mission, or to disobey in any way. Having sixty Crusaders aboard made certain of that — there were only forty Naval Marines and 150 crew to manage, and the Crusaders were much better armed...

And, Audrey thought to herself, *if we act up, our families pay.*

Life as a Naval officer in the Genesis Fleet was not good. Hell, life as any member of the technical class on Genesis wasn't good. The planet's society had been divided by the same antiquated prophecies that had *Grendelsbane City* and a massive fleet of 2,400 warships flying towards the dead world called 'Earth'. Those of the Church classes were the superiors, and they held all the power, on the ground and in space.

And just to remind the 'heathen' Navy of the social situation, they put Shaspas aboard every ship, with companies of Crusaders. Say the wrong thing and you'd die for it...

"The sentence is therefore death by spacing. May the Gods take you into their arms and show you the errors of your ways, my son."

Shaspa Charters said that with relish, and Audrey couldn't help but wince.

This was her second in command — her XO had been careless, said something he shouldn't have said, and now he was going to die. Just like that. This was the life of a Naval officer...

The trial, if that's what it could be called, was being held in a conference room in the Crusader section of *Grendelsbane's* hull — a section of the ship connected to all others by a single entryway which the Crusaders could easily control. The walls here were painted a shade of crimson, creating an atmosphere of blood, and it never failed to intimidate Audrey when she came in here.

She was an experienced combat officer — as far as experience went in the Genesis Navy these days — but these Crusaders held the power of life and death over her and her crew, and she knew it. It would be foolish to pretend otherwise, as Justin had discovered.

"Crusaders, take him to the airlock," Charters said dramatically. He was standing at an altar looking down at his prisoner, and at the assembled audience for the trial. "May his fate remind the rest of you Naval heathen to remember your Gods."

Audrey's jaw clamped down. She was here watching this with twenty officers and crew — the only ones who'd known Justin well enough to brave coming into this section to see the 'trial', and to show him whatever meager support they could as he died.

Every one of those Naval people had just been baited by the Shaspa, but their discipline held and they didn't say anything. If they had, Justin would have had company in the airlock.

Two Crusaders had been flanking Charters' podium, and now they moved forward and took hold of their prisoner by both arms. He didn't struggle, and his face remained impassive. They hauled him up the aisle between the halves of the audience gallery — Naval personnel on the left, more Crusaders on the right — and then out the hatch.

The Naval personnel began to file out next, and Audrey led the stony silent crew out into the corridor, finding the already narrow hall crowded even more by rifle-wielding Crusaders standing at intervals all the way to the lock.

None of the people with her would try something foolish to free Justin, but if they had, the Crusaders were ready to gun them down. The Church soldiers would be *happy* to gun more Naval people down...

The lock was mercilessly near the trial room, and the Crusaders wasted no time opening its inner hatch and pushing Justin in. The ArcMajor retained his dignity, and refused to speak. As the hatch shut behind him, he turned and peered through its small window, his eyes finding Audrey's as she came to a stop several meters away.

He nodded to her once, and Audrey nodded back once. That was the sum of their communication.

Shaspa Charters passed Audrey in a flourish, his ostentatious red cape flowing behind him, like a wing of blood. He stopped before the airlock and then turned back to the people assembled in the corridor.

"May the will of the Gods be done. Crusaders, send him to the void."

One of the Crusaders keyed the airlock, and Justin was jerked violently away from the window.

Charters closed his eyes and looked up at the ceiling, "Oh mighty Gods, your punishment has been executed. May you take your child Justin into your arms, and show him the light of truth. Amen."

"Amen," the Crusaders present repeated. The Naval crew remained silent.

Opening his eyes, Charters looked down, and his gaze settled on Audrey. She stiffened at the attention — she was no more immune to being spaced than Justin had been. The Church didn't care about annihilating the entire command staffs of ships — the ability of a warship to fight and fly wasn't as important as the faith on that ship, at least according to these red-clad fools.

Stepping forward and coming close to her, Charters' expression shifted to its most patronizing, "ArcColonel, I know the loss of your second will make your duty more difficult. I am sorry that these circumstances have come to pass, but remember it was not I, but your man, you defied the will of the Gods, and brought this about. It is he, and by extension you, who are at fault. But the Gods are generous, and they forgive you. You must look now to your duty."

Audrey locked herself in place. She refused to let herself think what she wanted to think, because if she thought that she wanted to kill this man, she might well do it, and then her ship would be damned, and the families of all the crew aboard would be rounded up and executed on Genesis.

She had to be still.

"It is not right that one so blessed in beauty by the Gods should look so sad. If you seek righteous happiness, you may always visit me later this evening," as Charters said that, his lips curled up in a smile, and his hand reached up and caressed Audrey's cheek.

She couldn't hit him. She'd be dead.

He drew his hand away, then looked her up and down, waiting for her answer.

"I am content with the happiness the Gods have provided me, Shaspa. I appreciate your kind offer, but the love of the Gods will satisfy me for now," she had used that answer many times — it was an answer the Churchers couldn't dispute, and it had kept her out of the beds of many Shaspas over the years.

It was humiliating to say. It was even more humiliating to *have to say*.

And knowing that, Charters grinned, "Very well, the love of the Gods it shall be. Now leave this section, return to your duties."

Audrey bowed her head, then turned and followed as her crew filed out of the Crusader section of *Grendelsbane City*. They marched in silence, every one thinking how much they'd love to kill that bastard and all his Crusaders... and everyone knowing they couldn't so much as whisper those sentiments in the corridor.

Or they'd be next.

Audrey's skin crawled, and her jaw hurt from being clamped down so tight. She tried to force her head to clear, but it wouldn't. She needed time to cool down, and to figure out what to do next.

CHAPTER 1

"What the hell am I supposed to do without an XO?" Audrey's enforced calm had not survived the day, and now she sat at her desk and nearly shouted at the screen built into it.

On that screen was ArcColonel Bill Wallace, of the Heavy Cruiser *Darymanis City* — one of *Grendelsbane's* sister ships and squadron mates. Audrey wasn't sure she really had friends — or if any Naval officer could truly have friends — but Bill was close enough. Now that they were connected via tightbeam communications, she could vent to him about her loss of that morning.

Bill's face was grim as Audrey made her exclamation, and he then slowly shook his head, "You'll have to appoint a new one. We don't have choices out here, Audrey."

"Of course we don't..." she flopped back in her chair and shook her head. "But..."

She stopped herself. There was no 'but' in this. She needed a new XO, and she didn't have any recourse to take against the Crusaders.

Some hoped, of course, that on this long venture out of Genesis — the furthest away from Genesis any crewed ship had ever been — there'd be a chance to take some revenge on the Crusaders... to give them some of their own medicine and then somehow keep word of what had happened from getting home. But she didn't entertain any such notions.

No, the only way to hurt the Crusaders without word getting home — and thus, without families being executed — was to kill them all. And there was no chance of that happening... they were on every ship in a 2,400-strong fleet. It'd take a massive effort of coordination, and a real alternative...

None existed.

"You have to do this quick, Audrey. We'll be in Earth space by the day after tomorrow, you'll want your new XO to have as much time as possible to get settled before we get there," Bill was watching Audrey's expression twist from angry to beaten, and tried to get her mind moving in a different direction.

"What, in case some aliens have taken the planet over and we need to fight?" she didn't sell that absurd suggestion particularly well, and Bill shook his head impatiently.

"Your Shaspa asks to go down to Earth and your XO isn't settled in, there'll be landing organization problems. Another execution, probably."

Bill was always thinking ahead — that was one of the things Audrey respected about him. And he was quite right — they'd get to Earth, find it a dead, empty rock, and the Crusaders would be in a rush to get down there, to do their part in fulfilling that ridiculous Quest prophecy.

And as much as they repressed and tormented the Naval types, they needed Audrey and her people to get them to the surface.

Bastards.

"I'd rather run into the Larosians than see them have their prophecy," Audrey chewed out those words quietly, her eyes drifting away from Bill's face.

Her compatriot nodded, "We could use a good fight. Even if we'd lose it. You go get your new XO appointed, and try to calm down if you can. Keep cool... I don't want to have this same conversation with your successor."

Audrey nodded slowly at the dry advice, and without further words she deactivated the secure line to *Darymanis City*.

She needed a new XO. And maybe if she was lucky, they'd find Larosians at Earth the day after tomorrow. Then they could all die gloriously for the Gods.

ArcLieutenant-Commander Sonya Fletcher was woken by a soft knock at her door. She was a light sleeper, so as soon as she heard the noise she sat bolt upright, pulling her auto-pistol from the holster that hung over the post of her bed. A nighttime visit from randy Crusaders happened now and then — she'd had a friend suffer through that, and she'd long ago decided that she wouldn't let it happen to her.

But as she raised the pistol and swung her legs over the side of the bed, Fletcher realized that Crusaders probably wouldn't knock. She still got to her feet, and moved away from the bed into the shadows at the side of her cramped, dimly-lit cabin. She reached out and keyed off the lock, then held her breath.

"Come in," her reply was quiet. The hatch opened, and Audrey poked her head in.

"Sonya...?"

Audrey was looking at the empty bed when Fletcher stepped forward from the shadows, lowering her pistol, "Skipper... glad it's you."

"Sorry about the hour. I didn't just want to call over, though," stepping into the cabin fully, Audrey shut the hatch behind her and locked it.

"That's fine," Fletcher returned to her bed and holstered her autopistol. "What can I do for you, ma'am?"

Wasting no time, Audrey pulled a couple of rank bars out of her pocket and tossed them onto the bed, "You're my new ArcMajor. I need you to start first thing tomorrow."

Fletcher was just turning to face her ArcColonel again when the bars clinked onto the bed, and she froze in place, "Ma'am?"

"You're it. I'm sorry, Sonya, I don't know if you want it, and frankly it doesn't matter if you don't. I need you as my XO... you're the only other really qualified person I have."

Fletcher swallowed and stared at the rank bars.

Going up in rank in the Genesis Navy wasn't always a good thing. As the execution had proved, rank did nothing to protect people from the Crusaders... if anything, moving up made a person a higher profile target.

Fletcher didn't want that, but then it didn't sound like she had much of a choice either.

"Pick whoever you want to take over for you in Operations," Audrey went on. Fletcher was *Grendelsbane's* Operations officer, in charge of the general working of the ship's systems. Now she'd be XO, responsible for *all* goings on aboard the Heavy Cruiser...

"How long until I'm out an airlock, do you think, ma'am?" Fletcher's question was sharp, and Audrey hoped she didn't actually pale when it was asked.

"Be smart, and you won't have troubles. We just have to watch what we say... very carefully..." the words sounded defeated to both women, but what else could they be?

Justin Webb had been executed for having an opinion — for believing that it was ridiculous to send 2,400 ships on a mission to a dead world, when half or more of those ships could have stayed at Genesis and protected the planet from the Larosians.

This Quest fleet was the largest formation of human ships ever assembled — four times the size of the biggest fleet ever to be sent against the Larosians. Why did they have to take all of it on a useless mission to a mythic planet?

Because the Kroggs said so. For some reason, the alien friends of the Church — the creepy black-carapaced creatures who'd given the fleet much of its technology — wanted it out of system. They didn't want the Genesis Navy in Genesis space, to fight their Larosian enemies...

It was curious to Audrey, and Justin had wondered about it too.

Wondering had killed him.

She couldn't let it kill Fletcher as well, "Look whether we should be out here or not, we *are* here. Sonya, you have to be smart. The crew needs a firm hand at XO, and if I lose you I've got no one else to help with that. You have to stay smart, alright?"

Fletcher nodded slowly.

This was the life. There was nothing else to do but your duty... until your duty got you killed.

CHAPTER 2

Shaspa Frederick Charters lowered himself into his office chair and then laid his hands before him on his desk, "I think we have suitably reminded them of their place."

Sitting across from the Shaspa was Crusader Sergeant Michael Benson, and that junior Holy warrior nodded, "I concur. I walked the decks of the Naval section earlier, sir, and they were suitably subdued."

"As they should be. Humble before the Gods and this mission," Charters said that fiercely, and then shook his head. "I tire of the lack of faith here, and it has only grown worse as we've moved away from the hallowed soil of Genesis."

Charters had spoken of this problem before with Benson, his most trusted Crusader. It was as though being further away from the families who would be punished for insolence had somehow given courage to the Naval types on this ship. Other ships were reporting similar sorts of loose behavior and adventurism — the discipline and faith of the Naval heretics was fluid at the best of times. It was gaseous now.

"When we find our paradise at Earth, sir, they will be silenced," Benson offered that comment quietly. "Or their blood will consecrate its soil."

A short laugh escaped the Shaspa, "Michael, my brother, your attitude never fails to impress me. You are truly one with the Church and the Gods."

Benson bowed his head slightly, then raised it again, "I thank you for that praise."

The two red-clad men sat silently for a moment after that, then Charters leaned back in his chair, "We must be prepared for more indiscipline, though, my friend."

Frowning, Benson shifted in his seat, "But the crew seems humble now, sir."

"Now they do. But when we reach Earth, and when they have the chance to sabotage our Holy landing on the planet... that will be the time their faith and obedience will be tested. Think about it, brother, when will we be our most vulnerable?"

The Shaspa's question pushed Benson into thought, and after moments of patient consideration, he nodded his agreement, "Of course, sir. When you lead our Holy contingent to Earth, they might sabotage your craft, or attempt to do some harm while part of our complement of warriors is away."

It seemed unlikely to Benson — one thing the Naval scum were not was courageous — but it was wise to be prepared in case the devils rose from their gulags and gave the heretic officers and crew of this ship the spine to challenge the will of the Gods.

"When we reach Earth space, it might be necessary to make an example of one of the crew — a warning against such activity," Charters had already thought on this problem, and as always, the Gods had blessed him with a logical course of action.

"Of course. Perhaps the new second in command — a warning again that no one is safe," Benson suggested, but Charters was already shaking his head.

"No, brother. Both the ArcColonel and the new ArcMajor she will appoint are of too much value to me when we return from the Quest. You will have second choice after I select, if it pleases you."

Benson was a man of the Gods: he did not personally subscribe to Charters' own school of thought — that heretic women might only be saved by congress with sanctified men. Many among the ranks of the Church believed that they could purify the Naval women, give them a better (but still poor) chance at entering the gates of heaven. Benson knew them to simply be damned, and he had no interest in spending intimate time with any of them.

"I appreciate that offer, sir, but perhaps you could handle both. It is not for me."

Charters grinned and nodded, "Very well. But continue to collect evidence against them for me, would you? It will make my proposition for their cooperation much more effective when I have sufficient evidence to have their families flayed."

"Of course," Benson bowed his head again. "If not ArcColonel DeBrooke or ArcMajor Fletcher, then who would you seek to use as an example?"

Charters paused again with a frown, "That is for you to decide, Benson. Anyone you think appropriate, though if possible do not waste a woman who can be saved. Our men deserve the chance to save souls after their excellent conduct on this long voyage."

"Very well," Benson's head remained bowed. He'd pay close attention to the Naval crew around him, and as soon as the ship reached Earth, the chosen man would be tried and spaced. An offering to the Gods, in a way.

Gods' will.

"Gods, are you hearing this?" Communications Technician Second Class Kyle Puncher shook his head as he pressed his headset tighter into his ear.

"They're both sick," Communications Technician First Class Deanna Sykes agreed in a whisper.

The two technicians were monitoring the ship's comm hack into the Crusader section. Every ship in the Genesis Fleet had one of these — it was an unofficial requirement of survival aboard a ship with Crusaders on it. During regular maintenance, an enterprising comm tech would bypass a few relays and gain secondary access to all the comms in the Crusader section of the ship, and then volunteers from the ship's comm staff would take shifts in auxiliary control listening in, gathering information.

If a hunt was about to begin for people committing a certain type of heresy, warning could be passed along to make sure the crew avoided that behavior. Such forewarning was one of the few advantages the Naval personnel aboard *Grendelsbane City* had... Puncher and Sykes were taking full advantage of it now.

"We'll need to warn the skipper. About both things," Sykes said after a moment. "Gods let them never get evidence like that on me."

Puncher nodded slowly at Sykes' oath, and the two technicians went back to listening.

"Charters wants to save both our souls," Fletcher spat out the words. "I'd like to castrate him."

Audrey DeBrooke's eyebrow climbed at the forthright statement as Fletcher sat herself down on her ArcColonel's couch.

"As soon as we get over Earth, he's going to look for a man to kill, to set another example to keep us in line when we start dropping Crusaders onto that rock," Fletcher went on. "Word's spreading that we need to be quiet tomorrow. And some people are saying we should stop them if they try."

Audrey's other eyebrow climbed to sit level with the first one, "Someone's saying we should *fight*?"

Fletcher had been in the XO's job for just a day, but already she was performing her role very well — she had her fingers firmly on the pulse of the ship. If whispers were being traded suggesting that the crew should resist the Crusaders, they had to be stopped.

The last ship to attempt a mutiny had been the Battlecruiser *Cardinal Saint*, back in Genesis space. The crew had openly attacked Crusaders, and the ship's Naval Marines had even taken up arms and begun firefights with Crusaders throughout the ship.

Five hours after it started, every member of the Naval crew on that ship had been killed — either in a firefight or by spacing — and their families all across Genesis were rounded up and publicly executed.

It wasn't that the Crusaders on any one ship were a match for the crew of that ship, it was that there were so many Crusaders nearby, ready to come aboard in support of their 'brothers'. And that families on Genesis had no defense at all from the Church's warriors.

The whole fleet would have to rise up, and somehow the eight million Crusaders they were escorting in those massive Colonizers would have to be completely destroyed.

Otherwise, any uprising was suicide, and homicide. Mass murder.

Audrey couldn't let it happen on her ship.

"We have to spread the word to stay calm. We can't get into this out here... they'll kill us all before they give ground. And if word gets back to Genesis..." she hated the caution in those words as she said them, but it was prudent. It was necessary.

Fletcher's mouth was a thin line, but she nodded slowly.

They were not in control of their own ship.

"So... tomorrow. We must have absolute discipline tomorrow," Audrey said softly, rubbing her eyes as she sat back in her chair. "Tomorrow we find Earth, and when they discover that it's a dustball, they're going to want to take it out on us."

"Yes, skipper," Fletcher nodded her reply.

Earth tomorrow...

CHAPTER 3

Audrey stepped onto *Grendelsbane City's* bridge early the next morning, having failed to sleep very well.

"Give me an ETA, Helm," she announced her presence with that order, and the officer of the watch quickly checked his board.

"Looks like we're making better time than the last recon probe did, ma'am. We're only an hour out."

Audrey nodded as she crossed the bridge to her chair, "Very well. Ship status?"

"Cruising stations and all quiet ma'am," the officer of the watch reported with a nod.

That was good, though not unexpected; the Crusaders weren't going to begin scrutinizing until later today. Word had been spread overnight through the usual back channels — officers had told their senior non-commissioned personnel, and the spacers were informed after that. It only took a few hours for a warning like that to reach everyone aboard the Heavy Cruiser.

Hopefully everyone would take it to heart. There could be no indiscipline over Earth, or they'd all pay...

Audrey tried to stop her thoughts on that line — she didn't need to dwell on the risks of simply doing her job. She needed to make sure her ship was ready for the parade it'd soon be a part of.

A parade to a diseased dustball of a planet...

Why the Churchers believed Earth would be some lush Mecca still baffled Audrey — according the Holy books, it was supposed to have been killed by a plague of the Gods, only 700 years prior. There was no reason to think the planet could have recovered from that sort of devastation in so short a time.

Seemed to her that a war of the Gods would leave deep, lasting scars.

But what did she know? She was just a Naval officer, and worse than that, a woman.

Audrey continued to ponder in frustration, despite her efforts at self control. She sat silently on the bridge and waited.

"Begin final flux deceleration protocol," ArcMajor Fletcher gave those orders as she paced the bridge. "Engineering, keep a close eye on the levels. We've never been in sustained flux for anything like this long."

Grendelsbane began to groan slightly as its high acceleration from the trip to Earth began to bleed away. Flux drive was an effective system of interstellar travel — Audrey couldn't dispute the speed with which it had carried the fleet to Earth, so many light years from home.

That said, it could still fail and kill you quickly, and without too much mercy.

Well, I suppose it wouldn't qualify as successful if it did that…

"Beginning final deceleration routine. We'll reach sublight speeds in thirty seconds," the officer at Helm reported.

With those words, Audrey came to her feet and approached Fletcher from behind, "Helm, as soon as we're at maneuvering speed, close us up with the squadron. Let's do it smartly."

Grendelsbane City had always handled reasonably well — in squadron maneuvers, it had always held its own, hitting its formation marks at the right times. Today Audrey wanted the ship to do the same. Perhaps if it performed flawlessly on the approach to Earth, Charters wouldn't come after one of the crew…

No. No he'd come for one of them, just because he could.

"Sensors, stand by to link into the squadron scanning grid. I want to see the make up of the system just in case," Audrey stifled her grim thoughts with more words, and the appropriate officers acknowledged her.

Grendelsbane shuddered slightly as the last of the high speed it had been keeping bled away, and the Heavy Cruiser coasted to sublight velocity.

"Telemetry beginning to come in. Tying into squadron grid," the Sensors Officer reported, and Audrey nodded.

"We're close to formation. Moving us into our slot," the ArcLieutenant at the Helm added quickly.

Audrey's crew didn't need to be told what to do at this stage — squadron maneuvering was almost second nature to the crew of the warship. That was one thing they trained in endlessly, as ArcGeneral Hastings said it was the only chance human ships had in a fight with Larosians. They either fought in tight, well-coordinated formations, or the Larosian Warcruisers could kill dozens of them without breaking a sweat.

"Put the scans up on the main screen as they come in. And make sure to funnel them down to the Crusader section in real time. The Shaspa will want to see everything immediately," Audrey managed not to sound too disgusted by the second half of those orders.

A couple of moments passed before the sensor data started to stream in from the squadron flagship *Cottswald City*, and then the rest of the fleet's positions began to appear on *Grendelsbane's* screen. There were so many ships in this Quest fleet that for a moment those were all that appeared.

"So far so…"

The screen chirped angrily at the appearance of unknown icons.

"Ma'am, signal from flagship: unknown vessels ahead!"

Audrey's mind switched gears instantly — worst case scenario, these were Larosians...

"Eight ships in a line, ma'am!" the Sensor Officer's nerves were making his reports hurried, and Audrey frowned and stepped closer to the monitor.

"Anything from flag? Are we going to General Quarters?" Audrey asked the question in a level tone.

"No ma'am."

Dammit, I don't want to get caught out...

Audrey had been an ArcEnsign during the last battle with a Larosian force, some six years prior. Of 800 crew on the Dreadnought she had been aboard, she was one of twenty-one survivors.

She didn't want to lose her ship now...

But there were 2,400 Genesis ships here, and *Grendelsbane* was in the rear third of their formation. Surely eight unknowns couldn't be that much of a threat... if the Genesis ships were *ready* for a fight...

Come on, give us the order... Hastings, dammit, give us the order...

The order to prepare for battle had to come from the top. Individual ships in squadron formations couldn't go to General Quarters on their own without specific orders from command — squadron unity to be preserved at all costs.

"Get the crew on its feet," Audrey turned away from the screen. "We're not at General Quarters, but I want people close to their stations."

That was cheating but she'd take no chances.

What the hell is flag doing? They need to get us to quarters... we're defenseless... and who are these unknowns... the Gods?

The last thought nearly brought an absurd smile to Audrey's face, but she killed that expression.

Fletcher closed with her and lowered her voice, "Eight ships... if they're hostile, we can handle them, right?"

"I would imagine so. But... well, I never thought I'd see 600 ships get flattened by twenty-five. Then the Larosians proved me wrong," Audrey could afford to be honest about some of her doubts with her XO... she felt that she needed to admit them to someone.

"Signal traffic, ma'am... between *Genesis* and the unknowns."

Looking back at the screen Audrey and Fletcher watched a dotted line lance from the icon of the flagship to the dots of the unknown force.

"We're being ordered to GQ-yellow, ma'am. Transmission from flag says the unknowns are designated 'Earthers' and are claiming non-hostile status."

"Ship to General Quarters code yellow," Fletcher repeated the order immediately, and a klaxon rang out through *Grendelsbane's* deck, rushing its crew to their standby stations.

Audrey's frown deepened and she peered hard at the eight icons on the screen, almost hoping that staring more intently would reveal something about them.

"Earthers?" she whispered the question to herself. She then raised her voice slightly, "Sensors, power up the long range probe scanners. Give me a look in-system."

"Yes ma'am. They'll be up in two minutes."

Audrey folded her arms and softly bit her bottom lip.

Earthers...

Shaspa Charters and Crusader Sergeant Benson stood at the head of a dozen other cloaked warriors, standing in one of several chambers in the Crusader section that was displaying the feed from *Grendelsbane's* sensors.

"Are they the Gods, sir, or heathen seeking to halt our Quest?" one of the Crusaders asked his question humbly.

Frowning, Charters shook his head, "I do not know, brother. But the High Chancellor's ship communicated with them. We must trust that he has the wisdom of the Gods filling his mind. He will discover the truth."

"I hope they are the Gods, and not foes, sir. I do not trust the Navy to fight well for this most Holy Quest," another Crusader declared his feelings with due alacrity.

One could only ever decry non-believers in loud tones.

Charters nodded at the sentiment, "Yes brother, you are right. In fact, arm your men, and prepare to send a squad to the bridge. If these unknowns prove to be heathen foes, we must make certain the Navy fights as it should."

"Skipper... Gods' dammit, reading a huge force coming out to meet us from further in system... over 1,000 ships! Many more than 1,000!"

The Sensor Officer didn't even try to contain his panic as he reported, and Audrey had a hard time blaming him. If these *Earthers* were anywhere close to the Larosians in terms of technology, that many ships would be more than a match for the Quest fleet.

Thousands...

"More ships coming in from the outer system, too, ma'am... it looks like they had picket squadrons out, and now they're all concentrating here!"

Audrey swallowed and nodded at the anxious report, then looked at Fletcher, "What're you thinking, Sonya?"

"If they're friendly, why in hells gulags are they all coming up?" Fletcher didn't sound particularly calm herself. She'd never faced the Larosians — she'd been only eighteen when Audrey had survived the last encounter with those aliens in the old fleet. Most of *Grendelsbane's* crew was under twenty-five; Audrey herself was only twenty-six.

The Genesis Fleet was culled every few years by the Larosian squadrons... only a rare few made it to their forties or fifties.

ArcGeneral Hastings was one of those few... surely she wasn't going to sit at code yellow and watch these unknowns come on.

Come on, let us protect ourselves...

"Orders from flag, all ships to General Quarters!"

Thank you.

"General Quarters! All hands to battle stations! Charge armor, activate lasers, load missiles! Prepare for combat maneuvers!" Fletcher wasn't bothering to keep her orders below the level of a yell. The adrenaline was flowing now — the possibility of a huge fight...

"Keep the flux drives idling, just in case we need to move fast," Audrey wanted to say 'in case we need to retreat', but knew that sort of honesty was too much for her people just then.

Grendelsbane's crew raced to upgrade the ship's readiness from code yellow to full General Quarters, and the lighting on the bridge shifted to reflect the dangerous status.

"All hands report ready for action," the new Operations Officer reported after a moment.

"The other unknowns are accelerating... I think... I'm getting huge energy readings now, but I'm not seeing hulls... the unknowns in front of us are extending some sorts of guns through hatches... rail guns maybe, ma'am."

Audrey frowned — rail guns? That was old tech. Maybe the *Earthers* were *behind* Genesis tech, not ahead of it. That'd be a nice change...

But it seemed pretty evident that shooting would begin soon — unless Hastings was getting soft. The first shot was essential to victory...

"Unknown fleet arriving now... strange readings... but here they are. Gods... skipper, it's about 1,800 ships total. They're lining up in eight-ship formations... those guns are getting extended."

"Stand by for combat maneuvers," Audrey turned to her crew quickly. "Helm, make sure we stay close to our squadron mates."

Heart rates on *Grendelsbane's* bridge were soaring. Battle would be joined soon...

"More signal traffic, ma'am..."

Audrey turned back to the screen and watched dotted lines pass from the unknowns to *Genesis* and back. What was being said? Was it an ultimatum?

"Everyone hold fast, we wait for orders..." Audrey didn't really need to repeat that — *Grendelsbane* was so far back in formation, there wasn't much chance the ship would become engaged before a thousand other Quest ships.

Time dragged out, minutes seeming like hours.

"What're they doing?" Fletcher came close to Audrey to ask the question.

Shaking her head, Audrey kept her eyes on the screen, "I don't know."

Minutes passed, and no one moved.

Audrey found her jaw starting to pain from being clenched, and her folded arms were held so tight against her they were cramping.

What's going on...

"Orders from flag... we're to reduce to General Quarters code yellow again. The High Chancellor is going aboard the unknown... Earther, sorry... the Earther flagship. With the ArcGeneral."

Audrey took a few seconds to process those words, and then she blinked her mind into action. Fletcher managed to react in about the same time, despite her own surprise.

"Back us down to yellow," the XO said.

Then she looked at Audrey, "Talks?"

Audrey nodded, "Well... let's hope the Earthers are welcoming us..."

They'd have to wait to see.

CHAPTER 4

The next hours passed very slowly. Though officially only at condition yellow, none of *Grendelsbane's* crew moved from their action stations, and Audrey didn't leave the bridge. Word had spread fast about the composition of the force that was now standing opposite the Quest fleet — everyone knew there were 1,800 ships out there.

And while an advantage of 600 hulls might have sounded good to an outside observer, Audrey and her crew knew very well how easily 600 Genesis ships could die. The Larosians had taught them that lesson...

"Anything?" Fletcher was pacing impatiently next to the communications panels, and the ArcLieutenant there simply shook his head.

"Nothing. Sorry, ma'am."

One shuttle had already come back from its meeting with the *Earthers*... surely there would be specific word of what was to happen next...

We're cruisers, they don't tell us anything until the last minute.

Audrey shifted in her chair and continued to stare at the screen. She wanted something to do — she wanted some indication of what was going on...

"They are heathen beasts. They have attempted to undermine our faith, claiming that the Gods were but men, and that prophecy is a lie," Shappa Bactule was delivering the news of Lord High Chancellor Bingham's meeting with the Earthers over a secured, secret channel, and Shaspa Charters watched the broadcast with a stern gaze.

"It is essential that we prepare ourselves for a battle against these Earthers," Bactule continued. "And we must be wary. The harlot Hastings has already been seduced by their evil temptations. We believe they may attempt to turn the Naval heretics against us, to gain a tactical advantage."

Charters had been waiting anxiously to hear about these unknowns, hoping to the Gods that the 'Earthers' were in fact the guardians of paradise, here now to welcome the coming of prophecy. Instead it seemed quite evident that the creatures were demons from the gulags of Hell — the last test of the faith and devotion of the Quest.

And the Naval class had no faith or devotion. They were scum, and Charters could immediately feel the rightness of Bactule's concern — of *course* DeBrooke and her crew would gladly give into the temptation of these Earthers. The Navy was weak before the Gods.

"The High Chancellor has ordained that we prepare a unique plan. We must prepare to take our own ships away from the Navy — we must be ready to purge their crews if they try to turn to the side of the Earthers. I will oversee the training of some of our brothers aboard the Colonizers in the ways of ship operation... if it comes to it, brothers, we will finish this mission ourselves."

Bactule paused, and Charters breathed deeply. Here was the coming of prophecy, with new challenges and new demands. Would the Crusaders be forced to undertake the filthy work of the Navy? If they were, they would do so gladly: it was their honor to be part of prophecy, no matter what work was required of them.

But it would be a challenge...

"For now, brothers, I must lead a party of our most faithful to Earth, to see what these Earthers have made of our world. The decisions will be made about the fate of the Navy when we return. Until that time, you must make your plans for all contingencies. Prophecy is upon us."

With that, Bactule vanished, and Charters sat back in his desk chair and sighed. The road ahead might be difficult... but faith would see them through.

"These Earthers are entirely different than humans... but they were very courteous and civilized. They've offered to take humans on a tour of Earth, and they've asked for separate delegations from the Navy and the Church. I'm putting together a group to go down on our behalf now, will advise on further details as they become available."

ArcGeneral Elizabeth Hastings' message faded from Audrey's screen and she sat back in her chair. That particular transmission had been heavily encoded so the Crusaders couldn't see it, and Audrey could understand why — Hastings almost sounded impressed by the Earthers. And now the Earthers were going to be giving guided tours of Earth? What was their angle?

Well, it'd be up to Hastings' chosen people to find out, and Audrey knew for a fact she wouldn't be one of them. The rumors of the 'Top Flight' order in the Genesis Fleet were widespread enough — it was known that Hastings had her own clique of preferred people who she trusted to help resist the Church in whatever ways they could. On one level, Audrey approved of the resistance... on another, she was rather bitter about the elitism of the organization. Whatever she felt, though, she could be certain it would be Top Flight officers who were heading to Earth.

The rest of the fleet would have to sit on its hands, looking down its missile tubes at those same Earthers.

Only time would tell if this was to end in a shooting battle.

•••

"I hear the Earthers look just like us, but have silver eyes."

"Not what I heard. I heard they're like lizards."

"No way."

Several spacers were whispering to each other across a galley table as ArcMajor Fletcher passed them on her way for a quick dinner. Overhearing their talk, she came to a halt and turned around, "You five, keep that talk to yourselves. We're not here to speculate on the Earthers."

The spacers knew they shouldn't have been so careless in their speaking, so they looked up with slightly guilty nods, "Yes ma'am."

Fletcher frowned at them for a moment, then headed for the galley counter. Looking down and whispering even more quietly, they began again.

"I heard from a guy who heard from a guy who heard from the pilot of Hastings' pinnace that they're like animals from the scriptures. They're covered in fur but shaped like humans, mostly."

"That's ridiculous. The chances of animals becoming humanoid are pretty much astronomical."

"Yeah, what are they, walking teddy bears?"

The whispering went on.

Audrey sat in her chair on the bridge, watching as eight Earther ships formed around the Genesis vessels carrying the Naval and Church personnel, then turned and flew in system. The Earther ships certainly moved smoothly on the sensor displays...

But what sort of hosts were they going to be? Hastings had sent along more information, and had made it clear that the Earthers did have the superior technologies every Naval officer feared they had... if it came to a fight, the Genesis Fleet would lose.

Something the fleet was accustomed to, by now.

Tomorrow would tell. Whether Audrey approved of Hastings' cliquishness or not, she could be certain that the aliens wouldn't be able to mislead 100 Top Flight personnel: if they were hostile and just looking to wrong-foot the Navy, Hastings' people would figure it out.

Of course, it wouldn't be Hastings who got to decide if there was a fight with the Earthers — the Churchers would have that privilege. What if they wanted a fight but it wasn't needed? What if the Earthers were as friendly as they said they were, but the Church refused to play nice?

Audrey shifted in her seat and let out a sigh at the thought. For years the Navy had wondered whether the Larosians were really the bad guys. Obviously, they'd killed thousands and thousands of humans... but many in the Navy silently wondered if the Kroggs were in fact the galactic evil-doers, and that they'd just found the humans of Genesis to be a useful pawn in their war against good Larosians.

It was bad enough that countless Naval personnel had died fighting the Larosians at the behest of the Kroggs... would this fleet die fighting the Earthers because the Church couldn't let go of its ridiculous prophecy...

We'll know soon enough. Hopefully the Earthers are just bastards and I can at least be glad to be fighting them when they kill me. Or maybe they'll be nice, and the Church will deal with them...

Sighing again, Audrey leaned back in her chair and waited.

CHAPTER 5

ArcMajor Fletcher was silently pacing *Grendelsbane's* decks that night, trying to quell her own questions about this whole situation. She needed sleep, but as long as she was wondering about who these Earthers were, and what was going to become of this damned Quest, she wasn't going to get any.

Because the Heavy Cruiser was still at General Quarters condition yellow, the night lighting throughout the ship remained at full brightness, and there were people moving to and from their action stations even in the small hours of the morning watch. Fletcher nodded to everyone who passed her, noting the harried looks on all of their faces.

They had been at action stations for coming up on three days now — ever since they'd arrived in this system — and that sort of constant readiness was exhausting the young crew. Just as it was exhausting Fletcher — she needed what sleep she could get. But she couldn't sleep, because she was thinking about the Earthers, and all the rumors about who they were.

Right now, the Top Flight people Hastings had sent on to Earth were supposed to be bunking down on an Earther ship. Unless the Earthers had a mind to eat human flesh, what nefarious plan could there be behind letting humans aboard one of their ships? They were offering tours of Earth, welcoming people from the enemy Navy onto their vessels...

Are they friend or foe, dammit?

Just as that thought passed through Fletcher's head, she instinctively came to a stop, and bowed slightly at the waist. She'd seen the red cloaks of two Crusaders coming around the corner ahead of her, and long years of bowing to the Church made her reaction automatic.

The men passed without seeming to notice her, and as they continued up the corridor Fletcher had just come down, she eyed their backs.

What are they doing down here? We're decks from their section.

A frown started to form over the ArcMajor's brow, and she turned and continued the way she'd been going, moving with more purpose. Had they just executed someone? Were they looking for evidence of shaken faith? It was the middle of the night... Crusaders tended to spend nights in their own section.

Why would they want to be down here, near *Grendelsbane's* flight bay, at this hour?

Hurrying along, Fletcher turned a corner and arrived at one of the hatches that granted access to her ship's flight deck, home of its small craft. Keying the door, she stepped through and looked around.

No bodies, no sign of any trouble at all. She spotted one of the senior spacers on deck and approached him, waving to get his notice as she came closer.

"Chief," she nodded as they stopped in front of each other.

"Ma'am, what can I do for you?" this man looked exhausted, just as Fletcher knew she probably did, but his tone remained professional.

Fletcher bobbed her head back toward the hatch, "I just passed two Crusaders in the corridor. Looked like they'd come from here... were there any problems?"

The Chief's face darkened and he shook his head, "They were here, ma'am. But they just walked around, looking at things and muttering to themselves. We figured they were looking for signs that we were weak in faith."

Fletcher began to nod very slowly, and then looked around at the deck. There were five spacers on duty — the flight bay was considered low priority during General Quarters, because there weren't too many logical reasons to launch small craft during a missile fight.

So were the Crusaders expecting that the five people here were more likely to be faithless because they weren't on a combat-critical duty?

Or were they looking for something else...

"Thanks Chief. Keep sharp."

"Yes ma'am," the man nodded, then went about his business.

Fletcher turned back to the hatch.

What are they at?

If Audrey actually had been sleeping, she might have been annoyed at Fletcher's knock, but since she couldn't sleep, the distraction was actually welcome.

The news that led to the visit wasn't, however.

"I don't know, just have a bad feeling," Fletcher was sitting on Audrey's couch, and as the ArcColonel pulled her housecoat tighter around her and sat down, she frowned.

"You don't think they were out hunting for a faithless victim?" the skipper studied her XO.

Fletcher shook her head, "My gut says it was something different. When they went past me in the corridor they didn't even look at me... if they were looking for some*one*, they should have been checking everyone in green they came across. They didn't even seem to notice me."

"Well, we know you and I are off limits by Charters' order..." Audrey chewed out those words, but Fletcher shook her head again.

"I know, skipper... but... I don't know, why would you check out a ship's flight bay? Aside from looking for people, you could be checking it out to see how easy it'd be to secure."

Audrey froze in place at the implication, "You... wait, secure?"

Fletcher nodded, "If you had to take the ship. If you wanted to keep the crew from escaping."

"That's a lot to suggest, Sonya," Audrey leaned forward slowly. "You think it's that drastic?"

Fletcher shrugged, "I have a real bad feeling, skipper. And if it's that... well, we need to be at least aware of what's going on."

Audrey's chin dipped and she rubbed her brow, "Get word out to keep us informed of Crusader sightings. Just in case."

"Yes, ma'am."

Shaspa Charters found holding meetings in an airlock to be slightly disconcerting, but he needed to be certain that these discussions were in no way overheard by the Navy. There was always a chance, unlikely as it might be, that the Naval scum could tap the intercoms of other rooms in the Crusader section, but the airlock had no such intercom. It was a shrine of silence, like the Cave of Unity in the scriptures.

"Our patrols have checked the entire ship, sir," Crusader Sergeant Benson reported in a reverent tone. "Your predictions were correct: the crew appears exhausted, and at this status of General Quarters yellow, they are scattered such that securing the key sections of this ship should not be difficult."

Charters smiled at the positive report, "That is very good news, Michael. The Shappa will direct our actions upon his return from Earth tomorrow, but I believe his original mission for us will only be confirmed by his time among the Earthers. The Navy is weak, they will never stand against the beasts. Our brothers from the Colonizers, who are being trained in the ways of ship operation, will lead our struggle."

Benson bowed his head at those words, "Yes sir."

Charters turned away from the Sergeant, looking out the small window in the outer door of the airlock as his smile broadened. For centuries, the Church had tolerated the Navy because scripture had told them to. Now, the Quest would at last give them a chance to be rid of the non-believers...

CHAPTER 6

Audrey was swallowing a stimulant pill when the sensors panel chimed on *Grendelsbane's* bridge.

"The Earth trip is returning, ma'am, under escort from those Earther ships."

She nodded as she took a swig of water to chase the stim, then felt an almost-instant rush of new energy as the chemicals in the capsule entered her system. Putting the cap on the bottle of water she'd taken to the bridge with her, she handed it to a passing ArcEnsign and then climbed out of her chair.

"Alright, we should have news soon. Alert the crew that we may need to go to condition red at short notice."

Well, the fact that they're coming back together means we probably won't have any reason to fight... unless the Church decides they want to scrap...

Fletcher reached the bridge a few moments later, just as the small craft began leaving the two Genesis ships that had carried the officers and Churchers to Earth. On one of those shuttles, Hastings' senior crony, Sarah Manchester, would be waiting to give her report. Bactule would be on another... and whatever those two said would probably have the most influence on what happened next.

"How long do you think until we'll know if we need to start shooting?" Fletcher asked quietly.

Audrey shook her head, "I don't know. But..."

She didn't finish that sentence. She couldn't say what she was hoping out loud.

But I hope we don't have to...

The waiting lasted several hours, and Audrey and Fletcher passed the time together on *Grendelsbane's* bridge. Minutes seemed to drag out into days, and as the silence continued to dominate, both women grew more tense.

Stimulants could never replace sleep, but they were all either officer had at this stage — most of the crew were in the same state. For days, they'd been staring at that Earther fleet down missile tubes. Waiting for combat was the most stressful pastime imaginable, and at this rate it was going to seriously hurt the effectiveness of *Grendelsbane's* people...

"Signal going from *Genesis* to... to division flagships, ma'am."

The report from the communications officer sounded about as exhausted as Audrey would have expected. She turned with a frown, "Just to flagships?"

Nodding, the ArcLieutenant confirmed, "Only to the other ArcGenerals and ArcLieutenant-Generals, by the looks of it."

That figured. After all this waiting, Hastings was only going to pass word down through the chain of command. Being right near the bottom of that chain, Audrey and *Grendelsbane* would have to wait for news.

Charters was summoned to his screen by the chiming of his comm. A transmission had been sent from *Genesis* to all ships, on the secure channels that the Navy could not detect. The Shaspa wasted no time in opening the message, and Bactule appeared.

"Plans will be carried out in two days. Remain vigilant, and prepare for the triumph of our Gods."

A smile came to Charters' face with that message. As he had predicted, the visit to Earth had only stiffened the Shappa's resolve.

Excellent.

"Ma'am, flagship is calling all ArcColonels to meet. You're requested to be aboard *Cottswald City* in one hour for discussion of squadron tactics in an engagement," the communications officer sounded somewhat confused by the signal as he read it out, but it wasn't his job to interpret, just to report.

Audrey glanced at Fletcher and nearly let herself shrug. Signals had gone from the divisional flagships down to the squadron flagships only a few minutes before, and now the ArcBrigadier of *Grendelsbane's* squadron wanted a face-to-face?

Well, I suppose this'll either actually be a meeting about tactics, or something's up…

"Send my acknowledgment, have my pinnace readied."

With a nod to Fletcher, Audrey left the bridge.

Charters was pulling on his uniform robes when a knock came at his hatch.

"Come in," he turned to face the door as he buttoned up his tunic, and Benson stepped into the cabin.

"Sir, the ArcColonel is going aboard the squadron flagship for a meeting about tactics against the Earthers."

A frown formed on Charters' brow as he finished tugging his uniform into place, "Indeed? According to Shappa Bactule, the Earthers gave no indication that they would attack. The High Chancellor has issued no such orders, and without orders from him, I doubt Hastings would be so daring. I think this might be a meeting for other purposes, brother Michael."

Benson replied with a nod, "I do not trust the Navy, sir."

Charters collected his autopistol from its place on his desk, sliding it into the holster on his hip, "Join me, Crusader Sergeant, for a walk."

Nodding again, Benson followed Charters out of his cabin, and they proceeded down the corridor to the airlock. Stepping in, they shut the inner door and Charters turned to his loyal Holy warrior, "They may be preparing to refuse orders to fight. Perhaps they hope if they all refuse at once, we will not kill them for their faithless insolence."

"Could they know about the plan to remove them?" Benson's question was a prudent one.

"I don't think so..." Charters' words were soft, and his eyes narrowed thoughtfully, "...no. No, Crusader Sergeant, if they were aware that we were building the capacity to replace them, I doubt they'd be so foolish as to overtly meet in person. They think we are unaware of their impending treachery. We must watch DeBrooke and Fletcher. They will be at the head of any attempt to make this ship compliant to the Earthers. It will be a waste of savable souls, but we will kill them if necessary."

The Shaspa's words were filled with truth, and Benson bowed his head at their wisdom. True aptitude and foresight could only come from men strong in their faith, to whom the Gods were willing to communicate. Benson was not so blessed, but he knew to follow a man who was.

"We will be watchful, sir," the Crusader Sergeant affirmed his faith, and Charters nodded.

"Good. And I will inform the Shappa of our suspicions."

The Navy would regret any foolish actions it took in the coming days...

And in two days, we can eliminate them altogether. I hope they do not act before then... DeBrooke and Fletcher should be taken alive...

Charters smiled silently to himself.

CHAPTER 7

"*Mutiny?*"

Audrey was the first to blurt out the word in surprise, and ArcBrigadier Simon Guerin's eyes shifted coolly to her, "Yes, ArcColonel, you heard right."

What Audrey had just heard *couldn't* be right. One night with the Earthers and all the Top Flight idiots Hastings had sent out to Earth had decided to commit suicide by betrayal? They wanted to mutiny, lock down every ship in the Genesis Fleet and run to the Earthers?

"Sorry, sir, but I'm with Audrey: this is sounding a little too good to be true," Bill Wallace, the skipper of Audrey's division mate, *Darymanis City*, came to her defense.

Guerin nodded, "Yes, it did to me too. But this is big, it's coming right down from the top. Hastings is organizing it, and she wants every ship in the fleet on board. If we all go at once, the Crusaders will be taken right off guard. They can't fly our ships. We'd be able to dictate terms."

"Or the Earthers will destroy them?" one of the other ArcColonels in the squadron asked sharply, and Guerin shrugged.

"No one's said that to me. I can only guess that the Earthers will kill them while they're defenseless unless they surrender. And then when they surrender, we get our ships back, and we take the Churchers home as prisoners, and demand society be changed."

Oh just that easy... Audrey's skepticism was powerful... and she couldn't contain it.

"I'm sorry, we've known these *Earthers* for a couple of days, and now we're going to trust them to help us mutiny? What's in it for them?"

Guerin didn't seem to appreciate the tone of Audrey's question, and he glared at her, "They get a chance to end this without killing us, or possibly dying themselves. Look, I don't pretend to understand them. I've never seen one. But how close to mutiny is your crew right now as it is, Audrey? Mine's pretty damned close. We all do it together, we might just pull it off."

Bill Wallace leaned forward, "Yeah, but if we don't, then all our families die. Hastings is so convinced by these Earthers that she's willing to put my family on the line?"

Guerin nodded, "Yes."

Looking to Audrey, Bill shook his head, "I don't know. It's a huge risk to take on the word of an alien race I've never seen."

"Well I'll make it easy for you, Bill. It's an order," Guerin's tone had an edge. "We're doing this all together, all across the fleet. If any of us don't do it, we all will probably pay. And come on, you know you *want* to. We can get away from the Crusaders, get our own alien allies."

The Kroggs support for the Church was one of the things that made the structure of Genesis society so unchangeable, that was true. Audrey had to admit that the prospect of having a powerful alien on the side of the Navy alone sounded great... but in her short life, she'd seen a lot of things that 'sounded great', and had ended up being horrid.

Though, as always seemed to be the case for a cruiser skipper, she didn't have a lot of choice. Guerin couldn't really order her to *mutiny*, but he was right: what if the rest of the fleet went, but she didn't? If Hastings was organizing this silently from the top, then every ship in the fleet would be on the same mission.

What if 2,399 ships went, and *Grendelsbane* didn't?

Dammit...

"You have two choices. You can abandon ship and get to your life pods and small craft for a run out of the fleet, or you can try to take your ship from the Crusaders. I know for *Cottswald*, we're going to abandon. I plan to lockdown all systems on an intruder alert, then we're heading to the pods. All Navy small craft and ships are going to be given a special transponder so the Earthers can identify us and give us escort."

Guerin's explanation didn't do much to calm Audrey's racing mind.

Abandon ship?

Well I'm not leaving my ship to that bastard Charters...

"I'm not leaving *Grendelsbane* to those bastards," she voiced her thought almost immediately, and again Guerin glared at her.

"Well that's your choice. Good luck with your Crusaders."

The way he said that, Audrey could almost hear him saying 'It's been nice knowing you.' Trying to deal with sixty Crusaders in firefights in the corridors of a warship would be tough.

"I'll take *Darymanis*," Wallace looked at Audrey when he spoke. "Division mates stick together."

He smiled thinly, and Audrey nodded back. She was still too lost in the insanity of what was being said to appreciate Bill Wallace's decision, and the prospect of having his support.

The rest of the skippers of the twelve-ship Cruiser squadron were less daring. Isolating the Crusaders for long enough to get the crew off a ship was much easier and safer than trying to capture the ship. Fewer things could go wrong, fewer people would die... but the Crusaders would then have the ship.

Not that they knew how to fly the ships, but still... Audrey wasn't giving up her ship, her only leverage, because Hastings said the Earthers were trustworthy. If... *when*... it turned out that the Earthers were too good to be true, her crew would have a real chance of getting away, while all those who escaped in small craft would be trapped.

That was fine with Audrey.

The meeting broke after an hour of discussions, and as Audrey left the briefing room — still not fully accepting all she'd heard — Bill Wallace hurried after her.

"Audrey," he called quietly, then waved her to walk next to him.

She grudgingly accepted the offer, and as she fell into stride alongside him she spoke quietly, "We can't talk about anything out here."

He nodded, "I know. Just... well, we'll stick together in any fight... against the Earthers. Division ships stick together, no matter how much trouble there is... from whatever aliens we're facing."

Audrey couldn't tell if her fellow ArcColonel meant the Earthers or not. Certainly, he meant that during this ridiculous mutiny, *Darymanis City* and *Grendelsbane City* would cooperate closely... but after that, when they were among the Earthers, would they be sticking together then? Or did Bill believe the hype?

"Of course," Audrey couldn't ask for clarification, in case there were Crusaders nearby. Silence was essential. Whether she thought this plan was a good idea or not, it had momentum and organization from the top. The only way to make certain it wasn't suicide for all involved was to see to it the Crusaders weren't tipped off about it.

Bill and Audrey walked together all the way to *Cottswald City's* flight bay, where they departed in separate pinnaces.

CHAPTER 8

Audrey was tense as she answered the knock at her door. Her autopistol sidearm was in its holster on her hip tonight — a small comfort during troubled times — and she tried not to wrap her hand around it when she opened her hatch. If it *had* been a Crusader at the door, come to kill her for planning mutiny, that pistol would be her only slim hope...

But it was Fletcher, looking pale and anxious, and with her own sidearm snugly fitted to her hip.

"Sonya," Audrey nodded as the ArcMajor stepped in, and then closed the hatch behind her.

"I've passed the word. The officers are worried, the ordinary crew that I've heard from can't wait," Fletcher was whispering, even though Audrey had her bug-jammer on.

"Good," the ArcColonel spoke up more loudly, trying to project confidence that truly didn't exist.

She'd been back from *Cottswald City* for several hours, and after discreet meetings with *Grendelsbane's* senior staff, word was filtering down. Captain Davidson, commanding the detail of forty Naval Marines assigned to the Heavy Cruiser, was planning his attack on the Crusaders, and the crew was getting ready to assist.

"The crew are quite happy you said we won't give up our ship," Fletcher continued, rounding Audrey's coffee table and seating herself. "They don't even seem to care who these Earthers are... they just want a chance to kill the Crusaders."

The impetuous crew...

Audrey let out a sigh, "Are the officers worried about who we're running to?"

"Some of them," Fletcher sat back in her chair. "But... well, most of them don't care. They want to string Charters up, castrate him... there's angry talk. I've been reminding people they absolutely have to keep it quiet, but I don't know how long we'll have before the excitement gets to people."

Nodding, Audrey sat opposite her XO. Hastings hadn't given an exact timeline for the move — some time in the next day or two. The crew just had to contain themselves that long...

"Did the ArcBrig convince you about the Earthers, though... I mean, you really think this is right?" Fletcher looked up and locked eyes with Audrey, and the ArcColonel swallowed.

"I want to get out from under the Church," she said quietly. "I'll deal with the Earthers after that."

There were so many variables. The Earthers *had* to have an agenda, Audrey just had no way to know what it was. So many Genesis Navy personnel were so desperate to get away from the devils they knew... they could be running into the arms of more devils they didn't know.

But Hastings had decided, and now it had to be done...

"I hope Hastings and Manchester and the rest of those Top Flight bastards know what they're doing," Fletcher was nearly whispering again, her anxiousness making her feel sick.

Audrey nodded, sharing the queasiness with her ArcMajor.

"Look at it this way," she offered quietly, and her XO looked up at her. "This is the same as being ordered to attack the Earthers — it's a death sentence. But we *might* have a way to survive this one. So at least there's some hope."

Fletcher swallowed, "Except, if it fails, my sister and my mom will end up in a Crusader parish somewhere, and my dad will be shot."

Audrey blinked a couple of times, and then nodded.

"Except that," she rasped out the word. "So let's just do everything we can to make it work. Pray Gods it does..."

The Crusaders were standing outside Charters' cabin, anxiously awaiting the contents of the latest order that had arrived from *Genesis*. Benson was in front of them, his rifle slung over his shoulder and his head dipped, silent prayers being sent to the Gods for success and triumph in prophecy.

Almost as if to answer those prayers, Charters' hatch opened, and the Shaspa emerged into the corridor, a confident smile on his face.

"Brothers," he said softly, aware but not fearful that he might be overheard by the intercoms that *could* be tapped. The will of the Gods could not be stopped by eavesdropping. "Brothers, tomorrow, at the noon hour, we begin our quest for prophecy. Tonight you must take time to pray, prostrate yourselves before the Gods and be filled with their strength."

The Crusaders held up their heads, and then bowed them again. Their spirits reached up to the Gods of the Unity National, and their praise and joy filled the corridor. In reply, the Gods sent them strength and power to complete the Quest.

Charters could feel the power in this corridor. Gods' will would be done...

One drink to calm anxious nerves had turned into three, even though Audrey knew it shouldn't have. Vortexes were strong drinks, but she knew well how to mix them — in the academy, when she'd been young and innocent, she'd mixed them at parties.

Then, after her Dreadnought had been destroyed by the Larosians, and she'd been haunted in the night by the faces of her dead shipmates, she'd learned how to mix them quickly.

Now, she and Fletcher were doing the worst possible thing: they were trying to use them to relax.

What both these officers needed was a good night's sleep, to get them off the stims. Instead, they were adding alcohol to the mix, which wasn't going to sharpen their wits any...

"I just hope the Earthers have good booze," Fletcher laughed senselessly. "If we can drink with them, they'll be alright."

Both Audrey and Fletcher were, at least, good Genesis spacers: they had a high enough tolerance for alcohol that they weren't drunk yet.

They were just in much lighter spirits.

"I don't know, I'm hoping what they say about them being animals is true. They should be all cute and cuddly. Maybe I could keep one..." Audrey blurted that out dumbly, and before Fletcher could agree or goad her, the comm chirped and interrupted.

Audrey scowled, "Who's wrecking our girls' night?"

She hopped up and crossed her cabin quickly to her desk, keying the panel there to bring up an encrypted signal.

"Ooh, it's from Hastings," she keyed it open.

"All ships, all ships. We just got intel that Bactule is planning to spring some sort of trap to kill us all and replace us with Naval-trained Crusaders. Don't know how, but we have to move fast. His plan kicks off at noon, so we have to do this tonight. I'm sorry for the short notice, but if we go at 02:00 we can catch the Crusaders while they're praying for success or some damned thing. Make the preparations."

Audrey stared at the screen, and felt her stomach start to churn. She got to the bathroom before it voided its contents, and by the time she got back from that run, Fletcher had left the cabin to spread the word.

CHAPTER 9

Captain Colin Davidson didn't have a good plan for dealing with the Crusaders, and that much became clear to Audrey as soon as he reported to her cabin an hour later.

"Colin, we have *two hours* to get this right," Audrey was trying not to stare at the chronometer on her wall, and the Marine nodded.

"I know that, ma'am, but they have all the advantages. The way this ship was *built* gives them all the advantages. If I try to get into their section through force of arms, they can cut me down in the entry corridor. That's why they only have one way in…" Davidson was barely twenty-three, and this was his first time commanding a Marine detail. He wasn't ready for this sort of operation — at least not on such short notice.

Audrey's head was foggy, the detox pills combining with the Vortexes and the stims to put her in a sticky, stifling haze. But she wasn't about to let her crew down: she was fighting through that haze.

"Well what advantages does that give us? The one entrance, I mean. We can drop the bulkheads leading in there on an intruder alert lockdown…" she rubbed her temple, pacing across her cabin floor as she did.

"That could hold them for a while, ma'am, but they're going to get out of there eventually. How long is it going to take to get this ship to somewhere where we can get some help in killing them?" Davidson's question was again much too panicked for a man of his rank.

Audrey shook her head, trying not to allow herself to get irritated, "I… there's no way to know how long. We need to kill them, though."

"If we just abandoned ship, the bulkheads would be enough, ma'am. They'll hold the Crusaders long enough for us to get off…"

"*No*," that answer was sharp, but as far as Audrey was concerned, it had to be. "If the Earthers turn out to be troublemakers, I want this ship. I want the ability to get me and you and all of us the hell out of here. Is that *clear*?"

Davidson swallowed and stiffened.

"Good, now *figure out how to do your damned job*," Audrey's words were quite harsh, but Davidson had it coming.

He nodded hurriedly, "I'll get volunteers from the security staff… if we rush them… we might have a chance."

Audrey huffed and rubbed her forehead, "Listen, Colin, no *might*. Do it. All our lives depend on you getting this done. Clear?"

She wasn't keeping her cool, which was a mistake. She knew it, but she couldn't help herself — she was far too edgy after the drink, the detox pills and the cumulative use of stims.

"Of course, ma'am," Davidson said it tightly, then turned to leave.

Looking at his back, Audrey shook her head. If the Crusaders were going to space anyone, it should have been this guy...

That was too far. Stop it now, you need to get a handle on yourself. You can't behave like this, you're the skipper around here. Get your head on straight. There will be no spacing...

"Wait."

She said that before she quite realized what she was thinking.

"Colin... get me someone from engineering. Get ArcLieutenant Kenzie. Get him up here now. Quietly."

She had an idea.

Sergeant Benson found himself unable to sleep. In a man of his rank and experience, that was perhaps a surprising quality, but the excitement of what was to come in scant hours was too much for him to contain. While he ordered that his Crusaders rest for their long day to come, Michael Benson remained awake, and paced the decks of the Crusader section with his rifle slung over his shoulder.

It would be good, at last, to put this Quest entirely in the hands of the faithful. Had Benson been of a higher rank, and had he been asked to advise the Chancellery on this Quest, the exclusion of the heretic Navy would have been his only recommendation. It would be a sacrifice for those in the Church assigned to the duties once reserved for the Naval class, but on a mission of such importance as this Quest to Earth, could a faithful man truly think that any role, however lowly, was unworthy of him?

Alas, it was not for Benson to decide. He was but a soldier — one humble servant of the Gods, an executor of their will. Those who knew much more than he did, men like Shaspa Charters, were much better equipped to make such decisions.

And now, they had decided as he would have. At last...

Passing a chronometer in the corridor, he noted that the time was turning to 01:20 hours. Very soon, the great purge would begin...

"Sergeant!"

The call from behind surprised Benson, and he turned quickly at the urgent summons. Shaspa Charters had stepped out the door of his cabin and now waved, "Michael, join me please."

Benson could detect a tension in the Shaspa's tone, and with a frown he hurried to the door to the Shaspa's cabin. Charters stepped aside to let his

Sergeant enter, then shut the hatch after him, "There is word of an uprising on a Battlecruiser. It seems the heresy of the Earthers found purchase with one of the weak women."

Stiffening, Benson swung his rifle off his shoulder and held it in front of him, "Do we expect the same reaction aboard this ship, sir?"

Charters was hurrying to his desk to replay the urgent message that he'd just received from Shappa Bactule, but he stopped at that suggestion, then looked back.

"I hadn't thought so, Sergeant. Perhaps attentiveness is warranted... but I do not imagine that the foolish heresy of one ship will spread. If the Navy was seeking to rise up, they would not do it one ship at a time — they would not give us warning time. No, I think this is just one officer... Manchester, that harlot whose parents published heresy... she is the leader of it."

Charters had reasoned through that answer as he'd given it. When Bactule's alert had come in, it had seemed only to be a piece of important news. The rebellious Naval types on *Warlock Prophet* would soon be crushed decisively, and the people of the Navy would be chastened moving into the last day of their lives...

"Michael, this will work to our advantage tomorrow. We can assemble the crew in one place to tell them the dangers of rebellion, as demonstrated by the crew of *Warlock Prophet*. Then we can show them what their punishment as a group will be."

Benson took comfort from the righteous confidence in Charters' voice, and he nodded, lowering his rifle from its ready position, "Gods' will, sir."

Charters nodded with a smile, "Gods' will, brother. Come and watch the message."

Two sections away, ArcLieutenant Kenzie, *Grendelsbane's* chief engineer, entered a crawlspace with a hand lamp and a tool kit. Standing at the open access panel to the chute, Sonya Fletcher kept a lookout for unwanted observers.

"Make it fast, Vlad. We don't have a lot of time to get this right," she said softly. With a wordless nod, Kenzie hurried into the dark passage.

It was 01:25. *Grendelsbane City* was due to be liberated in just over half an hour...

CHAPTER 10

Audrey stepped out of the main armory with an autopistol in her hand, and its drop holster clipped to her thigh. Around her were twenty of *Grendelsbane's* crew — all that could be armed from this main armory. Throughout the ship, weapons were being passed out from arms lockers, so nearly three quarters of the Battlecruiser's personnel would be armed when the fight started.

But there was no plan.

Nearly three quarters of the crew amounted to 110 men and women, and the Naval Marines added another forty, bringing the total to 150... that sounded like a lot, but the sixty Crusaders they were going to try to contain would be much better armed, and better trained. With no plan, there was no guarantee that this mutiny would succeed.

We'll probably all end up shot.

Audrey tried to quiet her inner doubts. Her mind was clear of the post-drinking fog, but the loss of the fog was exposing the ridiculousness of this situation to the light of reason. On *two hours notice*, they were going to try to launch an attack that would dislodge sixty Crusaders from this ship?

Keep calm. Don't let the crew see.

"We have a plan, ArcLieutenant Kenzie is working on it right now, but the fleet is going to mutiny in..." she checked her watch "...four minutes. When they do, Charters' Crusaders are going to come looking for us... so we have to meet those bastards. I want to contain the Crusader section."

There was a murmur of uncertainty mixed with anger and even *hunger*. These people wanted to kill Crusaders — that was certainly their right — but they also were under no illusions that it'd be easy. The 'loudmouths' who, in whispers, would always talk about wishing for just this chance to get their revenge, were now silent. The Crusaders were good shock troops. The bastards...

"We're going to try to override their hatch and lock them in... but if that doesn't work, or if they can shoot their way through, we need to keep them tied up. We have to be stubborn," for all her doubts, Audrey was reasonably certain she was sounding confident. "Clear?"

The nods she received in answer weren't particularly inspiring, but at this stage she couldn't be particular.

"Good, let's move."

•••

Fletcher's fingers were playing on the handle of her autopistol as it sat in its holster on her thigh. She wanted this done... they were down to *no* time and Kenzie still hadn't managed it...

"Come on," she muttered quietly, and as she checked her chrono, she held her breath.

It was 02:00 hours.

Benson was sitting across from Charters, watching the latest update as the Crusaders from a squadron near the troublesome Battlecruiser closed to board.

"Those crafty scum," Charters shook his head. "How dare they shoot down our noble warriors in space... a horrible way to die."

With a nod, Benson glanced at the chrono, "Our brothers from the nearby squadron should hopefully meet with more success..."

The feed suddenly winked out.

Benson and Charters froze in surprise for a moment, thinking at once that there must be a technical fault in the comm grid. Then, at the same time, they both realized that the reality could be much more sinister.

"Call our brothers to arms," Charters was on his feet instantly, arming himself as he did. He then turned to his screen and, "Initiate Crusader Lockdown Faithful!"

"Should be... now..." Audrey was crouching with the forty crew she'd joined at the armory, and the Marines under Captain Davidson. They were just down the corridor from the Crusader section, and their wait was about to end...

Then the lights shifted color to red, and a klaxon sounded.

Audrey looked upward in surprise... they'd activated their lockdown!

"How the hell... did they know we were coming?" one of the crew hissed immediately.

Gods help us... I have to get to a control terminal...

Audrey could theoretically overturn a Crusader lockdown with her own intruder alert lockdown, not that she — or anyone — had ever tried that before. She had to try now, though. With the Crusaders in control, there'd be no way to lock down their section.

"I'll get it overturned. Colin, take them in, hold the Crusaders!" holstering her auto-pistol, Audrey straightened up and started sprinting down the corridor. She had to get to auxiliary control... she could try to regain command functions from there...

"How the hell did they know we were coming?" another spacer protested, but without trying to answer the now-pointless question, Captain Davidson led the horde of armed Naval personnel down the corridor towards the Crusader section.

• • •

From sleeping soundly to formed up in just a moment, the Crusaders of Shaspa's Charters company did him proud. They lined up now in the corridor outside his cabin door, absent only the two men who he'd sent to watch the entrance a dozen meters around the corridor.

"Brothers, the Naval scum on one of the Battlecruisers mutinied tonight. Now we have lost telemetry from the flagship. I fear that we may be dealing with an insurrection, and as such, I have woken you. We cannot wait: we must eliminate our own heretics now, before they cause trouble. We will move cabin to cabin in teams of five. Sergeant Benson will take a team directly to the Naval Marines barracks, and deal with them there. I will lead a team to—"

Rifle fire cracked from around the corner, and Charters' head jerked to cast his gaze in that direction, "Or perhaps we will all fight the heretics here and now!"

Wasting no time, he hefted his own rifle and called to his men, "Brothers! Come brothers, and fight those who would defy the will of the Gods!"

The men followed him.

Davidson's squad had two sets of portable breastworks, and now one of them stopped three explosive rifle rounds that had been coming for his face.

Popping up again, he sprayed the corridor ahead with his rifle, trying to keep the heads of the Crusaders down. The two who'd been guarding the entrance had seen him coming, and now they were proving more difficult to hit than he'd like.

"Come on, let's go!" a spacer roared from behind him, and before Davidson could open his mouth to stop the woman's brash command, a handful of Naval personnel had sprinted around the breastworks.

They were cut down without mercy, and as they fanned out in the corridor ahead of the Marines, they blocked the lines of fire.

"Dammit I said *stay where you are! Stay out of our fields of fire!*" Davidson leaned up and roared those words back at the disgruntled spacers sheltering behind. Despite their fear, they all wanted to be in this fight… they just had no training for it.

Gritting his teeth, Davidson looked back down the corridor… just in time for the spray of rounds from Shaspa Charters' rifle to punch through his forehead and to shower those behind in brain matter.

Davidson's body dropped heavily to the deck, and some of his Marines started to lose their composure, rising a little too high over their breastworks in shock or anger. The Crusaders were fanatical zealots, but they were also a cohesive military unit, well armed and in control of the situation.

Marines started dying, and as Naval personnel rushed to take their place, the ill-trained spacers and junior officers died even faster.

•••

Fletcher heard the cacophony of rifle fire just around the corridor and gritted her teeth. She needed to be there with her crew, Gods dammit.

Just as that thought occurred to her, she watched a party of a dozen officers and spacers jog through the intersection down the corridor from her, clearly heading towards the Crusader section.

"Vlad you bastard, come *on!*" Fletcher's temper was slipping out of her grasp, and she now pounded the rim of the hatch he'd gone through with the flat of her palm.

"I can't work fucking miracles!" there was no mistaking the utter panic in his voice as he screamed back. "It's their lockdown! They... they fucked it all up... I can't..."

Fletcher dropped into a crouch and turned to look into the crawlspace, "You bastard! *Find a way! People are dying out there!*"

They didn't have long.

The screams of spacers in agony were echoing all the way to the entrance to the service chute Audrey found to take her up to the Aux Control deck. Every scream cut right through her, and she chewed her lip as she resisted the urge to run back to her people — she should be there with them...

But she had to override the lockdown. She should have thought this all through better... she should have locked down first, been ready for this... she'd been so foolish... drunk...

Move it. No time for this.

Only the hard inner voice convinced Audrey to open the hatch to the service shoot and make her way up to the next level. She had to break the Crusader lockdown — she had to drop bulkheads and seal the Crusaders in...

In the meantime, her crew died.

CHAPTER 11

Shaspa Charters had never been in a firefight before, but as his Crusaders dropped several sets of portable breastworks in front of him, he felt years of training taking hold of him. With the help of the Gods, he was proving himself equal to the task of putting down these Naval heretics. He had killed their Captain himself!

"Grenades!" Benson was next to Charters, and the Sergeant's command was instantly executed. Four Crusaders lobbed their bombs into the air, dropping them with practiced ease behind the Naval fighters' meager protection. The explosions were followed by wails of agony.

"Brother Finnigan, take a team and cleanse the living," Benson gave the next order, and taking advantage of the shock of that volley of grenades, ten Crusaders leapt forward past their own breastworks.

The Navy cowards didn't fire on them.

"Behind us, Shaspa!"

Charters had begun to feel slightly smug, but that warning forced him to correct himself. More heretics were coming, these from the opposite direction.

"Join me in the attack, brothers!" he surged in that direction, leveling his rifle at the green-clad heretics who had appeared clumsily in the corridor behind him.

The sight of dozens of red-robed Crusaders surging up the corridor at them proved too much for the cowardly scum.

"Get back," their leader screamed without dignity, firing her autopistol very badly as she tried to retreat. Charters felt the power of the Gods surge through him, and that power channeled into his mind and his eyes, making his aim true.

The woman's chest burst under the fire of his explosive shells, and then the brothers flowing up the corridor behind him fired as well, knocking down five of the unbelievers before they could escape around a corner.

Slowing to a stop, Charters looked back over his shoulder, "Sergeant Benson, take half the men in the opposite direction. Let us cleanse this ship!"

Fletcher heard the rifle fire getting closer, and drew her autopistol from its holster as soon as the haggard remnants of the Naval fire team fled into the corridor she was standing in.

"What's going on?" she demanded, taking a few steps away from the hatch she was guarding.

"They're coming!" one of the spacers gasped, then turned his pistol back on the intersection.

Fletcher's mind raced, and for a moment she raised her pistol and aimed it towards the intersection. They had no chance of surviving a firefight here... they'd be cut down in the open corridor...

"Keep retreating," she barked as she realized that. Holstering her own weapon she crouched and started struggling into the crawlspace behind ArcLieutenant Kenzie. "Lead them past us. We *have* to finish what we're doing here!"

The spacers all looked at Fletcher in surprise, and then seemed to freeze as they tried to understand what she was saying. The ArcMajor cursed inwardly — Audrey hadn't told the crew the whole plan, so these spacers must have had no idea what was going on...

And taking time to try to understand it killed them all — Crusaders swept into the intersection and shot down all of them in a flurry of rifle fire.

Sonya Fletcher wanted to scream and to shoot back... instead she shut the hatch and hissed at Kenzie to be silent as he worked.

Audrey reached the deck above the Crusader zone and opened the entry hatch, only to be greeted by the muzzle of a rifle. A nervous spacer quickly yanked the weapon away from her face as he recognized her, and Audrey nodded to him.

"If they start coming up the chute or the lifts, we have to stop them. I'm going to Aux Control," she brushed past the spacer and two of his friends as she said those words, then broke again into a run.

Auxiliary Control was just ahead, and there was a spacer with an autopistol guarding the door. Audrey nodded to the woman and hurried past her into the compartment. The consoles here were all abandoned — they were of no use to the spacers and officers who would normally have watched them, because the Crusader lockdown had disabled all command function.

But perhaps Audrey could get that function back, drop some decompression doors to contain the Crusaders...

Holstering her pistol, she got to work. She wasn't a flag officer... would she be able to make this work?

Fletcher tried not to breathe as she heard the fall of Crusader boots just outside the hatch. Had they seen her come in here... did they know she was hiding?

Seconds stretched, and blood pounded in her ears. She had to hope...

Come on, go past us. Don't see us... come on you bastards... come on...

Her thoughts were jagged, and she realized her hands were shaking.

The silence was deafening.

Then Vlad Kenzie intruded in it.

"I got it! I got it to work!"

With all the adrenalin in his veins, the ArcLieutenant yelled that with far, far too much enthusiasm — and volume.

Fletcher didn't even bother to turn to hiss at him to order silence, she just raised her autopistol. In the confines of the crawlspace, she was lying on her back with the feet up against the rim of the hatch, so when the first Crusader yanked it open, she was able to get a reasonable shot. The man in red fell, but the Church warrior right behind him lined up on her and sprayed.

She had nowhere to go: the explosive bullets punched through the bottom of her torso and shredded her.

ArcMajor Fletcher died lying in the dark.

With bitter timing, then, the comm attached to her belt sounded: "Sonya? Sonya I've overridden the lockdown. Are we good? Sonya?"

Audrey had felt such a wash of relief when the Crusader lockdown had crumpled before her intruder alert code. Now the Navy had control of *Grendelsbane's* systems again — the way they would have if Audrey had thought things through better in the first place.

But the relief didn't last. Sonya wasn't answering her comm.

The bastards had gotten to Sonya... was this entire plan about to collapse? Did Kenzie get the work done before they'd been discovered...?

There's one way to find out for sure... you need to do it before you lose containment.

The cold reality behind that thought shook Audrey's fingers into motion, and she tapped a layout of the deck below onto the screen of the console at which she sat. She swallowed and started identifying emergency pressure doors to drop in the corridors.

She cursed the Crusaders, and then she started activating the necessary controls.

Shaspa Charters was in no hurry — the Naval fools seemed determined to come to him, to engage the Crusaders in open corridors, where their chances of survival against Church marksmanship were nonexistent. It suited him.

Perhaps fifty heretics were now dead, including the foolish Naval Marines who had been in the front line of the failed blockade on the Crusader section. There would be many more dead Naval fools soon...

There was a dull thud ahead — one unlike any Charters had yet heard in this firefight. The Crusaders ahead of him increased their pace, and rounded the bend in the corridor, ready to meet any treachery.

Then the leading Holy warrior turned back to his Shaspa, "The way is blocked by a pressure door!"

Before Charters could respond, a new set of warning klaxons began to sound.

The spacer who'd been watching the door to the Auxiliary Control room edged in behind her skipper as she heard the console chime, "Ma'am?"

Audrey blinked and looked back over her shoulder, "Turnabout is fair play, spacer."

The words were said bitterly, and there was little disguising the anger in them. Audrey wished they'd felt more satisfying — that what she was about to do would satisfy the hunger she'd long entertained. She was about to end the Crusaders... but with so many of her own people obviously dead now, that wasn't something to celebrate.

She just wanted it over with. She wanted them gone... then she'd have to count her dead...

Without any ceremony, then, she overrode the Church security protocols on the airlock in their section, and simultaneously opened both its inner and outer doors.

"Good job with the override, Vlad..." she whispered to herself.

Charters was lifted from the deck and the breath was torn from his lungs. He let go his rifle and tried to reach out to grip something as the atmosphere was torn out of the ship around him. He realized, as the seconds of his death seemed to slow, that the heretics had found a way to override control of his airlock.

Now, the platform from which unbelievers were sent to the Gods would be the death of the faithful on this ship.

He would go to the Gods, and apologize for his failure in the face of Naval treachery.

Making a half-hearted attempt to stop his flight to doom, Charters reached out towards a door-frame — the one, in fact, to his cabin. As he'd reflected upon the irony of his death, he'd traveled far through the corridors, and was already back in his own section.

He must have impacted door frames along the way, for there was a great pain in his ribs.

As he reached out now, a hand clutched his: it was Benson, his trusty Sergeant Benson.

Gritting his teeth, the Sergeant was holding onto the opposite side of the frame to Charters' cabin. The men locked eyes with each other, and as they did, the suction stopped: the atmosphere was gone.

Dropping to the deck, they nodded to each other — brothers in faith — and then they both froze, bloated, burst and died together, hand in hand.

Gods' will.

•••

In Auxiliary Control, Audrey rested her face in her hands for a moment, and forced herself not to think about any of her own people who would have been caught in the section she'd just decompressed. She hoped there hadn't been any...

Her comm interrupted her sad thoughts, "Ma'am, bridge here... we're in trouble... we've got all sorts of destroyers coming in to join us. We need you!"

Of course they did — *Grendelsbane* was still sitting at the rear of the fleet.

Well, she'd have to do something about that. She'd have to get this ship out of here, probably in company with Bill Wallace. She'd have to go to Earth, find an Earther, and ask that Earther whether it was as good as Hastings seemed to think it was. Because Audrey DeBrooke had just lost plenty of good people on the promise that the Earthers really were that good.

She got to her feet and left Auxiliary control moments later.

Shortly thereafter, Andra Ursla's 111th Flying Squadron saw *Grendelsbane City*, *Darymanis City* and their consorts safely out of the Genesis Fleet.

EPILOGUE

Grendelsbane City came through the Battle of the Belt with scrapes and burns, but essentially intact.

Essentially.

Audrey DeBrooke bitterly repeated the word in her mind as she folded her arms across her chest and looked around the flight deck. One of the hits they had taken from a Church laser — a graze only, thank Gods — had blown out power relays across the flight deck, so jagged pieces of paneling had been fired off walls at great speed, leaving dents and sections of torn alloy all over.

Hardly the crisp, refined look a good ArcColonel sought for her ship. Her engineering and repair crews were working hard now, trying to make good the damage, but they were still understaffed — there'd been no time to bring aboard replacements for people like Kenzie since the battle.

In time, Audrey imagined Hastings... no, it was *Manchester* now... would assign some of the personnel who'd abandoned their ships to the Church to *Grendelsbane's* crew. That would help, perhaps, though Audrey wasn't sure she'd be able to welcome new faces particularly well.

The carnage on her ship had kept her from thinking very highly of too many of her fellow Genesis Naval types — especially the leaders. What had Hastings been thinking, trying to bring off a mutiny that vast on such short notice?

And who were these Earthers, really?

Though days had passed since the end of the fighting against the Church, Audrey still hadn't seen one, let alone met one. Sure, she'd seen their ships fighting, and that was impressive enough — some 'Commodore' called Ursla had bailed *Grendelsbane* and *Darymanis* out of their captivity at the rear of the Genesis Fleet, and then in the Battle of the Belt those Earther ships had proved incredibly powerful...

But she could have said the same of the Kroggs before this all started.

Powerful didn't mean good.

Well, you're about to get your answer, aren't you? Here they come.

The Earthers — not the Genesis Fleet, the *Earthers* — were the first to be sending a team of engineers to assist with repairs aboard *Grendelsbane City*. On one level, Audrey could understand that Manchester was trying to re-sort the Genesis Fleet from nothing, and thus didn't have extra engineer crews organized... but it still felt wrong to her. Why couldn't the top brass of her own fleet get their act together, while these Earthers could?

As these thoughts dogged her, Audrey watched a shining silver pinnace slide impressively through the force field at the end of the landing bay, and with an austere grace, park itself across two guest landing slots — the Earther ship was much larger than the usual Genesis small craft.

It landed with no bang, hiss or whine, and as Audrey approached it cautiously, she realized it wasn't going to start venting coolant at her. Impressive technology, to be sure — the ramp was even lowering silently.

Now she'd get to see what these Earthers were about. She had her suspicions already. Like the Kroggs, they'd undoubtedly promised help for 'nothing', and they probably had an agenda all their own. Audrey didn't like that thought much, though perhaps it would be good to have some nasty aliens on the side of the Navy... the Kroggs were on the side of the Church, after all.

"Um, excuse me. Sorry, would you be Captain... sorry, I mean *ArcColonel* DeBrooke?"

The question surprised Audrey — she hadn't heard anyone come down from the pinnace, but sure enough, the rich, warm voice had come from a figure standing right in front of her... from quite a thing.

It was an Earther, and Audrey stared at it. It had white fur, a long mouth and nose, pointed ears, and a royal blue uniform that looked parade-ground crisp. Its words had been perfectly enunciated, and its tone warm and friendly... and... for some reason she felt at ease.

That last part hit her abruptly and struck her as odd. She frowned at the white thing as she tried to process that feeling — it was almost instinctive, in her gut. She'd seen a Krogg once, and it had made her skin crawl... this thing didn't. Maybe it was because it came from the same world as her ancestors... maybe it was because it was an evil creature trying to lull her into a false sense of security...

It coughed politely, and then smiled.

"Sorry, I should have checked... I'm guessing I'm the first Earther you've met?"

The question didn't lose any of the earlier warmth, and Audrey realized she'd been staring — probably quite rudely. Before she could answer, the creature chuckled and extended his hand, "I'm a wolf — an arctic wolf, to be specific. Lieutenant Zed Dune, chief engineer from *ENS Galatea*. Pleased to meet you, ma'am."

It was all too much for Audrey to process quickly — she was still consumed by looking at this strange creature. She took its... *his* hand on sheer auto pilot, and nodded a couple of times without thinking.

"Audrey DeBrooke... welcome..."

She stammered to a halt, then blinked her mind into action again, "Sorry,

I'm ArcColonel DeBrooke... welcome aboard... Lieutenant."

Zed Dune's smile grew, "Thank you ma'am. I'm really not sure what we can do for you yet. This is actually my first time meeting a human too, so I can't say I know much about your systems. But we'll do our very best, I can assure you."

His first meeting with a human? How can he be so calm about it?

"Sorry, if you're wondering why I'm so relaxed, I should say that I've watched plenty of old movies from the human times. I do know what humans look like... this must be a real new experience for you and your crew," Zed somehow knew what she was thinking.

"Did you just read my mind?" Audrey countered in a flat and serious tone. The Kroggs were supposed to be able to do that... some of them, anyway.

Zed cocked an eyebrow, "Hm? No, just guessed. Sorry, I'm getting ahead of myself..."

Audrey noticed that Dune's engineering team had disembarked, and they came in all different shapes and sizes... one of them close to three meters tall. All human activity on the deck had stopped — everyone was staring at the Earthers, but they all seemed friendly and welcoming of the attention.

"So what can we help with?" Zed pressed the question gently, and Audrey recognized that he was trying to help push her out of her mental tailspin.

"Um... well I'll take you to engineering. You can meet my head of repairs and figure it out from there. Alright?"

Zed nodded with another rich smile, "Works for me..." Then he paused and cocked an eyebrow, "Will he fit?"

As he asked the question, he bobbed his head towards the big fuzzy brown Earther that stood nearly three meters tall. Audrey frowned and shook her head, "Sorry... we don't have anybody that tall... well... in humanity."

Zed chuckled and nodded, then glanced back, "You'll have to help out on the flight deck, Rom."

The Earther grinned, "I like the head room, boss."

They were all so *happy*. Audrey couldn't think of a better way to put it — her crew was under so much stress, but these Earthers seemed so relaxed.

"Follow me," her tone was perhaps too sharp, and she turned away from Zed with some effort — she still wanted to stare at him.

"Ma'am, actually, if I could talk to you quickly while they go ahead," Zed said softly, and she stopped in mid-step and nodded.

"Alright..." she turned and pointed to a couple of officers on the deck. "Take our guests to engineering please."

As the rest of the Earthers (save for 'Rom') headed off the flight deck, Audrey turned back to Zed, and found his smile had gone.

So this was it — the other shoe was about to drop. They were all smiles and jokes at first, but now this white wolf was going to lay down the rules. If she wanted the help of their superior engineers, she'd have to play ball, the way Hastings evidently had. She'd known these bastards were too good to be true.

"We all heard about the crew you lost in the mutiny, ma'am. Took a little digging, but when we were assigned to assist you, we looked. On behalf of my skipper, and for all of us... we're sorry. And thank you."

Zed's soft words locked Audrey in place. Zed studied her face for a moment, then cocked an eyebrow, wondering if he'd said more than he should have... but his instincts told him to wait silently.

Audrey didn't have any reply for a moment. She'd heard nothing like that from her own chain of command — Manchester and Conroy and the rest were all so wrapped up in trying to fix this shadow of a fleet that none of them had sent word down... not so much as a message of congratulations.

She realized she was staring again, so she tried to talk, "I... uh... sorry. We don't get that sort of commentary around here much. We're a Heavy Cruiser, they don't tell us much, and they thank us even less."

A frown seemed to crease Zed's brow, "Don't tell you much?"

Audrey nodded, "Yeah, you know how it is... well what's your ship again? Is it comparable to a cruiser?"

Zed nodded, "We're a 36-gun frigate... similar to a Battlecruiser, I believe."

"So you probably don't get much news from the top... from your fleet commander. Right?" Audrey half shrugged.

Zed looked genuinely surprised, "Um. No, we hear from First Lord Caine all the time. He keeps us informed of the strategic situation... why we're doing what we're doing... the usual. You don't get that?"

Audrey nearly started staring again, her surprise on the one hand pleasant and on the other almost bitter. Maybe if this *Caine* had been her fleet commander, she'd have had enough warning to properly plan the mutiny.

"We don't get much," she said finally, forcing herself to smile. "But thank you for your thoughtfulness, Lieutenant."

"Not at all... we... well, it's what we do..." he paused for a moment. "I can't imagine what it must be like to live without it. If we lost our communications lines to the top, I think we'd all probably leave the service."

Audrey chuckled now, waving Zed in the direction of the exit from the flight deck, "What, just up and leave?"

Zed nodded, "Indeed. Let me guess, you don't have a volunteer fleet... mandatory terms of enlistment, I think they used to call it."

Putting one foot in front of the next kept Audrey's continuing disbelief from growing too acute. She'd known this creature... she'd known *Zed*... for five minutes, and yet she already *liked* him. And he was already making her envious.

"Let's... let's not talk about that right now, Zed. I'll get depressed. I shouldn't say this to you, or to anyone, but I'm not impressed with my fleet command right now. And I can't just leave."

Zed cocked an eyebrow and looked sideways at her as they walked, "Why not?"

Audrey came to a stop, her face becoming quizzical, "Well... *because*..."

Halting and looking back at the ArcColonel, Zed realized he was probably getting a little bit ahead of himself. Humans probably would probably frown on talk of... what was it they called it in the movies... *desertion*, right. This was ArcColonel DeBrooke's first meeting with an Earther... probably better not to overload her with the culture differences.

So Zed changed the subject, "Sorry ArcColonel, I'm getting ahead of myself. Let's talk about... people. You lost your XO and your chief engineer, I understand. Tell me about them. Tell me the funniest stories you have about them. I never got to meet them, and I'm sure that's my loss... so tell me about those people."

Audrey had to blink several times to bring her mind round to that question, and then to process the genuine interest in it. It seemed a morbid thing to ask — why did he care who the dead were?

"Why do you want to know about them?" she asked, her tone cooling again.

Zed's face seemed to neutralize, and he took a step towards her, "They were your friends. If they were my friends, I'd want every chance I could get to tell people about them, to tell the funny stories... to remember them, so they can live on."

Audrey was silent.

"And besides, they died, ultimately, defending my home. It's the least I can do to learn their names, and remember them myself," Zed followed up softly.

In that moment, despite all her better judgment, Audrey DeBrooke realized she liked Zed Dune, and that she liked Earthers. She understood why Hastings could have trusted them so quickly. Something felt *right* about the Earthers.

That didn't excuse Hastings' complete lack of planning, or Manchester's silence since the end of fighting, but at least this all had perhaps — perhaps — been for a good reason.

"Well... my XO was an ArcMajor called Sonya Fletcher. She would have loved to meet you, I think..." Audrey started walking again, and with a smile, Zed fell into step next to her.

The Quest had come to an end, and a new journey was just getting started.

Zed Dune, for one, was looking forward to it.

THE ENTIRE SERIES FROM ICEBERG PUBLISHING

THE
EQUATIONS NOVELS

The Earthers evolved after humans were driven from the Earth by an intelligent bio-weapon dubbed 'Omega'. They are faster, stronger, smarter, wiser, *better* than humans, and they are the only hope for the survivors of the human race as an interstellar war between two great alien powers absorbs the galaxy. But all is not as it seems, and the humans and the Earthers face challenges that overshadow the wars of alien empires and threaten to destroy their civilizations...

The Equations Novels by Kenneth Tam

Book One: THE HUMAN EQUATION (Oct 2003)

Book Two: THE ALIEN EQUATION (May 2004)

Book Three: THE RENEGADE EQUATION (Dec 2004)

Book Four: THE EARTHER EQUATION (July 2005)

Book Five: THE GENESIS EQUATION (July 2006)

Book Six: THE VENGEANCE EQUATION (July 2007)

Book Seven: THE NEMESIS EQUATION (July 2008)

Book Eight: THE DESTINY EQUATION (July 2009)

The Equations Novels are complete, but there are spinoff series and new stories in the Earther universe still to come!

For more information, please visit
www.earther.net

ALSO AVAILABLE FROM ICEBERG PUBLISHING

KENNETH TAM'S
DEFENSE COMMAND
SERIES

The Earth Empire has holdings across the solar system and though it is plagued by piracy, politics, and the press, it remains, in 2231, the leading bastion of human civilization. But the former colony of Mars — with its new 'Imperium' — is hostile to the Empire, and now the Martians are causing trouble.

Learn about the Martian War from one of the heroes of the Empire's Defense Command, the irreverent then-Commodore Ken Barron. Written twenty years after the events, these books are his 'reminiscences', told with caustic humor and providing insight into an often-misunderstood period of Imperial history!

THE MARTIAN WAR

1. THE ROGUE COMMODORE (June 2006)
2. THE ALMOST COUP (June 2006)
3. THE HAWKE MISSION (Nov. 2006)
4. THE INDEPENDENT SQUADRON (Nov. 2006)

Omnibus 1. 2231: Mars Against Empire (Jan. 2010)

5. THE GALLANT FEW (June 2007)
6. THE JUPITER PATROL (June 2007)
7. THE SINOPE AFFAIR (December 2007)
8. THE DARK CRUISE (December 2007)

Omnibus 2. 2232: Chase Into Blackness (Jan. 2010)

9. THE CANARY WARS (July 2008)
10. THE FORGE FIRES (July 2008)
11. THE MERCURY ASSAULT (July 2009)
12. THE FLEET CLASH (July 2009)

Omnibus 3. 2233: Reap The Whirlwind (Jan. 2010)

13. THE MARS CONVENTION (Forthcoming)
14. THE EGESTA CRISIS (Forthcoming)
15. THE PAX TERRA (Forthcoming)
16. THE ARTICLES OF EMPIRE (Forthcoming)

Omnibus 4. 2234: Victory From Peace (Forthcoming)

Books 17-20, and Omnibus 5, coming soon!

For more information, please visit

WWW.DEFENSECOMMAND.NET

ALSO AVAILABLE FROM ICEBERG PUBLISHING

HIS MAJESTY'S NEW WORLD
by Kenneth Tam

1919. The British Empire and the United States have been colonizing a new planet for nearly 40 years. But there are secrets yet to be uncovered on His Majesty's New World...

His Majesty's New World novels by Kenneth Tam

Book One: THE GRASSLANDS (April 2008)
Book Two: THE FRONTIER (April 2009)
Book Three: THE REPRISAL (Forthcoming)

For more information, please visit

www.newworldempire.net